OVERLORD

The Eighth

Kelly Turnbull Novel

OVERLORD

By

Kurt Schlichter

Paperback Edition ISBN: 978-1-7341993-9-0
Overlord - Kurt Schlichter - Paperback - 092823 – Complete - v75

Cover Design by J.R. Hawthorne

For Irina

ACKNOWLEDGEMENTS

These books are not a solo endeavor. I want to thank everyone with a particle of participation in this project (knowing or not), but that's a whole book in and of itself. Let me try my best.

First comes hot wife, Irina Moises, who was there every step of the way, including at the beginning when I was workshopping titles. She read and edited many drafts and was always insisting that we do just one more read because she is racist against typos.

Thanks to friends and supporters like Drew Matich, Matthew Betley, Larry O'Connor, Cam Edwards, Glenn Reynolds, Chris Stigall, Tom Sauer, Hugh Hewitt, Duane Patterson, Pat and Robert O'Brien, Seb Gorka, Ned Ryun, Christian Collins, WarrenPeas64, Big Pete, Jim Pikl, Jim Hanson, Nick Searcy, Dana and Chris Loesch, A-10 jockey Dale Stark, Dan Bongino, LTC(R) Russ Smith, and many more. And to those I can't name because I'm so controversial, or they are so shy, thanks!

Scott McKay showed me around some of New Orleans, and that might just play a role here.

Thanks to Bill Wilson of Wilson Combat for his technical expertise on weapons and ammo.

Thanks to Adam Kissel, who always volunteers for a detailed copyedit and gets some great wine and my gratitude in return!

My cover artist, J.R. Hawthorne *aka* Salty Hollywood, whose covers are the best in the business. They look like no one else's covers.

Thanks to everyone who has followed me on Twitter and all the Gladiators at *The Schlichter Arena* on Locals.com. A big shout out as well to everyone who reads my columns at Townhall.com!

And I must, of course, thank every one of you hundreds of thousands of folks who have read this story from beginning to end! I am trying to keep it up to snuff!

And, finally, I always thank Andrew Breitbart because he started me down this road. Hope you dig the latest, Andrew!

KAS, October 2023

PREFACE

Astonishingly, this is the eighth novel in the Kelly Turnbull series. I never really thought I would write two, much less eight.

Let's set the time frame – this is the latest chronologically. The last book, *Inferno*, told the story from after Number IV, *Collapse,* when United States forces have invaded and occupied part of the formerly blue West Coast. *Inferno* showed that the reunification of the USA with (part) of the People's Republic of North America was not quite as smooth as some expected.

Overlord picks up after the events of *Inferno*, so that would be in the mid-2030s in our hypothetical timeline. But remember, after eight books and eight years and all sorts of insane developments, like Trump and Biden, there may be some canon and actual timeline glitches. And I don't want to hear about how my geography of a certain famous historical site is slightly off. I urge you to ignore them and don't sweat it. Just enjoy the ride!

People still tell me that they thought my depiction of the woke future was crazy, but now it seems to be coming true. I mean, luggage-thieving nuclear waste administrators who identify as who knows what? I mean, really?

I don't want this to come true. It's a warning. Remember that when the *Bulwark* dorks wet themselves over my books again.

I hope you find *Overlord* as much fun to read as it was to write but remember – do what needs to be done to ensure that these books never come true.

So the people shouted, and priests blew the trumpets; and when the people heard the sound of the trumpet, the people shouted with a great shout and the wall fell down flat, so that the people went up into the city, every man straight ahead, and they took the city.

Joshua 6:20

BOOK ONE

1.

"Welcome to the jungle," Kelly Turnbull whispered to himself as he gazed out the prop-plane's port-side window at the green carpet of rain forest rolling along 10,000 feet below. He paused, forgetting how the rest of the song went except for a few more words.

"You're gonna die," he said absently.

"What was that, Mr. Turnbull?"

The voice had a pronounced West African accent, with each word articulated clearly and precisely, as if the man sitting across the fuselage from him on a canvas jump seat spoke for a living. In fact, he did or, rather, had until he had been selected by the United States government for a new position back home. Dr. Adam Akebe had been a professor of history at Duke University in red America for about five years since he had been forced to flee with his family from Liberia's current dictatorship, a dictatorship allied with both blue America and the red Chinese. Duke itself had been completely purged of communists, critical race theorists, and similar charlatans following the Split years before. Those academics whose tenure was terminated mostly emigrated to the People's Republic of North America, where their ideology was embraced instead of banned. Dr. Akebe was one of the replacement faculty – he focused on ancient Greece and spoke Greek as well. He never would have gotten a professorship in the People's Republic, as he was far too serious about his subject to tolerate the insanity that passed for modern scholarship. He had applied to Princeton in blue New Jersey after escaping ahead of the new Liberian President Nathaniel "Machete Nate" Sawyer's killers, but the faculty recruiting committee had found, fatally, that his Ph.D. dissertation on the foreign policy of Greek city-states "completely ignored the trans experience, the oppression of indigenous folx, and the legacy of colonization." His evaluation had darkly hinted that the African gentleman's scholarship amounted to "white supremacy."

The new Duke University swooped him up, and he settled into exile in the new United States. Students flocked to his courses. He also became the most prominent external critic of the Sawyer regime. There were few internal ones – those still inside Liberia tended to end up chopped into small chunks. And then one day, a man named Clay Deeds knocked on his door, accompanied by a large, somber fellow who called himself Kelly Turnbull, and appealed to his patriotism for his homeland.

"Nothing," Turnbull grunted in response to Dr. Akebe's query about his choice of lyrics, before adding "Mr. President."

"I am not president yet, Mr. Turnbull," Dr. Akebe said, his dour face breaking into a smile. It was hot inside the dirty, noisy cargo plane, but Dr. Akebe was wearing a crisp white dress shirt, sans tie, under his sport coat. He peered at Turnbull through thick, black rimmed glasses. "That is where you come in, you and your friend."

"Friend? What, am I just a pasty in the cupboard?" said the exaggerated Cockney-inflected voice of the third man in the cargo hold of the rickety Czech-built Let L-410 turboprop. A woodland camo–painted L119A1 Close Quarter Battle Carbine, basically an M4 with a ten-inch barrel, was on his lap. He had said his name was Derek Kirby. It probably wasn't.

"That's not a thing," Turnbull told the English soldier. "Pasty in the cupboard."

"Oh, now you're an expert in English idioms?" the Brit replied, smiling.

"I'm still not sure if you even are English," Turnbull said, only partially joking.

"I'm Welsh," Kirby said.

The Brits had wanted a piece of this op too, so there was Kirby. Kirby and Turnbull had history.

"You always seemed a little soft for the SAS," Turnbull observed.

Kirby scoffed. "What do you know about the Regiment? What color is the boathouse at Hereford?"

"Pink with lavender trim," Turnbull said. "Like your panties."

Kirby paused for a second, then erupted into laughter. "Bloody American."

"Red American," Turnbull specified.

Dr. Akebe smiled thinly, not offended at the ribbing between the warriors. He understood it even if he was not a soldier himself. Men going into battle, men living on borrowed time because a bullet fired at them went an inch to the left instead of smashing into their skulls, must laugh or go mad. It was true among his beloved hoplites who fought at Marathon and Thermopylae, and it was true twenty-five hundred years later here in West Africa.

The bush plane carrying them into Liberia had come from an airfield outside Ouagadougou. In fact, the chance to add Burkina Faso (and Liberia, for that matter) to the long list of countries Kelly Turnbull had visited in his travels on behalf of the United States of America – even if the USA would deny that sponsorship if ever pressed – was a small but not insignificant reason he had let his friend and handler Clay Deeds talk him into taking this mission. After all, how many people ever got to visit the former Upper Volta? But then, how many would ever want to?

Now here, flying over the jungle in an ancient transport flown by a couple of Polish pilots with SIG pistols in their shoulder holsters – he did not want to speculate who was actually the owner of Air Dahomey and the crew's real employer – Turnbull was wishing he was back home in Texas in the US of A.

"It's easy," Clay Deeds had told him, much as he began every conversation where he tried to get Turnbull to take on a mission.

"It's never easy," Turnbull said. They were at Kelly's ranch, with a whole pack of dogs frolicking around them. But Gibson, the Belgian Malinois he had picked up in Washington state – sometimes called Hillaryia – sat nearby giving Deeds a death stare. Turnbull did not rebuke his animal. He felt the same way.

"This shouldn't be so bad," Deeds replied. "You get him in, turn him over to his army, off they go to mount their coup. You fly home."

"Let me count the ways this can go wrong," Turnbull said. In his head, he was already up to twelve before Deeds spoke again.

"Let me be clear, Kelly," he said. "The whole thing is already set up. You drop him off in Bong..."

"Bong?"

"Not what you think. Bong is a county. Liberia has counties. It was founded by freed American slaves that came to Africa in the nineteenth century. That's why the flag looks like ours, why the capital is Monrovia, from James Monroe."

"I'm familiar with him. I've spent a good part of my life enforcing his doctrine."

Deeds ignored him.

"And it's why Nathaniel Sawyer is named 'Sawyer.' The Liberian elite has always been the descendants of the American expatriates."

"I'm not sure that's where his cannibalism came from."

"Really? Because you seem to get chased an awful lot here in the Americas by people trying to eat you," Deeds observed.

Turnbull considered this for a moment.

"Point taken. But why the hell do we care about what's happening in Liberia?"

"Rare earth elements. Liberia used to be known for blood diamonds. Now the mining companies – who are our friends in this endeavor – have found neodymium, dysprosium, and terbium deposits. We need them. And we need to keep China and the blues, who are Sawyer's backers, from controlling them."

"So, you are going to start a civil war over a bunch of elements at the ass-end of the periodic table?"

"No, we are trying to avoid one. You are going to escort the man who is going to take over without another civil war into the country and hopefully he will take power quickly with a minimum of bloodshed and we will have a friendly government."

"I just thought of another dozen ways this could go wrong."

Deeds looked his friend in the eye.

"I need you, Kelly."

"So does my fiancé. And so do my many dogs."

"Look, you are still a light colonel and Lorna is a warrant officer. You do this and that's your reserve duty. You'll have done your part this year. Sooner or later, the red US is going to push into the blue Northeast to finish the reunification, and they will need everybody and who knows how long that lasts? I am offering you quite a deal."

"I just went and got your H-bomb back, again," Turnbull said quietly. "Along with bringing in the general who was trying to run a coup here, and who, by the way, our government hasn't even been able to hang yet despite a mountain of evidence."

"Kelly, I need you," Deeds said.

Turnbull sighed, and Gibson growled.

The plane entered Liberian airspace heading east from Ivory Coast. To the north, near the border with Guinea, was the low, green Mount Nimba, the highest point in the country.

"Listen up," came a voice over the intercom redolent with a Slavic lilt. "We are coming into Gbarnga in a few minutes. Strap in. The airfield is beat all to hell."

"Who do you think will be waiting for us on the ground?" Kirby asked. He opened the bolt on his rifle and confirmed a 5.56mm round was seated in the chamber.

"Hopefully the people who are supposed to be waiting for us," Turnbull said. He checked his own Heckler & Koch 416. It was ready to go. He put it aside and drew his Wilson Combat CQB .45. It checked out too and he slid it back into his holster. Dr. Akebe was watching him closely.

"You want a piece, Doctor?" Kirby asked, sounding a little like Michael Caine. "I have an extra Glock."

"The people of my country do not need another generalissimo," Dr. Akebe said. "They need a man of learning, who leads without a gun. Like Major Digby Tatham-Warter from your country, Mr. Kirby. A British Army company commander at Arnhem, the bridge too far. He carried an umbrella into battle. His men would follow him anywhere."

"I'm impressed," the Brit replied. "You want to come home with me and be our PM?"

Dr. Akebe smiled. Turnbull frowned.

"You do you, but I'll stick with my guns," Turnbull said.

The aircraft dropped through scattered clouds as it descended into the airfield. Gbarnga itself was not a large town, just about 35,000 people, but it was the capital of Bong County.

"This is the cradle of revolutions in Liberia," Dr. Akebe said. "The first civil war started here. And the third."

"And the fourth too, if we blow it," Turnbull observed.

The plane was dropping rapidly now toward a long, simple asphalt landing strip. Near a cluster of low buildings was the reception committee, a half-dozen trucks with markings Turnbull could not make out.

The landing gear extended, the plane touched earth and bounced, then shook as it hit a pothole. But the Polish pilots held steady – this was not the kind of mere dirt patch they were used to, so they were way ahead of the power curve.

The aircraft slowed and came to a stop, the props still spinning, and it turned around and began to slowly roll toward the buildings and the trucks. Turnbull noted that no one was shooting at him. That was a good sign. And a nice change of pace.

"Doctor, you stay inside when we pull up. I'll go out and make sure our hosts are who they are supposed to be. Kirby will stay with you."

"Why am I staying with the package?" asked Kirby. "No offense, Doctor."

"Because we won the Revolutionary War, so the American is senior," Turnbull said.

"How about the War of 1812?" Kirby snapped.

"You limeys burned Washington DC, so that counts as another American win."

Kirby conceded, and when the plane came to a stop and the engines wound down, Turnbull opened the door. The hot, moist jungle air blasted him. He scanned the area, his rifle hanging off him but readily available.

A tan, middle-aged white man in khaki cargo shorts and a tall, steely, similarly uniformed African soldier approached. More soldiers, STRAC and disciplined, stood back with the vehicles. The African troops carried FALs, older rifles but well-maintained and still deadly with their 7.62mm rounds. The two men approaching them carried what looked like Galils, but Turnbull figured they were probably 5.56mm South African Vektor R4 rifles.

Turnbull jumped down to the tarmac and instantly felt the heat through the soles of his boots. He stood fully erect and held out his palm.

"That's far enough," he said as the pair was a few yards away. "Who are you?"

"Rand Sipkis," the white man said, his Afrikaner accent thick and syrupy. "Colonel Sipkis. I'm commander of the bee-wham-ack security forces."

"Bee-wham-ack?"

"Bong West African Mining Conglomerate. We're the nucleus of Dr. Akebe's army." Turnbull noted the BWAMC emblem on the uniforms and ranks as well. Sipkis wore epaulets with two stars and what looked like an oak leaf – a South African Army colonel.

His comrade wore one star, a kommandant, roughly a lieutenant colonel. They both carried side arms, Glocks of some variety.

"I am Kommandant Bangizwe," the other officer said in accented English. "Welcome to Liberia."

They looked like the photos he had been provided by Deeds, but Turnbull pulled his phone out and confirmed it anyway. Better safe than dead.

They were who they said they were.

"Your new president is on-board," Turnbull told the pair.

Sipkis and Bangizwe laughed bitterly.

"Not our president," Kommandant Bangizwe said. "I am Zulu, from South Africa. We were all driven out by the damn communists."

Imprisoned as a terrorist, Nelson Mandela had tried to build a united nation in South Africa following his release, but after his death the African National Congress had devolved into yet another kleptocracy. Like its neighbor Zimbabwe, it embraced racial hate instead of reconciliation. After they had been stripped of their rights, the majority of the citizens of European ancestry had fled. Next were those of Indian ancestry – they were driven out too. Finally, the ANC turned on the Zulus living on the eastern coast, but the great warrior people had resisted efforts to subjugate them. There was bloody civil conflict in the mid-2020s – the People's Republic of North America had, of course, backed the communist race baiters – and there was a diaspora of Zulus throughout Africa. Many had been welcomed to the red United States.

"I'd love to share stories of killing communists with you, I truly would, but I need to get going, so let me go fetch him and we will be off," Turnbull said. Sipkis nodded and Bangizwe called back to his troops in a language Turnbull did not understand.

Kirby was at the door of the battered L-410 now, and Turnbull nodded to him. Then he froze.

A noise in the distance.

Turnbull pivoted and Sipkis and Bangizwe were both listening intently. It was far off, but the sound was clear. Bangizwe shouted at his men and they sprang into action.

"What is it?" Kirby asked from the doorway, his rifle at low-ready.

"Helicopters," Turnbull said. "And from our hosts' reaction, I'm thinking they aren't friendly."

"Shit!" Kirby swore and disappeared inside the aircraft.

"There's no OPSEC in this damn country," Sipkis said. "We need to move."

Dr. Akebe jumped out of the doorway to the ground, and Turnbull took him by the shoulder ungently.

"Time to go," he told the professor.

"What is it?"

"Someone knew you were coming," Turnbull said, pulling the man with him toward Sipkis.

The engines on the plane revved, and Turnbull instinctively bent down though he was not underneath the wings. Sipkis grabbed the other shoulder and together they pulled/pushed Dr. Akebe toward the vehicles.

"Welcome home, Mr. President," Sipkis said.

"Not the welcome I had hoped for," Dr. Akebe replied.

The helicopter rotor noise was getting louder.

"If you are going to go, you need to fly now!" Sipkis told Turnbull as they frog-marched the professor toward a Land Rover with the "BWAMC Security" emblem on it. There was a belt-fed German MG3 machine gun, a modern update of the dreaded Wehrmacht MG42 of World War II, mounted on the roof.

"I'm supposed to hand him over safely," Turnbull said. "And he's not safe yet."

They reached the Land Rover.

"I have him," Sipkis said. Around them the other vehicles were revving up and their crews were manning their own mounted machine guns. "You can go."

Turnbull turned and looked down the length of the airfield. There were two black dots in the sky, dots which were rapidly getting larger in size. He knew exactly what they were, McDonnell Douglas MD 500s, the civilian version of the AH-6 light attack helicopter, except someone had de-civilianized them. There were side-mounted machine guns, and several dudes were hanging off the sides with rifles.

Kirby was on the ground now, running toward Turnbull with his weapon in hand. Behind him, the aircraft was pulling away.

"They're never going to make it!" Turnbull said.

"They're Poles. They expect to die," Kirby said. The L-410 began taxiing down the runway as the two MD 500s began to dive. They ignored the aircraft. They were after Akebe.

The bullets began to hit just as the sound reached them. A line of holes tore across the truck's fender. The right chopper continued firing, with a swarm of rounds tearing into a wood-paneled warehouse, blasting it apart.

Sipkis shoved Dr. Akebe into the vehicle as the gunner on the roof opened up. Hot shells rained down on them.

The pair of choppers passed overhead, with the gunners hanging off the skids firing down. One of the BWAMC soldiers caught a round in the skull and dropped. The rest fired back if they were not engaged in getting their vehicles moving.

"I guess you are coming with us," Sipkis said to Turnbull. In the distance, the helicopters were turning for another gun run.

"Guess so, since our ride just bugged out." In the distance, the L-410 was trundling down the runaway and getting airborne, unmolested.

"Time to take our leave," Kirby said. Around them, several vehicles pulled out and began moving.

"Where did Sawyer's mob get helicopters?" Turnbull asked.

"A gift of the Chi Coms – the Kurylenko Group."

"Ukrainian mercs?" Kirby said.

"Yeah, pretty good flyers," Sipkis observed, hefting his Vektor.

"Damn well should be. We Americans trained them and now they are trying to smoke us," Turnbull spat. "Just fantastic."

The choppers began another pass.

"Better split up," Sipkis said, his accent getting heavier as the stress increased. "Make them choose who to chase. Get in."

"Not yet," Turnbull said, taking up his HK416 and sighting through the optic. There were two guys hanging off each side of each chopper armed with some sort of Kalashnikov variant with lots of optics and shiny gadgets. They were firing a bunch of rounds quickly, but not particularly effectively.

Turnbull took aim, placing the red dot on one of the shooters and then trying to figure the lead.

He exhaled as he pulled the trigger. His rifle bucked. The target jerked and fell forward out of the aircraft. He hit the ground with a thud as the helicopters passed overhead again.

"Should have had a safety strap," Kirby observed. More rounds impacted nearby as the dead man's friends sought to avenge him.

The other vehicles pulling away had confused the pilots, since it was not clear which one had the target aboard. One of the helicopters veered off in pursuit. The other chose wisely and turned for another gun run at the vehicle holding Dr. Akebe.

"I have had it with these bastards!" Sipkis shouted. He ran to the back of the vehicle.

Kirby was firing single shots, but fast. Turnbull joined him. The three survivors had learned from their comrade's fate and had pulled back up into the fuselage, but their legs were still exposed.

Turnbull took aim and joined Kirby in squeezing off more shots even as the aircraft's side-mounted machine guns sent a stream of rounds directly past their position. One shooter's knee exploded, and he rocked back then forward and out face-first from about a hundred feet. In his heavy body armor and gear, he barely bounced.

"Got him," Kirby said.

"No, he was mine," Turnbull said.

"Yanks," the Englishman sniffed. "Always taking credit."

"Like for saving your ass in World War II?"

Sipkis came around the back of the Land Rover with what was some sort of man-portable missile tube.

"That's a Blowpipe," Kirby marveled at the ancient anti-aircraft missile. "Did you rob a museum?"

Sipkis ignored him and took aim.

"Better clear off," Kirby said, and he and Turnbull ran. Sipkis fired and was engulfed in dust and smoke. But from the cloud came a white streak on a path that bent toward the fleeing chopper. It hit the tail rotor, vaporizing it. The MD 500 spun wildly and hit the ground on its side. Segments of fractured rotor shot out of the fireball and the noise of the explosion washed over them.

"It'll be easy," Turnbull said mockingly. Oh, would Deeds ever pay for this.

"Come on," Sipkis said. "Before his *maat* comes back for another go."

Turnbull walked the perimeter of the BWAMC *laager*, noting that Kommandant Bangizwe had posted his attentive pickets at reasonable intervals through the jungle. Satisfied that their camp was secure, he returned to the command post at the center behind the outward-facing vehicles. He was still concerned about the number of locals hanging around inside the perimeter, cooking and doing the labor for the mercenaries.

"Security looks good," he told Kirby, who was drinking from a plastic water bottle. "But too many eyeballs inside the wire."

The Brit nodded.

Dr. Akebe sat nearby at a table, looking remarkably poised for a civilian considering the circumstances. The sun was going down, but it was still ungodly hot.

"Sorry you boys got stuck with us," Colonel Sipkis said. He placed his rifle against a folding chair and sat down inside his open command post.

"So are we," Turnbull said.

"You could try driving east out to Ivory Coast," Sipkis suggested.

Kirby shook his head.

"Seems like a good way of getting cacked."

"Lots of guerillas to the east, though," Sipkis said. "We really only hold the road southwest between Gbarnga and Monrovia. And their intel is quite good."

"Yeah, you have an operational security issue," Turnbull said.

"In fairness, so do they. There are no secrets here. Information passes at light speed," Sipkis said.

"They know you are coming," Turnbull said.

Sipkis nodded.

"Yeah, they do. But we've dealt with this sort of thing before. My guys and I are experts in facilitating governmental transitions."

"You do seem to be a bit heavy for guarding mines," Turnbull assessed.

"I got a battalion of Zulus, all experienced and trained. Five line infantry coys and a headquarters company. Fire support element too. They are in position around Monrovia, waiting for my go."

"Opposition?" asked Turnbull.

"There are a few Chinese and People's Republic troops, mostly around their embassies, but some in the field as trainers or security for their own civilians. The Kurylenko Group is the real combat power. The red Chinese are paying for them. It has a couple companies and leads the government troops, who are basically a mob. Young, high, and a generally nasty bunch. Don't get taken alive, that's all I'll say."

"What about the populace?"

"Ready for peace. That's the thing. We get in and place the Doctor in charge, decisively, and hopefully they fall in line. But there's a problem."

"There's always a problem," Turnbull said.

"Machete Nate. As long as he's loose, there's no transition. We come into town in force and he fades back into the bush and builds up another army of drugged-up psychopaths."

"So kill him," Turnbull suggested.

"Easier said than done. He's got Kurylenko Group PSP," Sipkis said, referring to the President's physical security protection team. "We go in in force and they can evac him if it looks hairy."

Turnbull said nothing for a moment. Sipkis looked at him expectantly.

"Are you kidding me?" Turnbull sputtered.

"It's divine providence, you and your *maat* here," Sipkis said.

"Is this joker saying what I think he's saying?" Kirby said.

"He better not be," said Turnbull.

"Look," Sipkis said. "You boys obviously can take care of yourselves, and no one really knows you are here. They know about Dr. Akebe, yeah, but not his bodyguards. If a few of my guys disappear to go on a mission, everyone will notice. You two hop in a Land Rover and head east toward Ivory Coast and you're forgotten. No one will expect you to show up in Monrovia."

"That's not my mission," Turnbull said.

"Or mine," added Kirby.

"Boys," Sipkis said. "You don't strike me as the kind of guys who let mission parameters stop them. Besides, no one will be coming in here to fly you out until the deed is done."

Kirby looked over at Turnbull and shrugged, grinning.

"Plus, you're American," Sipkis said. "They will think you are People's Republic. No one will suspect you."

"Great," Turnbull said. "I'll get busy selecting my pronouns."

"Of all our choices," Kirby said contemplatively, "this sounds like the least terrible."

"It's the best option for everyone," Sipkis said.

"Not Machete Nate," Kirby offered.

Turnbull reflected on how annoyed Lorna would be if he came back later than expected from reserve training – he did not tell her he was on a job for Deeds. Facing down a tyrant and his merc bodyguards seemed the path of least resistance.

"Fine," Turnbull said. "I'll kill your bloodthirsty, psychotic warlord."

"No," said Dr. Akebe, who had been listening intently. "You cannot kill him. His justice must come from the people of Liberia, not a foreigner, if we are to become a true nation again."

"You know," Turnbull said. "I relied on justice back home and the guy who should be swinging is still breathing and he's a folk hero."

"This is non-negotiable," Dr. Akebe said forcefully.

"I wasn't negotiating," Turnbull relied.

"Come here," Sipkis said. He stood and walked off with Turnbull out of earshot. Turnbull sighed, then got up and followed.

"Listen, you and Kirby infiltrate and do what you have to do," Sipkis said. "Akebe is an idealist in a hellhole. Trust me, I know how Africa works. He will deal with whatever the situation is. And then you go home."

"And you get your money," Turnbull said.

"*Ja*," Sipkis said, defaulting to Afrikaans. "I get my money, but I would rather have a home to go back to if you want to know the truth."

They returned to the group.

"I'm up for it if you are," Turnbull told Kirby.

"Sooner we finish, the sooner we get home," the Brit replied.

"Remember what I said," Dr. Akebe told Turnbull. "You foreigners cannot deliver justice to Sawyer from the barrels of your guns."

Turnbull said nothing.

They headed out ostentatiously, so that everyone saw their departure. One of the sergeants would drive them in a Land Rover, but they did not head east. Instead, they went north, making it known they were headed to Guinea. Then they took the western fork of the main road outside of Gbarnga and turned southwest toward the capital on the Monrovia-Kakata Highway.

The road was somewhat secure, with occasional BWAMC vehicles in some of the many villages they passed through. Most of the loyalist forces in this area had pulled back into the city. If there were Sawyer troops out there in the bush, they chose to let the Land Rover pass.

The road itself was a wreck. Some areas necessary for the mines were well-maintained but other stretches were a disaster. Infrastructure was not President Sawyer's forte.

It was a long drive to the BWAMC forces front line outside the capital, passing out of Bong County through Margibi and into Montserrado, the home county of Monrovia. Near a town called Careysburg, about ten or fifteen miles west of the city, they encountered a BWAMC infantry coy – "coy" being a common term among European-based armies for "company." Its job was to secure the road. Past its forward line of troops were the loyalist forces.

Turnbull and Kirby met discreetly with the commander, a young captain who was distracted by some poorly aimed mortar rounds impacting a few hundred meters from his position. The moon was high in the sky giving more illumination than Turnbull would have preferred, but it was what it was. With the captain's permission and advice, they moved to the front line and advanced past the most forward positions through the jungle on foot for several hours.

"Worse than Belize," Kirby complained quietly, referencing the site of the rain forest phase of the SAS assessment course, and wiping some ants off his neck. Turnbull was to his front. This was, in fact, worse than Panama, where he had done his own jungle training.

Off to the right, they heard voices and saw flashes. The local Sawyer-aligned troops were exercising neither night nor light discipline. That was fine with Turnbull. The pair pressed on unseen.

The jungle was thick, and the moist air made it seem almost like they were swimming through a hot tub. It would get cooler soon, and then the sheen of sweat coating them would get cold. The jungle, Turnbull was reminded, sucked.

They found a hide position about three miles in, a copse of trees on a small hilltop with good fields of fire across the surrounding area. There were no paths running nearby, no reason for anyone to wander by. The loyalists would hold to the roads and the towns – they would not be tramping about patrolling the boonies. The main road was to their north, and the Monrovia suburbs really started not far ahead. It was a good place to rest and figure out a plan.

"This mission seems pretty half-assed," Kirby observed. He was cleaning his rifle in the moonlight as Turnbull stood guard with his. When he finished, they would switch off.

"Maybe a quarter-assed," Turnbull said. "Just kind of wander into town, find the most guarded guy there, whack him – or not – and then something-something peace breaks out."

"Well," Kirby said. "At least we have the element of surprise."

"Because no one would expect anything so stupid," Turnbull snarled.

"Look, we aren't getting out of here until Machete Nate gets dead, so I say we fry his kipper and go home."

"Fry his kipper? That's not even a saying. Who are you?"

Kirby grinned and went back to wiping the carbon off his firing pin. Turnbull used the pre-programmed sat phone Sipkis had given him to call in their status.

"We go tomorrow night," Sipkis told him. "No matter what."

They stood-to at dawn, both men ready to fight and oriented outward on the two most obvious avenues of approach to their position. They lay silently, listening and scanning for targets.

Some kind of deer-like creature trotted daintily by. The birds were calling loudly. In the distance, someone honked a horn. But there was no assault on their little position. After a while, they sat up and ate some of the rations Sipkis had provided, drinking water from the bottles he had supplied them.

"Maybe if we can get a few hundred meters away from him, we can drill him and run," Kirby suggested. Turnbull nodded.

"That's my choice if we can. He has close protection, and the Ukrainians will know what they're doing."

"You sure?"

"I helped train them back in the day. The war with Russia ended and a whole bunch of guys with very marketable skills flooded the market."

"So, from a distance."

"If we can. I still don't know how I got talked into this."

"Ah," Kirby said. "I know. You're one of those guys who lives for this."

"Let's try to just live period. I'd hate to die in this armpit."

They made their way further west through the jungle. Now there were fewer trees and more buildings, usually farmhouses. They were both wearing civilian clothes, or at least civilianish if you took away their chest rigs and rifles – 5.11 Tactical khaki shirts and pants over boots. They would get pegged as outsiders, but for which side was the question. Western fighters all looked the same. The locals might or might not call the cavalry in on them, but the pair looked like fighters, and like they should be left alone.

They kept out of sight as best as they could, choosing to break through the brush where possible. Where it was too thick or there was a river, they would emerge out on the road and walk down the shoulder. When they had to expose themselves to prying eyes, they acted like they were exactly where they belonged. The locals who did see them looked them over and went back to their business. Apparently, the locals were familiar with foreigners with guns tromping about.

On one such isolated stretch of road, they turned a corner and came face-to-face with a white SUV with government markings parked on the muddy shoulder. Two men stood looking under the open hood; they had AK-74s. Turnbull caught a glimpse of a colorful patch – very colorful, since it had at least two dozen stripes and slashes in various hues – on the right shoulders of their camo shirts.

"Crap," hissed Turnbull, who kept tramping down the road as if nothing was amiss. "People's Republic."

One of the soldiers glanced up, puzzled.

"Hey, you see some civilians?" the soldier asked. "You know...not African-American ones."

"You mean white?" asked Kirby.

"I don't want to presume their race," the soldier said. "My pronouns are..."

Turnbull jerked up his rifle and fired a suppressed burst into the soldier's chest. The soldier sprawled back into the mud. The second went for his own weapon, but Turnbull pivoted and fired twice. The rounds passed through his face just below the nose and out the back on a garish scarlet spray. The body dropped into a muddy puddle with a "plop."

"Hell, Turnbull!" Kirby snarled, his own weapon up and searching for targets as Turnbull lunged forward.

Turnbull cleared the vehicle and, satisfied there were no other enemies, relaxed a bit. Kirby did too, but he was appalled.

"Did you have to smoke them? They thought we were friendlies."

"How long would that last?" Turnbull asked. They were always getting shot. The question was when, and no time like the present. "Now, we need to get this crate off the road and out of sight. The stiffs too."

"You're one cold son of a bitch," Kirby said, grabbing the boots of a dead trooper.

"I'd rather choose when to have the gunfight than let them," Turnbull said. "Also, screw them."

"Civil wars never are civil, are they?"

"Nope," said Turnbull, grabbing a foot.

They hauled the dead into the brush. A quick search revealed little of interest in their pockets and vehicle. The two had cell phones, but they could be tracked. Kirby smashed them. The dead men also had plastic passes with blurry photos on lanyards to hang around their necks, which Turnbull took. The vehicle refused to start – it would barely crank – so they put it in neutral and pushed it into the tree line. It would be invisible to casual passersby.

Delighted that they had not been observed, Turnbull and Kirby got walking again. But the number of people along the road grew as they headed west and the terrain went from forest to light urban. They reached a village that lined the highway, Kofoayealah. Its roads were packed, as well as dusty and rutted. The buildings were worn and tired. Women in colorful skirts walked along the edge of the road with outrageously large baskets or plastic bins full of whatever upon their heads. Boys wandered in groups, laughing and joking, wearing soccer jerseys or old t-shirts. The PR was obviously on scene, buying local affection with clothing giveaways. One pre-teen wore a pink Target t-shirt bearing the words "My Penis Does Not Mean I Am A Man."

There were few military-aged males outside, as they were likely to be shanghaied into service with Machete Nate's forces. His face stared down at the passersby from dozens of posters, often torn or defaced. This place was about to become a war zone yet again. It happened with depressing regularity. All that changed were the perpetrators and the purported *casus belli*. That was probably why the people were not taking the latest threat particularly seriously.

Except for the occasional passing army patrol, which Turnbull and Kirby took cover from, it was business as usual in Kofoayealah. Someone with guns was going to be in charge, and it made very little difference who that was.

The locals kept their distance from Turnbull and Kirby, who figured they had at best an hour to find a ride before someone found the dead PRNA soldiers or word spread of the two heavily-armed strangers in town and someone with a lot of firepower showed up to investigate. They had little choice – the jungle was giving way to the ramshackle townships that encircled the half of the capital not facing the Atlantic, and they would have to ride or die.

"Hey Kelly," Kirby said, gesturing up the road. There was a white SUV, a Nissan probably, with the black letters "PRNA" painted across the hood making its way slowly down the rutted road. On the side, black letters spelled out "Apology Corps."

Turnbull nodded toward the sign of a fertilizer shop, and they ducked out of sight along the side. Turnbull carefully peeked around the corner and saw the SUV continuing on toward them. Turnbull whispered his plan and Kirby nodded.

"Sounds good," he said, gripping his rifle. It was hard to tell if he was being sarcastic.

When they heard the vehicle out front, Kirby dashed from his hiding place, waving his hands. The SUV slid to a stop, both sets of occupant eyes forward. The two in the front seats did not see Turnbull sidle up to the open passenger side window, rifle forward.

The SUV's side windows were down. A tremendously fat woman in a large, floppy-brimmed hat turned to face him from the passenger seat. She was sunburned and, like the female driver, was in her mid-twenties. Both wore the yellow unisex jumpsuits of the People's Republic Apology Corps.

"Where have you been?" demanded the angry behemoth.

Turnbull's kill plan was to put two bullets in her face, then to pivot right to get a better angle and next put two in the driver's mug. But he did not execute it. Instead, he stopped and made sure his muzzle was aimed off to the side.

"We've been looking for you," Turnbull said. Kirby was walking up to the driver now, who regarded him suspiciously.

"We didn't want you. We don't need you," the fat one hissed. "We are perfectly safe."

"Well, here we are," Turnbull said, thinking that the woman might explain what she was talking about in response to an open-ended response.

"You are not driving," the driver told Kirby through her open window.

"Okay," Kirby said, following along with Turnbull.

"You can get in back, but you cannot interfere with our work," the large one told Turnbull. "Your so-called 'security' is patriarchal bullshit."

"I hate patriarchy too," Turnbull objected.

"Get in!"

Turnbull glanced up at Kirby and nodded almost imperceptibly. They went to their respective back seat doors, pulled them open, and piled in. They slammed the doors shut and the driver accelerated.

"Are you from the People's Republic Anti-Colonial Military Land Forces?" she asked. The term "Army" had been recently banned as triggering and racist.

"Sure," Turnbull said. He thought for a moment. "So, what are your pronouns?"

"She/her," the driver said.

The fat one sniffed. "I refuse to participate in language constructs that inflict violence on marginalized communities."

"I'm that too," Turnbull said. "Pronouns are a tool of oppression."

"He/him," Kirby said.

The fat one scowled and grunted. She was wearing black eyeliner and looked like a Cure fan who had eaten several other Cure fans.

"He/him centers the phallus," the big one told Kirby.

"He's always centering his phallus," said Turnbull, shaking his head slowly. "He just refuses to do the work. And if you're wondering about his accent, he's from Boston but identifies as British."

The PR aid worker looked back at them coldly.

"Well, we don't have time to help you grow. We have an important job, and if we have to have you along then you need to stay out of our way."

"Absolutely," Turnbull said. "But they only told us to provide security for you. What's your job?"

"The role of the Apology Corps is to battle white supremacy, patriarchy, and climate change among those indigenous peoples who have suffered harms from the old United States. The racist US has a long legacy of oppression to undo."

"That's important work," Turnbull said. "So, are we headed back into Monrovia?"

"Don't call it that!" the driver shrieked.

"The locals call it that," Kirby said defensively, and Turnbull rolled his eyes. It would only encourage the pair.

"They don't know any better. And calling them 'locals' is racist."

"See?" Turnbull said. "Look what I have to put up with."

"He's probably cis," the fat one said. The SUV shuddered as it hit a pothole.

"Well, I'm trying to be more flexible," Kirby said.

"We're going to a neighborhood in the capital to help the community," the driver said. "We have been here for a month and never needed gunpeople with us before."

Turnbull glanced over at Kirby. These two and their PR Apology Corps SUV would likely get them waved right through the military checkpoints.

"Things are getting rough out there," Turnbull said. "What have you heard?"

"That the Liberian military people have fought off the sexist and imperialist forces," the fat one said. She did not say "soldier" because that term was also offensive.

"Well, that's a relief," Turnbull said. "How far?"

"About an hour," the driver said. "We would be there already if we did not have to come out to find you."

"Well, I am glad you did find us because I think we both will learn and grow experiencing your work," Turnbull said.

Kirby rolled his eyes.

The SUV continued west back toward Monrovia – the pair never explained what the new, non-triggering name for the capital should be. They passed through several checkpoints along the main road, and were generally waved through, though once Turnbull had to flash the passes they had liberated from the dead PR soldiers. Luckily, the guards did not take a close look at the photos.

Monrovia proper, or at least the portion with the main government buildings, was located on a peninsula that ran along the southwest coast. Across the water and extending inland were the poorer areas, vast stretches of cheap buildings housing the mass of the population. The military patrolled it, and life was continuing on largely as usual, but the tension was palpable and evident to everyone, except the two Apology Corpspersons. It did not seem to have occurred to them that the calm could change into a storm in a moment.

The Dandawailo neighborhood was located in the northeast of the city, several miles inland from the Atlantic. The businesses were mostly closed, and the poverty was evident. There was also no power – to please the World Economic Forum, Machete Nate had banned all non-renewable power sources in order to minimize Liberia's infinitesimal carbon footprint, with predictable results. Signs were out, as were the few streetlights. Traffic crawled even though there really was not that much to begin with.

Several times, hard men hungrily looked over the SUV, and met Turnbull or Kirby's eyes. A slight shake of a rifle and the predators wisely thought better and sought softer prey.

Neither the driver nor her hefty friend noticed what was happening. They instead spent the ride complaining about how racism had harmed this "African-American community."

Turnbull held his tongue.

After a long, painful attempt to read a map and follow directions, during which Kirby was told he was a sexist pig for attempting to share his land-navigation skills, the SUV pulled up at what looked like a Pentecostal church. They could see a few dozen people milling about inside the sanctuary through the open door – probably open because there was no electricity to power the air conditioning, assuming there was any.

"Ugh," the fat one said. "Christianists. Well, it is not their fault they don't know better."

"Simple people and their superstitions," the driver said. "They fear their sky daddy when they should fear climate change."

"And transphobia," the fat one added, struggling to get out of the vehicle.

"Carry the gifts," the hefty one commanded Turnbull and Kirby. Kirby looked at Turnbull, who rolled his eyes, and they went to the rear of the vehicle. There were several jugs of cooking oil in the back, as well as several sacks of flour. The white bags were printed in blue with the words "A GIFT OF THE PEOPLE OF THE PEOPLE'S REPUBLIC OF NORTH AMERICA IN HUMBLE CONTRITION FOR THE HATE CRIMES AND ENVIRONMENTAL RACISMS PERPETRATED UPON YOUR PEOPLE." Turnbull and Kirby carried them inside and put them on the floor.

The several dozen people gathered inside were arrayed in a semi-circle, with the two yellow-clad Apology Corps workers in front. The seminar began inauspiciously, with an attempt to perform a land acknowledgement descending into a bitter shouting match between members of two clans who both claimed the rightful ownership of the area. Turnbull and Kirby prepared to step in if it became too heated.

Moving on eventually, the corpspersons directed the discussion, which was translated from English (it was an official language in Liberia) into local languages, toward the real meat of the seminar. They began to quiz the locals on their feelings regarding various oppressions, spending ten minutes trying to translate "microaggressions" into Kpelle and Kru since it made no sense to them in English.

The corpspersons' frustrations grew as the seminar progressed, especially when the group burst into laughter at the notion that a man could become a woman and that some men got pregnant. Turnbull suspected that the locals thought it was some kind of hilarious translation mistake, but he also noted that they were all eyeing the gifts – apparently, those were the reason the people were indulging these bright yellow foreigners with the bizarre ideas.

It went downhill further when the large one excoriated them for "the erasure of fat folx" after noting that none of the audience was large. This time, the audience did not laugh – it simply made no sense to them. Then one woman asked, "Is your husband rich, because you are very fat?" The bulging bride ran out to the SUV crying and the people lunged forward toward the gifts.

Turnbull saw it all going south, and he grabbed the driver ungently and pulled her outside. She was in danger of being trampled.

"They have not earned their gifts yet," the driver protested as the audience divided the spoils. Turnbull did not comment on the racist nature of the concept of "earning" – that was basic PR dogma. His years infiltrating the PR had made him immune to irony.

"Get in," he directed the driver. Her hefty partner was already in the front passenger seat, literally shaking. The driver got behind the wheel and Turnbull joined Kirby in the back.

"Go!" Turnbull ordered.

"Don't tell me what to do!" the driver protested.

The barrel of Turnbull's rifle pressed into her neck.

"I'm done with you. I'm counting to two and if you aren't moving, I cap you both and take the wheel. Two."

The driver cranked the engine. Her friend stopped blubbering and stared.

"Here is how this goes," Turnbull said. "You get me into Monrovia proper and I don't kill you. That's the deal. And you don't talk."

"That part is key," agreed Kirby.

The SUV rolled forward. Behind them in the receding distance the audience was carrying away the food.

"Why are you doing this?" asked the driver.

"You're talking," Turnbull said, pressing in the barrel. "The People's Republic is abandoning the racist and sexist and, uh, transphobic government of Machete Nate in favor of a new leader who centers the decolonization agenda of the indigenous peoples. Anyone still supporting him is committing actual violence on marginalized communities. We could not let you know until now."

"I don't understand," the fat one said.

"That's because of your own racism and fatphobia," Turnbull said. She burst into tears again.

"So, President Sawyer is...," began the driver.

"A white supremacist," Turnbull replied.

"And cis," the fat one added.

"So very cis," Turnbull said.

"What the hell?" Kirby said leaning in.

Turnbull whispered back: "Once they drop us off, they will head back to the embassy and tell what happened and that might just tie the PRs up in knots for a while until they figure out whose side the PR forces should be on."

"We're sorry for our own structural racism," the driver said.

"We need to do the work to truly embrace anti-racism and anti-fatphobia," the larger one added.

"Yes, you do," Turnbull said. The SUV hit a pothole.

They headed west toward the Atlantic, with Kirby reading the map and navigating. They passed easily through a pair of checkpoints. Eventually, they reached the main road. Running north-south along the coast was United Nations Drive, and they took that south over the bridge across the Mesurado River to the peninsula. There was another checkpoint on the bridge, but the Apology Corps SUV was not hindered. They continued south through the city to the Antoinette Tubman Stadium, a decrepit soccer field.

"Let us out here," Turnbull said. "You know where the embassy is?"

The driver nodded. The old United States embassy had been taken over by the People's Republic ambassador after the nation had broken relations with red America. This was common – many nations recognized only one or the other of the remnants of the old USA. She drove off with her miserable friend.

"We need to go," Turnbull said.

"The map says the executive mansion is to the south," Kirby said. "Maybe a mile. Do we have a plan yet?"

"Not even remotely," Turnbull said. In the distance, several miles to the south at the base of the peninsula, they could see helicopters lifting off from the old Spriggs Payne International Airport, which was now under Kurylenko Group control.

They headed toward the presidential residence. The sun was falling out over the Atlantic, and in an hour there would be a curfew. The roads were getting packed with people rushing home. There was an abandoned gas station, and Turnbull broke out the shards of shattered glass and eased himself inside to hide out until things simmered down.

In the distance, there was the noise of gunshots and explosions, light initially but growing.

"Show time," Turnbull said.

Turnbull called Sipkis on the sat phone again.

"You're still alive? Good!" the South African said. "I cannot talk long. The war is starting."

"I noticed," said Turnbull. "Any intel?"

"We think he is at his command post in the Executive Mansion, so I think you have no chance."

"Maybe," Turnbull said.

"Maybe you wait and try to ambush him as he runs away to the bush."

"We'll play it by ear. Out." Turnbull hung up.

"Stuck in the middle of somebody else's war again," Kirby observed, his back against the wall and his suppressed rifle across his lap.

"It gets old," Turnbull said. "But so does being stuck in the middle of your own country's war."

"I did Afghanistan, Yemen, Second British Civil War, a bunch of other jobs," Kirby said. "Nothing ever changes."

"Did all those, too. And more."

"Busy," Kirby said.

"I get around," Turnbull said.

"The Second Brit Civil War got bad after you left," Kirby said, not mentioning that the first was technically "The English Civil War," but that the second civil war in that green and usually pleasant land included fighting all over the British Isles and Northern Ireland, not just England. Kirby continued. "Guerilla ops on the damp Scottish moors. Mountain warfare in Wales. House-to-house in bloody Manchester. But it still beats this tropical battlespace any time."

"Beats London," Turnbull grumbled.

"You only say that because you got capped in the arse." He giggled.

"Yeah, your war was a bitch," Turnbull replied. "And so was "Queen Meghan."

In fact, Turnbull had been the one to duct tape her mouth shut after they snatched her from the enemy beachhead near Port Wenn in Cornwall to deliver her to the Free English forces for trial. Turnbull finally having to shut her up seemed to relieve everyone, not least of all her feckless husband, who had been arrested with her. Sadly, the communists did not immediately stop fighting after the royal pretenders were captured in the joint US/UK mission, Operation Privacy, where he and Kirby had teamed up the first time. Turnbull stuck around long enough to receive an embarrassing flesh wound in London, and was long gone by the time the Free English retook Manchester and Birmingham after horrific urban battles. The leftists had to be rooted out until the Treaty of Stonehenge ended open hostilities and the United Kingdom adopted a neutral foreign policy (though the government still quietly favored red America). But the United Kingdom was no longer so united. Scotland was left a cold, communist hellhole, and an active PR ally.

The roads were clearing of the relatively light civilian traffic, though patrols of military vehicles continued to pass by at regular intervals. The sun went down and then the noise grew louder – dull thuds to the east, with occasional gunfire.

"It's started," Turnbull said.

"Makes for a nice distraction," Kirby observed.

"Hopefully those nitwits from the Apology Corps ran their mouths at the embassy. If I know my bureaucrats, they will keep any PR forces out of it until they figure out whose side they are supposed to be on."

A louder explosion went off in the south.

"Airport?" Kirby speculated.

"Maybe," Turnbull replied. "I'd hit the airport if I was Sipkis."

"We gonna go kill this Machete Nate bloke or what?" asked Kirby.

"Why not?" Turnbull asked rhetorically. "We're supposed to capture him, but in the end, I think Dr. Akebe can live with his head on a stick."

"How do you know if Dr. Akebe will be any better than this Machete Nate guy?"

"I don't," conceded Turnbull. "I'm pretty far past believing any politician."

"Well, we get to shoot one. Think of how many people would love to shoot a politician."

"Come on," Turnbull said, standing up and confirming through the broken windows that the coast was clear.

They began moving through the deserted streets tactically, taking cover whenever some military vehicles passed. The first they dodged had "TKG" in red painted on the doors of their Toyota SUVs. The men inside looked focused and Slavic. They evidently shopped where Turnbull and Kirby did.

"The Kurylenko Group," Turnbull said.

"Close security," Kirby said. "That will be a problem."

"Well, we still have the element of surprise," Turnbull said.

"I know," Kirby replied. "Because no one would be stupid enough to do this."

The Capitol Hill section of Monrovia held the Capitol Building and the adjacent Executive Mansion. The mansion was an architectural atrocity, something that people probably thought looked futuristic in the early Sixties when it was erected, but it was simply five stories of ugly. President Samuel Doe had used it as a residence, the site of bizarre religious rituals and sacrifices during his reign in the 1980s. It burned down in the early twenty-first century but was rebuilt just as awfully as before.

The lights were on – apparently the roaring diesel generator on the grounds was exempt from climate concerns. An ornate black metal fence, maybe ten feet high, surrounded the grounds, with guard posts at each corner. The main gate out front had a crew of maybe six to eight guards with AKs. Occasionally, a small pack of vehicles would enter or depart with minimal fuss. A dozen or so were parked out front before the building entrance.

"No way to break in," Kirby said.

"Why not walk in?" Turnbull said.

"What, just sally on through?"

"We have the passes."

"With other blokes' pictures?"

"Do those guards look particularly diligent?"

"Are we even sure he's in there?" asked Kirby.

"Look, we are not getting out of here unless we deal with this guy, so why not rip the Band-Aid off?"

"What, is that some American saying?"

"Yeah, it means just do it. If it goes bad, we have a fair chance of being able to break contact and get away."

"Fair," Kirby grumbled. In the distance, there were more artillery noises.

"Try and look PR," Turnbull said, standing up and walking to the sidewalk. Kirby followed.

"I need a yellow suit."

They walked casually down the sidewalk, weapons hanging loose, broadcasting their total lack of any care in the world.

The metal main gate was open. Blocking the road was a red and white wooden bar that could be lifted to admit vehicles. A wood guard shack was to the left and had a light inside. There were phones on the table. The Liberian soldiers looked at the approaching pair quizzically. There was not a lot of pedestrian traffic at the Executive Mansion.

Turnbull lifted up his blue pass and Kirby did the same, casually, as if it was nothing out of the ordinary.

The guard shouted something behind him in a language Turnbull did not know, and a lieutenant in a green beret stepped forward, his ancient AK still tucked under his arm.

"People's Republic," Turnbull said. "Here for the meeting. Open up."

"Meeting?" asked the lieutenant.

"You want to be the guy who makes us late for the president?" Turnbull asked. The lieutenant pondered this for a moment and seemed on the verge of speaking when a pair of lights appeared moving in toward the gate.

It was a white Toyota SUV with "TKG" painted on the door.

"Shit," Kirby hissed almost imperceptibly.

"Stay cool," said Turnbull.

The SUV pulled up to the gate and stopped. The driver leaned out of the window. Three more Kurylenko mercs were in the vehicle.

"Open the gate!" he shouted.

"Are you here for the meeting?" the lieutenant asked.

"What meeting?" replied the driver. He looked at Turnbull and Kirby.

"Who are you?" he demanded.

Turnbull stared back.

"Assassins!" Turnbull yelled, drawing his Wilson Combat .45, and opening fire on the vehicle.

The first two shots hit the driver in the face and neck. The second hit the thug in the passenger seat as he went for his tricked-out AK-12.

Kirby was pumping Glock rounds into the backseat, joined by the lieutenant who sprayed down the vehicle on full auto.

They ceased fire. A piece of windshield glass dropped and smashed on the dashboard. The SUV idled and rolled forward into the gate and stopped.

"You saved the president," Turnbull told the lieutenant. The lieutenant seemed disoriented.

"We need to go protect President Sawyer!" Turnbull shouted.

Without another word, Turnbull took off inside the compound, followed by Kirby. The compound was coming alive with activity. They sprinted for the building.

Turnbull dropped the .45's mag and replaced it, then slid the pistol back into his holster. He brought up his suppressed HK416 rifle as he ran.

There were a trio of confused guards at the front door. He flicked the selector switch to "AUTO" and sprayed them all. They sprawled across the concrete floor of the entrance way.

In the distance, there were more explosions and the sound of helicopters.

He and Kirby were inside the grand entrance hall, with each covering up the winding stairs and to the sides.

"How the hell did we pull that off?" asked Kirby. "Where now?"

"Up," Turnbull said.

A Kurylenko merc appeared at the top of the staircase as they climbed and was hit by four shots before he knew what he was looking at. They passed his crumpled body and headed to the elevator.

There was a button at the top of the panel that read, "PRESIDENTIAL SUITE." And there was a keyhole.

"Wait," Turnbull said. He ran to the dead Ukrainian and rummaged through his pockets. He found a key attached to a ring. He ran back to the elevator and put the key in the hole.

Turnbull punched the button and the doors shut.

They both took aim at the door, assuming the worst about who it would open up to.

It opened up to a pair of bewildered Kurylenko mercs who did not expect them. Turnbull and Kirby each took one, both aiming for the heads to avoid dealing with the Kevlar chest plates in their carriers.

Both men fell back, their rifles clattering.

Turnbull and Kirby burst out of the elevator and attacked over the dead bodies. It was a very large, open room, suitable for gatherings and conferences, with a variety of tables, chairs, sofas, and the like. Dark wood panels lined the walls, and crude portraits of the presidents of Liberia – except those who the current Supreme Leader despised – hung unevenly around the circumference. And the floor was covered in a thick, dirty white shag carpet that appeared to have been teleported in from a Marin County rumpus room circa 1977.

Machete Nate Sawyer was there, bending over maps on one of the tables, next to one of his generals in full general regalia. More importantly were the half-dozen Kurylenko mercenaries. Standing beside the president was evidently the mercenary leader, a blond, thick-necked specimen wearing major rank. He had a long, thin scar across his left cheek. And when he saw Turnbull and Kirby, he went for his AK-400.

Kirby engaged one of the mercs to the left, putting several shots into him. Turnbull wanted to take out the major, but there was another merc closer who was raising his weapon and Turnbull had to engage him first. The man caught three rounds, the first probably stopped by his chest plate. The second and third went into his neck. He flew back over a gold and white upholstered couch.

The major opened fire with tight bursts, joined by the other mercenaries and their AK-12s. Turnbull and Kirby both went to ground. A nearby lamp disintegrated under the hails of bullets, and the ugly couch was shredded by 5.45x39mm rounds.

Unfortunately, none of the mercenaries' weapons were suppressed – Turnbull's ears rang. He rose up and fired several bursts back. A portrait of President Samuel Doe was riddled. The Liberian general made a break for it. Kirby put one in his head and he went down.

Turnbull dropped back and reloaded as he assessed the tactical situation. They were outgunned two-to-one, not counting the surviving Liberians. But they held the elevators.

It was a good, old-fashioned stand-off.

Turnbull just hoped no one had grenades.

"What now?" Kirby asked, sliding in a fresh mag.

"I'm thinking," Turnbull said.

"American!" came a voice across the room. "You cannot win."

Turnbull rose up and fired a burst in the general direction of the speaker, who he expected was the major.

"You have already killed several of my men, and I expect you will kill several more, but in the end you will die!"

"Everyone dies, Ivan," Turnbull said. "I want Sawyer. I don't care about you and your thugs. Give him up and go."

"Ah, but my principal insists that we honor this contract until completion. So, you cannot have him."

"Well," Turnbull said, crouching behind the couch. "I guess we have a dilemma."

"Not for long," The Ukrainian replied. He shouted out instructions in Ukrainian.

"I don't savvy a word of that tongue," Kirby said. "But I damn well know what it means."

"Get ready," Turnbull said, lifting his rifle.

A phone rang.

No one moved. It rang again. It was over near the major and his client. Someone – it sounded like Machete Nate – started arguing. Vasilev told him, in English, to shut up.

The phone rang again.

"You getting that, Ivan?" Turnbull asked.

"It is Major Vasilev," the Ukrainian shouted back. "Ivan is Russian!"

"Don't care, Ivan."

"You should care that it is my principal, so please keep the shooting down so I can hear." Unintelligible conversation commenced.

There was a noise up above them, on the roof. It sounded like helicopters. And men exiting them.

"Oh, shit," said Kirby.

"That's not good," Turnbull said.

"American!" shouted Vasilev. "It appears the situation has changed."

"We'll shoot your new friends too, Ivan."

"No, it's not that," the major said. "The president is yours."

Over by Vasilev, Machete Nate was screaming obscenities. There was a slapping noise, and he went silent.

"You're giving him up, now that your friends are here?" The men on the roof were coming down the stairs toward the presidential suite. Turnbull took aim at one of the doors up to the roof.

"American, you misunderstand. They are not my friends. They are my employers. My new employers."

The doors down from the roof opened. The first man out, Vektor rifle at the ready, was Kommandant Bangizwe. He was followed by a dozen of his Zulu infantrymen. They poured into the room.

"How about that?" Kirby said, whistling thinly. "A Welshman saved by Zulus!"

Turnbull rose, aiming at the Ukrainian officer as he placed his AK-400 rifle on the table with one hand. With the other, he held and absolutely miserable Machete Nate Sawyer by the back of his collar.

"Kommandant Bangizwe, I am Major Markus Vasilev of the Kurylenko Group, at your service."

Bangizwe smiled and lowered his rifle. The other mercenaries relaxed. So did Turnbull and Kirby.

"What is happening?" Turnbull asked Bangizwe.

"We bought their contract," the Zulu officer replied. "The Kurylenko Group works for us now."

"It was expensive, too," Vasilev said. He still held the president tightly until two Zulu troops relieved him of his whimpering prisoner.

"You may go," said the kommandant to the mercenaries. They gathered their gear, slinging their rifles, and walked toward the elevators.

"It is just business," Vasilev said to Turnbull. "But you killed a lot of my men, and I will not forget."

"You sure take things personally for a mercenary," Turnbull replied. The half-dozen Slavic survivors were looking at him hard.

"My weakness is that I take things personally," Major Vasilev conceded. "In other circumstances, I would act on my feelings."

"Don't hold your feelings in," Turnbull said, his weapon ready to jerk upwards. "Express them." Turnbull figured he would get four of the six Ukrainian mercs before they got their guns unslung. Hopefully Kirby would take out the other two.

"Not today, American," Vasilev said. "Some other day."

"Looking forward to it," Turnbull said. Vasilev smiled enigmatically, and then he led his men into the elevator. The doors closed, and Turnbull relaxed. Then another man came out of the doorway from the roof, guarded by two Zulus.

"Dr. Akebe," Turnbull said. "I mean, 'Mr. President.'"

The professor was as unflappable and as composed as always as he strode into the Presidential Suite. Machete Nate was shaking as he watched his replacement walk over to him and regard him curiously. Turnbull and Kirby joined him.

"Alive, like you wanted," Turnbull said. "Ready to face justice."

Dr. Akebe looked at him sadly, drew a Glock pistol from his coat and shot Machete Nate Sawyer in the forehead. The body dropped to the floor and twitched.

Dr. Akebe casually replaced the weapon in his belt.

"I thought you didn't want me to kill him," Turnbull said.

"I didn't," Dr. Akebe said. "It had to be a Liberian. I know my history. And this was justice."

Turnbull sighed as Sawyer twitched out the last of his life on the shag carpeting.

"If I let him live," Dr. Akebe said, "I would be guaranteeing further war. That's what history teaches us."

The Doc had a point.

2.

Denton Q. Quinn, Esq., wore a navy-blue suit with subtle silver pinstripes that cost more than the guard who was checking his identification made in a year. His shoes, of rich Corinthian leather and also ridiculously expensive, tapped on the institutional linoleum floor as he waited.

"It looks in order, sir," the guard told him, handing back his Texas driver's license and the piece of paper that was the order from federal judge Raymond Burke granting him access. The guard looked at Quinn expectantly. There was a US flag on the shoulder of the officer's uniform; a nametape read "FEDERAL BUREAU OF PRISONS." After a moment of uncertain quiet, Quinn broke the silence.

"Do you want to inspect my briefcase?"

"No, that won't be necessary, sir. Please follow me."

The man came around from his post and led the way down the white cinderblock hall. Quinn followed. It was a long walk, almost a hundred yards. Cameras covered every inch of it. There was a four-way intersection at the end, with each radiating corridor marked with a letter. From down corridors A to C, Quinn could hear the noise of men at the other end, even through the metal doors. But the fourth corridor was silent.

"He has D wing all to himself," the guard said when they reached the metal portal at the end. He pulled a set of keys from the pants pocket of his uniform and inserted it into the lock. The mechanism clicked, and the guard pushed the heavy door open.

"Sir?" the corrections officer called out inside the room. "You have a visitor."

Quinn had practiced law in Texas for decades, since well before the Split, and he had walked into a lot of prisons to see the billionaires, politicians, and celebrities who had sought him out as their attorney. He had expected Federal Correctional Institution Beaumont, located between Houston and the Louisiana border, to be like the others, squalid and ugly. But he had never seen a prison cell like this one.

It looked like a hotel suite. There was fine furniture and a library of books in the shelves lining the walls. A computer sat on an oak desk. The bedroom was off in a separate room. You would never know you were in a high-security prison if you had not gone through a dozen metal doors to get there.

"General," the guard said politely to a fit man in the prison's blue shirt and dungarees uniform sitting on a leather easy chair with a book in his lap. A glass of something brown sat on the wooden table beside him, probably from the open bottle of Macallan double cask 18-year-old single malt scotch whisky that stood nearby. It was an impressive enough pour in the real world, not least of which because the communist government of Scotland had destroyed the brand by replacing the skilled distillers with equity hires that promised to "decolonialize so-called 'scotch' and reimagine it in a non-patriarchal and exo-European context." But to have it in this place was astonishing.

General Karl Martin Scott looked up beatifically.

"You have a guest, sir," the guard continued politely.

"Thank you, Jimmy, that will be all."

The guard nodded. "Ring me if you need anything, sir," he said, then ushered Quinn inside the suite and closed the metal door behind him. It clanged shut and the locking mechanism engaged. The suite was comfortable, but it was still a prison.

"It's like the jail scene in *Goodfellas*," Quinn said, marveling. "Do you get steaks every night too?"

General Scott smiled. "The guards here are patriots. They know I've been wronged, that the current leadership of our country is corrupt and afraid, so they take good care of me."

"Very good care, I'd say. You live better in here than most people live out there," Quinn marveled.

In the past, they had met in attorney-client conference rooms. Judge Burke's order required the US government to allow Denton unaccompanied access to the general's housing. Judge Burke would experience the gratitude engendered by doing so down the road. Burke was one of many powerful friends of the general on the outside.

"How are you, Denton?" the general said, motioning his attorney to sit. Quinn did, in a comfortable leather recliner.

"I am concerned, and not just about you and your trial," the lawyer confessed.

"I am guessing they have put the trial date off again."

"No, they are setting it, and sooner than I would like. They would never try you if they could get away with it, but I suspect they feel they have to get it over with," Quinn said. He looked around the room then back at the general.

"I suspect they are listening," the general said. He bent in and spoke in a low voice. "If we need privacy, I have a place we can talk where we need not worry about prying ears."

He sat back upright. Without asking, the general took another crystal tumbler and poured Quinn two fingers, then handed it over. Quinn put it to his nose, inhaled the smoky goodness, and sipped. Then he lowered the glass.

"It must be difficult, going from a commander to...," Denton paused.

"A convict?" the general replied. "Though I am technically not convicted yet. They treat me well, the guards I mean. Most support me. The government should technically have me in a military prison, but they were afraid to put me back in the custody of the Army. A wise decision. They keep me alone here, probably so they can ensure that I do not tell anyone what I know and to keep me from being killed by some prisoner looking for fame. But when I do interact, many of the inmates support my cause. The scum of the earth. Killers, thieves, disgraced former teachers serving time under the DeSantis schoolhouse anti-pornography laws. Even the lowest of the low still have a spark of patriotism. But back to the matter at hand, my trial."

"It is a delicate problem for them. They will never publicly mention the ... allegations involving...," began Quinn.

"I know what you mean, Denton. They are charging me with corruption and murder. They want to tar my reputation, make me into a mere criminal. The other charges, all false of course, are too explosive to bring in open court."

Both men understood that the United States government could never charge their country's greatest, most popular living general with trying to steal a hydrogen bomb to use to spark a coup that would install him as dictator. It was too much. The millions who adored him would never believe it. They would see it as a power-play to sideline their champion. The split-off red states, still locked in a war with the remnants of the blue People's Republic, was already growing unstable. That could tip the country over the edge into chaos.

"When they do try you, they will attempt to do just what you said, smear you by turning you into a greedy thug. And they will make sure you cannot speak out."

"A kangaroo court, but I will still have my say, and that will roil the waters," the general said, chuckling. "Kelly Turnbull should have killed me when he had the chance."

"I don't know who that is, and I know everyone," Quinn said. It was true – Denton Q. Quinn knew everyone there was to know in the Lone Star state. He was not hired for his courtroom acumen – he would buy the right attorneys to argue the case when the time came. His role was as a fixer. When a problem needed solving, a deal needed to be made, a threat delivered, a judge manipulated, you sought out Denton Quinn. And you brought a truckload of money. Of course, the general never talked money. His friends, some of the most powerful men in the country, wrote the checks. The very big checks.

"Kelly Turnbull is the gentleman who brought me in. He's a pawn. He works for others."

Denton nodded. The arrest of General Scott had been part of some black operation, an operation so deep that his many contacts in the US government could only provide him with hints and clues about it. He knew of Clay Deeds, though he suspected that was not the operative's real name. Denton Quinn did not concern himself with mere functionaries like this Kelly Turnbull fellow. But apparently the general did.

"Mr. Turnbull and I have unfinished business," Scott said sourly, swirling his scotch. "The same with his master, this Clay Deeds fellow."

"General, you have more pressing concerns."

"I thought that all I had to do was wait for my trial and sentencing," Scott said, lifting his tumbler and taking another peaty sip. "Or for the people to rise up and throw off the current regime."

"There is another option," Quinn said, looking around the room again.

"Another option?"

"It is a radical one, an unexpected opportunity."

"When I was commanding, I always tried to do the unexpected. And to make the most of my opportunities."

"You mentioned a place where we can talk?"

The general regarded the lawyer for a moment. A bead of sweat was forming on the attorney's right temple. Whatever he had to say was making Denton Quinn nervous, and a man did not get to be Denton Q. Quinn by getting nervous.

"Follow me," the general told Quinn.

They stood, and he led the lawyer out to the walled field that was his personal exercise yard. The guards stayed back a respectful distance as the two men began to talk.

Dr. Seb Gorka was on Kelly Turnbull's F-150's radio, talking about the new June 14th Donald Trump birthday national holiday, as well as the campaign to rename the new American overseas territory of Greenland "Trumpland." Gorka was in favor. Turnbull did not mention to his fiancé that they had met, or that the host was a decent shot under fire.

Lorna reached down and clicked the radio off.

"I need you to cooperate at the fitting," she said.

"Why a fitting? Can we just go to a Sears or something?"

Kelly Turnbull was sitting at the wheel of his Ford pick-up in Dallas morning traffic on I-35, with Lorna beside him. In between them was Gibson the dog.

"Sears has not been a thing for decades," she said. "And you are getting a wedding tux that fits."

"I'd rather go back to Africa."

"When were you in Africa?" she demanded, and Turnbull knew he had said too much. "Last month? Were you there last month? You told me you were at a training course."

"I meant the Toto song," Turnbull said, backpedaling. Or was it Poco?"

"'Africa?' 'Africa' is by Weezer."

Turnbull let that go, and Lorna let go her fiancé's travels – she knew his work was secret even from her with her own clearance. But the wedding thing was still bugging him.

"The only reason I am doing a fancy ceremony instead of paying a preacher $100 to hitch us is that I want to stick Clay Deeds in a sky-blue suit for a night," Turnbull said. "And then feed him some scotch and watch him sit in some sticker bushes. That would make it all worthwhile."

"That's very specific."

"I've given it a lot of thought."

"Well, I intend for this to be a nice wedding," Lorna said. "On the plus side we will not have a huge guest list since the only people you don't hate are undercover."

Turnbull veered right onto the off-ramp down to the surface streets. Gibson was attentive, looking out the windshield. A Dallas police car passed them down the exit. There were a Remington 870 pump and a Springfield SOCOM 16 in the rack in the back window of the Ford. Turnbull had his Wilson .45 on his hip. Lorna was carrying her 9mm Smith & Wesson Military & Police 2.0. The cop in the passenger seat nodded, and Turnbull nodded back. Just a couple of patriotic citizens exercising their right to keep and bear arms.

At the bottom of the off-ramp there was an underpass. There were several billboards there, one for Dan Bongino's Queens-Style Pizza Parlors ("Our Secret is Our Service!"), and another featuring a smiling, balding Vivek Ramaswamy touting his "Elite Billionaire Bit¢oin $$$trategy Seminars," but they was not what Turnbull noticed. The underpass was free of derelicts and trash, which was to be expected in the red, but what caught Turnbull's eye was something you did not see much in the post-Split United States of America.

Graffiti.

"Free General Scott" was spray-painted across the concrete face of the overpass.

"Hang him," Turnbull muttered, Lorna saw it too.

"Why do you always get pissed off when General Scott comes up? I mean, more than you usually do about everything."

"Not a fan," Turnbull said. He had not mentioned their run-in in San Francisco in the liberated western US. He typically did not mention much of anything – not merely because he disliked human interaction but because it was safer for his bride-to-be not to know. The threat was not hypothetical. A bunch of Scott's boys gunning for him had blown out one of her kidneys. She had recovered, but Turnbull was determined to keep her safe. And that meant keeping her in the dark, at least about some of the details.

Like Scott's involvement in the stolen H-bomb.

"They say his trial is coming up," Lorna said.

"Finally," Turnbull growled. "It's been months."

"I don't get the animosity. You would think you'd like him. He pretty much wants to kill every blue he meets too."

"Maybe I don't like officers."

"You are one."

"I'm not a general. Or a politician."

"You are definitely not political," Lorna replied. Her phone beeped as the map program indicated a turn. She pointed. "Left here."

Turnbull parked right in front of the Olivetti Tailor Shop, a store front on a quiet Dallas city street near a taco shop and a gun store. The front display windows held several headless mannequins modeling suits and tuxedos. Lapels had gotten thinner, and they looked odd to Turnbull's eyes – he was a child of the aughts. And what he knew of fashion would not fill a thimble.

He followed Lorna inside. The new Oliver Anthony song "New War, Old Story" was playing quietly in the background. Turnbull was not a fan of music in general, but he had heard it and understood how it was becoming an unofficial protest song for those tired of the endless war with the blue.

He put current events out of his mind. The sooner he got fitted with his monkey suit, the sooner he could be out of there.

Olivetti the tailor was short and round, but his stylish dark suit was set off by a bright red tie. You could barely detect the bulge of the Walther PPK he wore in a black leather rig under his right arm. There was a citizen pin on his lapel. He gave the dog a skeptical look, but Gibson was well-behaved and the customer was always right.

The man knew his customers, though. Several of the mannequins displayed various holsters, mostly leather. Some were quite elaborate. Fake plastic guns filled them. The American citizen of the mid-2030s was always packing.

Turnbull endured the fitting stoically. Every prospective tux was fine with him; none was fine with Lorna, and he would have to take the current candidate off and don a new one over and over again. But Turnbull figured it was the least he could do since he had inadvertently gotten Lorna shot. That he had killed everyone with a hand in the attack – with the exception of General Scott – made him feel a bit better.

But the fact that Scott was still drawing breath gnawed at him. Dr. Akebe would have smoked the traitor given the chance, and if Turnbull could have turned back time, he would have capped the sonofabitch and tossed him out of the rear of the C-130 that was bringing the prisoner to Dallas.

In retrospect, that would have been more appropriate due process than turning him over to a judicial system that was neither swift nor sure. It had been six months – six months! – and no trial and no hanging yet. It was almost like before the Split, when justice was delayed and denied with grim regularity.

"This one," Lorna announced. "The midnight."

Turnbull was swathed in a tuxedo he could barely distinguish from any of the others. Olivetti walked around him.

"Yes, the midnight," he agreed after considering it for a moment. Then he bent in and began pinning and marking it for tailoring.

"It's black," Turnbull said.

"It's midnight," Lorna corrected him. He shook his head. She shook hers back.

"I have a nice citizen pin for your lapel. It was my dad's," Lorna told Turnbull. Her late father had been a Marine in Desert Storm, so he was instantly a full citizen following the Split. No service, no vote.

Olivetti tugged and pulled on the jacket.

"Will you be wearing the .45 on your hip or thigh? Or do you need me to make a space for a shoulder rig?"

Turnbull frowned. He had not considered his wedding gun. That was a big decision.

"He's a 1911 man," she said. "Though the Wilson has seen some use."

Turnbull glanced down. The .45 on his hip was a bit scuffed.

"We'll think about it," Lorna said, and Olivetti nodded.

Turnbull was removing the jacket when his cell went off. Gibson and Lorna looked at him hard. He did not get a lot of calls.

Turnbull picked the iPhone off the pile of street clothes he had left on a chair and looked at the caller ID.

"I have to take this," he said, walking to the back.

Lorna knew better than to argue. She watched him go and turned to Olivetti.

"I need you to alter it for a right shoulder rig," she said. "It's a surprise. I'm getting him a Wilson SIG WCP365 as a wedding gift. He'll wear that."

"Lucky groom," Olivetti said, nodding. "I have a SIG myself to use for the fit. And the perfect black leather rig."

Turnbull hit the button to answer but did not speak until he got to the far back of the shop. He was out of earshot near a rack of dress shirts, though the dog came along so he was not technically alone.

"What do you want, Clay?" Turnbull said.

"I need you now," Clay Deeds said with finality. Turnbull usually bickered about assignments, but Deeds's tone made it clear there was no time for that today. And Turnbull detected a note of concern in his handler's voice. Even after their many missions, he had rarely heard that.

"I'm reading your location as an Olivetti's Tailor Shop," Deeds continued, sounding unsure of his phone tracker's accuracy.

"I'm with Lorna trying on wedding clothes," Turnbull said. "You're invited, by the way."

"I think that your nuptials might be delayed," Deeds said. "I have a vehicle on the way to you to bring you to me. There'll be a plane ready for you at the airport. Is there somewhere Lorna can go where she'll be secure?"

"Is she in danger, Clay?"

"I don't know, Kelly. I don't know much of anything except that this is bad."

"Tell me what you can over an open line."

"It'll be all over the news soon enough," Clay Deeds said. "General Karl Martin Scott has escaped."

3.

The corrections officer opened the door to the general's suite carefully, so as not to wake him abruptly. It was nearly one in the morning, and the US Marshals here to escort the prisoner on his surprise transfer were not particularly friendly. The guard had checked their papers and called his higher headquarters for confirmation. It was confirmed. The general was to be placed in the custody of these men immediately for transport to the United States Penitentiary Yazoo City along with several other transferees.

It was strange, very strange.

The guard flipped on the light and the general was there on his chair, fully dressed and sitting in the dark enjoying a scotch. USP Yazoo City, in Mississippi, was no vacation spot – he would not be getting the same treatment there, which might be the point of the no-notice transfer.

Except General Scott did not seem surprised.

"General, I'm sorry, but you need to go, and right now. There is no time to pack – we will send on what we can."

"It's all right," Scott replied. "Thank you for everything, Jimmy."

The marshals who were running the transfer were no Jimmys. They were brusque and undeferential, and like the two other men being transported with him, he was chained hands and feet. And they were in black tactical suits with vests and M4s. They hustled the general into a borrowed light gray US Bureau of

Prisons bus and walked him to the rear and chained him in hand and foot. The sergeant who brought him in tugged on the chains – they were solid.

"You're only doing your job," General Scott said.

"Shut your face, convict," the head marshal said. The general simply smiled.

A Chevy Suburban in Marshal Service livery led the small convoy. Next came the bus and then another Marshal Service Suburban. The guards were tense and silent except when they were shouting orders, usually for the passengers to pipe down. There were a driver and two guards, one of them the hostile sergeant, on the bus. A wire mesh kept the guard and the prisoner sections separate. The prisoners were seated with space between them. This did not stop them from trying to talk to each other.

"Why the hell are they taking us now?" a bald, thuggish looking man asked. "Transpo is usually after breakfast."

"Shut up!" the head marshal shouted.

"It's him," said the other prisoner, gesturing with his close-cropped afro back toward the general. "They want to make sure the general here gets where he's going, so they are changing up the schedule. And why are marshals taking us, not regular guards?"

"Sorry about the inconvenience, gentlemen," Scott said.

"Shut the hell up!" yelled the head marshal.

"I'm with you, General Scott," the bald man said. "I was in the 4th ID. I'm a citizen!" "ID," in this context, referred to an "infantry division."

"Thank you for your service," the general replied, without sarcasm.

"You must have messed up to be going to Yazoo, General," said the bald veteran.

"I know I did," said the other prisoner. "Punched a screw."

Scott did not reply, and the man turned his attention to the warders at the front of the vehicle.

"Hey guards, why the hell aren't we taking an airplane? We'll be all day to Mississippi. I'm gonna have to pee soon," said the other prisoner.

"Hold it!" ordered the head marshal.

"You're going to need a mop if you don't get me to a pisser or hand me a bottle," the prisoner replied sullenly.

The border was only a few miles west of Federal Correctional Institution Beaumont on I-10, and the advantage of leaving early was the traffic was light as they crossed over into swamp country. Long segments of the drive east were on the raised roadway over the swamps. The other two prisoners stared out the window, taking in the sights under the full moon. At Yazoo City, which was a maximum-security joint, they would not be seeing much of anything for years.

General Scott simply sat looking forward and smiling slightly.

Baton Rouge was coming up. It was hard to see from the back of the bus, but at the I-12 and I-10 split, the bus kept south on I-10.

The bald prisoner took no notice, but the other did.

"Hey dummies," he yelled. "You can cut across I-12 instead of going down through New Orleans. Save 20 minutes. Not that I give a shit. I ain't in a hurry."

"Shut up," yelled the leader. The driver was following the directions on his nav computer's screen.

"You take as long as you like!" the convict answered. Then he looked over at the general. "I'm from here."

Scott smiled.

The little convoy rolled on for over an hour. The sun was just coming up. Traffic was light.

"I gotta take that piss now!" shouted the convict as the three vehicles passed through Kenner.

Scott did not. He had intentionally dehydrated over the last 58 hours, except for a final snootful of scotch.

There was some discussion among the marshals up front at Metairie, and the convoy slowed down.

"Piss break?" the convict yelled.

"Shut up!"

The lumbering bus followed the lead Suburban as it got off the interstate at a cloverleaf and headed north through the city. Scott caught a glimpse of the signage – "North Causeway Boulevard."

"Where the hell are you going?" wondered the convict. This was a surface street, and the prisoners marveled at the shopping center, the Cheesecake Factory, and the Trader John's, Trader Joe's having stayed in the blue to satisfy the screw-top Chardonnay needs of the PR's many, many unhappy wine women.

In a couple minutes, they came to it – the causeway north over Lake Pontchartrain. The sun's tentative early light illuminated the vast estuary ahead as it stretched nearly to the horizon. The causeway was actually two low, parallel bridges elevated on pilings pounded into the bottom, each one supporting a two-lane highway. The two bridges were of nearly equal length, with the original causeway that opened in 1956 23.86 miles. The second was about .03 miles shorter; it opened in 1969.

It was the longest bridge in the world for decades until Guinness World Records considered handing the title to a bridge in communist China. There was a controversy which was solved by naming it the longest bridge in the world that was purely over-water. The issue was mooted in the early 2020s when Guinness World Records disestablished itself after apologizing "for its inexcusable legacy of ableism and white supremacy through its focus on 'achievements' as well as its racism and embrace of cisnormalism by stating categories that falsely accepted the gender binary." The group also specifically apologized for its fatism regarding the famous photo of the world's heaviest twins riding dirt bikes.

There was little traffic this early, just a few civilian vehicles headed up to Mandeville at the northern terminus. To the rear, a ways behind, was a Bekins moving truck. The bus rolled out over the water, bracketed by the Marshal Service Suburbans, just as the sun rose to the east. Scott simply smiled and waited.

The baby-puke green US Army bus pulled up to the front gate of Fort Polk, the legendarily remote US Army Joint Readiness Training Center (JRTC), and stopped at the entrance. The ancient vehicle was packed with about 50 soldiers, with their M4 rifles and day packs, though they would have seemed older than the troops you might find in a typical active-duty infantry company. But the gate guards likely would have written it off as reservists coming into the base for training. Thousands of active and reserve soldiers went through the JRTC training program here every month, and if the guards did a deep dive on every bus full of soldiers that appeared, even after midnight, they would create a traffic jam that blocked up Entrance Road for a mile through the small town outside the base gate. This would have enraged the proprietors of the tattoo parlors, the Korean BBQs, and the pawn shops that made base communities such a delight, and that would not do. The commanding general had enough headaches.

Instead of checking all their identification – though the men all had ID cards – the sergeant at the gate chatted briefly with the captain who descended the steps and then quickly waved the bus through. The captain's American accent was perfect, which was why he was playing the company commander. Unless the gate guards spoke Ukrainian, and they did not, they would not have understood a word of what the rest of the troops had to say.

The bus made its way past the billets and base operations offices, past the morale, welfare, and recreation facilities and past the various warehouses and equipment yards along Louisiana Avenue. Main Post was dead quiet at 0113 hours; off in the field, back in the endless training areas out there beyond the tree line, there were 24/7 ops training underway. You could occasionally hear a pop of an artillery simulator or the rip of a burst of machine gun blanks. But for the vast majority of the permanent party folks unlucky enough to be assigned there in the armpit of the Army, it was nighty night.

The bus lumbered on, with the leader – who was not the captain, since the leader's accent was quite pronounced – standing up and issuing his final orders. He had a scar on his cheek. His men listened intently, both because the major was squared away and because he was quite willing to blow out the brains of any one of them who threatened the mission in order to encourage the others.

They had seen him do it, back in Ukraine, in Africa, in Asia, wherever they had been hired for a job that normal men, men with either morals or common sense, would refuse to do. He would get them through it and paid, but the price was instant obedience. The alternative was the ugly end of a Makarov.

Polk Army Airfield lay along the eastern edge of Main Post; beyond it was the endless, trackless woods of the JRTC training ranges. There were a couple of prop planes – an RC-12 electronics support aircraft and a C-12 transport – parked near the row of hangars, but the bulk of the airfield inventory was the helicopters. There were a couple dozen UH-60 Blackhawks parked in neat rows, and perhaps a dozen AH-6s.

The bus pulled into the parking lot at the base of the tower. The airfield was dark – as promised. There were no aviation night ops that evening but several air traffic controllers would be working the tower in case the units out training in the bush needed a MEDEVAC.

The bus stopped in front of a cyclone fence gate that led to the airfield and dropped off six men. It then idled in the dark. The away team was led by the English-speaking captain, who actually was a captain within the Kurylenko Group. They moved toward the tower and they took their weapons. They looked very much like American soldiers, except for the suppressors on the end of their rifles.

Major Markus Vasilev stayed in the bus. He would have enjoyed a cigarette, but he was too disciplined for that. Incredibly, American soldiers did not smoke inside buildings or in their vehicles. It was hard to imagine, but it was true. Many of his men likewise jonesed for a Marlboro. Their hosts, who had picked them up from the ship that snuck them into Gulfport, had provided them cartons of the marvelous American cancer sticks as they holed-up in a bleak warehouse waiting for tonight. But none dared light up as the bus idled.

The captain called back over the Motorola about ten minutes later. It was done. His American accent had gotten the air traffic controllers to open the tower door. After that, it was a matter of shooting them all before they could make a cell call to the military police.

Major Vasilev nodded to Sergeant Drago, a Slavic behemoth who exited the bus with his bolt cutters. The lock to the gate was promptly disposed of, and the beefy NCO pushed the wheeled gate open. The hit team rejoined them, and then the bus went through the open portal onto the tarmac. Vasilev checked his watch. Right on time.

The aircraft they needed were the three positioned on the south ends of the two lines, a trio of Blackhawks and a trio of Little Birds. The bus stopped a respectable distance away, and it disgorged its passengers onto the airfield. The men moved with a purpose. The pilots took their helmets from their day packs as they ran to their aircraft. The rest of the men followed. Each had an assigned place, so there was no need for any discussion.

The six aircraft were not tied down or locked up – why would they be? The men loaded into the six helicopters even as the driver took the bus back outside the tarmac and parked it. He set the fire bomb for six a.m. local time – it was easier to burn it out than to wipe it down to eliminate DNA, prints, and other evidence. Then he ran back to one of the AH-6s and sat on the floor of the open side door with his M4 on his lap, chuckling quietly in Ukrainian with his comrades. There were safety straps they could use, but like his friends, he eschewed such feminine luxuries.

The rotors cranked and roared to life. The few people who noticed the helicopters lifting off assumed it was either a training iteration or a MEDEVAC – probably not the latter since there were six choppers rising into the air instead of just one, and none bore a red cross on a white field. They got up a few hundred feet, turned east and flew out in formation over the trees toward where the sun would be rising in several hours.

The AH-6 has a 206-mile range; the Blackhawk a bit over 350 miles. Their final objective was much farther than the Little Birds could fly, so they made for a hasty forward air refueling point – a FARP – set up in a remote field about 170 miles away from Ft. Polk, just south of Clinton, Louisiana, and far from major roads and prying eyes.

The FARP consisted of several cargo trucks and a repurposed CONOCO civilian fuel tanker filled with JP-8. Men on the ground guided in the six aircraft with flashlights and panels, and they powered down. The fuelers went to work, refilling the Little Birds and topping off the UH-60s. The truck rolled to them, and at each stop the men dutifully drove a grounding spike into the dirt. A spark from static electricity could ruin their whole day.

As the fuelers fueled, the armorers set to work. It was two Hellfire missiles per AH-6, plus ammo for their machine guns. Some of the men wondered what could be worth this expense, but they suppressed their curiosity and did their jobs. They were not paid to wonder, but to do.

They were on the ground perhaps thirty minutes, time to refuel, arm up, and take a leak. On Vasilev's order, they mounted up again and took off. The ground crew would police the area for evidence, dispose of the tanker and trucks, and redeploy to the rally point.

The helicopters flew southeast, into the early hints of dawn on the horizon ahead.

They were about ten miles out from Metairie. The convicts were enjoying eyeballing the rising sun over the water enough to temporarily forget about the lack of a rest stop. Dawn, something taken for granted by the free, was a particular treat for the imprisoned.

General Scott, instead of looking east, glanced to the northwest. Nothing. He understood that while all seemed calm here, the electromagnetic spectrum on the designated frequencies was probably quite active.

"Damn, what's with that truck?" the driver said. He had a rearview camera, not a mirror, and one of the marshals glanced at the monitor then turned to look through the cage mesh and out the barred back window. Scott turned too. The Bekins moving truck that had been behind them all the way from shore was now stopped and turned across the causeway, blocking both northbound lanes. It looked like smoke was starting to billow out of the cab.

"Driver probably fell asleep," the other marshal said.

"He didn't crash, though," the head marshal said. "I'll call it into 911 anyway."

The three-vehicle convoy kept moving at about 55 mph. A few civilian cars were with them in their pack, but no more cars were coming behind them. Now the sun was getting higher. It had to be nearly seven.

Scott looked out the window. There were six helicopters flying low in the sky a hundred feet above the dark waters of Lake Pontchartrain, just as Denton Q. Quinn had promised. Their white strobe lights flashed; Vasilev had ordered the choppers to keep them turned on to help avoid aerial collisions. That the beacons could be seen by people on the ground was about to become a moot point.

Scott identified them instantly – three AH-6 Little Birds and three larger UH-60 Blackhawks. The AH-6s broke low and in a line, while the UH-60s stayed higher. They were on an intercept course.

"Must be an Army exercise," the head marshal said from up front, but there was a tinge of doubt in his voice.

As Scott watched, there was a flash on the side of one of the Little Birds, and a missile jumped off the side rail trailing white smoke as the rocket streaked toward the bridge ahead of the gray prison bus.

"Shit!" yelled the driver.

Scott could see, through the mesh and the front windows, the Hellfire slam into the rear driver's side quarter panel of the lead Marshal Service Suburban, detonating on impact. The SUV exploded in orange flame, gray smoke, and clouds of atomized metal. It flipped and tumbled forward, the energy of the 55 miles per hour momentum dumping out on the surface of the roadway. Parts and pieces of it littered the road.

The driver threw the bus's steering wheel left hard to avoid the debris, and the vehicle was thrown into the left lane. Scott expected the jolt, but the other convicts were slammed hard and the marshals who were not driving sprawled in the front cage.

Another missile tore off the rail of a different bird. It was aimed at the rear Suburban, but it overshot the target and flew into the water of the lake, blasting up a white geyser of water and foam.

The bus was still moving, and the oversteer caused it to slam hard against the causeway's concrete left wall, sending a shower of sparks along its side and against the windows. The convicts swore and took cover, which Scott watched with bemused detachment and curiosity about how the attack would proceed.

The smoking, ruined hulk of the front Suburban came to rest in the midst of the roadway, straddling lanes, and the driver of the bus overcorrected again to the right. The convicts and the marshals were thrown in the opposite direction, while Scott held on. The angle was wrong to try to avoid the wreck and get through between it and the causeway wall. The bus's right front side clipped the concrete eastern wall and the bus came to a halt. It now almost blocked the two lanes of the causeway heading north.

The second Suburban, having just dodged a missile, skidded to a halt about twenty feet from the bus that now trapped the Suburban and several civilian vehicles. The marshals, most of them vets, instantly deployed out of the Chevy with their M4s, and it was a good thing – a few moments later a third Hellfire found its target and blasted the empty Marshal Service SUV to fiery bits.

The helicopters passed overhead with a roar and Scott heard the sound of rifle fire from above and from the causeway.

Up in the front guard cage, the marshals were in a frenzy. The bus was wedged against the causeway wall at the front door, so even if the three marshals wanted to get out, they were trapped. The driver was trying to restart the vehicle. The lead marshal was on the radio calling it in – "We're under attack by helicopters!" he shouted into the mic. The third marshal just gripped his M4.

The convicts knew the score.

"They're here for you, general," the one who had to pee said, looking back at Scott.

"Take me with you," said the bald one.

Scott said nothing.

The AH-6s flew above the causeway behind the bus, with the shooter passengers sitting with their legs hanging off the sides engaging with the four marshals who had gotten out of the second Suburban. The rate of fire was high. Scott saw one of the marshals fall amid a hail of bullets that kicked up puffs of concrete around him. But another marshal made his shot, and one of the mercenaries pitched forward and out of the aircraft, splattering face-first on the number one lane.

"Should have worn a safety strap," Scott noted to himself.

One of the UH-60s hovered over the empty lanes about 100 meters ahead of the bus. But now any of the traffic not caught behind the crippled bus was long gone up the road. The Blackhawk disgorged eight men, including the hulking Sergeant Drago, who carried a large, heavy weapon in his thick arms. They made for the trapped bus. Two paused to spray rifle fire into the smoldering hulk of the Suburban.

While it was a mission to take a prisoner, they were not going to be taking any prisoners.

"What the hell are they doing?" the lead marshal said, gripping his own rifle. The approaching men did not even bother trying to breach the front glass with their own M4s. That was a non-starter. Instead, they set up a perimeter while Drago walked obliquely to the front of the bus with his Barrett Model 82A1 .50 caliber rifle and lifted it to his shoulder.

"Shit!" yelled the driver from his seat as he cranked the engine one last time before Sergeant Drago fired.

The round entered from the left side, punching through the armor as if there were no armor at all. The mercenary chose the angle with care to ensure that the heavy slug did not go all the way from front to back and inadvertently take out their target. As it were, it vaporized the upper thorax of the driver, spattering the mesh between the guard cage and the passenger compartment with red, meaty chunks of fresh government employee.

The convicts were shrieking and the two surviving marshals were too, but Scott watched it all with a detachment that belied his presence in the midst of the firefight. He was chained to his seat, so there really was nothing to do but watch and see how it played out.

Drago fired again from the shoulder, then again, and there was chaos up front and more gore. Scott had a good view of the mercenary firing out the left windows from his seat. He speculated to himself that the mercenary's shoulder was going to hurt like hell tonight.

Drago fired twice more into the marshals' cage, and there was no more noise from up front. The convicts were both yelling, but Scott ignored them. He was busy watching one of the other Blackhawks come over top of the bus and disappear from sight as it hovered above.

Scott's attention went back to the firefight behind the stuck bus. The third UH-60 had dropped a squad a few hundred yards to the rear. That group was sweeping forward but seemed to be pinned down not only by the surviving marshals but by civilians in the trapped cars who were engaging the attackers with their own weapons. Scott admired their spirit.

The surviving marshals now numbered two, and they were fighting hard against the shooters in the choppers making passes above. The AH-6s now came in closer, and at least one of their shooters paid with his life before the last two marshals went down fighting. The gunbattle with the civilians was still on and the AH-6s now went to join that.

The nearby defenders dead, the attackers could enter the next phase. The hovering Blackhawk came in lower over the bus, and there were four separate thuds. Jumpers. There were men on the bus roof. The UH-60 veered off.

Scott watched, waiting for the next development. He did not wait long. There was a loud machine noise on the roof, and a silvery metallic beak poked through the ceiling of the bus on the right side, then another on the left. They began to cut – each one was a pair of metal shears that was tearing through the roof like a tin can. They cut in a rough parallel about two feet apart. The roof was not armored, as it never occurred to anyone that someone might try to break in through it. They had not considered the Kurylenko Group.

After about four feet, the two parallel cutting tracks turned into each other until they met, creating three sides of a rough rectangle with a little glint of morning sun shining through the cuts. The shears withdrew, and to one of the long sides two bolts about a foot apart powered through the roof. Then feet began kicking in the metal until it came free. A face with a scar on the cheek appeared, with a suppressed pistol ready, scanning down inside the bus. They had cut a door in the bus's roof.

The face disappeared and down flopped a metal chain ladder – the two bolts anchored it. Major Vasilev was the first down – he did not use the ladder but dropped into the center aisle, pistol ready. The general's eyes met his, but the major ignored him and then moved to the front leading with his weapon, a suppressed HK USP Tactical .45. At the mesh he paused and looked over the carnage. Someone in the marshal's cage said something Scott could not make out – apparently Drago's Barrett had not killed everyone. Vasilev replied with three suppressed shots then turned back.

Another mercenary dropped inside. He wore a pneumatic tank on his back and carried the metal shears that had cut through the roof. He and Vasilev moved up the aisle to Scott, ignoring the convicts who were peppering them with questions and demands for freedom.

"General Scott," Vasilev said.

Scott nodded. The other mercenary moved in with the shears and snipped through the chains at the general's feet and hands. Scott rose up and stretched.

"Now cut me out too – I gotta whizz," said one of the convicts. Vasilev raised the USP and shot him in the forehead, then the bald one as well.

"Let's go," General Karl Martin Scott said.

Post-Split, Louis Armstrong New Orleans International Airport was still Louis Armstrong New Orleans International Airport, even if it was not always such a wonderful world. Turnbull landed there in a Citation M2 Gen 3 jet that Deeds had set up, and it rolled to a remote corner of the airport where an Airbus H135 helicopter in the livery of GasPro, an oil rig support company, was waiting. The short flight out over Lake Pontchartrain took only a few minutes, but from miles away he could see the flashing blue and red emergency vehicle lights on the causeway's northbound lanes. As he got closer, he saw a moving company big rig blocking the southern end of the chaos, and a gray bus blocking the north. There was wreckage, and lots of man-sized tarps on the road. They flew over the spectacle, and as he looked down, he saw what appeared to be a rectangular hole in the roof of what looked like a prison bus.

"What the hell?" Turnbull said under his breath.

The chopper deposited him several hundred yards north of the crime scene. Clay Deeds was there, with a small team of surly personal protection guys Turnbull had seen with him before. The leader of the four-man squad was a shave-headed bulldozer named Rothko, first name unknown to him. The barrel tip of his MP7 submachine gun poked down below the hem of his blue suit jacket. The guards all wore Oakley shades.

"I wanted you to see this clusterfark and tell me what you think," Deeds said as the group started walking south past the cop cars, ambulances, firetrucks, and coroner vehicles. Many had left their flashing lights on, giving the tableau an even more surreal and unsettling vibe.

Deeds continued.

"They stole six helicopters out of Polk last night. Blackhawks and Little Birds. Capped three soldiers in the tower. The aircraft were fueled and ready, but not armed."

"They had to refuel somewhere between here and there," Turnbull said. "The Little Birds don't have the range."

"We're looking for where that happened," Deeds said.

He stopped at the shattered Suburban that had been the first casualty.

"That looks like a Hellfire," Turnbull said, incredulous. "Where do you get Hellfires?"

"Good question, Kelly. I'm not sure we will like the answer," Deeds said.

"They refueled and rearmed. This was planned to the gnat's ass."

"And they were not playing around," Deeds said, pointing to the wreckage. "They did head shots on the marshals in there. They did headshots on *everyone*. Marshals. Civilians. No survivors."

"They knew it was a murder beef so they didn't hesitate," Turnbull said.

"Eleven marshals. Seven civilians. Two convicts. And one missing prisoner."

"General Karl Martin Scott."

"Who the hell could do this, Kelly?"

"I could, with my guys," Turnbull said. "But I have an alibi."

"They got the convoy isolated out here on the water. We can't figure out who set up the route, but it was intentional. Insiders. They were moving Scott because the Bureau of Prisons guards were co-opted and were letting him live like a king. They chose marshals because they were not compromised like the Bureau of Prison guards."

"And they were expendable."

Turnbull and Deeds, trailed by his bodyguards, walked past the prison bus. It was lodged against the causeway wall at an angle nearly blocking the roadway. There were several large holes in the left side by the driver's seat.

"We think they used a .50 cal to shoot up the guard cage on the bus," Deeds said. "Back there a few hundred yards is a Bekins moving van stolen out of Baton Rouge a week ago. They used that to block the causeway behind them. The cab is burned out. No evidence. Now, there were witnesses going south on the other roadway. One was former 101st Air Assault, so he identified the aircraft. He said they fought from the choppers. He also said one of the Blackhawks dropped guys on the bus roof. We figure they cut through the roof, capped the surviving guards and the other prisoners, then hustled Scott out."

They walked on. There were a lot of shells on the road, and a lot of tarp-draped bodies. Cops in uniform and plain clothes were taking photos and video. They gave Deeds and his crew a wide berth.

"One hell of a firefight," Turnbull said.

"We're pretty much only finding 5.56mm casings," Deeds said. "I want to show you something."

They stopped at a runny, vaguely man-shaped red splotch on the concrete roadway.

"Our guys got at least one of the bastards," Deeds said.

"Looks like someone fell out of his chopper," Turnbull said, considering.

"They recovered the body before they left. They poured bleach on the blood to make sure we can't get any DNA."

"It wouldn't come back with anything anyway," Turnbull said. "They're not American."

"What are you saying, Kelly?"

"I'm saying I saw this on the last mission you sent me on. Kurylenko Group. Ukrainian mercs. It was in my debrief. They like helicopters and they don't strap themselves in."

"I know them," Deeds replied. "They are on the ground in the blue. They train the People's Republic Army, or whatever they are calling it this week."

"I don't imagine they are popular on the other side," Turnbull said. "They seemed to know which bathroom to use."

"Why Ukrainian mercenaries, Kelly? Why not disaffected US forces?"

"They have the skill set, they have OPSEC, and if one takes a face-plant into the asphalt there are no parents asking questions. Plus, there's no hesitation about killing other Americans."

"This op goes deep," Deeds said. "Half of America wants Scott free. There are already people online celebrating."

"I should have killed him when I could have," Turnbull said. "But no, I had to trust the justice system. I'm not going to make that mistake again."

"You have to find him, Kelly."

"Any idea where he went?"

"Radar tracked them flying out over the swamps. Then, poof."

"He's in the wind. No way they planned all this without an ironclad out for Scott and for the mercs."

"I need you on this," Deeds said.

"I assumed," Turnbull said. "Though when you assume, you make an ass out of you and me."

"I don't know who to trust in our red government," Deeds said.

"How about nobody?"

"My people will dig from our end. We'll find you a lead and vector you in when we do. In the meantime, my people are securing Lorna."

"And the dogs," Turnbull said. "Don't forget the dogs."

4.

The barrage of four 155mm shells hit the concealed forward observation post almost simultaneously, kicking up chunks of black earth and tearing apart the already scarred and battered trees caught inside the burst radius. Bits of wood and clods of dirt fell lazily from the smoky sky. The thunder of artillery rolled over the ancient battlefield once again.

There were no casualties because Major George Ryan, Jr., had walked into the position unannounced and saw Private First Class – soon to be Private No Class – Dunwoody having a hushed conversation on his old iPhone 23 as his sergeant peered north out over the no-man's land that ran across rural Pennsylvania. Junior Ryan let out a string of obscenities. The private nearly vapor locked.

The soldiers bolted and took cover a hundred meters away in the ruins of the Eternal Peace Memorial that had once dominated the northern edge of the Gettysburg battlefield. Seconds later, the shells came down on the abandoned OP. They shut their eyes and let the noise, the debris, and the blast waves wash past them.

The once-proud monument that was providing them cover had been reduced to a heap of pulverized concrete and marble by prior direct bombardments. Now the steps were the only recognizable part of the ruins. The major and his party, along with the 19D scout sergeant and the hapless PFC Dunwoody, huddled behind several large chunks of marble that lay on the grass and waited out the strike.

The four high-explosive rounds, point detonating as they impacted the rich Pennsylvania earth, were probably from a Chinese Norinco AH4 155mm towed howitzer battery ten to twenty miles away to the north. Their target section had locked in on Dunwoody's cell phone signal. That's why Ryan had nearly had apoplexy when he saw the trooper jabbering away on it.

"You dipshit!" the sergeant said to his subordinate when the explosions subsided, grabbing him and pushing him against the rock. The soldier's Kevlar helmet made a loud CLUNK as it made contact. The private's eyes were wide as plates.

"General Scott escaped," he blurted out. "They ambushed his bus, killed the guards, and freed him."

The sergeant paused.

"My girlfriend," the private panted. "She called to tell me and I forgot not to answer it."

The sergeant slammed his man's helmeted head into the stone again.

"You can't even have a cell phone on!" the NCO shouted. That was the rule, no cells on within 30 miles of the front line. The People's Republic Army – wait, now it was called the "People's Republic Anti-Colonial Military Land Forces" – had electronic warfare units that triangulated on cell phone signals and called in arty strikes. Of course, the US forces did that too.

"You and your girlfriend nearly got us all killed," Ryan growled. He had seen the phone call and grabbed the scouts and got the hell out of Dodge, and not a moment too soon. The enemy gunners were fast – it was probably Chinese "volunteers" manning the Chinese equipment. The Americans were lucky to be alive.

"But what's this about General Scott?" Ryan continued.

"He's escaped. He's gone," the private sputtered.

"Good," said his sergeant. Scott had a lot of fans in the ranks.

From a distance, to the south, there were booms. The division's M777A2 medium towed howitzers were firing counterbattery back at the AH4s. The US targeting radar read the shells' trajectories coming in and plotted their origin. If the Chi Com gunners had not picked up and pulled out of their positions practically the instant after pulling the lanyards, they would be finding the DIVARTY's 155mm shells raining down on them in a few seconds.

Ryan was now the executive officer of 5th Battalion, 327th Infantry, second-in-command of about five hundred paratroopers. The battalion was a reserve unit, technically, but he had been in it fighting for over a year. He had been a company commander and had jumped into San Mateo during the invasion of California. When the former XO departed – he got killed by a sniper near Chambersburg – Ryan was acting S3, the operations officer. As the senior captain, he moved up and got his gold oak leaf. Now he was second-in-command.

But a lot of the other captains who started the war were dead. And a lot of the troops, too.

The 101st Airborne Division had been moved from the West Coast to the East Coast, and here they were on the front line of the war against the People's Republic. Early on, US forces had pressed north. This front was a supporting effort, with most US forces in the west, and it did not get too far north. The war settled into a static battle, and once again Gettysburg became part of the frontline in a war between the states.

The 5-327th Infantry got a long frontage, too long really, when it relieved the shattered 28th Infantry Division a month before. The men grumbled that an elite unit trained to attack deep into the enemy's rear via parachute or helicopter was wasted in a static battle holding ground like some leg infantry unit. But Ryan had seen the classified reports from higher, and the situation was grim.

Casualties were higher than anyone expected, and there were now even desertions, something you almost never saw earlier in the war. It was received wisdom that citizens did not desert, yet now it was happening. And the troop pipeline was emptying. Everyone who wanted to be a citizen was already under arms.

The reservists who made up the bulk of the red American military were getting called back for a second or third tour. The elite Screaming Eagles were holding the line here against what was left of the People's Republic because there was no one else.

Ryan and his escort left the sergeant to his wall-to-wall counseling of the private who had almost gotten them all killed. It was not technically legal for a sergeant to beat the snot out of a junior enlisted man, but there was no time for nonsense like nonjudicial punishment or court martials when a simple attitude adjustment would be far more effective and efficient. Ryan was just glad that he did not have to report any more casualties to the battalion commander.

His driver called in and got the all-clear from the air defense section – no enemy drones detected. It was safe to move. The remotely piloted aircraft could spot artillery too, and a couple of HUMVEEs heading down the Chambersburg Pike would be an inviting target for Chinese AH4 cannons, whether the ones that just took a potshot at them or another battery. Artillery was the primary killing system here, that and direct attack drones. Rifle fire, which mowed down men here like wheat being scythed 170 years before, was rare. The two sides kept their distance. The PR was too weak to push the US out of Pennsylvania and the US, its combat power draining, was too weak to push forward through the PR lines. This theater had always been the orphan campaign. The Pacific thrust had been the priority, but it bogged down at the Oregon border. The Chinese and the Russians fed in enough forces to keep the PR alive, but not enough to end the war. Stalemate was in their interests, if not in the interests of the inhabitants of North America.

The rutted and charred landscape passed by as the two vehicles sped toward the battalion main command post. Ryan hated to go back there. He belonged in the field, visiting and checking and correcting. As XO, he was the designated bad cop, the hard ass, the dick. It gave the CO the illusion of being a nice guy, which Lieutenant Colonel Badham was not. A high school track coach in civilian life, but with a half dozen combat tours, Badham was competent and demanding. He knew that anything less meant men in black plastic bags being shipped home to mommy. Like Ryan, he could accept necessary casualties, but not unnecessary ones.

Were any of them necessary?

Ryan lay back in his seat as the engine whined, annoyed that this insurgent thought had infiltrated back into his consciousness even after he had tried to banish it. He knew the PR like few of his men. Many of them were too young to even remember a time before the Crisis that brought America to the edge of civil war and the Split that tore it asunder. They grew up in the red United States; all they knew of the PR was that it was a bunch of communists who wanted them enslaved or dead. That's what was taught in US schools, along with the reality that there were only two genders, that climate change is a hoax, and that 1776 represented the founding of America.

And what they learned about the People's Republic was true, but not the whole story. Not by a longshot. The true story was much worse. Ryan had been a soldier in the border skirmishes before the collapse, getting his citizenship before serving two full years because some PR bastard shot him. Then he had, through chance, been paired with Kelly Turnbull, assuming that was his real name, and had gone into the People's Republic in search of his sister. That had opened his eyes.

Before all that, to him the PR's inhabitants were just a bunch of semi-comical cardboard villains. Their bizarre language. Their ridiculous notions of gender. Their stupid, ever-changing flag. But then he saw what they did, how they broke fellow Americans, murdered them, and tyrannized them. He had enlisted in a special operations group and gone back into the blue on missions on his own. And he grew to hate the PR with a cold fury none of his troops, except those who had escaped its clutches and come to the new United States, could imagine or understand.

But still, was this war necessary? After all, it was endless wars that could not seem to be won that helped set the conditions for the Split. Of course, there was much more than that, like a regime that centralized power and disenfranchised normal people, a cultural war upon them, and even the politicization of the legal system to persecute dissenters. And now, that last part seemed to be happening here in red America. Ryan had been outraged when General Karl Martin Scott was arrested. He was a hero, a general who got results instead of being bogged down. His criticisms of the war's execution were well-known and, to Ryan's thinking, legit. Scott would have been a strong presidential candidate, except he was sidelined with charges that seemed to be trumped up at best.

And yet when he was sitting with Kelly Turnbull on the porch at the ranch kicking back Shiners and the subject of General Scott came up, Turnbull turned more ferocious than usual.

"He's a piece of shit," Turnbull said. "And guilty of a lot more than the crap they are trying to nail him on."

That's all Turnbull would say. He was not giving up any more. Ryan sensed a history, but Turnbull was not talking.

And now Scott was loose, broken out apparently. Ryan was in some ways glad the general was free, because the hell with the government. But then, that meant someone had crossed the line into internal fighting here in the United States itself.

Could a country in a civil war break out in another civil war? And if it did, what side would he be on?

The former Chase Tower was on Ross Street and loomed over what had been the Dallas Arts District. The high-rise rose up fifty-five stories and used to be one of the top ten highest buildings in the city until the Split and Dallas's elevation to capital of red America. Now dozens of buildings dwarfed it, many new but some old like the green I.M. Pei–designed one from the Eighties that was twisted around and looked like a pine tree.

Renamed the Smith & Wesson Tower, it was still a prestigious address.

Kelly Turnbull looked up to the top, then mentally counted down two floors.

"I assume you hit terminal velocity if you get tossed from the fifty-third floor," Turnbull wondered aloud, shielding his eyes from the sun as he stared into the sky.

"Alive," Clay Deeds chided him. They were standing by the hood of a Chevy SUV. His team of about a dozen operators in plainclothes, led by his lead guard Rothko, waited in bunches near their own idling black Suburbans. "Alive is the whole point."

"No promises," Turnbull replied. He drew his Wilson .45 and did a chamber check. As always, there was a hollow-point seated in the pipe. He put it back in his holster.

"Denton Q. Quinn was the last visitor Scott met with," Deeds said. "We've sweated the prison guards and they don't know anything, but they did say he and Quinn were alone and we know they talked outside of range of the microphones. We need to know what was said."

"We're just going to have a nice, reasonable talk," Turnbull replied. He took a long cardboard box marked "Lone Star Floral" off the hood, put it under his arm, and started walking down the sidewalk to the entrance of the S&W Tower. There were no bums, derelicts, or hobos as there would have been before the Split. It was not allowed.

"Alive!" Deeds shouted after him.

The lobby of the building was wide, airy, and very busy, with people in suits going to and fro from the wide bank of elevators. Turnbull admired the FN SCAR rifle of one man and how it went so nicely with his suit. It was important to coordinate your assault rifle with your clothing, and his was a real assault rifle, fully automatic, just as guaranteed by the Second Amendment.

Others packed less firepower, but it being Dallas, a lot of the open-carry pistols were polished chrome. In contrast, Turnbull was dressed down. He wore his jeans, a button-down shirt, and his beat-up 1911 pistol on his hip.

There was no security desk or check-in downstairs – since most everyone was packing, there was no reason to bother. If someone got frisky, he was going to get ventilated. From the number of citizen pins on the lapels of the passing workers – probably fifty percent – there were a lot of ex- and reserve military. You did not have mass shootings in red America anymore. You had, rarely, the *beginning* of a mass shooting, and then you had the would-be murderer shot to pieces by armed citizens who would then be publicly awarded "The President's Medal for Criminal Elimination." The award was red and white and shaped like a cross-hair, and if you wore the miniature pin on your lapel, you rarely bought your own drink.

Turnbull walked straight over to the express elevator that serviced floors 46-55, making sure to exude the vibe that he belonged there. He passed a display in the foyer that was sponsored by the Department of Families which consisted of several nubile young women passing out literature about the importance of marrying early and breeding often. The USA was determined not to allow itself to slip into the demographic freefall that was plaguing most of the rest of the West – notably not Hungary and Poland though. Kelly noted the irony that allegedly uptight prudes of red America had an aggressively pro-sex agenda.

He unconsciously began quietly whistling the reworked Ted Nugent tune that had been the early theme for the campaign, now retitled "Wang Dang Patriotic Poontang." The octogenarian guitarist had recently given up his title as "American Rocker Laureate" to Congressman Kid Rock.

Turnbull got in the elevator car with a half-dozen others. Most were wearing citizenship pins. One middle-aged matron had her ancient M1 Carbine – the wood furniture was polished and inlaid with some shiny gems – slung over her back and Turnbull had to scoot over so that the chrome barrel did not accidentally wallop his face.

"I just hope General Scott gets past this crap," one man in a blue sport coat packing a comically large Smith & Wesson Model 29 told his companion.

"This false prosecution stuff is like something out of the People's Republic," his companion replied. He was in a charcoal gray suit cut nicely to make room for his black CZ 75 pistol.

Turnbull ignored them. By the time they got to the 53rd floor, only the lady with the World War II–era carbine was still in the car. The door opened and she went out first. Turnbull followed.

The foyer of the offices of Quinn, Dunn and Duffy, PC, was done in blonde wood and large glass panels that separated off the actual offices from the entry area. There was a dual glass door that led back there, and Turnbull noted that it had an ID swipe for access. Directly ahead of him, under the name of the prestigious law firm and its symbol – a Q that appeared to be eating the two Ds – was a pretty woman in a pantsuit manning a wide desk.

Turnbull approached her, carrying the flower box. She was on the phone, with a modern German Luger in bright pink lying next to her keyboard. She had a phone headset on and ignored Turnbull as he came to a stop in front of her.

"Chief Justice Pikl's chambers for Mr. Quinn," she said, connecting the call.

Her eyes flicked up at the newcomer.

"Delivery," Turnbull said, lifting the flowers. "Mr. Duffy."

"Mrs. Duffy," the receptionist sniffed. "Put them down here. Where do I sign?"

"Uh, just a second, I really gotta hit the head. Can I...," Turnbull began. The glass doors opened and two lawyers – you could tell they were lawyers by their pale skin and beady eyes – walked through. "It's okay, I got it!"

Turnbull walked through the closing doors and into the offices. Behind him, the receptionist was telling him to come back but the doors shut behind him.

Turnbull moved with a purpose down the path between the row of cubicles and the window offices, trying to look like he was supposed to be there. No one seemed to notice him; they were all occupied with their own tasks. Most looked like lawyers or support staff, but some he made as plainclothes security. None bothered him. He aimed at the northwest corner of the massive suite, figuring that Quinn would have the corner office with the best view of the New Capital Mall built where the old Love Field used to be.

Turnbull guessed correctly. Quinn's office was located right at the northwest corner. There was a thug in a nice suit he certainly did not buy for himself looking down at his phone while seated on a couch outside the closed blonde-wood double doors. On the doors was a brass plaque: "Denton Q. Quinn, Esq., Counselor at Law." The thug had a black Mossberg 590 pump shotgun leaning against the wall. Across the foyer from him a serious looking middle-aged woman sat at the desk just outside the doors and securing access to them. A Marlboro dangled from her mouth and smoke hung in an angry cloud above her head. She had dyed hair – the gray roots showed – that was piled high like that old band the B-52s. They were a lot of fun, but had chosen to go with the blue after the Split. Turnbull read somewhere that the surviving bandmembers had disappeared into the PR gulag archipelago after one of the periodic cultural purges had resulted in "Private Idaho" being condemned either as "aggressively militaristic" or "pro-capitalist."

Turnbull walked up to the desk, and the thug registered only the vaguest interest when he glanced up and immediately returned to his phone game. The secretary regarded Turnbull silently with her smoking butt held upward in her right hand. The ashtray on the desk was overflowing. A nameplate read "Mrs. Russell." She had no gun in sight.

"I need to see Denton Quinn," Turnbull said.

"Mr. Quinn," the secretary corrected him. "Is unavailable."

"He'll see me."

Now the thug was on his feet and walking over, unsure if this was actually a problem but not taking any chances.

"I told you. He was unavailable," Mrs. Russell repeated.

"And I told you he would see me."

"Hey…," the thug began and Turnbull spun and punched him in the throat – actually a bit lower so he would not crush the man's larynx. It had the desired effect – the thug fell to his knees wheezing desperately, forgetting anything other than his need to take a breath. Turnbull slugged him with a hard right to the jaw and the thug sprawled across the rug.

The secretary dropped her cigarette and went for her desk drawer. She pulled it out, revealing a cocked and locked .45 among the papers, pens, and cigarette packs. Turnbull thrust his right hand out and grabbed her right wrist as her finger tips danced on the weapon's grip. He locked tight and his eyes scanned the desk until he saw the blue button. He picked up her M1911 pistol with his left hand and used the butt to slam down on the button. There was a buzz, and the double-doors to Quinn's office popped open a crack.

Turnbull let her go and walked to the entrance, dropping the mag and racking out the round in the chamber. He tossed the gun to the side and pushed through the doors.

Quinn sat in a rich leather chair with a telephone receiver to his ear about forty feet away behind an elaborate oak desk. The blonde wood walls were covered with photos and awards representing his life as Texas's foremost *macher*. There were huge glass picture windows behind him – you could see the New Capitol, the New White House, and the Trump Monument, among other landmarks.

He put his phone down in the receiver without saying "Good-bye" and stared at Turnbull, incredulous at the visitor's presence in his inner sanctum.

"What the hell are you doing in here?" he demanded. He thought Turnbull was probably some lost maintenance worker. He found the intrusion an outrage.

Turnbull pivoted and pulled the doors shut, hitting the manual lock, then turned back to the lawyer. Then he started walking.

Quinn was staring, considering his options. Turnbull took the most dangerous one off the table at the threshold.

"I know you are thinking about grabbing whatever sissy gun you have stashed in that desk and, if you do, I am going to splatter you all over that chair."

Quinn had not been considering that – he had no gun and never carried one. That was for minions. Not being armed was a power move when everyone else was packing. But not in this situation.

"Who the hell are you?" he demanded.

"I am looking for General Karl Martin Scott," Turnbull said, closing the distance from door to desk across the finely woven Afghan rug that covered the hardwood floor. "I hear you and the general recently had a chat."

"I don't discuss my clients with the police, detective," Quinn said.

"I am not a cop."

"Then who are you?"

"A concerned citizen with zero patience," Turnbull said. There was now pounding on the doors behind him, but Turnbull figured they were designed to keep the bad guys out of the office. The problem with that was there was no allowance for when the bad guy was already inside the office.

"You are making a grave error, sir."

Turnbull came to a stop in front of the massive desk. Quinn was still seated, and he was wearing a blue pin-striped suit with a lavender shirt and a paisley tie that matched his pocket square. A citizenship button was affixed to his lapel – Turnbull suspected this was one of the few individuals granted citizenship without a hitch in the military for "special services." Yeah, this guy definitely serviced the elite.

"A grave error, and I mean the word 'grave' in its literal sense, would be you not talking right now," Turnbull said. The banging on the doors behind him was getting louder.

Quinn pushed himself back from his desk but did not get up.

"You think I'll bend to ham-handed threats?" he said. The noise from his security men outside in the foyer had given him a courage infusion.

Turnbull drew the .45 and blew a moderately-sized chunk of Quinn's left thigh all over the floor. The round passed through the outside flesh of his leg, through the chair, and into the bottom of the floor to ceiling window behind him. Besides the mess, there was now a crack through the length of the glass pane.

Quinn fell on the floor, screeching, grasping his thigh over the gaping flesh wound and shredded fabric. Behind them, the frantic pounding increased exponentially. Turnbull watched him, the Wilson in his hand.

"You shot me!" Quinn howled.

"Sorry about the pants. I'm going to ruin the jacket next. Where the hell is Scott?"

"I can't!" Quinn shrieked.

Turnbull blew a chunk out of his upper right arm. He was trying to miss the arteries and veins, and it appeared he had succeeded. As much of a mess as it was, it would have been much worse with active spurting.

"Back to your pants," Turnbull said, making sure Quinn saw he was aiming at the wounded attorney's crotch.

Quinn merely moaned.

"I mean it," Turnbull said quietly, but Quinn heard him loud and clear even over the noise from his men as they tried to break in.

The .45's yawning barrel hovered over the sobbing lawyer.

"Three," Turnbull said. "Two." He did not announce that it was a countdown to castration. He figured Quinn was a smart cat who would figure it out.

"Okay!" Quinn shouted. He was wrapped up in his own arms, one hand grasping his thigh, the other his bicep. Red was dripping through both sets of fingers and pooling on the rug.

"Good," Turnbull said. He had been wondering what he would shoot off next after the field expedient circumcision. The window was cracked, so he had considered kicking through the glass then hanging the man out of it fifty-three stories up by his Gucci loafers.

Quinn groaned again. Something that sounded like a saw roared to life out in the foyer.

"Like, now," Turnbull commanded.

"The blue," Quinn gasped.

"What about it?" Turnbull asked. He did not understand.

"That's where he is. The blue!" Quinn shut his eyes and moaned again.

Turnbull's mind raced – that had never occurred to him. It was some faction, some rogue element here in the US. What the hell would Scott be doing in the blue? They hated Scott as much as he hated Scott.

"Bullshit," Turnbull replied, taking aim at the lawyer's junk.

"No, no, it's true, I swear, it's true."

"Don't lie to me," Turnbull said, still not trusting the attorney. After all, the lawyer's lips were moving.

"They reached out to me," Quinn said over the sound of whatever cutting tool his men were using to get through the doors.

"You talk to the blue?" asked Turnbull.

"I talk to everyone."

"If you are lying to me, get used to sitting to pee," Turnbull warned him, finger on the trigger.

"They reached out to me. I made some calls. Connected people. Set things in motion."

"People in our government working with people in the blue?" Turnbull said, thinking it through. Whoever did it had to have help on the inside. It still did not make sense.

"Why would the blue want him?" Turnbull asked.

"I don't know," Quinn said. He was looking pale and clammy.

The cutting tool was some kind of rotary saw and the blade sliced through at about five feet and was cutting downward. Sawdust was kicking up into the air.

"I think you do know." Turnbull took aim.

"I'm just the damn messenger!" Quinn howled. "All I know is the blues want to make a deal with him."

"A deal?"

"That's all I know!"

The activity at the door was getting louder.

"Stay there," Turnbull told him unnecessarily.

He turned and walked a few steps until he was at an oblique angle to the door they were cutting through. He aimed the .45.

The cutting stopped. There was a ruckus outside the door, a loud one. No shots but lots of muffled thumps and yelling.

The tritium sights of the .45 floated over the face of the door as Turnbull waited. It took a minute to settle down.

"Kelly, it's all right," shouted a muffled voice from the other side.

Deeds.

Turnbull lowered the gun.

"It's all secure," Deeds shouted.

"Be right back," Turnbull told Quinn. He walked to the doors, one of which now had a jagged saw cut running down it vertically. He unlocked the doors and opened them up.

Deeds was there, in a vest marked "FEDERAL POLICE" and carrying a SIG. The rest of Deeds's security detail were similarly garbed. They were as much federal law enforcement as he was the Easter Bunny. They packed long weapons. A half-dozen of the disarmed Quinn, Dunn and Duffy plainclothes security thugs were on their knees, fingers interlocked behind their necks, under guard.

"How did your discussion go?" Deeds asked.

"Illuminating," Turnbull said.

"And Quinn?"

"Alive," Turnbull answers. "Though not exactly intact."

Deeds grunted and entered the room. His face changed – dismay? Turnbull looked back.

Quinn pushed his leather chair into the cracked window. The glass shattered outward, showering the street below with shards.

Turnbull and Deeds started toward him as Quinn crawled toward the hole, the wind whistling through.

He got his hand on the edge and began pulling his legs with him. Deeds was running now. Turnbull simply raised the .45 and shot Quinn in the left butt cheek.

Quinn shrieked and grabbed his shattered ass. Any notion of climbing out the window dissipated in a pink cloud of vaporized gluteus maximus.

Deeds got to the injured man and pulled him back away from the window. Turnbull walked over and slid the .45 into his holster.

"You could have grabbed him," Deeds said. "Was that absolutely necessary?"

"Probably not," Turnbull replied.

5.

General Karl Martin Scott assessed that he was not quite a prisoner, but not quite free either. The cuffs and chains were gone and the Ukrainians – he instantly pegged his liberators as Ukes, having served as a secret advisor to the Ukrainian Army during the war with Russia – were respectful. But there was no question where he was going. They got him up and out of the bus, through the bloody battlefield that the Lake Pontchartrain Causeway had become, and onto a UH-60 Blackhawk.

A medic checked him over to ensure he was undamaged as they lifted off. He allowed the examination without objection and observed the Ukrainians' actions in departing. They capped all the potential witnesses and extricated all their dead and wounded. It looked like they were spreading bleach on any of their own blood – they had taken several casualties getting him out, but he did not feel any resentment from his hosts.

Mercenaries, he assessed as the aircraft rose into the sky. Quinn had not told him to expect that, but he suspected it might be hired guns instead of American patriots. After all, he knew his ultimate destination, and not all patriots would be willing to go that far.

Why did the People's Republic want him so bad they would break him out of prison to get him? If they wanted him dead, they could have just left him in the United States' hands. The reds would get around to hanging him eventually.

Whatever was happening, it had support in the red. There was no way this could have been set up without insiders in the USA.

The medic finished his exam and turned to the man who, back in the bus, Scott had instantly identified as the leader. He had a scar on his face and his men seemed to fear him.

"I am Major Vasilev," the leader told the general over the noise of the rotors. "We have an hour flight in this helicopter."

"My thanks to you and your men. Good work."

Vasilev nodded.

The Blackhawk flew low and fast into the rising sun across the shimmering lake, the other aircraft behind it. They made landfall and flew on until they hit the swamps. The dope runners of prior decades had used dozens of airfields scattered among the endless trees, with the authorities largely unable to cope with the sheer volume of traffic. That stopped after the Split, when the US won the drug war by escalating to shooting drug smugglers. It is all fun and games flying in a $10 million load of coke in a Cessna until someone blows you out of the sky with a Sidewinder missile, turning you into a flaming cloud of white Bolivian party powder.

In fact, that concept became a hit movie post-Split – "Cocaine Croc" starring Lady Gaga, Senator Nick Searcy, and action movie star Dave Reaboi as cops fighting PR drug dealers and a giant water lizard. During the climax, the heroes realized that the saurian had a taste for leftists, and in the end, they left it on its own to continue doing the Lord's work keeping the swamps red in every sense of the word. Of course, crocodiles are not native to Louisiana – alligators are, but the alliteration prevailed.

The primitive airfields were still out there, a bit overgrown but still a generally open patch surrounded by forest. The helicopter set down on one that was deep in the swamp, but still next to a road – dopers had to get their wares out and the Ukrainians needed to get to their next stop.

They shut down the Blackhawk and some began wiring it even as the other aircraft landed and unloaded, and were themselves wired. The men each took a labeled trash bag that contained jeans, shoes, and a civilian shirt, and their black uniforms went into them with all their gear except their rifles and spare mags. Those they would not give up quite yet. The men, now in mufti, handed back their full trash bags to the disposal team. The bags would all find their way to an industrial furnace.

Once changed, each man went to a designated van. There were a half-dozen vehicles, all of them with markings of local churches or swamp tour companies. The mercs ensured that the local sheriff's deputies would not be interested in any unfamiliar vans that day. They were looking for the red 2027 Dodge Charger that their sheriff had pulled over that morning. Its occupants had sped off toward New Orleans after they shot him.

Sergeant Drago called Vasilev over to the plastic tarp that served as the casualty collection point. Three dead from the causeway were lying in a row, wrapped up like burritos in plastic tarps. There were seven wounded mercs. Four were ambulatory and had returned to duty patched up. One was stable. Two others were gut shot. They looked sweaty and moaned. Drago shook his head and Vasilev shot them both in the forehead with his HK USP. Scott, who remained with the major, said nothing. Nor did the other men, who continued working as the disposal team wrapped the fresh corpses in plastic tarps.

Bad luck for them. They knew what they signed onto.

Vasilev confirmed with each van leader that all the assigned men were accounted for and gave the order to depart in five-minute intervals. The disposal team finished loading the trash bags and the corpses into the disposal truck. They would find their final rest in the industrial furnace as well.

The vans maneuvered along tough country roads until they reached slightly better roads, finally reaching State Route 607 north. It was only then that Scott found out they were actually now in Mississippi. It was a couple miles to Interstate 10 and they turned east.

As they approached the exit for the Gulfport-Biloxi Airport, Vasilev turned on the radio to a local news talk station. After three gun store ads, the *Larry O'Connor Show* returned. His guest was Bethany Mandel, the motherhood activist with twelve children who was supporting the "Four or More Kids" campaign. She was explaining that procreation was patriotic.

"I did my part," O'Connor said defensively.

"I guess," Mandel replied, sounding unconvinced.

Vasilev waited for the newsbreak, and there was nothing of interest in the headlines, just the usual war news and gossip about the latest Ben Affleck/J Lo marriage – both had made a beeline for the red when the People's Republic announced the 92.7% "Fairness and Anti-Racist Income Tax."

Almost two hours after the battle on the bridge and the news of General Scott's escape had not made the wires. Vasilev turned the radio off. The airport exit was just west of Biloxi.

An Embraer ERJ (Embraer Regional Jet) 145 in Con-Am Charter livery sat on the runway at the private aircraft terminal. It had landed an hour before after flying in from a small airport near Pensacola. The Con-Am pilots lay dead in a ditch on the outskirts of the airfield near where the Kurylenko Group pilots had taken it from them. The flight plan on file was to Mexico City.

At about the time the Embraer closed its door on the last of the mercenaries, which was coincidentally about the time that the disposal team finished tossing the last body into the furnace, all six of the helicopters detonated in fireballs out in the swamp.

Now, twenty hours later, General Scott was at his final destination. He sat looking out of the skyscraper's window – he saw it was the 54th floor – down at the long stretch of green – actually, there were patches of brown where the neglected trees and grasses died – that extended north toward Harlem. He was drumming his fingers on the arm of the elaborate French couch as he observed, waiting for what would happen next.

He had made the trip from the Gulf Coast by plane south to Mexico City, then back circuitously north around Florida and up the Eastern seaboard far out over the Atlantic. It was a chartered Bolivian Airlines 737 that the red Americans would hopefully not shoot down. The US did not molest them. The Kurylenko men were with him the whole way.

They had flown into what had been Kennedy Airport. Of course, that name had to change, as Kennedy was probably fascist and definitely cis, but it was not changed to an actual new name. Every faction demanded recognition when the debate began as to the new name. The most recent candidate had been the Ocasio-Cortes-Harris-Marcuse-RuPaul-Mulvaney-Guevara International People's Airport, but this was deemed "too cis" even with 40% trans representation, as well as "too ableist, too Northern Hemisphere-centric, and too complicit in the erasure of Otherkin." The dispute had not been resolved even after a decade; it was simply referred to as "the Airport."

Scott took an AH-6 helicopter from the tarmac toward Manhattan, riding next to Major Vasilev and escorted by five other Kurylenko aircraft. He said little, and simply watched. He concluded that someone in the blue had his own private army, or hers, or xis.

The choppers flew in formation over Brooklyn, which seemed to have undergone whatever the opposite of gentrification was during the decade plus since he had last been in New York City. Looking down, it looked like a dystopian wasteland. Looking ahead, the skyline was dominated by the century-old "Decolonization State Building," where King Kong had famously suffered his death at the hands of the colonialist and speciesist people of pallor.

Their destination was clearly Midtown. After sweeping in from the East River, the squadron turned north at what he recognized as Broadway. The sun was setting in the west, but the areas outside the secure zones were largely dark, except for the flickering of what were probably innumerable cooking fires.

Midtown, however, was aglow with electric lights, especially in Times Square, where the colors flashed and sparkled. The large pre-Split video monitors still blared, showing the world that the People's Republic was still a first-world nation, though uttering that colonialist/racist/imperialist term was a felony.

Shapes danced and shimmied on the towering screens, depicting people of all kinds, diverse externally but uniformly weird to his red American eyes, while they cavorted across the screens. "SEXUALITY IS A CONTINUUM," flashed one, which then changed to "LOVE KNOWS NO AGE" as an elderly dude lasciviously petted a girl who could not have been older than twelve. Another was a recruiting ad featuring a general in a skimpy leather harness and leather puppy-mask holding his kneeling staff by a half-dozen leashes that led to their camouflaged collars. The legend read "JOIN OUR PACK – THE PEOPLE'S REPUBLIC ANTI-COLONIAL MILITARY LAND FORCES!" Scott now had an idea where all the freaks and perverts that the red Army purged from the senior ranks of the old US military following the Split had found a home.

The fleet of helicopters slowed and hovered over a tall skyscraper not far from the southwest corner of Central Park. There was landing pad, and apparently the Kurylenko Group had made it its base of operations. Vasilev hustled him out of the aircraft, into the chill of the dusk, and they ran to the access door with heads low to avoid the whirling blades.

The next day, after a relaxing sleep in a magnificent bed, Scott was drumming his fingers on the arm of that costly French couch. There was nothing to do but wait. He looked around. There were other equally fine chairs and tables in the suite. There was a black telephone on the coffee table between the couch and the seats. It was a luxurious space for a conference, and he wondered who he would be conferring with.

As he sat alone, he stared at the giant unhoused encampment in Central Park beyond the wall that bisected it, dividing the green space into the Midtown Secure Zone and the ungoverned chaos of the rest of the island. Of course, the term "unhoused" was no longer used – it was a misdemeanor to demean the unhomehaving. He had read intelligence about the city prior to his detention. Outside of the Security Zones where the rich people still on the island lived, it was unstable. No doubt it was even worse now, months later.

Scott wore a very nice suit, English, and in his size. It was a nice change from the prison garb. He had learned about clothing after his original retirement, serving on corporate boards and mingling with politicians before coming back to take on the challenge of finishing the North American War, as the rest of the world called it.

He missed the good life.

The door to the suite opened, He knew the face.

"President Richard Harrington," Scott said, standing. "Chairman of the People's Republic *politburo*."

My title is 'Temporary Rotating Executive,'" Harrington corrected him. "It's a recent change."

It was. The title previously had been "president," then "prime minister," then "president" again, then several other titles, until six months prior when it became "Temporary Rotating Chief Executive." But that changed just a month previously to "Temporary Rotating Executive" because indigenous peoplx took offense to the word "chief."

"In any case," Harrington continued, "it is a true pleasure to finally meet you in person."

His voice left doubt as to his veracity. He smiled like a cobra. For Harrington, this was not a weakness. He enjoyed projecting ambiguity.

He did not extend a hand to shake. Hand-shaking ratified and affirmed patriarchal violence.

"It is somewhat odd to be face to face with you," Scott said. "Considering you were at the top of our capture or kill list."

"And you on ours," Harrington said, gesturing for the general to sit again. He sat himself.

"The contention was that you were quite the war criminal. Murder, looting, transphobia," Harrington continued.

"Am I here to be tried?" Scott asked, settling back onto the couch.

"Oh, I think we need to get past all the respective unpleasantness," said Harrington. "I understand your own people have similar concerns with you, beyond the ones for which you were imprisoned."

"I was told there was an arrangement to be had," Scott said, changing the subject.

"And so there is," Harrington replied.

The door opened again. Three servers entered, a lovely young woman with tea, a handsome young man with small finger sandwiches, and a nonbinary with blue hair and a large metal stud through xir nose carrying a silver tray heaped with grapes. They came forward, placed them on the antique wood table between the men, then stood waiting.

"As an administrative matter, you may take whichever you wish, or all of them," Harrington said. "Our intelligence files on your preferences were unclear. They think cis, but so many of you are repressed and hide your true nature. There are other options as well. Do you enjoy furryplay?"

"Let's focus on our business," Scott declared, not bothering to camouflage his irritation at the tangent.

"As you wish," Harrington said, shrugging and turning to the servants. "Dismissed."

The trio filed out of the suite, and Harrington continued.

"I am simply attempting to make clear that you are welcome here. Very welcome."

"You should tell me for what, Mr. Chairman."

Harrington grimaced as Scott reached down and took a cup of tea off the tray.

"That word again, 'chairman.' We do not use that term. It's actually a crime. Sexist language. I believe it is a felony if charged as an aggravated microaggression."

"I don't care about your ridiculous word games, Harrington," Scott said.

"Well, you had better start if you want to be the president of the reunited United States."

Scott put down the tea cup.

"What did you just say?"

Harrington smiled and ignored the question.

"As Temporary Rotating Executive, I am the Chair*being* of the Supreme Political Bureau of the People's Republic of North America," Harrington declared. "Meaning that I am no one."

Scott said nothing, waiting. Harrington went on.

"Oh, the other eighteen Council members endlessly argue and debate, except for the two of them who refuse to speak in solidarity with either decolonialism or climate change, I forget which. I simply act as ringmaster for the circus. And it is not even our own circus. The Chinese, and to a lesser extent, the Russians, truly rule. Chairman – he does go by 'chair*man*' – Zhou makes that quite clear. The People's Republic is basically a communist Chinese vassal state, left in chaos with one overriding purpose."

"To facilitate the rise of communism and wokeness?" the general suggested.

"Oh no," Harrington scoffed. "Nothing like that. The purpose of the PR now is to ensure that the war continues and that America cannot unify, because a strong, unified America is the only potential threat to Chinese dominance. Look at Europe. It is exhausted. Only Great Britain, which is neither great nor fully Britain anymore, even tries to resist."

"And what do you envision that I can do?" asked Scott with genuine curiosity.

"You are the one figure who might possibly unite the United States again."

"But your people hate me."

"And they will continue to hate you until told differently. Of course, we cannot be too abrupt in shattering their expectations. We will have to introduce you slowly as our national savior. For your part, you will need to understand and demonstrate our values and norms."

"You mean be woke?"

Harrington grimaced again. "That word is likewise a hate crime. It will take you time to learn our ways, but learn you must."

Scott picked up the tea cup again and sipped. It was good.

"And the reds?" he asked. "What do you expect from them?"

"I know the outlines of what you were *really* imprisoned for, and it was not overzealously prosecuting the war on the People's Republic."

"And what do you think that was?" Scott asked.

"I think that you were plotting a coup," he said. "And I think you expected to kill many thousands of your own countrymen to do it. I am not sure of the details, but that is what my information tells me. Now you tell me, since we must be transparent – is it true?"

Scott smiled.

"It is. I sought to overthrow the feckless American government, and I intended to sacrifice tens of thousands of innocent Americans to do it. Is that what you wanted to hear? Is that enough to convince you that I am willing to do the same thing on a larger scale with a reunited United States?"

"You do not know how happy it makes me to hear you say that," Harrington said. "Because it erases any doubts I might have had about how committed you might be."

"Of course, the red American leadership knows all this, though it is a state secret. They might…hold it against me."

"They might not have that option," said Harrington. "A critical mass of red America adores you. In fact, your escape shows that there is some enthusiastic support in the red for our endeavor. When the conditions are right, if you tell the Americans to accept peace and unity, they will. After all, no one has proven a fiercer foe of the People's Republic."

"Only Nixon can go to China," Scott said.

Harrington sighed. "It's a hate crime to mention Nixon. He was a racist."

Scott ignored that.

"I see obstacles."

"Yes," Harrington said. "The conditions must be right. And one condition is demoralization and despair. The American military is wavering ever so slightly, but not enough to compel the people to change course. That requires a disaster."

"Your forces do not have the power to inflict one," Scott said.

"But you do," Harrington said. "With your help, they can make a mistake, a grave strategic error, and that will set the conditions for peace. Naturally, the logical unifying figure would be General Karl Martin Scott."

"With you playing an important role behind the throne," Scott said, eyeing the Chairbeing.

"I only wish to serve my country," Harrington said. "Not countries. One country, again."

Scott said nothing. He was looking out the window.

"General?" Harrington said, a bit concerned.

"You say you need to inflict a demoralizing defeat on the Americans. That's quite a sacrifice. Though for peace, perhaps it will be worth it. But what are *you* prepared to sacrifice?"

"Anything," Harrington said. "And anyone."

"Has your order of battle changed?" asked Scott.

"I am not sure what you mean, general," Harrington said. "I am not a person of militaryness."

Scott sighed. "Before my detention, your forces were largely deployed on a front line across New Jersey and Pennsylvania to Pittsburgh, Columbus and up to Chicago."

"That's been the front line for some time. There's a stalemate."

"And north of that – are there any other forces deployed back from the front?"

"As I understand it from our generals, who sometimes seem focused on non-military issues, we have few soldiers behind the front in reserve. Some Chinese units, mostly in northern

Pennsylvania, but well behind the front it is mostly People's Security Force units that track down insurgents, racists, transphobes, and the like."

"As I thought," Scott replied. "We long ago understood that if we could crack the line and get through, your front would become unstable and collapse."

"But you have not done it yet. Why?" asked Harrington, unsure of where the general was going.

"We do not have the combat power to break your lines, and if we try, the Chinese units in northern PA will counterattack. That's why we looked for an alternative."

"An alternative?" asked Harrington.

Scott was rolling now, back in general mode.

"We asked where we could break through and move north to a position where we could destabilize the PR's front, and do so far away and fast enough to neutralize the threat of a Chinese counterattack. There was only one place where it was possible."

Scott looked at his co-conspirator, grinning. Harrington shrugged.

"Here. New York City."

"I don't understand," admitted Harrington.

"We wargamed it out and drafted a plan. Our forces smash through the lines in New Jersey and eastern Pennsylvania then combine with Army airmobile and Marine forces to invade and secure Manhattan from the air and the water. It would be a huge symbolic victory to capture what was once the greatest city in the world, and it would destroy blue morale. Operationally, holding Manhattan would threaten the entire flank of the front line, but also allow us to attack north into a totally undefended New England. The PR's East Coast defenses would collapse."

"It's a crime to call New York 'the greatest city in the world,'" Harrington said. "It's racist and colonialist, but the plan sounds brilliant."

"No, it's idiocy," declared Scott. "At least, that is what I thought. We were ready to do it – a lot of the logistics work was done – but I quashed that plan."

"I don't understand," confessed Harrington.

"The plan sounds wonderful on paper. So did the plans for many defeats through history. But it relies on false assumptions."

"Like?"

"Like that your forces make a series of implausible errors. You would need to pull forces out of New Jersey and PA in a deployment for some reason, and the ChiComs would need to not get suspicious. That would solve the first problem, which is fighting all the way up to New York City quickly. A fast strike means that the ChiCom reserve cannot move to block the attack, and if they try, US air power attrits them on that long move and they cannot not get into position to stop the US in time."

"Conquering Manhattan does not sound like a disaster," Harrington said. "We need a disaster."

"Manhattan *is* the disaster. It's a quagmire. Over a million people on a densely packed island. You have to fight for it and then feed it once you take it. Besides the militias, the PR has armed psychos and criminals, and has fed them drugs to get them to fight since before the Split. In urban combat, that would be devastating. Their resistance would suck our forces – and it will take a lot of forces – into a meatgrinder. Speed is key, but you cannot take New York City fast. Once you hit Manhattan, not to mention the other boroughs, your attack comes to a dead stop. It sounds great – 'We have recaptured New York!' – but actually taking it would be a debacle."

"In other words," Harrington said, seeing clearly. "It would be exactly what we need."

And it would be what he needed. Manhattan was already only barely governable, with the various militias and street gangs the *de facto* government in most of the island and the drug-fueled crazies roaming the streets. Midtown was still under People's Security Force control, but only barely. Manhattan was already lost, though no one could ever dare admit it – the propaganda apparatus of the People's Republic portrayed it as a veritable paradise, enough so that gullible young people would travel there without permission and end up drowning in the urban cesspool if they could not learn to swim fast enough. It drained money and food and troops and for what? Give up New York City and the blue government are really only giving up a giant problem.

"And you said this plan exists?"

"It does, and I barely stopped it a year ago. It has its advocates, and they are convinced it will work. If I sent word to my friends in the armed forces and in the government to execute it, it could happen."

"How quickly?" asked Harrington, intrigued.

"A couple weeks," Scott replied. "The pieces are in place. You will need to move some PR forces to clear the way."

"I can arrange it."

"You will not want to evacuate the island, of course," the general said. "Casualties are the point. You need to make Manhattan an armed camp."

Harrington admired the general.

"You are refreshingly cold-blooded, General. These are your own troops who will be casualties in this bloodbath."

"Soldiers die," Scott said. "That's what they get paid for."

"I think you will make a wonderful president. Once the disaster becomes apparent to the red, you will arise and call for peace. You will offer to broker a deal. And you will be the obvious savior."

"This is a high-risk proposition," Scott observed.

"And high reward," Harrington noted. "The Split was never going to be sustainable. Reunification was unavoidable, by bayonet or by agreement. We are simply bowing to the inevitable. Obviously, the rest of the Council will not be aware of our plan. I doubt that they would appreciate a plan that eventually ends with them all against some wall."

"Obviously. But I need something else before we agree to go forward."

"What's that?"

"Revenge," Scott said. "It is personal and petty and I want it."

"Then you will have it."

"The men who took me to prison. They would be a problem anyway, but we can kill two birds with one stone by killing them."

"Then they will die. Who do you want to leave this mortal coil?"

"I am not sure where to find Kelly Turnbull, but I suspect that problem would be solved by solving the problem of one Clay Deeds."

"I am familiar with these names," Harrington said coldly. "And I agree that the world will be a better place without them. "He reached forward and picked up the receiver of the phone on the table. Putting it to his ear, he said, "Send me Major Vasilev."

Then Harrington hung up.

"This was a rare productive meeting," Scott said.

"Yes, it was, General," said Harrington. "Or rather, Mx. President." He pronounced it "mix."

Scott did not correct him.

"One other thing," Harrington said.

"Yes?"

"What is the name of this operation to take Manhattan?"

Scott smiled.

"Overlord."

6.

"I am at over 312,000 followers for @FullMetalGalt," Casey Warner informed Kelly Turnbull from the passenger seat of Turnbull's F-150. He was looking through his chunky black glasses down at his phone and bursting with pride.

"I know all those words," Turnbull replied. "Just not in that order."

"@FullMetalGalt? My Twitter alter ego." Casey said, as if explaining something to a child. "We've actually talked about this before."

"I wasn't actually listening," Turnbull said. "Because social media is stupid and I don't care. Also, you can be tracked using the Twitter app, so turn it off."

"I'll take the risk," Casey answered sullenly. "No one knows who @FullMetalGalt is, only that he's based."

Casey's FN SCAR 16 CQC carbine was lying across his lap with the stock folded. He wore a blue blazer with brass buttons and four more 30-round 5.56mm mags inside slipped into the purpose-sewn pockets. His 9mm CZ 75 SP-01 Tactical pistol was on his thigh in a custom leather holster, since they were going somewhere nice.

Turnbull scanned the road ahead less from a particularized concern than from habit. Downtown Dallas was moderately busy, but if there was not a war on with a big chunk of the working age populace in uniform, it would have been much more crowded. A higher proportion of those still here were noncitizens, but not being able to vote did not seem to bother them much. No one was shooting at them, unlike the citizens.

"One minute out," Turnbull said, glancing at his nav system. "We're early."

"When's Clay supposed to show?" Casey asked.

"Twenty mikes. I guess we can sit in the bar."

"I can sit in a bar for twenty minutes," Casey said. "I've been there before with Clay. Good people watching. Lots of celebrities. I saw Jesse Kelly there once. He's like seven feet tall."

"He did a good job as Secretary of Anti-Communist Reconstruction," Turnbull remembered. The post-Split campaign Kelly spearheaded to remove leftists from any position of authority in government, business, culture, and academia in red America had been called OPERATION I TOLD YOU SO.

Turnbull saw the U-shaped driveway up ahead and hit the turn signal.

Flesh took up the first floor of one of the many skyscrapers in downtown Dallas, and this one was only a couple blocks from the Smith & Wesson tower where Turnbull had paid a visit to General Scott's mouthpiece two days before. In fact, he could see the building in the distance. Turnbull steered the truck off the street and into the driveway. There were BMWs, Porsches, and other swank vehicles. He idled behind a Maserati with a gun rack.

There was a valet stand in front of the entrance, and behind the polo-shirted valets, their matching shoulder holsters all bearing Glock 17s, was a walkway leading up to the front doors of Flesh. In the middle of the path was a giant statue of a polka-dotted cow. It was supposed to be whimsical, but Turnbull found it stupid.

"Why couldn't we go to a Sizzler?" he grumbled as he pulled to a stop. "Does Flesh have a potato bar?"

"Your problem is that you are a barbarian, Kelly," Casey sighed. "Flesh is the hottest steakhouse in Dallas, and even Clay probably had to call in favors to get a ressy."

"Ressy," Turnbull sneered. "Just talking to you is dropping my T."

His door opened and Turnbull's hand fell to the Wilson handgun on his hip. The valet paused for a moment until Turnbull relaxed.

"Keys, sir?"

Turnbull handed them over. His key ring had a small Leatherman tool attached.

"You can leave your long weapons or check them inside," The valet said as Turnbull stepped out onto the pavement. He wore a blazer too, with his nicest jeans. They were not that nice. He was seriously underdressed.

"I'll leave the rifle," Turnbull said, gesturing to the HK417 in the rack in his rear window. He had picked that as his evening long weapon because it just felt right with the vibe.

Turnbull pocketed the valet ticket and walked around the truck to Casey, who had his SCAR. The valet took the truck and headed across the street to the parking structure where they parked the rides.

Turnbull and Casey started up the walkway past the bovine monument.

A plaque gave the piece's title: "SACRED COW."

"What kind of animal is a cow?" Casey asked.

"What?" asked Turnbull, confused.

"A cow. What kind of animal is it? Like, a doe is a female deer. A mare is a female horse. A cow is a female what?"

Turnbull considered the query for a moment.

"Stop talking, Casey," he said.

They went inside through the glass double-doors. Flesh was fancy. It reeked of money and entitlement. Turnbull would have felt more at home on Venus.

He paused inside, admiring the Flesh Wall of Fame. Talk superstar Dana Loesch's portrait was up, a signed still from the famous episode of her Fox reality show *Here Come the Loeschs!* where her hubby Chris brought home a full-grown Komodo

Dragon. Photos memorialized such diverse and distinguished individuals as late-night TV host Chris Stigall, Supreme Court Chief Justice Pikl, and former congresswoman/current musical theater star Lauren Boebert each finishing the "Flesh 72-Ounce Porterhouse Challenge" were hung next to Senator/famous actor Nick Searcy's autographed still from his *Justified* spin-off sitcom, *That's My Mullen*. And action hero Matthew Marsden was represented a photo of the star as his iconic character Elvis Michael Caine from *The Destructonator* movie franchise, signed with his catch-phrase, "Cheers, you commie bastards! You've been destructonated!"

Turnbull took it all in as he waited for the couple in front of him to be seated.

"May I help you?" inquired a pretty young woman at the hostess stand when the couple was taken into the dining room. Her name tag read "Coulter." She wore a tight black dress with a chrome Walther PPK in an understated holster hanging off her belt. No citizenship pin.

Turnbull left Casey to deal with her. He located the exits and the kitchen door, then scanned the scene. He spotted a few citizenship pins. Lots of rich people – it looked like a bunch of older men were out with their adult daughters tonight.

The décor was minimalist, befitting a steakhouse. It was all dark wood and white linen. The walls were decorated with portraits of whimsical cows in top hats and monocles where the walls were not covered by racks of wine bottles.

"Joey Ramone, party of three," Casey told the hostess. "We're waiting on our third."

He had picked the alias that Deeds had used to reserve the table. The young woman did not blink.

"I can seat you while you wait," she said, scooping up menus. "Do you want to check your carbine first?"

Casey nodded and stepped over to the gun check window. Another pretty girl with a name tag reading "Kristi Teagarden" manned the counter. The law required gun checkers to wear a nametag with their full name.

"Just the rifle or the handguns, too?" she asked.

"We'll keep our pistols," Casey said.

She handed him a claim ticket and Casey handed over his SCAR and the spare mags.

"Nice," she said, admiring it. Miss Teagarden then turned and placed the gun in a rack next to an impressive variety of firearms.

"I could date her," Casey whispered to Turnbull.

"In your imagination," Turnbull said.

They followed Coulter the hostess to their table near the rear wall. It had excellent lines of sight. Turnbull took the seat that backed up against the wall.

Casey opened up the wine list and began scrutinizing it. The French wines were limited, as much of France was under sharia law. There were, of course, no Californian vintages either. The vineyards of Napa, Sonoma, Paso Robles, and Santa Barbara had – except for the ones owned by the Newsoms, the Pelosis and other members of the PR nomenklatura – been redistributed to marginalized peoples as reparations for the vintners' complicity in the old US system of oppression. Naturally, that was a disaster, with most of the vines dying and the winery facilities being scavenged and looted.

"There's a great Idaho red from Nampa," Casey said, not raising his eyes up off the page.

"Napa?" asked Turnbull.

"Nampa. Nampa is a thing."

"Didn't Steve Martin serve Kermit the Frog and Miss Piggy one of the finest wines of Idaho?"

"If you weren't a troglodyte, Kelly, you would know that Idaho is the hottest wine region in North America, at least right now."

"I'm just not fancy like you. I drink beer like a man. When did you become a wine snob?"

"The word is 'sommelier,' and I learned everything I know about wine watching that 'Red Wine' show with the Conservative Wine Guy, Drew Matich."

Casey considered his options, and ordered a Matich-approved Famici Malbec from the Snake River Valley. He made a great show of swishing it around in his glass, commenting on its legs, sniffing it, then taking a swallow.

"I get hints of shoe leather and tobacco," he declared, placing the glass back on the table. Turnbull gulped down some of his own.

"I get hints of red wine," he said, placing his glass back on the table.

"Savage," sniffed Casey.

"Gentlemen," Clay Deeds said as he approached the table. Rothko and the rest of his security men were semi-inconspicuously stationed around the dining room and by the entrance. People seemed to notice him – he was clearly someone. That made Turnbull uneasy. But then, this was very public – nothing was likely to go down with all these people around. He relaxed a bit.

Deeds sat, his back to the people staring. He wore a tan suit and a purple paisley tie that few cis men could pull off.

"I see you two got started celebrating without me."

"Casey was introducing me to the finer things in life," Turnbull said.

"And it is about time. In any case, I wanted to recognize your impending nuptials by taking you out. How do you like Flesh?"

"Are they going to be upset if I ask for ketchup?"

"Oh, Kelly," Deeds said.

The waiter poured some of the cab into Deeds's glass. He also went through the process before tasting it.

"Good, but I miss California wines. The sooner we can get Napa and the rest producing again, the better, but it is going to be a decade before they can once again consistently bottle anything you would not use to clean engine parts."

"The blues ruin everything," Turnbull said. "Now, when do we go back in to get Scott?"

Deeds looked around. The other tables were set off a few extra feet, as he had asked when making the reservation, so they could talk freely if they did not shout.

"Good question," Deeds said. "Quinn did not know anything more about where Scott is than he told you. We pressed him and if he did know anything, he would have told us."

"I could come shoot him again if you want," Turnbull suggested. "Incentivize him."

"That's what we threatened him with. He was just a conduit. Of course, he was talking to front men, so there's deniability about the bigwigs here who were in on it."

"What's our government doing about this?" Turnbull said, expecting Deeds to answer "Nothing."

"Nothing," answered Deeds. "The jailbreak caught them completely off balance. They don't know what to do."

"I do," Turnbull said. "Send us into the blue to finish this once and for all."

"I'm in," Casey said, taking a sip.

"But the problem, gentlemen, is that we don't even know where he is. Do we send you back to Seattle to look for him in Hillaryia? Or New England? New York City? Chicago? There is still a lot of blue on the map, and he could be anywhere."

"We can't just cool our jets while he's out there," Turnbull said.

"Maybe you can take advantage of the situation to get married," Casey said.

"Hey Kelly, we found Scott. Cut short your honeymoon!" Turnbull said. "No, I need to do this first."

"It's not even official government policy to eliminate General Scott," Deeds said.

"It's my policy," Turnbull replied.

They clammed up when their waiter returned and recited the specials.

"We have a 30-day dry-aged prime Jim Hanson's Man Meat ribeye," the waiter said. He carried an old-timey Colt .45 pistol in a beaded leather holster.

"And some kind of fish," he added.

Turnbull got the special, but when it came, he could have sworn it was actually a New York strip. It didn't matter – Flesh may have been fancy but it knew how to cook a steak. Turnbull ate every bit of it along with the creamed spinach and whatever the hell charred broccolini paste was.

"Glad we got a chance to celebrate tonight," Deeds said, finishing his Idaho cabernet. "Be ready to go on short notice, Kelly, because when I find some intel we will need to act fast."

He got up and his security men stationed around the restaurant alerted. Rothko was speaking into his fist.

"Thanks for dinner," Turnbull said.

"I should let you pay," Deeds said. "You're the one with all the money from rescuing people out of the blue."

"I don't mind being put out of that business."

"Just stay out of sight," Deeds said. "Until I get something actionable for you. Do not draw attention to yourselves. Be inconspicuous."

"That's Kelly's specialty," Casey said.

Deeds snorted, then turned. His men closed in on him as he walked past the hostess station.

Several tables over, Turnbull saw a man dining alone dial his phone, put it to his ear, say a few words, then put it down. It was the first time Turnbull had seen a phone being used inside the dining room all night.

"Three tables over, sitting alone," Turnbull said to Casey. "Don't look."

"I saw him," Casey said. "So what?"

"He got on the phone as Clay was walking out."

"Maybe he's calling an escort."

"Maybe," Turnbull said. "But you'd think he'd have brought her to dinner."

"Clay's got a lot of security," Casey said.

"Watch my back," Turnbull said, standing up and dropping his napkin on his seat. The solo caller looked him over and returned to his filet. No gun apparent, Turnbull noted. But that meant nothing.

Turnbull began walking up toward the front door, passing the other diners who continued chowing down on their prime steaks and guzzling their Boise burgundy.

Nothing unusual. Coulter the hostess was on the phone and several customers were milling about the entryway. Through the glass doors, past the cow, Turnbull observed Deeds getting into the middle of three black Suburbans.

Then an orange streak tore downwards from a window on the skyscraper across the street and slammed into the front SUV. It exploded, and Turnbull pulled the hostess to the floor as the blast wave tore past the whimsical cow and blew out the front glass doors.

Glass shards blew over top of them, mostly absorbed by the dark wood of the hostess station. Some of the customers were not so lucky and lay bloodied and wounded on the Tuscan stone floor.

Turnbull turned over, trying to see through the smoke. He could see the gauzy outline of the cow statue. But he could hear gunfire – a lot of it.

He drew his Wilson .45 as two men in suits with some sort of AK rifles appeared out of the dust on the entrance way and opened fire into the steakhouse through the shattered glass doorway.

It was not aimed fire – it was suppression, and it worked. Most people inside the dining room dove to the floor.

Turnbull rolled out from behind the hostess podium and took aim at the one on the left. He fired one center mass shot that knocked the shooter backwards but not down. Turnbull tilted up and the next hollow point went through the man's forehead.

The other shooter noticed and shifted his aim down. A string of rounds slammed into the stone floor, knocking up little clouds of pulverized rock, the impacts walking toward Turnbull.

Turnbull pivoted, the front sight dancing over the shooter's face. He fired three times. The first two slammed into the man's jaw, the third taking off the top of his head as he fell backward, dropping his rifle.

Turnbull was up on his feet now, running to the gun check counter and dropping his Wilson's chrome mag. Behind him, there were three shots. He looked over and Casey was standing up with his CZ; a couple tables over, the solo caller was lying face down in his filet, a SIG pistol on the table in his dead hand.

Turnbull got to the gun check window. Miss Teagarden looked at him, stunned and confused.

"Long gun!" he shouted, reloading then holstering the Wilson. "Now!"

Miss Teagarden grabbed the closest weapon on the rack, a black Benelli M4 Tactical semi-automatic 12-gauge with an extra-long tube and eight buckshot rounds helpfully hanging in the shell holder on the side of the action.

"Thanks," Turnbull said, cracking the action and seeing red. He headed toward the door.

The frame of the glass doors was still there, but the glass itself was gone. Turnbull stepped through the frame, the shotgun at his shoulder and searching the smoke for targets. There was shooting, a lot of shooting, up ahead, but he could not see who was doing it. The wreck of the front SUV was on fire. The remaining SUVs were only hazily visible. There were shapes on the ground. He got to the bodies of the two men he had just knocked down.

There was movement to his left – a man in a black suit with an AK was moving toward the middle SUV and firing down at the men on the ground – probably Clay's security detail. Turnbull drew bead and fired. The shooter staggered. Turnbull blasted him again and he flew backwards, dead.

Turnbull sprinted forward, past the corpses, backing up against the stone cow and slipping two more buckshot shells into the Benelli's feed. He looked at the dead man he had just shot. Short hair, buzz cut, little or no neck. The others were the same.

"Ukrainians," he muttered, lifting the shotgun stock back to his armpit. Another finger of fire streaked down from a window of one of the surrounding high-rise buildings, this time slamming into the third SUV. The fire and debris carried by the blast wave roared past him, blocked by the cow statue, but it knocked back two armed diners coming out of the front entrance.

Turnbull shook it off, though his ears were ringing, and moved forward down the walkway, shotgun up and searching for targets. A shape appeared around the hood of the surviving SUV – Clay's ride – and he had an AK and was yelling something in a language that sounded Russian.

Turnbull acquired and fired, two shots directly into his chest. The man staggered back and Turnbull lifted the front sight to his face and blasted a load of buckshot into his mug. That took him out of the picture for good. Turnbull barely heard the gunshots because of the ringing.

He felt the spray of white granite on his face, and realized that it was from a bullet that had hit the cow statue. The flash was in a window on the second or third floor of the adjacent building where the rocket propelled grenades had come from, about 100 meters away. Turnbull brought the barrel up and fired twice, rushing forward to take cover behind the armored SUV that held Clay Deeds. Another round hit the hood as he dove behind the front passenger wheel. Several of Clay's security men lay dead on the sidewalk. Rothko was one.

He reloaded off the shotgun's side rack, as Casey and several armed diners moved down the walkway.

"Sniper!" Turnbull yelled, just as a red splotch blew across Sacred Cow behind Casey. Casey fell, dropping his SCAR.

Turnbull rose up and wheeled around, blasting the sniper's window with three shots, though at that range they would probably be ineffective for anything except keeping the shooter's head down.

Turnbull could now see beyond the SUVs onto the driveway. Besides the two burning Suburbans, there were a lot of bodies lying there and a lot of very expensive, very messed up luxury cars. Several black-suited shooters were engaging various targets with their AKs. One of the valets popped a mercenary in the head with his Glock 17. And an old lady was firing a Colt Commander at two more, or was until one of the Ukrainians let loose a burst of rifle fire into her.

There was a white Mercedes idling on the street with a couple of Kurylenko bastards nearby engaging targets. Two of the mercenaries, one of them a giant, were carrying a slumped figure between them to the waiting vehicle – Turnbull recognized the tan suit.

Clay Deeds.

He raised the scattergun and paused. That was not going to work.

Another round thudded into the hood. Turnbull lifted the sight and fired twice at the sniper position, but he was joined in suppressing the window by a half-dozen patrons who were outside and firing too. The sniper's window shattered under the impacts. One of the rounds must have connected because he stopped shooting.

Turnbull tore around the front of the SUV, shotgun up, seeking targets. A Ukrainian popped up from beside the wreckage, AK ready. Turnbull spun, but the mercenary was already flying backwards. Their waiter was standing just behind Turnbull with his old school Colt .45 revolver. He blew the smoke from the barrel.

Turnbull began running forward toward the white Mercedes sedan. The large mercenary was stuffing the inert body of Clay Deeds into the back. The man looked like a side of beef on feet.

Around the front of the sedan was another merc, this one with a scar on his face.

Turnbull remembered that face. Liberia. The major.

Turnbull fired twice, and the major dropped down behind the body of the vehicle.

The giant began to return fire with a pistol that looked like a toy in his hands. Turnbull acquired him in the sight, but checked fire – the buckshot spray could hit Deeds.

To his left, there was movement. A mercenary was running full speed toward the Mercedes. Turnbull shifted and fired two blasts. They caught the runner in the side and he staggered and sprawled on the street.

The Benelli was empty. Turnbull tossed it aside and drew his .45. A round went high over his head, and another whizzed close. Turnbull took aim at the giant but the ogre slipped into the Mercedes. The major did too – he was now behind the wheel. The sedan roared to life.

Turnbull held up, not wanting to hit Deeds, but the other diners out there did not hesitate. There were at least a dozen armed civilians in the driveway, several shooting at the Mercedes. It tore off down the street. Sirens sounded in the distance as the vehicle with Clay Deeds vanished.

The shooting stopped.

Turnbull did an about face and walked back toward the statue. One of the mercenaries rose up on his hands but a guy in a cowboy hat and a bolo tie shot him in the back with a double-barrel 12-gauge. None of the other mercenaries sprawled on the ground were moving.

Casey was half upright and leaning back against Sacred Cow. Several dead patrons, security men, and mercenaries littered the walkway.

"Can't believe I got shot," Casey said, a trickle of blood dribbling out of his mouth. "Or that you took only sixty seconds to start not being inconspicuous."

"Stop talking," Turnbull said, putting pressure on the wound. It gurgled when Casey spoke.

"You know why they call them sucking chest wounds?" Casey asked. "Because they suck."

"You're fine," Turnbull said. "Walk it off."

Casey smiled, then got serious.

"If I die, you need to take over @FullMetalGalt."

"Now you have to live," Turnbull said. He saw several of the patrons giving first aid to the other wounded – the veterans had all taken the combat life saver course and their training was taking over.

"They got Clay," Turnbull said as he pressed down to stop the bleeding.

"You're going to go get him, right?" Casey said. His voice was becoming weaker.

"My to-do list is getting longer all the time," Turnbull replied. He evaluated Casey as slipping into shock. There were lots of sirens, but where were the medics?

"Make sure you do Scott," Casey gasped. "Kill that piece of shit once and for all."

"And a certain scar-faced Slavic asshole," Turnbull said. "If I can find any of them." Turnbull reached over and picked up the SCAR, then handed it to Casey.

"Don't want to lose that."

"No," Casey said.

The flashing lights of the ambulances and cop cars were suddenly everywhere as they pulled into the driveway.

"I gotta go," Turnbull said. Casey understood and nodded.

Turnbull got up and grabbed hold of a passing valet who had a citizenship pin.

"Sucking chest wound," Turnbull said. "Put pressure on it and do not let off until the medics take over. Clear?"

The valet nodded – Turnbull was not in asking mode. The man knelt and pressed hard against the hole. Casey grimaced.

Turnbull walked through the chaos to where the valet station had been before the explosions knocked it over. He spotted his Leatherman and picked up his keys, then headed through the wreckage to the valet lot to get his truck.

7.

"Would you mind shutting up?" Clay Deeds asked. He was sore, his head hurt, and the handcuffs were cutting into his wrists. Drago, the gorilla that was always with Major Vasilev, slapped him hard across the face.

It hurt, but Clay Deeds did not intend to give General Karl Martin Scott the satisfaction of seeming to care.

"You're worms," Scott said. "You and your special operatives. Fighting in the shadows. Lying. Betraying. I despise you."

"The only traitor here is you, General," Deeds replied. "I don't count Major Vasilev because he prostitutes himself to the highest bidder, so there's no expectation of loyalty from him."

Drago looked to Vasilev, who shook his head. There was danger of excessive breakage. Besides, he was indifferent to the hostage's insults. He had been called much worse by other prisoners before they died.

Deeds was exhausted, having been sitting in his Suburban minding his own business after a delightful dinner when the vehicle in front of him exploded. Next thing he knew, all hell was breaking loose, and then Vasilev's shaved ape was pulling open his door and shoving a cattle prod into his ribs. From then on it was hazy, a lot of time hooded on car floors or in cramped boxes. There were airplane flights, and no provision of the necessities. They had tossed him into a shower after they finally removed the hood.

He was currently in what was actually a very nice hotel suite. It was impeccably decorated. The walls were walnut paneled. Was it the Mandarin? It reminded him of the Mandarin just off of Central Park, perhaps the Presidential Suite. Deeds had been in that suite with a president before the Split.

He could not see out the windows, which ran the length of one wall. The drapes were closed and the view would have confirmed or denied his suspicions. Still, he was pretty sure that's where he was.

But why not a dungeon somewhere?

"We're going to have some questions for you," General Scott said. "I'm curious about a number of things. But that can wait. We need your photo."

Drago picked him up. Deeds was in a bathrobe and unshaven – not his best look. The ape held a paper copy of the *New York Times* in front of him; it was about 8 ½" x 11". The headline read "GREAT VICTORY IN DEFENSIVE WAR AGAINST RACISTS." A headline that would have been the fold if there was a fold read "RECORD HARVESTS UNDER NEW FIVE-YEAR PLAN."

Vasilev walked behind him and opened the drapes a bit. He hid it well, but he was livid. The short notice mission had gotten almost a dozen of his men killed in Dallas. The reason they had taken Scott on the Lake Pontchartrain causeway was to avoid being surrounded by armed civilians spoiling for a fight. Everyone around the restaurant seemed to have a gun – young Igor had been taken out by an elderly woman blasting away with a pistol. It was madness, but then Vasilev was well-compensated for it even after the bounties to the families of the dead were paid.

Sunlight flooded into the room. Deeds twisted his head to peek through the open drapes. He was right – he could make out Central Park behind him. Vasilev walked back to Deeds's front and snapped the proof of life photo, then typed something into his phone.

Why had they opened the drapes instead of just turning on the lights if they needed illumination, Deeds wondered.

"They won't bargain for me," Deeds said. "As you know, General, most of our government will be happy that I am out of the picture."

"And terrified about what you will tell me about them," Scott replied. "But I'm not interested in ransoming you."

"Are you going to let me in on your plan?" Deeds asked.

Scott smiled, waiting a beat.

"You're bait."

Major George Ryan, Jr., was inside the battalion command post watching the war play out. There was a patrol in contact and the drone footage was displaying on the large center video screen. The fire support officer was coordinating artillery to help the recon squad break contact and retrograde south. No dead this time, thankfully, just two wounded. MEDEVAC choppers were inbound. A couple more Blood Citizens born. And for what? A pointless shootout in the Pennsylvania countryside. No ground gained.

Ryan kept a poker face, but the stalemate was getting to him.

What was the point? Hadn't endless kinetic war been one of the causes of the Split, along with endless communist freakshow culture war?

"Attention!" the noncommissioned officer in charge of the CP shouted. Lieutenant Colonel Badham entered ahead of several junior staff officers and muttered "At ease."

"What do we got?" he asked Ryan.

"Patrol from Alpha Company stumbled onto some blues. Firefight followed. They are moving back to our lines."

"Casualties?"

"Two, routine, MEDEVAC is inbound."

Badham nodded and looked around for the battle captain, the officer who coordinated the battalion command post.

"Lieutenant Redfern, take charge. I'm taking the XO."

The LT nodded and Badham turned and walked to the exit. Ryan followed. Outside the flaps of the tent, Badham kept walking off into the empty field, past trucks and hummers and whirring generators. It was raining lightly. They walked at least 100 meters, with Ryan's anxiety rising at each step. Finally, Badham stopped and turned. They were quite alone.

"What's up, sir?"

The commander was unhappy – Ryan could tell after working for him for so long. It was not yet clear just what he was unhappy about.

"Junior, the battalion is coming off the line."

That was good, Ryan thought. So why was the boss miffed? He waited as the light colonel continued.

"We go into the rear area, regenerate for a few days, then we and the Division will be joining the big push."

"Big push? An offensive?"

"Yeah," Badham said. "You remember that dumb idea about taking Manhattan?"

"That's on again?" Ryan said, incredulous.

"It's happening," Badham replied. "And soon. For some reason, the blues are pulling out of New Jersey and the Big Apple is right there for the taking. So, we are going to take it."

"Geez," Ryan said. "What's our piece of this?"

"The whole Division will air assault into Manhattan." Badham said. "There's no place to parachute in – not even Central Park."

Ryan gasped – this would be the biggest heliborne assault in history. Where the hell would they get so many choppers? His commander continued.

"It's not just us, though. We got Marines coming in by water and the legs and the tankers will push up through New Jersey and try to take the bridges and tunnels and cross. Otherwise, they get ferried over. We take the city, and the blue's whole frontline is threatened and collapses."

"Sounds like Market Garden," Ryan said, uncertainly. "A George Washington Bridge too far."

That play of using airborne forces to seize ground in the enemy rear and await the arrival of the ground forces had worked on the San Francisco Peninsula a year before, but in the original World War II battle, not so much.

"Yeah, they're trying it again," Barham said. "Except this time, they are calling it 'Overlord.'"

"You're kidding?"

"Nope."

Ryan sighed.

"I'll pass the word that we're pulling out. Who's relieving us?"

"Second ID," the commander replied. The blues particularly hated that infantry division because its shoulder patch was an Indian head and they found it oppressive to indigenous peoples.

"We have a lot to do," the executive officer said, his mind racing from the myriad tasks necessary to pull this off. As XO, he would be at the center of it. Good-bye, good nights' sleep.

"*We*, not you," Badham said.

"I don't understand," Ryan said.

"You're not coming with the battalion, Junior," Badham told him. "The whole 101st Airborne Division is air assaulting in and it needs Pathfinders. Two companies will go in a few hours before D-Day to secure the landing zones and key positions around them. You are commanding that mission. Division commander's orders."

Ryan just stared.

"Why me?"

"Because you operated in the blue in your other life. And you are not a dipshit."

"Not a dipshit. That's a compliment, I guess."

"Look, we expect the city will be largely clear of blue forces. It's chaos in there anyway, but you'll have two companies of crack infantry. You'll be the biggest, baddest street gang in Manhattan up until the cavalry comes. You just clear the way for the rest of us."

"And if you don't come?" Ryan asked. "Or if the rest of the forces get bogged down or a meteor hits or whatever?"

"Well," Badham said. "In that case you are royally screwed."

"Kelly," Casey said over the phone. "I need to see you. Now."

Turnbull was driving on I-35 and the call was on speaker.

"What is it?" he demanded. Casey had gotten out of surgery and was doing well enough to call him and pester him a couple times a day.

"I really need to see you," Casey said, sounding exhausted and serious. It had been three days since the gunfight beside the whimsical cow statue. Turnbull had been on his own, waiting for intel even though it was not clear who his new handler would be, or if he would even have one.

"Are you in danger?" Turnbull asked. He was nearing the Parkland Hospital exit. They had hauled Kennedy there after he was taken out by what was finally confirmed to be Ted Cruz's father's hit team. The post-Split revelations from the old CIA files had been pretty amazing, and ex-president Trump's reaction on his Truth Social account bragged "See, I Told you SO!! So Much WINNING!!"

Turnbull got out of the elevator on the sixth floor and saw the operatives immediately. They were vaguely familiar, but they both knew him. One motioned down the hall. Another operative waited by a door with an M4 on his shoulder. Turnbull walked past him and into the room.

Casey was on the bed, an IV port in his arm with a tube leading to a drip, and the monitor beeping. 120/79, blood ox 94%. The patient had an iPad in his lap and was typing. He looked up.

"Hi Kelly," he said. He was pale and there were bandages on his chest.

"I'm here," Turnbull announced. "What's the deal? Are you afraid they're coming back to finish the job?" Casey's SCAR was lying on the tray next to his bed right beside an empty apple juice carton and a fruit cup.

"Hit the door," Casey said.

Turnbull complied, then came back over to the bedside.

"Look what I got via text," Casey said, turning the iPad so Turnbull could see.

It was a photo, clearly from a cell phone, of Clay Deeds. He was alive, but he had looked better. He was in a bathrobe and unshaven and someone had clearly smacked him around a bit. He seemed to be in some sort of bedroom, or maybe a suite. The drapes behind him were open and beyond was a cityscape. He held a paper copy of the *New York Times* in his hand.

"The paper is today's," Casey said. "I checked online."

"Proof of life," Turnbull growled.

"Yeah," Casey said. "It popped up in my messages about an hour or so ago. Clay had my number in his phone."

"I tossed my last burner after the shootout," Turnbull said.

"Keeping up with your phone numbers is a giant pain," Casey said. "Anyway, as far as I know I'm the only one who got this."

"So, we know he's alive. Can you get anything more from this photo? Maybe enhance it or something?"

"What, like *Blade Runner*?"

"Which one?" Turnbull said. "There are eight." In fact, Robby Starbuck had just directed *Blade Runner: Tokyo Drift*.

"The first one," Casey said. "Spoiler – it's about a remorseless killer who turns out to be a robot. Could be your biography."

"Just analyze the picture with your IT powers," Turnbull snapped.

"I did," Casey said. "Look."

He put his fingers on the screen and spread them. The picture expanded.

"There's my super high-tech enbiggening tool," Casey said.

"That's a city skyline. Maybe a park. New York City?"

"Yeah, but where? I isolated some of those buildings and googled the images," Casey explained. The term "google" had become generic – he did not use the old Google site because it had stayed in the blue and was not available in the red. Even if it had been, it was essentially useless because even those few searches that were not barred for "racism" or "cisnormative bias" were preceded with a dozen trigger warnings and indigenous people's land use acknowledgements.

"They all came back as overlooking Central Park," Casey continued. "You can see some trees there. Anyway, I figured out where the buildings were and took the angles and reversed them, and I think this photo was taken in what is, or was, a suite in the Mandarin Oriental New York."

"Why is he not in a cell?" Turnbull wondered aloud.

"And why did they take a photo when they had to know that we would be able to figure out where they took it?" Casey asked.

"Unless they wanted us to figure it out," Turnbull said.

"Why would they do that?"

"Because they know I will come get him," Turnbull said. "Actually, that *we* will."

"I don't think I'm going anywhere for a while," Casey said.

"They'll be expecting two of us."

"So, you would not go in with sufficient numbers because that's just what they would expect you to do?" asked Casey. "I question your decision-making process."

Turnbull ignored him and continued.

"They wanted to make sure we know that Clay was somewhere we might have a chance to get him, not some supermax cell."

"You remember what a meme is?" Casey said. Turnbull looked at him, annoyed. Casey took the iPad, tapped it a few times and presented it back to him.

There was a gif featuring a bizarre alien creature – it looked like a bug-eyed newt mated with a hog – in an admiral's uniform on the deck of what appeared to be a space ship, with an intergalactic laser battle going on in the window behind him. Words flashed below him: "IT'S A TRAP!"

"What the hell is this?" Turnbull demanded.

"It's a trap, Kelly."

"Of course, it's a trap," Turnbull said. "And it's pretty clear who laid it. Those dead guys at the restaurant were Ukrainians and that means Kurylenko Group and that means Scott. He wants us to come after Clay. Because he wants us."

"Normally, it's good to be wanted," Casey said. "But this dude wants us dead."

"Clay is alive only as long as Scott and his buddies think that we might come to get him," Turnbull said. "If we don't, lights out for Clay Deeds, after they sweat him for every bit of intel he has."

"So, what are you going to do, Kelly?"

"Do?" asked Turnbull. "I'm going to go to Manhattan, get Clay, and put a hollow point in Karl Martin Scott's brain pan."

Scott looked out over the city from his 54th floor suite, sipping scotch. The former Mandarin Oriental New York, now nationalized and renamed the People's Asian American and Native Hawaiian/Pacific Islander Hotel New York, was one of the few hotels maintained at near-peak luxury for visiting VIPs and key members of the nomenklatura.

Scott was alone that evening, having declined Harrington's offer of company of whatever flavor or flavors he desired. Deeds was in another suite on the floor, under guard, ensuring he likewise remained out of reach of Harrington's potential competitors. Scott himself was the biggest secret; only Harrington knew he was in the blue. In the halls and the lobby, Kurylenko mercenaries provided security. People's Security Forces were banned from the hotel grounds.

The city was dark, at least beyond the secure zones' walls, since all the nuclear power plants were closed in the name of the environment, and all the coal and gas plants in the name of climate change. The city was under a People's Power Sacrifice, with the electricity turned off by popular demand – though no one ever actually voted for it. What lights there were down there came from generators or from fires. There were lots of fires, especially in winter. A fine layer of soot from the constant burning added to the filth of the city, though Scott was high above all that.

His plan was working. He had reached out and made his contacts, facilitated by Harrington's tech people who routed calls around the blue censors and the red firewalls. PR troops were moving out of New Jersey. According to Harrington, the Chinese and Russians were concerned and asking questions. But they were being told by the People's Republic Anti-Colonial Military Land Forces spokebeing John Kirby that it was just a routine redeployment of troops to facilitate conducting critical annual multi-division gender identity and cisnormative bias training maneuvers. The process was called OPERATION STONEWALL, though it was most assuredly not of the Jackson variety.

The plan was working so far. But there were many pieces and moving parts, and bringing them together would be a challenge. He sipped again, confident he was up to it. He would be victorious. He would be president of the reunited United States.

Down below, there were dozens upon dozens of campfires in Central Park outside the secure zone wall. Instead of a beautiful urban oasis, it was a criminal cesspit of social pathologies. That kind of indulgence would end once he was firmly in charge. Harrington was right when he pleaded with Scott to respect the norms of the blue. When in Rome, do as the Romans. But with power in his hands, that would all stop.

Harrington might not approve, but Harrington might not be there at all. Scott needed no power behind the throne, only the power to put him on the throne.

He sipped again. It was smooth. Harrington saw that he got the good stuff. Down below, people were dying from gin distilled in radiators.

Of course, the world did not need the kind of people who lived like that. It occurred to Scott that there were a lot of people the world – or at least, the reunited United States – did not need.

But there was one bit of business to take care of first. Clay's minions, the ones who helped humiliate him, who threw him in prison. Kelly Turnbull and Casey Warner needed to die, preferably unpleasantly.

That was his price to aid Harrington, and to his credit, the blue politician and schemer had come through and brought him Clay Deeds. Kudos to him for buying the loyalty of the Kurylenko Group. It was an effective outfit.

Now that Warner had the photo, it would only be a matter of time until they came to New York looking to get Deeds back. The fact that they must know it was a trap would not stop them from walking into it.

And then Deeds, Warner, and most of all the insufferable Kelly Turnbull, would die.

Scott sipped once more and smiled.

8.

Ernie Smith let Turnbull in through the back door of the facility, a sterile and generic office building on the outskirts of Dallas. It was not that Turnbull could not have walked in the front door with his ID. It was that Turnbull did not want to. There was the possibility that someone would attempt to take the place of Clay Deeds and presume to order him about and Turnbull preferred not to have to kick some schmuck's ass all over the spy org's headquarters.

He had his mission already.

"You got that focused look," Ernie said as they walked down the linoleum-lined hallway under the flickering fluorescent lights.

"Oh, I'm focused," Turnbull assured him.

"Word is that Deeds got taken," Smith said as he stopped at the door of the armory and swiped his key card. The metal door's locking mechanism clacked, and he pushed through. "I'm guessing that's why you're heading into the blue."

"For a guy no one is supposed to know exists, everyone seems to know Clay," Turnbull said.

"He's a player at the highest levels," Smith observed, walking inside. "Or was. You think he's alive somewhere in the People's Republic?"

"I know he is," Turnbull replied, following Smith through. "They told me."

"They?"

"Clay is bait."

"Which you're taking."

"I have a plan."

"So, you're going to go on a massive killing spree to get him back."

"That's the plan."

"That's always your plan."

Smith pushed the door shut. The lock engaged.

The armory was actually rows and rows of weapons of all types and sizes and calibers/gauges.

"Looks like *The Matrix* in here, Ernie. I like it."

"You said you needed guns, lots of guns. Well, I got lots of guns."

"Excellent." Turnbull smiled like a fat boy in a Cheetos factory.

They went up and down the aisles, discussing the firepower capabilities that Turnbull needed and the best way to achieve them. After a while, Ernie told him to wait up front. Turnbull did. Turnbull cooled his heels for a few minutes until Ernie approached with a cart.

"What do you have for me?" Turnbull asked. This was his Christmas morning.

The armorer smiled.

"You're going into the blue and want a visible carry gun that gives you the option of fitting in, to the limited extent you can," Smith said. He had lived in the blue for years until Turnbull had brought him out and into the red, so he knew of what he spoke. "You'll need something quiet, too, and you also need a shit hits the fan gun."

"That's correct."

Ernie picked up a pistol off the cart.

"Most of the bad guys in the blue seem to carry old US military Beretta M9s, right?"

"Yeah?"

"So, you need to fit in, but not with some old beat up junker that some LT schlepped around some Baghdad FOB." He handed over a brand-new black pistol. Turnbull noted the Wilson Combat markings and greenish grips.

"92G Centurion Tactical. Basically, a 92F/M9 that's been totally reworked but still looks like an issue model to the non-discerning eye. The slide's a bit shorter, and you can see the trigger guard is rounded, plus there's a light rail up front. Once I switch out the green ones for the ultra-thin black grips, anyone looking at you is going to think you have a plain old M9. But this weapon is high performance. And it's nine-millimeter, which means you can shoot the ammo that you find lying around."

Turnbull racked the slide. Tight, unlike most of the old, beat up Berettas out there.

"Seventeen round mags," Ernie said, pointing to six of them resting on the cart. "Federal HST +P 124 grain rounds."

"I'll miss my .45. You can watch her for me." He slid a mag into the Centurion, sent the slide forward, and dropped the hammer with the decocking lever.

"I'll keep her safe and sound. Now, look at this." Smith handed over a black polymer semi-auto pistol with a protruding, threaded barrel.

"FN Five SeveN Mk3 with a Trijicon RMR red dot optic. Shoots a high velocity 5.7x28mm bullet. The SS198LF rounds will punch through most soft body armor. I'll give you a suppressor and I've got four 20-round mags. That's your covert wet work gun."

Turnbull worked the action, then inserted a mag and seated a round in the pipe. Satisfied, he put the handgun back on the cart.

"Now the weapon for when you just don't care about being subtle, which for you is most of the time."

Smith handed over a black M4-style rifle, heavily modified and set up with accessories.

"This is your new recce rifle. I built it myself on an M4 base. Sixteen-inch barrel, so she's good for close quarter battle. Look at the optics – you got two. The first is an ATACR 1-8x24 variable power scope. It has an eight-times zoom to reach out and touch someone. But here is an Aimpoint Micro T-2 red dot reflex scope mounted forty-five degrees off, so you can switch from close to far engagements just by twisting the weapon. Got a designator and a mounted white light up front. The barrel is set up for a quick-attach SureFire SOCOM556-RC2 suppressor."

"Nice," Turnbull said, checking the action. Smooth.

"Ten 30-round mags, Hornady Black 5.56 NATO 62 grain full metal jacket."

"Okay," Turnbull said. "Anything else?"

"You are a walking arms room already, Kelly. Can you carry more?"

"I think I need a backup gun. I need a .45."

"You and your .45."

Ernie shook his head and turned and went back to his endless racks. Turnbull picked up the recce rifle again and started checking out the sights. Ernie came back after about five minutes. He was carrying something.

"I'm going to make this simple. Gen Five Glock 30." He handed over a short-framed black pistol, polymer, with three mags.

"Ten rounds each. Since you are a Wilson fan, it's .45 cal Speer GDHP 200 grain."

Turnbull loaded the small handgun.

"You got an ankle holster?"

"Sure, Kelly. That's four guns in four calibers. You satisfied yet?"

"Toying with a shotgun," Turnbull mused.

"I think you're good."

"Yeah," Turnbull replied uncertainly. "I guess."

"Here's a duffel," Ernie said, handing over an OD green satchel. "Let me go get those black grips for the Centurion."

Turnbull reluctantly took out his Wilson .45 and put it on the cart. He then started packing the duffel with guns and ammo. He had to break down the rifle to make it fit.

Ernie returned, having swapped out the green grips for black ones. Unless you were looking and knew guns, this would appear to be the same kind of Beretta the People's Security Force thugs typically carried.

Turnbull slid the Beretta into his holster. It fit. He then took the extra mags and placed them as well.

When he finished, Ernie handed him a small, heavy cloth bag, and manila envelope.

The cloth bag held gold coins.

"I cleaned out the bug-out stash for those and the cash," Ernie told him.

The envelope held a wad of PR bills bound by a rubber band, and a set of fake IDs. Turnbull looked them over.

"People's Bureau of Investigation," Turnbull said. "Do they still call it that?"

"As of last week," Ernie replied.

"Edward William Peyronie," Turnbull read off the credential. "Gender: 'Genderbent.' Oh, nice."

"I liked that too," admitted Ernie. "You're also differently-abled somehow and, I think, you're a druid of some kind, so you're privilege level nine."

Turnbull grunted in gratitude and put both items into his duffel.

"You're welcome," Ernie said. "Now go get our boy Clay back."

"I intend to," Turnbull said, zipping up the bag.

"Still, you're going in by yourself, right into what you damn well know is a trap. You think that's smart?"

"They're expecting two operators, except Casey's out of the fight. That's my edge."

"Great, you alone against the entire blue? Not sure I like those odds."

"Oh," Turnbull said, heading toward the door. "I'm not going to be alone."

The Tyler County sheriff's office in Middlebourne, West Virginia, was less a building than a thickened bunker – signs on the outside walls directed you toward the closest artillery shelter should the blues decide to start firing from over the border in Ohio. That had not happened for a while. The West Virginia front was quiet, at least officially. But there was always the chance the small town could find itself a combat zone.

Turnbull pushed open the front door and a female deputy with a citizen's pin and a FAL rifle leaning on the counter looked up, not too pleased.

"You can't bring that dog in here," she said.

"Gibson is a service dog," Turnbull said, walking up to the counter. "I'm looking for Tugg."

"*Sheriff Sweeney* is out on patrol," she replied, annoyed at the interloper's informality. "You and your *service dog* can sit and wait out here if you want." She gestured to some worn benches against the walls under the framed photos of long-ago West Virginia law enforcement officers.

Turnbull surveyed the office area beyond the deputy's counter. A few desks, some crackling radios, plenty of weapon racks. The sheriff's own office was at the back and the door was ajar – Turnbull could see inside.

"How about you get on the radio and tell him a guy named Kelly is here to see him? I think he'd want you to."

"I've known the sheriff for five years and I doubt it."

Turnbull pointed his finger behind her.

"You know that picture on the wall in his office with those Army guys in Mosul?" he asked. "I'm the one on the left, with the bloody bandage."

She squinted at him, considered, then picked up her cell phone and hit some buttons. After a short conversation, she hung up and led Turnbull and Gibson the Belgian Malinois around the counter and into the sheriff's office. Turnbull took a seat on a worn couch that probably dated from before the split with the British.

Fifteen minutes later, a portly and balding but solid-looking man in a tan sheriff's uniform walked in. His Smith & Wesson

Model 29 .44 magnum revolver rested in a holster hanging off his left side.

"Kelly freaking Turnbull," he said, brightening as he entered his office. "You look like hell."

"And you look like you haven't missed a meal since Iraq."

Sweeney smiled.

"Damn right. My wife can cook. No more plastic bag dinners for me."

He shook Turnbull's hand and walked around his desk, stopping and looking down at the war dog.

"Remember when the platoon adopted that dog and you got a case of the ass?" he laughed. "Since when do you like dogs?"

"I think they started to like me."

Sweeney sat down.

"Well, I'm betting you aren't a lieutenant anymore. I heard you went special forces after you rotated out of the platoon."

"Light colonel," Turnbull replied. "But I'm not on Army business."

"Yet I'm assuming this is not a purely social call," The sheriff said, considering. "So, what can your best squad leader from back in the day do for you?"

"I need a favor, Tugg," Turnbull said.

"You already owe me a favor. Remember how I got shot in the foot pulling you in when we got hit by those Al Qaeda assholes?" He jerked his thumb at a Purple Heart certificate framed on the wall next to a Bronze Star with a "V" device for valor.

"Everyone remembers his first Purple Heart. But I kind of lost count. And you're right about it not being a social call."

"Well, Kelly – still weird calling my platoon leader by his first name – I'm glad this isn't military, because we kind of have an arrangement up here."

"An arrangement?"

"Yeah, the military stays out of here and we handle this stretch of border ourselves. It's bad territory for the Army anyway, all cricks and hollers and hills and forests. You can't move mech and you can't move fast on foot. Hell, you can't move at all if you didn't grow up here. So, the military leaves us be and we keep this sector good and quiet."

"That's what I'm counting on, Tugg. That and the fact that the border here leaks like a sieve."

"Well Kelly, our boys gotta make a living, and they do, the same way they have forever – on the bleeding edge of the law. Moonshiners, tax smugglers, pot growers – whatever. A dozen generations of it right up to today."

"Tugg, I need you to introduce me to some boys who can smuggle people."

"People? Well, maybe I know some guys who might do a little of that," Sweeney said cagily. "Maybe."

"It's me, Tugg, not some boneyank. I know this is the terminus of the Underground Railroad."

Sweeney sized up his old friend.

"This ain't something we usually talk about with outsiders,"

"We bled together – me more than you that time – so I think I qualify as at least an honorary insider."

"Look Kelly, that's a dangerous subject. It's at the crossroads of money and religion. They bring back Christians and Jews, detranners and abort-refusers and others trying to get out of the blue. Not for free – the chickens gotta carry stuff with them, and not always nice stuff – but they are willing to backhaul fugitives on smuggling runs, mostly because the local preachers tell them it's a way of making up for their other misdeeds."

"I support them getting right with Jesus," Turnbull said. "This is not about shutting them down from bringing folks out of the blue."

"What's it about?"

"It's about smuggling folks *into* the blue."

"Like a boy and his dog?"

"Bingo," Turnbull said. "I want to ride the rails of the Underground Railroad, only the other way. North."

"Why the hell would you want to do that, Kelly? You got any idea what it's like in the blue, especially since the war started?"

"Yeah, I do, but that's where I'm going. Can you help hook me up with the people who can make it happen, or do I have to stumble my ass across those hills trying to do it myself?"

"Hell, don't do that. Instead of dragging out your wounded ass, I'll be dragging out your dead ass, you and your dog's too."

He ran his hand over his balding head.

"You sure you want to do this?"

"Yeah, I'm sure."

"When?"

"Now."

"Well, then let's roll."

"I consider this a personal favor, gentlemen," Tugg Sweeney told the dozen paramilitaries who were sizing up the outsider and his Belgian Malinois.

"Hauling some Army guy along with us? You're asking a lot, Tugg," Chase Hatfield said. He was their leader. He was wiry, with a scraggly beard, but intelligent if shifty eyes. His gear was dirty, but looked lived in. Turnbull assessed him and his crew as dangerous.

"I ain't asking, Chase," the sheriff replied. "You and your boys get left alone to do your thing, but when I ask for you to do me a favor, I expect you to do it."

The smuggler was visibly annoyed, but resigned. Keeping on the local constable's good side - or, at least staying off his bad side - was important.

"You're taking that hound?" Hatfield asked Turnbull, leaning on his battered Chevy Silverado, which had a M2 Machine gun mounted in the bed. An equally well-used M4 hung off his neck by a sling. He spit a wad of chewed Copenhagen on the dirt road. Several of his fellow Crusaders militia members shook their heads. They all wore a subdued cross on their camo uniforms' left sleeve Velcro shoulder pads. Calling themselves a militia instead of a gang gave them a lot of flexibility in their real work.

"Yeah," Kelly Turnbull told him. "I'm taking the dog."

Gibson, in a black harness, sat wagging his tail in the dust. The militia men kept a respectful distance.

"Your funeral, brother," Hatfield said. "I figure some of your hosts are not going to be thrilled with you bringing a dog."

"We'll work it out between us. When do I go over?"

"Hell," Hatfield said. "It's almost sundown. Anytime, if you're up for it."

"No time like the present."

Hatfield shook his head.

"We take a lot of stuff north, but we usually only bring people south."

"I go against the flow," Turnbull told him.

"Hop in," Hatfield said, gesturing to his ride. "We'll see if an Army guy like you can hang with us country boys."

Turnbull ignored the jibe. He pivoted to Tugg Sweeney and extended a hand.

"Thanks for the intro to these gentlemen," he said.

"Gentlemen," the sheriff scoffed. Hatfield and his compadres found that amusing as well. "They may look like hell, but they know every inch of this country. They'll get you in. They know it's a personal favor."

Sweeney and Hatfield's eyes met. Sweeney continued.

"And they know I'd consider it a personal affront if something happened to my old Army buddy."

"Damn, Tugg," Hatfield said. "I may be a crook, but you know I'm an honest one."

Sweeney grunted, and one of Hatfield's men dropped the tailgate on the truck they were standing next to. Turnbull picked up Gibson and plopped him into the bed.

"Tugg, you mind giving the preacher a heads up that there might be some refugees coming in tonight?" Hatfield asked the sheriff. "I heard a rumor."

"Yeah, yeah," Sweeney replied. "You stay in one piece, Kelly."

"I intend to." Turnbull tossed his pack into the rear and walked over to the cab as Sweeney turned and went to the driver's side.

The small convoy of technicals – all civilian trucks modified with weapons and bearing the Baptist Crusader militia logo – wound its way through the wooded hills, getting higher and higher and more and more remote. The main roads, Route 18 and Route 180, were blocked and locked. The convoy stuck to the back roads, roads only a local would know.

"Technically, this is a demilitarized zone," Hatfield said as he drove, cranking the wheel to avoid a fallen American beech tree that was partially blocking the road. There was a carpet of leaves on the asphalt, indicating only occasional traffic. "No active military allowed, only militias. Guess that arrangement is all gone to hell now that the red invaded the blue."

"Much fighting up here?"

"Nah," Hatfield said. "It's hard for you boys to move your soldiers in here, and harder if you don't know your way around. We're pretty much left alone on both sides. The blues know what we'd do if they started something."

"Do they try to stop the smuggling?"

"Hell, governments have been trying to stop us doing what we do for two hundred years. The blues used to hassle us, a little bit, but I think they needed us to do what we did. We would walk in medicine and good cigarettes, good liquor, whatever the blues couldn't make themselves. Normal porn was big up in the blue – cute adult all-American girls, no weird stuff. Stuff the PR outlawed as felony cis. Big market for normie porn, they called it. The blues generally left us alone but they leaned on the guys we sold our stuff to, took a cut, and shut their eyes."

"And you would bring out refugees? Anything else?"

Hatfield smiled, cagily.

"Well, there's always something people in the red want that they can't get."

"Specialty porn?"

"Sure. We still got our freaks. You city boys love that weird shit that the blues make."

"And you move dope too, I suppose," Turnbull observed. The blues grew a lot of pot, and manufactured a lot of other poison to keep their folks distracted.

"I gotta deny that. The red hangs dope dealers. Fast way to get people paying attention to you. The other stuff is harmless, pretty much, but not drugs. Like, in *The Godfather*."

Turnbull grunted. The money was probably too good for the Crusader militia to forgo smuggling drugs into the USA. He suspected that their buyers had to agree that the retailing would take place far from West Virginia. Trafficking drugs in town would turn guys like Tugg Sweeney on them in a heartbeat.

They came to a low hilltop thick with trees and pulled over and parked. Gibson hopped down off the back deck and sniffed around. Birds called, but otherwise it was still. The whole area was dull and gray, with the sky overcast and darkening.

"We need to walk for a bit," Hatfield said. "You up to it?"

Turnbull nodded and pulled his backpack close on the floor of the truck bed. He undid the straps and pulled out the components of his rifle. Hatfield watched as he assembled his weapon.

"That's a sweet piece," the smuggler said. "Brand new. Maybe you'll even see some action out here."

Turnbull ignored him, locking in a mag and charging it. Then he looked through the dual optics, focusing on a tree at the crest of the hill. He tightened the suppressor and pulled the strap over his head.

"Let's go," Turnbull directed.

"You look positively fierce," Hatfield said. His men snickered.

Hatfield and four of his men would go, each with a long gun. The rest of the crew would wait by the vehicles. Blue intruders on this side of the border were rare but not unknown, nor were competitors.

They tramped up the hill, pushing past thick bushes and trees, making more noise in the leaves than Turnbull would have liked, but the locals did not seem concerned and they knew the area best.

At the top, the panorama opened up from the claustrophobic woods. It was getting dark, but there was still sufficient light to see the terrain. Immediately below them, at the bottom of a long band of gray slate cliffs, was a deserted road. This was Energy Highway, a tribute to the coal that used to be mined nearby. Beyond that a few yards and running parallel was an abandoned railway. Past that and a line of thin trees was the Ohio River. It flowed placidly, with barely a ripple, and was maybe a fifth of a mile wide here. On the other bank were low hills, with a few white buildings spaced out along the shore.

"All evacuated years ago," Hatfield said, answering the question Turnbull would have asked him. "Officially evacuated. There might be some folks over there, living off-grid."

"Any OPs?" Turnbull asked. If he was a blue general, he would at least have some observation posts watching the border.

"Nothing permanent. Once in a while they get an officer who goes along on a patrol and then they actually patrol instead of just get outside the wire and hunker down until they go back to base. We'll wait for dark just in case."

"You got a boat?"

Hatfield looked at him as if he was stupid.

"Yeah, we got a boat."

9.

The outboard motor was probably not loud objectively, but it seemed like the roar of a jet engine to Turnbull. It only took a few minutes to cross the surface of the cloudy water, but it seemed like an eternity being exposed out on the river. Gibson sensed his master's discomfort and hung close. The West Virginian smugglers were quiet, but they did not seem particularly concerned crossing just after dusk. Hatfield clearly enjoyed Turnbull's agitation.

Across the river was the People's Republic state of Ohio, which had as yet not been renamed. It meant something like "beautiful river" in Seneca, but this was name appropriation and could not stand. The renaming would commence even though the nation was occupied with a war for its survival. Candidates for the replacement name under consideration included "Buckeye," "East Two-Spirit" (Indiana would be "West Two-Spirit") and "Obamaland," though that was odd in light of the recent PR decree that it was henceforth unlawful to deny that the former president had been born in Kenya.

The little boat pulled into a small inlet that cut into the shore a few meters and tied off on a gnarled tree. From the wear on the bark, this was the smugglers' usual anchorage. Turnbull did not approve – habits got you dead.

The men carefully stepped off and onto the dirt of the northern shore, and Gibson leapt over the side to land on the bank. Moving out, Hatfield took the lead, his weapon slung. The smugglers seemed carefree. Turnbull kept his rifle ready.

This side of the river had its own old road running parallel to the water, the former Ohio River Scenic Byway. The name had been changed by the People's Republic early on after the Split, even before the border zone had been shut down and evacuated as a prelude to armed conflict. It was now the Anti-Racist and Anti-Transphobia Byway. It was empty and clearly little used.

As they approached the road, they passed an old billboard with fading and peeling paint that faced south, depicting a militant mass of diverse people of all races, gender identities, plus several fursonas – the furries depicted included a mouse and a cartoon cow – all standing athwart a bunch of KKK members in full robe and cap get-up who were presumably coming north from West Virginia. Like the North Korean propaganda billboards along the Demilitarized Zone's 38th Parallel, this unsubtle display was designed to aggravate the enemy to the south. The smugglers paid it no heed and the little band made a fast crossing of the deserted road, heading toward a brace of decaying white buildings on the south slope of a range of low, wooded hills that ran parallel to the empty Anti-Racist and Anti-Transphobia Byway.

Gibson was on alert, keeping near to Turnbull but stopping to sniff every few feet. Turnbull would have preferred to have held up by the boat tie-up for a few minutes and let his ears acclimate to the quiet, but the smugglers were running the show and he was well aware that he was a free rider. He kept his weapon ready as they moved toward the buildings.

"You a little nervous?" Hatfield said, smirking.

"Let's get where we're going," Turnbull growled.

Turnbull paused to look up and down the dark, wide river. The sun was well below the hills, and there were no lights on either side. The river had once been lined with small towns on both sides. The people were all gone now, evacuated willingly or unwillingly, leaving the husks of their homes and businesses behind. This idyllic place had been the front in a war, even if most of the shooting was happening elsewhere. Instead of the Ohio being a great river that held a country together, it was now a scar.

Gibson alerted. Turnbull stopped. Hatfield noticed, and held up his fist. His men slowly and silently went low with their weapons up. Turnbull found a stump and listened, his rifle ready.

There were several voices, arguing and snapping at each other, coming from the buildings around them. There was pounding, and tearing, and the strain of things being pulled apart. It sounded not much different than the demo work Turnbull had done as a teenager making a few bucks pre-Split doing construction, except these guys were amateurs.

"Metal thieves," Hatfield whispered. "Must be desperate if they came out here looking for copper and such."

"We need to try to get past them," Turnbull said. He preferred not to waste ammo.

Hatfield nodded, then continued in a low voice.

"They are getting hungrier and hungrier up in the blue. They don't usually go out this far from the cities."

"Everything else must be stolen already."

Hatfield nodded again, and led the group around the building where the looters were doing their thieving, giving it a wide berth.

It was not wide enough. As they moved through the clump of old buildings, a pair of the looters packing crowbars piled out of another doorway and came face to face with Gibson. Their faces erupted with delight as they saw their next meal.

"A dog, bash it!" the lead looter shouted. He lunged, but so did Gibson. The man was not expecting to become a meal himself.

The Belgian Malinois hit him in the chest and the man tumbled backwards, the animal digging his teeth into the skinny thief's throat. The other looter stood there stunned, then he recovered and held up his crowbar to bring it down on Gibson's skull. Turnbull put two 5.56mm rounds into his chest. He crumpled. Gibson continued his toothy work.

The smugglers who didn't freeze were trying to unsling their weapons but Turnbull was already moving. There was noise from inside another building a few feet away, as the last two looters had heard the dinner bell and had no idea that their reservation had been cancelled.

The first one silhouetted himself in the doorway. Turnbull shot him through the forehead and stepped inside. The last one, with a steel pipe in his hand, looked at the gun and dropped his weapon.

"Hey, I'm cool!"

Turnbull shot him in the sternum and finished him with a round to the head, then exited. The smugglers, their weapons now out, stared at him, slack-jawed.

"Gibson, let go!" Turnbull hissed at the dog. The animal seemed almost disappointed as he disengaged his bloody snout from the looter's esophagus. Turnbull finished the moaning blue looter with a round to the head.

Hatfield surveyed the carnage, then looked at Turnbull. Turnbull's face was stone.

"Drag them into the building and out of sight," Turnbull ordered. "We need to move."

"You're one cold son of a bitch," Hatfield observed.

"This is not a game," Turnbull said. "This is a war. Maybe not right here, but it's a war. And I intend to win it. Now pick up those stiffs and let's move. Do it now."

They did it now.

The wooded hills to the north rose up to about 500 feet. The band group followed a draw and the dirt trail that started at the bottom all the way up to the summit. From there, the land flattened out a little, with only a hundred or so feet of variation going north. The smugglers moved confidently, indicating to Turnbull that they knew this ground intimately. They had been here before, probably a hundred times. And now their weapons were out. That, and the fact that they were giving the red killer a wide berth, pleased Turnbull, though Gibson remained on edge.

They walked several miles north and, in the distance, to the east and west, they observed occasional lights. Not electric ones – there was no power. These were cooking fires or oil lamps or candles. The PR had managed to take Appalachia back over a century in time in just a few years.

After more walking, a comparatively big building loomed ahead, one with candlelight in the windows. It looked like a church to Turnbull, but there was no outward sign of it being one. There was no steeple and certainly no cross. There was a sign, though – "Anti-Fascist Community Center." Below that was a land acknowledgement that apologized to some tribe Turnbull had never heard of for what long-dead people might have done to each other nearly three centuries ago.

"Wait here," Hatfield said. He slung his weapon and walked to the main double door. Turnbull, on alert, watched as the smuggler knocked and the door opened. Answering the knock was a tall, thin man who looked like he should be the undertaker in some western town burying gunfighters and horse thieves. Most everyone in the blue was thin, but even compared to the slim smugglers the man looked emaciated. He and Hatfield spoke briefly, and Hatfield pivoted to wave the crew inside. But not all of the crew – a pair of his men stayed outside, no doubt providing security.

Turnbull walked over with Gibson at his heel, weapon ready but held in as non-threating a manner as one could hold such a fearsome firearm. The interior of the Anti-Fascist Community Center came into view, illuminated by candles and a couple hurricane lamps. It was a church after all, with pews and an altar. A metal cross dominated.

There were several teens and a woman in view, all thin and tired-looking. The young people were not particularly small, since squirrels and other varmints could provide the protein they needed growing up, but none of them would have been a linebacker even if football had not been outlawed in the PR as "a white supremacist exercise in cis brutality." Ironically, the sport was not particularly popular in the red either, being so closely associated with disrespecting the flag and normalizing perversions pre-Split.

"I'm Reverend Clark," the thin man said to Turnbull as he took up the rear in entering the sanctuary. He had not bothered to introduce himself to the smugglers, indicating they were familiar with each other.

"Hello," Turnbull said, defaulting to his habit of avoiding giving his or any other name unless it was absolutely essential. "I hope you don't mind the dog."

"All God's creatures are welcome here," he said, closing the door. "Except the damn atheist communists."

"Yeah, reverend, we'll get along fine."

It was warm inside the sanctuary. There was a fire in the fireplace, and a pot of soup. Turnbull did not want to speculate on the meat it contained. Raccoon? Squirrel?

For their part, the teenagers stared at Gibson, fascinated. The minister saw that Turnbull had noticed.

"Most of the dogs were culled here a few years ago," the reverend told Turnbull. "Cats too. 'Useless eaters,' the blues called them. Now we are plagued with rats."

"They killed the dogs, huh?" Turnbull said. He added avenging that atrocity to his lengthy mental to-do list.

"I wish I could offer you some of our food, but we don't have any extra and you red boys look pretty well-fed."

"That's okay, father," Hatfield said. "You think they are on the way?"

"If they left when it got dark, they should be here soon. Now, I have to ask – who is your guest and his dog? They are not part of your posse."

"A favor," said Hatfield.

"A favor?" asked the minister, skeptical. "Just wanted to see the blue, see what the People's Republic was like and go home?"

"I'm not going home," Turnbull said.

"I don't understand."

"I'm going north, riding the rails as it were."

Reverend Clark looked at Hatfield, who shrugged.

"We did not have a lot of choice, padre," the smuggler said. "Like I said, bringing him and his dog was a favor. A favor to the powers that be who let us bring the sheep in your flock back to America."

"You're infiltrating north through our Underground Railroad," the reverend said to Turnbull.

"That's right."

"Do you understand how dangerous that is for us? The risk you'll be putting us in?"

"I know what I'm doing, reverend. This isn't my first rodeo. It's not even my hundredth rodeo."

"Yeah, father," added Hatfield. "He may look fancy but he's a stone killer."

"I can't promise you they'll take you," the reverend continued.

"You let me worry about that," Turnbull replied. "I can be very persuasive."

There was a quiet knock at the door, but no one moved to answer it.

"They're here," Hatfield said.

"We'll see how persuasive you are," Reverend Clark said to Turnbull, walking to the door and opening it.

There were four men outside, armed with AKs and carrying packs. The two associates of Hatfield were there too, but they did not seem worried. These newcomers were thinner than the reds and unshaven – definitely blue siders. They came inside and greeted the reverend.

The newcomers wore shabby uniforms that Turnbull did not recognize – he thought they were probably some flavor of blue militia, since there were faded, obsolete versions of the rainbow

People's Republic flag stuck with Velcro on their right shoulders. Like Hatfield's boys, these guys were clearly leveraging their semi-official status to ply their real trade.

"How many?" the priest asked.

"Seven," said the leader of the newcomers. "None of them are lame this time,"

"That's good news," Hatfield said. "Bring them up."

One of the newcomers disappeared into the dark. Their leader looked over at Turnbull and stared for a moment.

"I don't know you," he said.

"I'm the guy you're taking north," Turnbull said.

"The hell I am," the blue side smuggler replied.

"You may want to rethink that," Hatfield advised. "He's got a mean streak."

"I don't expect to ride the railroad for free," Turnbull said. "I'm going to buy a ticket."

"What do you got that I want?"

Turnbull opened his pack and took something small out of the bag Ernie Smith had given him. He tossed the shiny disc over to the blue smuggler.

"One ounce, pure gold."

The blue regarded it, astonished. He put it in his mouth and bit. The soft metal bent.

"That enough for a ticket to ride?" Turnbull asked.

The blue nodded and shoved the coin in his pocket.

"Where's mine?" asked Hatfield. Turnbull ignored him.

The blue smugglers brought seven wretched figures inside the church, clearly civilians and clearly not smugglers. Each carried a worn backpack, probably supplied by the smugglers. They were horribly thin too, and each one was a combination of terrified, tired, and disoriented. The congregants took their guests' burdens, sat them in pews, covered them in threadbare blankets, and got them some soup. None ate until the reverend gave the blessing.

The reverend left the travelers and walked back to where Turnbull stood, back to a wall and facing the front doors.

"Some of them come a long way. New York, Chicago, Canada," said Reverend Clark. "The red is the promised land."

"It's a lot less promising than it used to be."

"Is there food? Is there electricity? Do they shoot you for proclaiming Jesus Christ our Lord and Savior?" the minster asked.

Turnbull shook his head.

"Then it's promised enough."

The smugglers were doing their own thing, comparing the wares they would exchange. Hatfield examined and cringed at some of the magazines the blues brought, like *Non-Binary Babes*, *Frisky Furry Fantasies*, and worse, much worse. The blues, for their part, were thrilled with a shipment of copies of *Cheerleader Naked Party* and *Sorority Girl Hoe-Down*.

"There's a big market for cis porn. Pretty girls and guys together. It's illegal as hell here," said the blue smuggler to Turnbull, who had not asked.

"They'll eat up this weird stuff in Austin," Hatfield added, repacking the wares. Turnbull got sight of a mule on the cover of one of the magazines before it got stuffed back in a ruck.

The reverend just shook his head.

"Kind of strange seeing a minister associating with this kind of crowd," Turnbull observed.

"Do you think the Lord came for the folks who are already righteous? He came for folks like these," Clark replied. "These fellows have saved hundreds of Christians from de-religiousization camps or even worse. Who are we to question who He acts through?"

"Not me," said Turnbull. He walked over to the refugees. A couple were teenagers, the rest between their twenties and forties, though it was getting harder to accurately tell the age of PR subjects as their hard lives took a toll. Forty was now the new fifty and would probably be the new sixty soon enough.

Turnbull took a seat on a pew adjacent to the adults. They regarded him warily as they slurped their mystery meat soup.

"What's your name?" he asked one of the men, who put down his spoon.

"I'm Mike. He/him," Mike replied. "Sorry, force of habit. I hear you don't do pronouns in the red."

Turnbull nodded.

"Where did you come from?" Turnbull asked.

"New York," he said. Turnbull picked up the hint of an accent.

"What's it like?"

"Bad. And not just for us believers. We're all Catholic, but real pre-ban Catholic, not People's Catholic. An informer told the People's Religious Directorate that we were holding the Latin mass and the People's Security Force raided our secret church. The priest stayed behind to distract them while we got away. I hope he's not dead."

"How did you get here?"

"We had a contact. We thought maybe he could hook us up with the Underground Railroad, if it was real and not just a story. I guess it is real, since here we are. Where are we anyway?"

"Ohio. I assume you'll cross into West Virginia tonight. And then you're free."

"Free? Been a long time since I heard that word used in a good way. Not since the Split. You know, they teach pre-adults in school that 'freedom' is people of pallor supremacy."

"They say a lot of nonsense. The red is going to be an adjustment for you."

"You can really have a church without a license?"

"Yeah. And carry guns. And eat. And speak, except not communist crap or pervert stuff. We don't tolerate that garbage anymore."

"I don't know what we'll do when we get to the red," Mike said. "I'm a little scared."

"Freedom can be scary," Turnbull said. "I guess that's why so many people are so willing to give it up without a fight."

"I'm just worried that the PR will win the war. How long can the red states keep losing battles?"

"Oh, the media and its lies," Turnbull said. "Nice to see that there's something that hasn't changed since before the Split."

Hatfield approached them. His ruck was on.

"Time for you to go with your new guides," he said.

"Thanks for the help," Turnbull said.

"Try not to kill anyone else," the smuggler replied.

"No," Turnbull said. "That outcome is not in the cards."

Hatfield turned to his crew and his charges to organize them for movement.

Turnbull rose to his feet as the reverend approached.

"Good luck," Clark said, extending his hand. "God be with you."

"I'm going to need Him," Turnbull said as he picked up his ruck, reached in, and pulled out a gold coin which he passed the cleric surreptitiously. No sense tempting the smugglers.

It was a long walk through the woods to an abandoned fire station in Antioch, a tiny hamlet due north of the secret church. They passed a number of houses that appeared as though they might still be occupied, but even those were dark and decaying.

"Not a lot of farms," Turnbull said to the leader of the smugglers. Unlike Hatfield, this guy mostly kept his mouth shut.

"Lot of the farmers got pulled out to work collective farms. That all went to hell. They worked their asses off and most everything got taken away by the blues. So, they figured that if they were going to starve, they would do it sitting on their asses and they walked away. No farmers, no farms."

They took shelter in an abandoned fire station that had once housed a volunteer fire company of the kind once common in the region. No more. The blues had decided to "rationalize" and "centralize" the emergency services and took the equipment away to redistribute it more fairly. There had been no emergency services in Antioch for years, and the smugglers took over the fire station as a safe house. Turnbull noted a few pictures still on the walls of firemen in happier times proudly standing by their shining engine. The dust was thick on the frames. There was an official PR poster still tacked up, faded and dogeared. It showed a bunch of mostly fat firepeople of at least a dozen genders, including a couple in wheelchairs, with the legend "EveryBODY Can Be A Firefighter!"

The smugglers left Turnbull and Gibson there alone to wait for the next evening when someone named "Chaz" would meet Turnbull and his dog there. Turnbull got a sense of the layout of the immediate area in the dawn's light, and ate a blueberry power bar. He hid the wrapper.

Chaz pulled up to the station in a People's Republic Department of Sanitation and Hygiene pick-up truck and went inside. Chaz was apparently a woman, a sturdy one who wore a very used light blue surgical mask. She looked around and pounded on the door. Nothing. She was puzzled.

Turnbull was watching from the wood line about a hundred meters south. After the smugglers left and he had his snack, he and the dog had made their way out of the station for the trees. The soiled mattress on the floor in the fire station was tempting, but Turnbull worried that a reward for turning in a red intruder might be even more so to his guides. He found a spot to lay-up in and got some ZZZZs. Gibson, ever alert, was his intruder alarm.

Satisfied that Chaz was alone, he and the dog approached and took the driver by surprise. Chaz's arms went into the air at the sight of the gun.

"Don't worry, I'm your guy. Let's go."

She looked him over carefully.

"Wait, I have to unload."

The driver went to the truck and whispered into the bed. Three figures, each with a ratty backpack, got up and climbed down onto the ground.

They regarded Turnbull and the dog with some trepidation, and he noted that each of them seemed, at a minimum, gender ambiguous. Chaz herself was not particularly feminine – if she was a she. Turnbull did not try to guess.

"Forget it, Kelly," he told himself. "It's the People's Republic."

Chaz hustled the three refugees into the fire station and, as Turnbull loaded his gear into the ride, heard Chaz tell them that their guides would be coming soon and not to lose their backpacks. The smugglers would insist that the wares the chickens carried be delivered intact as part of the price of transit.

Chaz shut the door to the fire station and hopped behind the driver's seat. Turnbull was already in the passenger seat with his rifle between his legs and Gibson on the floor.

"Where are we going?" Turnbull asked.

"The next stop, north toward Akron. Keep looking down if we pass another vehicle. You're not fat, but you're not thin either and that might draw attention. Keep the dog down too. The dog will draw attention."

"People haven't seen a dog in a while?"

"Not one that isn't cooking over a fire."

"I don't recommend anyone try to put Gibson in a pan," Turnbull said. "That's a good way to lose your face."

The road was bumpy and the truck shook as Chaz seemed to hit every pothole and rut in the asphalt that they passed. Pete Buttigieg had, as one of his many jobs, been the People's Infrastructure Czar. He never actually fixed any potholes, but he did manage to outlaw complaining about bad roads as being racist.

"You bring a lot of Christians south?" Turnbull asked. It was not that he was chatty – he was looking for whatever information he could get on the Underground Railroad since his personal safety now depended on it. If that meant making the sacrifice of interacting with other human beings, it was a price he would have to pay.

"They weren't Christians," Chaz replied, her voice deeper than it should have been. "I mean, maybe they were, but that's not why they are trying to get out. Those were detransitioners."

"What?"

"They started transitioning, male to female, female to male, something else to something else, and then thought better of it. But you can't stop once you start. That's a crime. Puts the whole idea of gender fluidity in doubt. So, if you start and then try to stop, they will put you in a camp and finish the transition. Hormones, surgery. Everything. It's a one way trip. These are the ones who are trying to get out before the blues do it to them, or sometimes after it's been done. They say the red medicine can undo it. I don't know if that's true. I hope it is."

It was not true, sadly. Turnbull overcame the temptation to say so, as well as to ask Chaz about her own story. That was none of his business and he did not need to dig up something that had been buried.

Chaz went on. It seemed to have been a while since she had been able to talk freely.

"There's a war on but they have a whole directorate of the PSF that does nothing but hunt down detransitioners and abortion resisters. If you schedule an abortion – or if they schedule you for one based on their algorithms – you either go through with it, willing or not, or you find us and get south."

"The blues always had their own priorities."

"Is it really different in the red?"

"Yeah, it's really different in the red. It's not perfect, but we don't castrate people. At least ones who haven't raped a little kid or something."

"Minor attracted is an accepted identity here," Chaz said flatly, resigned to her country's barbarism. Turnbull had nothing to add. There was nothing to add to something like that.

10.

Lower Manhattan was smoky – that was the first thing Turnbull noticed as he looked over from Brooklyn across the East River at the saw-tooth skyline. A dark pall hung over the cityscape, casting an unsettling and unnatural orange glow to the tableau before him. And it looked decrepit, as if it had been abandoned yet the people were still there. Black spots where windows had been, their glass shattered, made the face of the high-rises look like a hillbilly's teeth.

Gibson growled. A couple of salty looking dudes were considering them from across the street, probably weighing their chances. Turnbull's recce rifle was broken down and packed away in his ruck, and his Beretta was under his loose leather jacket, but what they saw were Turnbull's eyes when he turned to stare back.

They considered their chances and wisely moved away.

Others along his week-long journey – much slower than he had hoped – had not been so wise. Moving across Pennsylvania, Turnbull had found himself in a barn with a dozen civilians while being shuttled across the former Keystone State – the new nickname was "The Non-Patriarchal Alternative State," since matriarchy was simply far too exclusionary. It was somewhere south of Elmira, New York. Laying up was not unusual. He had been passed from safehouse to safehouse on his trip backwards along the Underground Railroad, with varying degrees of welcome for him and the dog, and often he spent time with people going the other way, into the red. They were tired and thin, weak and frightened, and they kept away from the big man and his mean dog – though Gibson often reverted to puppyhood when little kids were around.

A trio of toughs broke into the barn that evening. They carried what looked like an old axe and a couple clubs, and they enjoyed the fear in the eyes of the refugees.

Most of the refugees' eyes.

The safehouse host was no help – he shut off his lamp and stayed in his farmhouse, but even if he was not involved, what could he do anyway except wait until the thugs had their fun? One of the three raiders spotted a girl of no more than fourteen as soon as they entered – Gibson had been letting her pet him earlier. The travelers were resigned to their fate; the thugs were expecting a fine time. They paid no attention to the dark, silent shape in the back corner who was holding something in his lap as they strolled over to the terrified girl, pausing only to backhand her begging mother.

Gibson was primed and ready, awaiting only his master's word. But Turnbull said nothing as he got up to his feet. At the other end of the barn, the desperate father flung himself at the attackers and a vicious swing of the club to the guy felled him. They turned their eyes back to the girl as Turnbull walked forward to a position a couple yards to their rear. Gibson walked beside him, tensed, his upper lip pulled back.

The presumed leader, club in his left paw, looked in the girl's eyes and said, "You're ours now, bitch," and put his right paw on her tear-stained cheek.

"Gibson," Turnbull said quietly. The dog's tail was wagging slightly as he leapt.

The three now noticed the big man behind them, but it was the dark flash of something black coming fast that focused their attention.

The leader saw what it was, or rather felt it, first. The average Belgian Malinois can generate 195 pounds per square inch, and what is being pushed are sharp teeth bred for ripping flesh. But Gibson was not average – when his jaws locked on the forearm of the hand that pawed the girl's face, the force was over 225 PSI. The ulna and the radius snap at about 160 PSI. And Gibson was not content to merely crush. He ripped.

Turnbull raised the suppressed FN Five SeveN Mk3 pistol and the Trijicon RMR optic's red dot danced across the face of the one with the axe. Turnbull fired twice, with the high-velocity 5.7x28mm bullets each entering an eye and spurting out the back. The third guy was running his options through his brain when two more SS198LF rounds went through his brain too, disrupting his musings and deflating him into a heap that flopped onto the ground.

The one with the dog shredding his arm was shouting, "Get it off me!" He seemed to be in a lot of pain, so Turnbull paused for a few moments – very long ones for the would-be rapist – to let Gibson get in a few more vicious shakes before he placed the barrel to the man's temple. The round went straight through and punched a hole in the barn.

Gibson let go of the now limp scumbag, disappointed, his snout a red mask of gore. The civilians were in shock.

"Look after him," Turnbull directed, pointing to the injured father. "Gibson, come on."

They went to the farmhouse and pounded on the door. Nothing.

"Open up," Turnbull said. "Now."

The farmer had been frightened by Turnbull when the man showed up earlier, and he did not even ask him for money – the farmer was one of the conductors who did it for cash or goods or whatever else the hapless victims could pay him. It was an open question whether he had tipped off the intruders for a premium. In any case, he cautiously opened up.

Turnbull stared back through the cracked front door.

"They're all dead," he said coldly. His gun hung in his hand, and the farmer saw it. "Who were they?"

"The Borden brothers, I think. Maybe Toby White. They're bad seed."

"Will they be missed?"

"Not for a while."

"You got shovels?"

"Yeah."

"Get them. You and your family are digging some holes."

"Me?"

"You. And if you're smart, you'll dig them deep in case somebody comes looking for these guys. Get to work."

Turnbull did not have to add that the farmer could always join the intruders in the rich Pennsylvania earth.

That incident was the only time Turnbull had had to use his weapons since Hatfield's crossing. A few miles outside of West Point, which was still a military academy but now flew even more multi-colored flags than before the Split, a PSF cruiser had pulled over the truck Turnbull was riding in the back of for the final leg into the New York City area. The driver had gotten the uniformed thugs to go away for a bribe of some fresh cheese from an upstate farm. They were wise to have accepted it – for about five minutes Turnbull had had the red dot from his FN pistol's optic laid right on the PSF sergeant's skull.

Now he was in town, looking across the greenish water at Manhattan. The bridges were closed, except to elite traffic. That was a problem. Even with his fake People's Bureau of Investigation credentials provided by Ernie Smith – he needed a license to be packing – he might not get past the bridge checkpoints. He would have to take the subway, which was allegedly still open.

That thought was not particularly soothing.

Turnbull dropped his pack and knelt by the dog, who was on high alert in the urban environment.

"There's no hiding you, so you're hiding in plain sight," Turnbull told the canine. He pulled a harness out of his ruck and slipped it onto the panting dog. Gibson was used to it, and it actually seemed to please him to wear it. There were black Velcro patches on each side, and Turnbull had specially made patches to stick on them.

They both read, "OFFICIAL ANTI-RACIST SERVICE NON-HUMAN COMPANION." Turnbull stuck one on each side of the harness. The guy who made them up for Turnbull back in Dallas had looked at him like he was insane.

"Let's go find a subway," Turnbull said.

He glanced at the dingy, peeling Brooklyn Bridge, which five years before had been painted orange to celebrate indigenous people for some reason, and led Gibson into the High Street station. There were no operating fare turnstiles – fares were racist and collecting them had been long ago abandoned. Now free, the subways were worth precisely what New Yorkers paid for them.

The long escalators down to the platform had long ago become inoperable. The people who once maintained them had retired, moved to the red, or been replaced according to the strict quota system that governed employment in the People's Republic. While the geographic origin of an applicant's great-great-great-grandfather was extremely important when it came to parceling out jobs, mechanical ability fell far below it on the list of qualifications. Even if someone knew how to fix the machines, the gears and the teeth of the steps were rusted solid.

Bums lay in their own filth on what was now a stairwell by default. At least one appeared dead – the hypodermic needle next to him on the step was probably the reason. And there was the odor. The bathrooms were long ago destroyed, but that did not silence the call of nature. The inhabitants answered it everywhere. The descent down to the station was like being lowered into a cesspool. Even Gibson seemed appalled, and he would happily smell other dogs' butts.

There were a few people coming up and going down, mostly working folks forced to risk the subterranean hellscape to get to their jobs. Many people in the PR were freeloaders, getting their welfare checks for doing nothing or claiming jobs like "poet." Other people were required to perform necessary tasks, and those jobs were both assigned and mandatory – no work, no ration cards, no food. These were "Designated People's Servants" and they had to work. They were the ones who sort of kept things going, and the government was very serious about them working. They had no choice but to ride the rails.

And then there was the trash – not merely the garbage that littered the concrete floors but the human detritus who gathered together throughout the subway station in little packs, scanning the regular people, looking for victims. And there were People's Security Force officers too, mostly bored and hardly proactive. A pair of them lounged with cheap cigarettes under a dingy sign reading "NO SMOKING OR SEXISM" that was illustrated by a large woman in a turban sitting in a wheelchair pointing at the reader and scowling.

There were lots of cameras. Turnbull knew from his review of the intel that they had been installed before the Split in an ill-fated attempt to control crime. Most of them probably did not work, and the lenses of those that still did were probably so fouled over the years that the images would have been indecipherable even if someone cared enough to monitor them.

The train platform had apparently not changed since the era of *The Warriors* – a row of metal beams with peeling paint held up the ceiling. The platform was long and the cement floor was splattered with who knew what. Gibson stepped gingerly, trying to avoid the larger deposits.

Along the walls, a dozen derelicts and hobos sat and stared with glassy eyes. One was injecting himself.

Gibson the dog drew glances, but no stares. Staring, one learned quickly, invited a response and that might escalate into serious trouble. A big man, not thin, with a dog – very unusual. And if he was out in public, presumably he was not worried about being out in public. The PSF officers looked him over as he calmly walked past. He ignored them, and they went back to their puffing.

Turnbull stood under the land acknowledgement plaque awkwardly bolted into the cement wall. He did not bother to read who the land had been stolen from, though someone had spray painted his own idea of the victim – "MY ASS!!!!"

Other posters, mostly faded, torn, and defaced, warned of the looming climate crisis, promised the end of "CISPATRIARCHAL POWER STRUCTURES," and demanded that PR subjects be alert to the peril of "RED RACIST SPIES."

"Got that one right," Turnbull muttered to himself.

Gibson growled at three young men who approached within about ten feet. They were staring – apparently, they did not fear trouble, or did not fear it enough.

"What's with that dog," one with curly hair and a bad attempt at a moustache asked. Gibson growled low and long.

"He smells racists," Turnbull said. "Are you racists?"

The trio seemed puzzled.

"I just want to pet the dog," the young man insisted.

"If you come a step closer, he'll rip out your throat," Turnbull said evenly. "He's a trained anti-racist non-human companion."

The dog was probably valuable, either alive or as dinner. The three were pretty thin and Turnbull noted that their eyes were red. The air reeked of strong pot – that was one commodity the PR made sure was always in stock – and these fellows had almost certainly partaken. Maybe it was spiked – angel dust was a cheap and popular way to hype up the high without the risk of an OD like fentanyl. All of it was given out by the PR government, so it could be any one or combination of them.

The trio thought it over, and Turnbull saw the glances of the other passengers around the platform. They did not want to draw attention by staring, but they also wanted to see how this drama resolved. Turnbull, for his part, realized that smoking these jokers probably meant dropping the PSF flatfoots too, and for all their derelictions, the People's Security Force tended to take seriously people shooting their officers.

The trio was still weighing its options when Turnbull pivoted to face them and pulled back his jacket just enough to flash his Beretta.

"I'm People's Bureau of Investigation," he said in a low voice so only they could hear. "And the only reason I don't kill you racists right now is the paperwork. Walk away. Move."

The pot was THC-enhanced, but not so strong as to make the young punks believe they could take on the guy with the big gun and the dog with the big teeth.

"Just messing with you," the leader said, breaking into a poisonous smile. He turned and attempted to lead his small posse away with a modicum of dignity.

A voice came over the loudspeaker, but it was distorted and came in and out. Turnbull had no idea what it said, but the other passengers did. They stirred. The A Train was coming.

He could hear the clattering down the tunnel, louder and more chaotic than he remembered from his pre-Split and even his post-Split rides on the subway. The train lumbered into view. It was covered with graffiti – literally every inch of it. But the one part that was not touched by the spray-paint was the painted-on PR flag. It was a rainbow banner with a bunch of designs imposed on it – triangles, squares, what looked like a cartoon gerbil. Turnbull recognized it as being the version of the People's Republic flag from about three years ago. He could tell because the candy-cane stripe for minor attracted persons was there on the bottom – it had moved upwards in later versions to make room for the gray stripe of elderly-loving "geronsexuals" and the brown stripe representing those into scat.

No one dared defile the painted flag. There were some crimes the PR took seriously. That, like practicing Christianity and denying global warning, was one of them.

The train creaked to a stop and the doors – most of them anyway – opened to release the passengers onto the platform.

They seemed relieved to escape to the relative safety and hygiene of the High Street platform.

Then the waiting passengers pressed in – the thug trio stayed behind, no doubt waiting for less challenging marks than Kelly Turnbull and Gibson – and the doors shut. It smelled worse than a cesspool, reeking of fluids, cannabis, and unwashed bodies, soap having been pronounced an environmental hazard and rarely available to the proles. At the far end of Turnbull's car was a disheveled man's crumpled body on the floor. He might have been dead, injured, or sleeping, but there were no Samaritans aboard who bothered to check. Most of the passengers simply found a place on the filthy ceiling to stare at during the ride under the East River.

Turnbull saw an unoccupied orange plastic seat that seemed relatively sanitary, perhaps rubbed clean by a thousand backsides this week. He sat and Gibson sat beside him, seemingly annoyed that Turnbull did not have to share the floor. A man at the front of the car, next to the body, began to sing an obscene pop song by an aging Megan Thee Stallion that was currently popular. There was one kid on the car with his mom, who ignored him as he mumbled along with the words to "My Vagina Speaks."

An obviously pregnant young woman and her mother stood next to him, hanging from the straps. The pregnant girl was obviously in distress, but Turnbull suppressed his urge to offer her his seat. Cispatriarchal acts of chivalry would draw attention. The girl looked like she was about to vomit, but her mother consoled her that within a few hours the baby would be gone and she would have her Abortion Validation Payment and they could buy some meat or maybe some cheese.

After a twenty-minute stop under the East River – the loudspeaker crackled but Turnbull could not make out the explanation – the train continued on. It jostled and jolted, and Turnbull doubted it would be long before the whole system simply collapsed. That was not his problem. His problem was the girl. The pregnant girl gagged a little, but mercifully did not throw up on him or the dog.

The A Train pulled into the Fulton Transit Center, which was only a couple decades old. It still looked like something out of Dickens, filled with hobos, losers, thieves, and normal folks just trying to get through it. Turnbull and Gibson wended their way out of station, but since this was a secure zone, he had to show his fake PBI credentials. Others showed their ID cards and, if you were not a Privilege Level 6 or higher, you needed to show a secure area work permit too. Those who could not were refused entry.

They got out of the transit center on Broadway. It was a dingy canyon of decaying buildings, with people hurrying along the streets. He could see the former Freedom Tower, One World Trade Center. It looked abandoned, just as the name had been. It was now the Anti–Hate Speech Tower. Nearby had been the 9/11 Memorial – that was long gone, initially replaced by a monument to the victims of Islamophobia, which itself had been replaced by a monument to victims of transphobia after believing Muslims had largely rejected the PR's pro-trans and pro-pederast agenda. The conflict had gotten so substantial that Islamophobia, like anti-Christian and anti-Orthodox Jewish discrimination, had been expressly legalized.

This was downtown, and it held the remaining financial institutions for the PR. As one of the secure areas of Manhattan, there were a lot of PSF officers around. They would glance at Turnbull and his anti-racism animal companion, assess him as bad juju, and ignore him. Anyone that big with a service animal was someone serious. Hiding in plain sight was working.

New Yorkers had always been fast, moving with a purpose. Turnbull had noticed that this had changed somewhat during his previous post-Split infiltrations in to the city, but now the people seemed agitated and in a hurry.

He put that observation aside for a moment. He had bigger things to worry about, like how he would accomplish his mission. Obviously, he needed to get to Midtown, where Clay was last being kept over a week ago. That meant leaving the downtown secure area, and the intel reports warned that it was pretty ugly out there in the unsecure zones. Once in Midtown in that secure zone, he had to scout the old Mandarin hotel, but how would he get in? And, assuming he found Clay Deeds, how would he get his boss out and off the island?

It again occurred to Turnbull, as it had several times during his trip backwards along the Underground Railroad, that perhaps this adventure was not particularly well-thought out. But what was the alternative – let Clay die?

Assuming he was not already dead.

"Come on," Turnbull told Gibson as they started to walk north. But then, he noted the agitation again. Something was up.

"What's going on?" he muttered. Ahead of him, a well-nourished man in a suit – probably a banker – pushed by him, rushing to a taxi and shoving aside a man dressed in a cocktail dress and pearls who was showing his ID and about to step inside.

"I'm priv 10!" the intruder shouted at the confused driver, holding out his ID card. "And I need to get out of Manhattan!"

The man claiming Privilege Level 10 looked like he stepped out of a Romney family reunion photo. For all Turnbull knew, he *was* a Romney – the former presidential candidate had made a huge show of going over to the blue right after the Split because "Red America represents the lack of diversity and hostility toward working people that I have always fought against."

In any case, the man in the dress was not having it.

"I'm a 10 too!" xe shouted, and threw the man in the suit to the sidewalk before slipping into the taxi. Painted on the side of it was "PRIVILEGE LEVEL 8 AND UP ONLY."

The banker sprawled in front of Turnbull, his suit defiled by the muck on the sidewalk. He did not seem to care about that. His eyes were wide and a bit of saliva strung out of the corner of his mouth. Turnbull initially assessed drugs, but realized it was not drugs.

It was fear.

Turnbull stopped and helped the man to his feet. Other people passed by them, rushing forward.

"What's going on?" Turnbull asked.

"Don't you know?" the man said, incredulous.

Turnbull said nothing, but held onto the man's forearm.

"The reds are coming," he said.

"What do you mean?" Turnbull asked.

"I mean they are coming. They have invaded, like they did in California. They are coming here, to Manhattan! I have to go!"

The man pulled away and Turnbull let him loose. The man turned and ran off up Broadway.

Turnbull looked down at his puzzled dog.

"Let's go."

BOOK TWO

11.

Captain Tobias Winfrey of the People's Republic Anti-Colonial Military Land Force's (PRACMLF) A Company, 1st Battalion, 22nd Infantry (Trans), looked out over their unit's area of operations at Columbia, Pennsylvania, and was quite proud of their command. With the help of their political officer, who called xirself "X," though even that sometimes caused confusion with the short-lived new name for Twitter, CPT Winfrey was fully focused on rooting out all residual racism and patriarchal leanings within their 100-being unit. That the whole company was composed of gender-fluid individuals – roll call in the mornings included both a check on whether the soldier was present and whether the soldier was still the same gender identity as the day before – did not mean the company could not become a tool of patriarchy. No, it must be carefully monitored because, like the various segregated units of oppressed racial/ethnic/other groups within the company's infantry division – including a platoon of differently-abled Samoan Two-Spirit folx – it could easily become a tool of white supremacy if the command failed to continuously do the work. A black commander of a black battalion – it was designated as a unit composed of "Persons of Africanness" because the term "black" had been designated as racist – within the division had just been arrested for white supremacy. Sadly, the price of anti-racism/sexism/transphobia-plus was eternal vigilance.

Of course, prioritizing internal conformity meant de-prioritizing other aspects of military life. But Winfrey – born Agatha – understood the expectation of the PRACMLF chain of command, and that was maintaining ideological purity. As for fighting, that was rarely brought up. The front was 25 miles or so to the southwest, far enough from Columbia that CPT Winfrey did not bother to order their troops to dig in and fortify the area. The fact that most units in the region had pulled out or were in the process of doing so – no one told them why and they never asked – made improving the company's defenses seem like even less of a priority.

But Winfrey, who qualified for command based on "lived experience" as a trans demi-gender thrice-spirit being, still understood the strategic value of the location. Columbia was a small town at the eastern landing of two bridges that crossed over the wide Susquehanna River, which runs northwest to southeast across Pennsylvania, and creates a nearly impenetrable obstacle. The former Wright's Ferry Bridge on the old US-30 – now denominated "PR-30" – and the former Veterans Memorial Bridge on Route 462 that ran parallel a few hundred meters to the south, were key crossing points on the main supply route to the front. The town itself had been cleared of civilians – with many of them sent to camps to remedy their backwards thinking – and the troops of A/1-22 found themselves alone in the empty village.

Nothing much happened in Columbia; it was quiet and safe duty with days marked by dull guard shifts and self-criticism sessions. Trucks ran back and forth over the bridges bringing supplies forward and, lately, bringing troops back from the front as part of the redeployment.

Oddly, considering their importance, the racist red forces had never bombed the bridges or hit the twin spans with missiles, but Winfrey did not give that much thought. As a commander, they already had much to do to ensure that their unit was a safe space to all gender identities, except that of those cis throwbacks. Those people were officially oppressors.

And CPT Winfrey was dealing with an uncomfortable personal medical issue. Their artificial penis, stitched together from flesh taken from their left forearm, was suffering yet another low-grade infection. Like fully a quarter of their troops, almost all of whom had undergone surgical gender reassignments, Winfrey was gobbling down antibiotics – the trans units in PRACMLF divisions typically consumed 60% of the entire divisional allotment. Still, they soldiered on despite the nagging ache in their groin.

Winfrey was up before dawn that day, meeting with X on the headquarters building's balcony overlooking the river while drinking cups of responsible coffee. It was only vaguely brown. Neither mentioned that the coffee kept getting more and more responsible. That could be seen as subversive, and while the two were friendly, both also knew the other could become an enemy in a flash.

It was a typical morning with typical company issues. There had been a fight the evening before between a two-spirit and a tri-gender soldier. X suggested consulting with higher headquarters on which one should be prosecuted – last week it certainly would have been the tri-gen, but the identities' relative place in the hierarchy might have changed. Winfrey sipped and readily agreed that this was the best course of action – X was a huge help in avoiding gaffes. X, who had a forked tongue and whose face was tattooed in a serpent motif, made a note to take care of it.

Across the river, an orange fireball erupted near the west end of the Trans Genocide Memorial Bridge, formerly the Veterans Memorial Bridge. Winfrey and X stared for a moment, stunned, holding their coffee cups. There was another explosion, and then another. And another.

"What the...," began Winfrey, but then they heard it – the sound of rotors. Lots of rotors.

Two dozen helicopters were skipping across the black surface of the Susquehanna, the dark broken by occasional orange flashes as the aircraft fired their weapons at Columbia. Winfrey watched as a finger of fire leapt off the rail at the side of one of the UH-60 Blackhawks and streaked into the town. The Hellfire punched into the battalion bathhouse not 100 meters north of where Winfrey and X stood, detonating with dozens of Alpha Company's troops still cavorting inside. And both heard the low growl of the rotary cannons just as a wave of 7.62mm rounds tore across the face of the headquarters building. The two officers clumsily dove for cover, their weak coffee splattering the floor.

"Eagle-5, this is Eagle-1," Major George Ryan, Jr., called into his headset's mic. Down below was the black water of the river, streaked with a few flecks of light from the rising sun to the east. He was looking out the open door, buffeted by the wind and sitting next to the gunner wielding the mounted six-barrel M134 Minigun that sprayed 7.62×51mm bullets at 3,000 rounds per minute.

"This is Eagle-5! Taking fire from the Vets bridge." Ryan could see fingers of orange tracers coming off the bridge roadway up toward his UH-60 Blackhawk.

"Get in there and suppress it," Ryan answered into the mic. "No damage to the bridge."

"Roger!" Eagle-5 banked hard toward the targets spraying rifle fire at the chopper. A stream of orange lightning reached out from its door gunner and hosed down the resisters. There was no more return fire.

Eagle-1 bucked and shook as a Hellfire leapt off the rails. The infantrymen inside were glad that the Army had added the missile racks to the assault gunships – whatever the Hellfires killed was something that would not be trying to kill them when they hit the ground. Before the mission, the targetters had identified the key buildings housing the 1-22nd – the barracks, the headquarters, the company bathhouse. The raiders were going to flatten them all and kill anyone who managed to escape the storm of missiles.

Eagle-1 banked right, the open right door of the chopper facing Columbia as the aircraft flew north along the river bank. The gunner spotted movement – it looked like some pick-up trucks with mounted heavy machine guns – and he proceeded to unleash hell upon them with the minigun.

Ryan surveyed the situation. A half-dozen black choppers were landing and dropping off their squads of infantry at the foot of each bridge – it was, of course, easiest to take a bridge from both ends and, back on the west side of the spans, other squads were doing just that. As for the People's Republic forces, there was nothing like organized resistance. There should have been dug-in positions overlooking the bridges and the open areas near them to stop just this kind of air assault. There was nothing. Whoever was in charge was not doing his job.

Their job, he corrected himself. He knew that the enemy force was part of a trans unit and intel had told him the commander used "they/them." But then, misgendering the enemy was the least worst thing they would be doing to the PR forces today.

Ryan had the chopper fly over the center of Columbia, and the door gunner sprayed several groups of PR troops who tried to fight back. Surprise was total, and the American troops on the ground were beginning to report in that they had seized their initial objectives.

"Let's get down there," Ryan told the pilot.

Eagle-1 dipped and headed toward the aptly named Rotary Park at the east end of the now-secured Route 462 bridge. The helicopter came in low and touched down, with the door gunner scanning for targets.

Ryan leapt off and hit the ground, rifle up, his radioman behind him. The rest of the squad poured out onto the dying, yet overgrown grass – lawn maintenance was not a big PR priority – and then the helicopter took back off to circle overhead and provide gunfire support.

The enemy headquarters was just north of the park, one of a number of buildings that had formerly housed shops and businesses. Ryan waved his arm in that direction.

"Follow me!" he said and took off.

The squad followed, spreading out. There was light gunfire in the distance, but none directed at them as they moved toward the enemy command and control node.

The building has taken some fire, and its western face was pock-marked with 7.62mm holes from the helicopter door guns. The Americans had not hit it with a missile because they wanted to take it whole – it might have some useful intelligence.

There were two dead bodies near the front door, probably guards killed by the choppers' fire. One corpse had lost its helmet and had bright red hair – not Irish red but scarlet. The other was a 6'2 individual wearing camo and make-up that made him/her resemble Lola Falana.

Beyond them was a main door, and it opened as Ryan approached. What came out was a PR soldier with a green political officer brassard, but it was the face that caught Ryan off-guard. It was the face of a lizard, a tattoo designed to make him or her or whatever look like some sort of human/iguana hybrid. And the iguana had an AK-74. It was hissing.

Ryan shot the creature six times; his radioman added another five. It fell onto its back and flopped on the sidewalk for a moment before becoming still.

Another shape appeared in the doorway, a captain who looked like a woman pretending to be a man. They – she, because the red paratroopers did not play pronoun games – stood in the doorway with hands-up.

Ryan rushed her and knocked her to the ground. He led a couple other troops inside to clear the headquarters building while downstairs his troops secured the prisoner. The command post was secure – in fact, it was totally empty. Apparently, all business stopped at night. Ryan shook his head.

There was more gunfire within the town that petered out over the next hour. Ryan convinced Captain Winfrey to radio out a surrender order to her whole company command, which helped end the killing quickly. He did not even have to put his gun to her head, which he would have done if necessary. Ninety minutes after his troops first engaged, he radioed headquarters that Columbia was secure in the hands of US forces – including the two precious bridges, intact and clear. The initial combat test of his Pathfinders was a "GO" with no dead and three lightly wounded. But New York City was not going to be this easy.

One of the sergeants made coffee – they brought their own. As Ryan drank it in his new headquarters, he looked over at the zip-tied captain in the corner. She might or might not have some good intelligence – the spooks would be talking to her soon. Right now, they were going over the papers and computers in the enemy headquarters.

"It's true," one of the intel guys told Ryan. "The PR forces really are pulling out of New Jersey and Pennsylvania, except for some skeleton forces like this one."

Ryan grunted. It was almost like the enemy was clearing the Americans a path to New York City. And the Americans were taking advantage of it. Right at that moment, the offensive was beginning. Red artillery was pulverizing the remaining front line RP units and US armor was going to punch through and come barreling north, including along old US-30 and across the Wright's Ferry Bridge his men had just captured. Then they would press on, all the way to Manhattan, where they would meet up with another axis of advance pushing through New Jersey and the Marine forces sailing up from North Carolina. Off to the west, a feint into the Chinese forces was distracting them and keeping them from interfering with the main American attack.

Then would come the climax of the campaign, the assault on the island. Ryan's Pathfinders would be waiting for the Americans inside Manhattan – assuming the enemy was as feckless there as it was here in Columbia. If it was not, that could be a problem. A terminal one.

It was all working according to plan. If it kept up, very soon, the United States would once again hold the Big Apple. And that would change the course of the war.

So why was he so anxious?

There was a moan. Ryan pivoted. It was the captain sitting on the floor, her hands bound before her with a white zip tie.

"I need a medic," the captain groaned.

"Are you wounded?" Ryan asked.

"No," she said, shaking her head in manifest distress. "My penis hurts."

General Karl Martin Scott's suite in the former Mandarin Oriental Hotel had been turned into a command post of sorts. He was now sleeping in another suite on the same high floor, and sleeping is all he did there. The rest of the day he was in the CP monitoring the battle. You can take the general out of the military, but not the military out of a general. The makeshift command post, with maps, computers, and video feeds manned – personned – by a diverse team of PRACMLF soldiers, was tracking the fight. This meant tracking the utter annihilation of the PR units remaining in Pennsylvania and New Jersey between the former front line and the island of Manhattan.

Harrington was no soldier, but even he could read a map. The People's Republic forces were falling back in disarray.

General Scott was smiling.

"You're proud of your red army," Harrington observed, devoid of emotion. It was not a value judgment, but a statement.

"As a wise man once said, I love it when a plan comes together," the general replied.

"I am no student of military science," Harrington continued. "But this seems to be a unique situation in which the general who planned the offensive also planned the defense."

Scott chuckled grimly.

"I had not thought about it like that," he replied. "I guess I am like Alcibiades."

"I don't know who that was," Harrington said, unashamed of his ignorance.

"A dead white male," Scott said.

"The best kind, myself excepted," Harrington said.

"It seems both of my plans are working," Scott continued. "The initial attack broke the People's Republic Army –"

"People's Republic Anti-Colonial Military Land Forces," Harrington corrected him.

"The reds broke through the front line just as I expected," Scott continued, pointing to locations on the map. "With the rear echelon forces withdrawn, there is no way to counter-attack. So far, the US Army has performed flawlessly. The Army air assaulted in and secured the bridges over the Susquehanna River here at Columbia before the offensive even started. With no reinforcements, there was no way for the blues to dislodge them with a counter-attack. US armored divisions are punching their way north now, blasting through any defensive lines your army can throw up."

"As I said, you are proud," repeated Harrington.

"Of course I am. Just remember, if this plan of yours works out, all of these will be our soldiers in a reunited United States."

"So true," Harrington said. "But before that happens, we have to kill thousands of them."

"War is about sacrifice," Scott replied absently. He was staring at the monitor showing a US corps moving fast north through New Jersey.

"This is where my logistics planning paid off. Before terminating Overlord, we cached a huge supply of ammo and fuel forward. We never moved it back south after I called the operation off. That's why when the red command saw the PR troops pulling out of the way, they were ready to strike quickly."

"With a little help from you talking to your comrades back home," added Harrington.

Scott smiled.

"There are many of us who believe like we do that reunification under a strong leader is the only way forward."

"Leaders," Harrington said. "I am not a potted plant."

Scott continued to smile.

The doors to the suite opened and a pair of beefy and gender-ambiguous PRACMLF security personnel – they would be "military police" in any other army, but the word "police" was considered triggering – entered holding up a disheveled prisoner. Scott gestured to bring the captive forward.

"Mr. Deeds," he said, looking the spy over. "You are a mess."

"The Mandarin's hospitality has deteriorated substantially after the change in ownership," Deeds replied.

"I am told that you are not being particularly talkative. You really should cooperate."

"No," Deeds said simply.

Harrington stepped back, watching the exchange. He approved of Scott's latent sadism – that would need to be encouraged to fully flourish. It annoyed him that Scott always seemed to want to justify his cruelty with military or political necessity rather than to admit the truth – that he enjoyed it. Harrington usually had no use for honesty, but Harrington demanded it when it came to people knowing themselves.

"If your friends do not arrive soon to rescue you, I am going to think that they are not coming and then we'll be free to use every measure to convince you to be more forthcoming," Scott said. "That should worry you."

"I think *you* should be very worried, General," Deeds said.

"I'm not," Scott laughed. "Would you like to see what's happening? Take a look."

The general gestured toward the bank of video screens. A PRACMLF soldier with ears surgically enhanced to resemble that of a badger got up from xis seat to let them have a clear view.

"Over there in western New York the US forces are tying down the Chinese corps with a feint. That keeps the Chinese from interfering with the axes of attack from Pennsylvania and New Jersey toward New York City. As you can see, those attacks are moving north fast, helped by the fact we have pulled most of the People's Republic units out of the way."

Deeds squinted.

"This is your ridiculous plan to take New York City," Deeds said, incredulous.

"Yes, and you are right – it was ridiculous, which is why I called it off. And why I have now convinced the United States to resurrect it."

"You are drawing the Americans into a quagmire," Deeds said as it became clear to him.

"Yes," Scott said. "A bloody quagmire that will make Vietnam or Afghanistan look like old Disneyland." Of course, Disneyland in blue California was now Transtopia, with the "Small World" boat ride now called "Flotilla of Fluidity" and entirely devoted to the countless gender identities, while the Matterhorn had been converted into a huge fiberglass representation of a sex toy. In the red, Disney had been dissolved following a horrific pedophilia scandal not long after the Split. Disney World in Orlando was now Patriot Land, featuring Ernie Eagle and a muscular, flying version of the sixteenth president called Super Abe. EPCOT was converted into a huge beer garden, since the only interesting thing to ever do at EPCOT was drink.

"And somehow you benefit from a quagmire, probably in conjunction with that creature," Deeds said, nodding his head toward Harrington. "I suppose you telling me about your scheme like Blofeld in a pre-Split Bond movie means you want something else from me besides information."

"Very good. You're smart, and that saves time. Let me make a proposal, Mr. Deeds. In the not-too-distant future, both the red and the blue are going to be so deep in the quicksand of this war that they will have no choice but to negotiate a peace. And then a war hero from the red and a visionary leader from the blue will step forward to lead a reunified America into the future."

"I can guess who those two are. Your proposal is going to be that I throw in with you and use my contacts, my influence, etcetera, to help."

Scott grinned. "That or a horrible death."

"And I suppose part of any deal is to call off Kelly Turnbull," Deeds added.

"Well, to get him into a position where I can deal with him," said Scott. "Merely calling him off is not quite sufficient to address what he's done to me."

Now it was Deeds's turn to smile.

"I think you ought to be more worried about what he's *going* to do to you."

12.

The guards at Gate 23, located at Broadway and Canal Street, normally paid little to no attention to the blue-shirted workers leaving the secure zone except to scan out their passes. There were a dozen of these sentinels, outfitted in black utility uniforms with vests and AK rifles, and they took one look at the big man with the big gun and the big dog with the anti-racism canine harness and decided he was not to be messed with. It was fairly common for unusual people to transit into the wilds of unsecure Manhattan, and they understood their command's main expectation – do not create problems. The lead officer waved Turnbull through without a word, not even demanding that he swipe his PBI credentials through the scanner. Turnbull and Gibson stepped outside of the secure zone and the gate clanged shut behind them.

The Downtown Secure Zone's wall ran northwest to southeast along Canal Street, fifteen feet high and topped with razor wire and a catwalk for armed patrols. With that behind him, Turnbull set off north on Broadway, unsure of exactly where he was going or what he would do when he got there.

"Adapt, improvise and overcome," Turnbull muttered aloud. The dog turned and cocked his head as he trotted along. The passersby saw nothing unusual in the big, scary man talking to himself. They were used to that.

The first thing Turnbull noted was the zombies. These were not merely the unhouse-having street people – of which there were plenty – but the actively semi-conscious who staggered about, usually bent over or shaking and twitching as if having a minor seizure. Their eyes were empty, and they drooled. Some stood in one place and shook. Others wandered aimlessly into the near-empty streets, heedless of anyone or anything in their path. At one corner, some of them had formed a line around a government van. It was a PR pharma facilitator giving them their daily drug ration. Another was walking among those too far gone to join a queue and simply slipping the packets into the zombies' filthy hands or the pockets of their rags.

There were a surprising number of what passed as regular people on the sidewalks, mostly thin, mostly ragged, and often staring at Turnbull because he was neither. They stared at the dog because he looked delicious. They ignored and simply walked around the zombies, who paid no attention to them either.

What was missing were the crazies that Turnbull had read about, drug-fueled but still functional fighters concerned only with food, pharmaceuticals, and inflicting pain. They swarmed in packs, indifferent to pain and fear. The intel reports said they mostly come at night. Mostly.

There were few cars, but a lot of old bikes. Apparently, bikes were a precious commodity. Within five minutes, Turnbull saw a man mobbed, thrown off his bicycle, and beaten by a gang of thugs. They did not kill him, which was something. Turnbull walked past and they looked him over but thought better of it.

While the mood on the streets was tense – people avoided eye contact and shuffled along quickly – there was none of the same kind of enhanced fear as back in the secure zone. Just the usual fear.

They don't know about the invasion, Turnbull thought to himself. But that was no surprise. These were the peasants. The masters of the universe in the secure zones would be the first evacuated, and probably the last.

He kept walking, not trying to hide his weapon or his dog, acting as though he belonged and daring anyone to say otherwise. People passed him with a wide berth, eyes downcast. He noted very few children. That made sense. He also noted that the entrepreneurial spirit of the city was not totally dead. Several times he was solicited to ride in one of the jerry-rigged rickshaws that carried the passengers the taxis used to.

There was a rumble behind them on the street, and Turnbull turned to see a line of four five-ton OD green military trucks – though the bright multi-hued PR flags painted on the doors of their cabs destroyed any camouflage effect – rolling up Broadway. It was definitely unusual because the people stopped to look as the trucks sped past, bumping and shaking as they dipped into the countless potholes.

The last one passed Turnbull, with the armed soldier riding shotgun sending him the stink-eye, and a few meters on it hit a particularly deep rut. The truck convulsed and shook, and continued on, but something long and black popped out of the canvas-covered bed and clattered in the street.

Turnbull stepped out in the road to confirm what he thought. It was an AK-47, an ancient one by the looks of it, but still potentially deadly. He became aware that all the people along the sidewalk had stopped and were looking at him to see what he would do. He moved on, leaving the rifle behind, and several people rushed into the road and proceeded to brawl over it.

Where were those truckloads of guns going?

He resolved to try to at least get north to the Midtown secure zone before finding shelter for the night. Whether or not he would attempt to enter the secure zone today was another issue, and he deferred a decision until he could scope out the situation.

The white spray-painted letters "UFT" were covered in red and black spray paint, though they still showed through if you squinted hard. Someone had sprayed "POUM" in red on the wall next to it to assert dominance.

Gangs?

Turnbull and Gibson kept walking. The high-rises on each side of the street bathed it in shadows. There were fewer zombies and unhousehaving here, but they were still in abundance. It was a couple hours until dark and things were sketchy enough in the daylight. Turnbull resolved to find shelter in the unsecure area and then to turn to figuring out how to accomplish his mission tomorrow.

"After all, tomorrow is a new day," he told Gibson, before remembering that quoting *Gone with the Wind* was likely a felony.

More vehicles were approaching. He had seen several pick-ups with scraggly-looking armed paramilitaries roll by but he had done a good job of ducking into doorways or alleys to avoid being seen. They were typically painted red and black, and he caught that word again, painted on the sides of the vehicles.

POUM.

This time, when two of the vehicles came south, he was caught mid-block between West 3rd and West 4th Streets in the middle of a concrete canyon.

Nothing to do but meet their gaze as the two vehicles stopped beside him in the middle of Broadway. But they did not stop recklessly, and the dozen or so paramilitaries did not seem particularly agitated. A civilian rickshaw even continued on around the stopped vehicles with its fare while a zombie stood with mouth open sort of watching as the POUM people disembarked.

"We have been looking for you," the leader said excitedly. He seemed to be trying to look like Che, and he certainly had the thinness, the silly goatee, and the beret down. He was maybe thirty-five, though figuring ages in the blue was harder than in the red as their life was harder.

"You found me," Turnbull said, his rifle hanging free. Gibson was alert and tense.

"Comrade Chico, he/him," he said, coming forward and pounding his fist on his chest. He seemed to be waiting for a response.

Turnbull did not bang his chest – he thought it was stupid.

"Comrade Eddie, he/him," Turnbull replied, using the name on his PBI ID card. "And my anti-racist animal companion is Gibson."

"Pronouns?" asked the militia leader.

"He/him," Turnbull replied. "Gibson identities as cis-canineist."

Gibson wagged his tail. Comrade Chico nodded gravely.

"Welcome to the POUM," the militia leader said. He proceeded to introduce the other comrades, along with their pronouns and, in several cases, their very specific gender identities. Turnbull did not remember a single name.

"We appreciate your being here to act as a liaison with the People's Republic, but you need to understand something," Comrade Chico said formally and solemnly.

"And that is?"

"First, we remain an anarchist collective dedicated to not just the urban marginalized but *all* marginalized persons. That's why the name change."

"Name change?"

"From Party of the Urban Marginalized to the Party of the United Marginalized."

"POUM," Turnbull said.

"Power to the marginalized!" Comrade Chico shouted. All of the comrades raised their fists and repeated the slogan.

"And we appreciate the so-called government's help during this crisis, but we remain committed to our collective anarchist vision based on true Marxist-Leninist thought and Kendian principles."

"Of course you do," Turnbull said. "As for me, I'm from the government and I am here to help."

"Like I said, we appreciate the government keeping its promise to provide support for our transformative anti-racism efforts in response to the red aggression. The defense preparations are going well. We have the first delivery of weapons and we will distribute them to the workers and unjobbed as requested well before the invaders arrive. But we do need a commitment from your government if we are to continue to work in allyship and cooperation."

"My instructions," Turnbull said carefully, "are to be an ally and cooperate."

"The UFT's political wrongthought is intolerable. For too long, we alone have struggled to stamp out their revanchist ideology and we believe that we must purge their poison before we fight the reds." Comrade Chico stared at Turnbull as if this made sense.

"Oh, the UFT is the worst," Turnbull said. "Very racist. Down with the UFT. Up with POUM!"

"Power to the marginalized!" Comrade Chico shouted, delighted. All of the comrades joined in raising their fists.

It was not a long drive to the POUM headquarters, just a few decrepit blocks. Up ahead was New York University, or at least what had been NYU. After several name changes – the most recent moniker was the "Lumumba-Zapata College of Decolonialization" – the university completely ended grades, faculty, and classes, and ceased operation. Now, the campus was something else, though just as communist.

Out front, banners reading "POUM" hung from the buildings. The anarchist militia had taken over much of the campus as its base of operations. But not the newish 181 Mercer Street building – the modern glass and steel building was a burned out pile of broken glass and ash.

The militia had a fleet of pick-up trucks and a couple gas tankers in an ersatz motor pool in Gould Plaza. As for numbers, Turnbull estimated a few hundred troops, mostly armed with old

AKs. The POUM could certainly not dominate the whole island. It probably controlled only a chunk of it. Whatever the UFT was, it most likely was just the POUM's next door neighbor and closest rival.

Even the damn gangs were commies here, Turnbull told himself. On the plus side, when they fought it was a win-win.

Comrade Chico seemed to be the leader, to the extent an anarcho-socialist collective had a leader, and Turnbull was eager to pick his brain, but as soon as they arrived at the base Comrade Chico was called off to a meeting. Another comrade whose name Turnbull did not catch showed him to his room. It was in an old dorm and smelled like a latrine. Turnbull turned over the mattress in the hope the underside was less unsavory. It was not, so he turned it back. Gibson was happy to sleep on the floor.

The anarchist meeting went several hours, hours that Turnbull used to sleep and then to gather information by wandering around. He spoke to a few POUM militia members, who were quick to share with him their thoughts on the latent racism that plagued their force, but also how it was dwarfed by the even greater racism – and sexism, and transphobia too – of the hated UFT.

"What's the UFT stand for again?" Turnbull asked one woman whose superficial weirdness was limited to her Ferdinand the Bull–looking nose ring.

"United Federation of Teachers," she replied, as if he was a child.

"Like, a teachers union?"

"Yeah, it was, but I don't think many are teachers anymore," she replied. "I would have thought an anti-racist liaison like you would know that."

"It must be the pot," Turnbull said. "I smoke a lot of marijuana."

"Oh," she said, satisfied. "Me too."

Gibson was wary, not growling but eyeing very carefully anyone approaching them. The POUM fighters seemed to be afraid of the animal – probably a smart course of action – and kept back. But apparently his teeth were not all they feared.

"Does he really smell racism?" a tremendously fat fighter asked, looking at the dog. Turnbull suspected the anarchist was thinking about how to cook Gibson.

"Yes," Turnbull said. "He literally sniffs it out. Want to see?"

The fat guy shook his head and moved away, probably concerned that the dog would sniff out the unconscious bias that countless struggle sessions had taught him lurked within them all.

Comrade Chico re-appeared, exhilarated by the long meeting. He seemed to enjoy the endless conclaves, as did the rest of the anarchists. Similar to militant atheists who love talking about God, these opponents of government seemed to spend an inordinate amount of time governing themselves.

"Have you and your non-human companion detected any racism?" he asked, dead serious.

"I think he smelled some latent sexism," Turnbull said. "But we were not able to narrow it down to a single individual."

"It's here," Comrade Chico said, concerned and looking around at his fellow anarchist as if he might be able to spot the villains himself. "It's worse than ever."

There was a flurry of shots from somewhere nearby. Turnbull's hand found his weapon's grip, and Gibson alerted, but Comrade Chico did not flinch.

"Just a pair of UFT traitors," he assured Turnbull. "Nothing to worry about. Like I said, their Maoist heresy is intolerable. We will need even more support from the People's Republic if we are going to fully purge it."

"Definitely. That will go in my report," Turnbull said. "Now, tell me about the defense preparations."

"We received a three truck shipment of rifles today, but two more trucks did not stop at our base. We are concerned with who is getting those weapons."

"I assume other defenders of the island."

"Not the UFT, right?" Comrade Chico asked, squinting.

"I am not sure where the other guns went."

"Well, the POUM should be the vanguard of the defense of Manhattan, just as it is the vanguard of anarcho-socialism!"

"That is above my pay grade, Comrade Chico."

"We know the crazies in Hell's Kitchen are getting weapons, too. There are lots of weapons flowing into the island. I am just saying that the POUM should be the leader of all the various factions."

"The anarchists should be the bosses?"

"Absolutely, Comrade Eddie," Comrade Chico said, sincerely.

"I will report that back to my people," Turnbull promised.

"The POUM's reputation is very well-known," Comrade Chico told him.

"Of course," Turnbull said.

"Representatives of all of the factions have been summoned to Central Park to arrange the next phase of weapons distribution. I am leading our delegation."

Turnbull nodded. "Properly so. Clearly, your force is one to be reckoned with."

Comrade Chico seemed happy with that reassurance. He led Turnbull and Gibson down to the meal area, where fighters were divided into two queues. One was a long line with the vast majority of the force, each getting a single dollop of gruel from a ladle. They carried their bowls to a row of picnic tables, though some furries dressed as collies or cattle placed the bowls on the ground and lapped up their dinners.

There was also a much smaller line of maybe a dozen fighters, all morbidly obese and including the tubby dude who worried that Gibson might sniff out his racist thoughts. They each got four dollops and some bread.

"The POUM proudly rejects fat genocide," his host told Turnbull as the corpulent comrades eagerly devoured their rations under the gaze of their hungry fellow travelers.

"Rightly so," Turnbull said. "Extra rations to maintain their size is an innovative strategy that I will report to my superiors. This is the kind of outstanding work that will get the POUM the attention and recognition it deserves."

"We can get in the girther line," Comrade Chico told Turnbull, taking him to the front of the tubby queue. "As a leader, I require more calories and you are an important guest."

Turnbull took a bowl for himself, with some bread, and a bowl for the dog. Turnbull placed Gibson's on the ground and the dog sniffed it skeptically, but then began lapping it up. He only paused to turn and snap at a middle-aged POUM member in a beagle costume who tried to sniff his butt.

Turnbull tasted his porridge and it was, as expected, loathsome, but calories were calories. He ate what he could but consumed all of the generic white bread. The fat guy from before was sitting across the table eyeing Turnbull's uneaten gruel, and Turnbull pushed it over to him.

"I appreciate your sacrifice to maintain the existence of people of heft," he told the huge man, who nodded and began to greedily devour Turnbull's leftovers.

"I have a confession," Turnbull said to Comrade Chico as they walked out of the dining area and into the Gould Square motor pool. "There is something I have not told you. But it is of the utmost secrecy."

Comrade Chico was intrigued. Turnbull went on.

"My mission here is more than to seek out latent racism and to liaison with you regarding the defense of Manhattan from the racist red forces. It is a mission only the POUM can help me accomplish."

Comrade Chico nodded eagerly.

"This is highly sensitive, highly secret."

"Comrade Eddie, you can trust me and the POUM!" Comrade Chico promised.

"I know," Turnbull replied. "You are the one group that is both tactically and ideologically sound enough that we can trust to help me with my mission. There is a prisoner in the Midtown Secure Zone. This prisoner is being wrongly held by revanchist counterrevolutionaries in a hotel there. I need to get inside and get the prisoner out. It's vital – if we fail our entire campaign to decolonize the paradigm will fail."

Comrade Chico blinked twice as he processed Turnbull's information.

"I understand," he said.

"I knew you would," Turnbull told him. Gibson sat and scratched his neck with his hind paw. Turnbull continued.

"Can you help me get there and get into the secure zone, then help me and my target get out?"

"Yes," Comrade Chico replied, though he was thinking and did not seem absolutely sure. "We can travel under the truce, but we need to get to Central Park to arrange our weapon and ammunition supply."

"Then we get my prisoner," Turnbull said.

"Yes, but who is this prisoner?"

"One of the most important and progressive voices in Marxist-Leninist-Kendi thought," Turnbull said. "Professor Deeds."

"*The* Professor Deeds?" Comrade Chico said as if he recognized the name.

"The very same," said Turnbull. "You've read Professor Deeds's work?"

"Oh yes," Comrade Chico assured him.

"Then you know what an important thought leader xe – xis pronouns are xe/xir – is. Obviously, if the POUM is able to help me accomplish this task, the rewards will be…"

"What?"

"Very rewarding. Like leadership of the defense of Manhattan and leadership after we repel the racist red invaders."

Comrade Chico's eyes were wide and there was a smile within the frame of his scraggly goatee. Turnbull smiled too for a moment, until they were interrupted.

"Comrade!" someone yelled.

The shout came from across the square. A half-dozen POUM members were crossing the motor pool toward them escorting a salty-looking woman – probably a woman, but Turnbull would not bet money on it – who carried a M4 on a sling and had a determined demeanor and cruel gaze.

The group got to about ten feet away when she stopped, as did her escorts.

"Who the hell are you?" she shouted at Turnbull, her beefy finger pointing at him.

"She says she's the liaison from the People's Republic," one of the escorts said uncertainly, not having heard her pronouns.

"Who the hell are *you*?" Turnbull replied.

"I am Deborah David Running Bear Cloudtree, and I am the designated liaison to this ridiculous POUM militia from the government of the People's Republic!"

Comrade Chico looked at Turnbull uncertainly.

"Gibson," Turnbull said calmly.

The dog growled, and Deborah David Running Bear Cloudtree looked down at him, furious.

She looked back up into Turnbull's eyes.

"You're a...," she began.

Turnbull pivoted his tricked-out M4 up and brought it to his shoulder, instantly firing a round through Deborah David Running Bear Cloudtree's forehead. A red puff erupted out of the back of her skull as the brain matter vaporized by the 5.56mm round passing through her head. She stood there teetering for a moment while her jaw worked silently, as if she was trying to finish her sentence, and then she collapsed straight down into a heap on the cement.

The comrades stood stunned, processing what just happened. Turnbull lowered his weapon.

"A racist agent," Turnbull announced. He reached down to pet Gibson. "Good dog."

"You shot her, Comrade Eddie," Comrade Chico mumbled, baffled and stating the obvious.

"That's what you do to racist traitors. You shoot them. My companion animal detected her. Her racist slander of the POUM confirmed it. Now search her corpse. See what you find."

The other comrades began going through her pack and pockets. They brought a handful of documents to Turnbull and Comrade Chico. Turnbull took her privilege card and examined it.

"A clear forgery," he declared, handing it to Comrade Chico. "See?"

The militiaman carefully scrutinized the card for a few seconds.

"Yes, definitely a fake," Comrade Chico announced. He began sifting through the other papers.

"I expect the rest of this includes forged orders," Turnbull said. "And I expect they will tell you to stand down or subordinate the POUM to the UTF or some other heretical faction."

"They do," Comrade Chico said incredulously as he scanned the documents. "These papers claim to be orders that the POUM give up control of its forces to something called the Manhattan Anti-Racist Defense Committee at the meeting in Central Park."

"I told you so," said Turnbull. "Do you believe a legitimate liaison would bring that kind of order to an organization as important as the POUM?"

"No," Comrade Chico said.

"It was clearly a trap."

"Yes," Comrade Chico agreed, nodding.

"POUM!" shouted Turnbull, raising his fist.

"Power to the marginalized!" the comrades shouted, raising their own fists into the smoky New York sky.

13.

"The bridges and tunnels are sealed. No one leaves. We fight and win or we die! POUM!"

"Power to the marginalized!" the others shouted.

"Our time slot at the defense meeting is tomorrow night at six," Comrade Chico continued. He was standing with Turnbull and several other comrades – including the fat guy – in the POUM command post looking over an old AAA map of Manhattan. "Gathering the factions together is much more efficient than going out to each group. The truce allows five representatives from every group to cross boundaries. The meetings have been going on all day. Every group, organization, and party in Manhattan has an assigned time to arrive and arrange the weapon and ammunition delivery. It's not just rifles and bullets either. Grenades, rocket launchers, anti-aircraft weapons. We will make Manhattan a fortress against imperialism!"

"Power to the marginalized," Turnbull said.

"You can help get us more stuff, right?"

"I'll use all my influence," Turnbull promised. He had no idea how he would play it, except that it would be by ear. He continued.

"Where do we go in Central Park?" Turnbull asked.

Comrade Chico put his finger down in Central Park right at the Great Lawn, north of where the Secure Zone wall bisected the park at 72nd Avenue.

"My nanny used to take me there to play as a little kid before the Split," Comrade Chico said, then clearly felt the need to explain. "My sperm supplier and fetus-pod were criminal looters and wreckers and I have totally repudiated their imperialism."

"Proper," observed Turnbull.

"We will have to travel across a lot of factions' turf," Comrade Chico continued. "But the truce is on until noon tomorrow. We can get you north of the Midtown Secure Zone, and once we are there and we have made our arrangements, we can rendezvous with some friends and get inside the Zone."

"How?" Turnbull asked.

"We have a lot of fellow travelers inside and outside of the secure zone," Comrade Chico said. "We're very influential."

"Clearly," Turnbull said, looking at the map. "We need to cross UTF territory."

"Like I said, there's a truce," Comrade Chico answered. "Everyone's coming to Central Park at some point, everyone who wants guns and ammo."

"But do you trust the UTF not to break the truce if they see us?" Turnbull asked.

Comrade Chico looked around at the other POUM members. They seemed skeptical.

"When there's no truce on, if they see us, they'll kill us," Comrade Chico said.

"Then they better not see us," Turnbull said. "Just in case."

"Well, the teachers have a lot of patrols and roadblocks. It will be tough."

"I know you will prove the POUM's worth."

"We will, Comrade Eddie – POUM!"

"Power to the marginalized!" they shouted in unison.

Turnbull added his fist to the collective fist-raise. Gibson looked at them like they were idiots.

The next afternoon, Comrade Chico selected three others to accompany him and Turnbull to the conclave.

"It's an elite team of specialists with the attributes we need to accomplish this mission," he boasted. "First and foremost, of course, is diversity – our true strength. Plus, it goes without saying, firm ideological conformity to the precepts of Marxist-Leninist-Kendi anarchist thought."

"Okay," Turnbull replied, unconvinced.

"Obviously, I am here to provide my combat skills and leadership," Comrade Chico announced. "I have also identified one of the workers living here in the POUM zone who has a job pass for the Secure Zone and works in the People's Asian American and Native Hawaiian/Pacific Islander Hotel New York. Plus, I am Latinois and gender skeptical."

He gestured at the rest of the team.

"These are committed anarchist revolutionaries who offer a fully diverse representation of sexualities and identities," Comrade Chico proudly reaffirmed. He introduced the first of them to Turnbull. The stocky Karla, no last name, they/theym, with bright green hair and a stud in theym nose, stared back at him sullenly. They did not offer theym hand to shake – maybe they did not like him, or maybe hand-shakes were racist this week.

"Karla is an expert in tactical driving, and they is a representative of the gendertweaked community," Comrade Chico explained.

"I am not fully genderqueer, just gendertweaked," Karla informed Turnbull. Turnbull did not ask they to elaborate further regarding theym exact sexual standing.

"The next team member is Paloma Warren, she/her," Comrade Chico said, introducing a 100-pound woman with not-great skin who was wearing quasi-Indian garb. "She is from Massachusetts."

"Are you related to Elizabeth Warren?" Turnbull asked.

"We share a bond of kinship and the blood of the First Peoples runs in both our veins," Paloma said defensively. "But I reject her counterrevolutionary descent into colonialism and her revelation as the red face of white supremacy."

"Me too. And your relevant skill set?"

"Besides being a First People person? My key skill is utilizing cisnormalized preconceptions of sexuality to gain an advantage over the phallocentric," Paloma said with a Boston accent.

"I see," Turnbull said, quelling any expression of his doubts. This was their *femme fatale*? He assessed her as a blue eight and a red three. And Karla was giving Paloma some serious side-eye. What was that about? Turnbull resolved not to delve into what was going on there.

"This is our final team member," Comrade Chico said, bringing forward the last of them. "This is Gerald the Giraffe, he/him. He represents the furry community and all oppressed alterbeings."

The man wore a complete giraffe suit, though he stood upright on his hind legs. Turnbull could not see Gerald's face due to the elaborate headpiece. Turnbull shook Gerald's outstretched plastic arm-hoof.

"I could not imagine entering into this important mission without full representation of otherkin folkx," Turnbull said. "And your skills – are you a good fighter, or what?"

"I have a lot of problems getting a good cheek weld with the stock of my AK when I am wearing my fursuit," Gerald replied, his voice muffled by the giraffe head he wore. "The eye placement in the headpiece also interferes with my sight picture."

"Kalashnikov failed to consider the furry community at all when designing the AK-47," Comrade Chico said, disgusted. "In any case, there is another issue."

"What's the issue?" Turnbull asked, and to his regret, he found out. There began a long debate among the other four team members over how to count Gibson in terms of diversity, in light of the speciesism inherent in referring to him – Turnbull reiterated that Gibson was he/him – as a "dog," but after a half-hour, Turnbull intervened and announced that considering

Gibson human would "deny his non-human status and devalue his existence." The others eventually agreed that the Belgian Malinois would accompany them in his non-human observer status on behalf of other forms of life. Gerald the Giraffe would fulfill the role of animal representative.

Turnbull was surprised the fat guy did not get a slot.

The diversity considerations resolved, it was time to address the minor remaining issues relative to the operation. Other than Turnbull, all of them carried AK-47s, along with some extra ammo pouches and ill-matching camo clothing. The brown and white pattern of Gerald's fur suit seemed surprisingly effective camouflage in the urban environment when he wore the whole thing. However, it was hot, so most of the time he had the head off, which impacted its concealment effectiveness considerably.

They would travel by a vehicle under cover of the truce, get into the Zone, do their job, and get out and return to POUM headquarters. The truce covered of all the organized groups, most of whom were more interested in killing each other than they were killing red Americans. The members of the little band each wore a bolt of cloth around their upper right arms to demonstrate that they were moving under the truce. Traditionally, the cloth would have been white, but that would not work for obvious reasons, so it was bright blue. They would ride in an old Chevy Suburban SUV which had a blue cloth tied to the roof rack. The "POUM" painted on the sides had been scrubbed off.

They left the motor pool and pulled onto the street, passing the dry and desolate Washington Square, which was home to a mass of lurching, twitching zombies high on whatever the PR was passing out to them. A pharma van was there distributing more junk. Most of them seemed to already have rifles.

"I've been advocating arming the marginalized for years," Comrade Chico said as he observed the tableau. He was sitting in the front passenger seat. Karla was driving. It was slow going – the streets were torn up and people wandered across the road not just at corners but wherever they chose to. Derelicts lounged or slept along the sidewalks, some with weapons next to them.

Turnbull was in the second row of seats behind the driver, Gibson next to him. Paloma and Gerald, who had his fursuit head off and in his lap, sat in the third row. They seemed excited to be in a vehicle – it had been a long time since they had ridden anywhere. Gas was, of course, at a premium.

They passed several abandoned and stripped electric vehicles on each block. Gas vehicles had been banned for Privilege Level 8 and below a years before, and when the power stopped coming on outside the secure zones the owners just abandoned them where they stopped. Now, there were almost no motor vehicles of any kind moving in the streets, but there were many carts and rickshaws – both kinds of conveyances powered by human beings.

"We are at the cutting edge of defeating climate change," Comrade Chico said proudly as they slowed to let a sweating man tug a pair of riders sitting in his homemade rickshaw across the intersection. "We have cut fossil fuel use by 99% in Manhattan!"

"Does that include the secure zones?" Turnbull asked. Comrade Chico chose to ignore the question.

Turnbull heard the whoop of a helicopter and cocked his head to look up. An unmarked AH-6 zipped above them through the concrete canyon heading north.

Kurylenko Group? Had to be – so they were still here in Manhattan. And that likely meant Clay was here too.

"I dare the racist fascist transphobes to try to take Manhattan from the people!" Comrade Chico crowed as the chopper flew past. "With the POUM and the People's Republic forces, the people are unbeatable!"

"POUM," said Turnbull.

"Power to the marginalized!" the others replied. Gerald's giraffe head tumbled off his lap when he lifted his clenched hoof in a salute.

Karla was taking them up 5th Avenue, and from the graffiti it was clear they were soon in UFT territory. The streets seemed noticeably less packed.

"Where are the people?" Turnbull asked.

"Classes," Comrade Chico said. "The teachers have a program they call "The Curriculum." It teaches all their revanchist Maoist thought. They require the people to spend at least three hours a day in classes learning it. They even take roll. People who don't attend don't get their daily gruel allotment."

"Teachers gonna teach," Turnbull said absently. It had only taken the teachers union a few years to go from labor organization to armed occupation force. The SUV passed an official United Federation of Teachers sign that read, "Tardiness = Hunger."

"Yeah, it really is a great innovation," Comrade Chico said, his voice betraying a hint of envy at what the UFT was accomplishing. "I mean, if you put aside the heretical revisionism they are teaching. We're definitely going to move toward at least three hours a day of teaching on Marxist-Leninist-Kendi thought to the masses."

"That's a great idea," Turnbull assured his host. "I will pass that on to my superiors."

Comrade Chico beamed.

The old Madison Square Park was on their left. It was now Randi Weingarten Park, named in honor of the former teachers' union official who post-Split oversaw the PR's reeducation camp network and later advocated for "humane euthanasia" of the "ideologically incorrigible." She had eventually disappeared from the scene – it was unknown if it was the result of some internal PR power struggle or if someone had taken her out of the picture with a high-powered rifle. Turnbull smiled a little and said nothing.

"A true herox," Karla said, using the approved ungendered term for "hero" and pronouncing the "x."

There was a roadblock ahead at the intersection of East 31st Street, with carts dragged out and left across 5th Avenue, and with the old Empire State Building looming beyond. The building had been attacked as "a patriarchal expression of phallic dominance over the skyline and the oppressed folx below" by the People's Renaming Commission not long after the Split, but the Commission found a way to channel those objections in support of their ideology. It was officially renamed "The Barack Obama Creating a More Just Society by Rejecting Cisnormality Building," and turned over for use by "oppressed peoplx." It was soon largely looted and abandoned even though the ex-president had been very proud of the renaming and how it recognized his long-hidden sexual versatility. His bestselling post-Split volumes, *The Audacity of Orgasms: The Erotic Poems of Barack Obama* and *Dreams of My Daddies*, were mandatory reading in every PR high school, at least those still operating. A subsequent surreptitious audio recording of Michelle Obama played in the red media – it was banned in the blue, of course – caught the former FLOTUS on Leonardo DiCaprio's yacht telling the fiftyish star's then-current 19-year old girlfriend that "Barack's skinny ass can stick his whatever wherever as long as I get to keep the beach house."

The SUV came to a halt, and Turnbull could feel the tension. There were maybe a dozen UFT troops on guard, and several standing off on the sidewalk instructing about two dozen unhappy pupils who sat on the filthy concrete paying, or feigning, rapt attention to the lesson. These unfortunates appeared to have been pulled off the sidewalk at random and subjected to this impromptu educational experience. The whole UFT area seemed to be in detention.

The UFT militia stared at the Chevy, since vehicles were uncommon, and moved forward warily. It was unclear how they would react to the blue banner of truce. Turnbull considered his options. He could get out his FN pistol and screw on the silencer, or prepare to go full rock and roll.

He lifted up his custom rifle and clicked the selector switch to "AUTO." If this went south, rock and roll it would be.

He then hit the button to drop the window.

The lead UFT member looked like a third grade teacher who had a hidden life as a secret serial killer. Her eyes were red, probably from the free pot the PR poured into the island, and she had her AK-47. The receiver was rusty; apparently no one had taught the teacher how to clean her gun.

"Who are you?" she demanded, adding, "She/her."

"We're under the truce. We are on our way to the meeting," Karla said, lifting her arm to show the blue cloth, and adding "They/Theym."

"Theym?" the UFT leader asked.

"'They, but with an 'm.'"

The UFT leader nodded. She/her did not appear particularly concerned about the vehicle. But she/her was also not yet ready to wave them through.

"Who are you? Art Trendies? Worker's Force? Spaz Army? TransElves? You're not crazies."

Karla paused, considering theym next step. Turnbull broke the silence.

"They're POUM," Turnbull said, flashing his fake People's Bureau of Investigation ID.

"Revanchists!" She/her shouted.

"You're the real revanchists!" Comrade Chico shouted from the passenger seat.

"Stop talking!" Turnbull shouted. He looked at she/her. "I am their People's Republic liaison to the POUM. Under what authority are you stopping us?"

"Authority?" She/her asked, puzzled.

"I represent the People's Republic government. Get me your...," Turnbull began, then paused to consider before continuing. "Your principal. No, your *superintendent*."

She/her went pale.

"That's not necessary," She/her said. "There's a truce and even these revanchist imperialist swine are free to pass through our liberated learning zone."

"What did you call us?" Comrade Chico shouted from the passenger seat. Turnbull ignored him.

"Drive," he told Karla.

She/her waved at her comrades and they pulled apart the cart barricade enough for the Chevy to squeeze through. Once past it, Karla accelerated up to her typical ten miles per hour.

"These parasites need to be exterminated," Comrade Chico said.

"The reds may do that for you," Turnbull said.

"We will defeat the red colonialist imperialist running dogs!" the man dressed as a giraffe shouted, caught up in the moment. He paused. "Sorry, Comrade Gibson. I did not mean to microaggress."

Gibson ignored him. Paloma Warren broke the uncomfortable silence.

"The people, united, can never be defeated!"

"POUM!" Comrade Chico shouted.

"Power to the marginalized!" the rest shouted, including Turnbull. It was now an unconscious habit.

"The southern Midtown Secure Zone wall runs along 42nd Street," Comrade Chico said. "We will need to go around it, all the way out to 1st Avenue and head north past the old UN Building. It gets sketchy, with lots of undisciplined factions. Most of them are not highly organized like the POUM."

Turnbull did not comment on the anarchists' pride in their level of organization.

They saw the Midtown Secure Zone wall up ahead and turned right, working toward the East River until they hit 1st Avenue where they made a left. There were several merchants on the sidewalks selling their cloudy home-distilled rot gut in old peanut butter jars.

They went through several other groups' areas and were waved through two other roadblocks because of the blue truce banner. The going was slow. There were a lot of people wandering at random across the streets. Most seemed to have a gun. Every once in a while, someone would shoot someone else. It did not seem to be a big deal. People generally kept walking if they did not stop to ransack the corpse.

"Arming the people is the best way to defeat tyranny, Comrade Eddie!" Comrade Chico said proudly.

"Oh, I agree with that," Turnbull replied sincerely. He noted that a good number of the newly minted paramilitaries seemed particularly unfamiliar with their new firearms, but enough guns in enough hands would still create a huge problem for the red invaders.

This invasion would be a slog and a bloodbath. So, why do it? It made no sense to him. He shook his head, glad that he would never be a general and experience the requisite IQ drop.

The SUV slowly lumbered forward through the masses thronging the crowded street. The old UN building, or what was left of it, came up on their right. The United Nations had pulled out of its massive headquarters within two years of the Split following the new United States' withdrawal and funding cut off. The UN headquarters was now in Hong Kong, where the communist Chinese used the zombie organization as another pawn to increase and enhance its influence with the Third World nations that remained as members in exchange for cash. The building itself had been ostentatiously returned "to the People to provide housing for the unhomed." A few years later, it was now a charred ruin, and Turnbull smiled as they passed by it.

Good riddance, he thought.

Paloma lit a joint and offered it to him. He declined.

"I never inhale."

"To my people, it is a sacrament," Paloma said, sucking in a hit. Turnbull's window was down and he turned to face out of it.

In a vacant lot there was a large crowd of people gathered around a pair of beaten-up tanker trucks with different versions of the PR flag painted on their sides. All the people in the crowd carried some kind of bowl or jug.

"The community gruel trucks," Comrade Chico said. "A very efficient way of distributing nutrition to the masses."

Turnbull had seen a few plots of dirt being tended to grow vegetables as they drove. In the POUM area, these were outlawed as "uncollectivist." He also noted that all the shops and bodegas were long ago abandoned and ransacked.

"Stores are an artifact of late-stage capitalism," Turnbull told his companions. "That is part of the Professor Deeds Thought."

"I am excited to meet him," Gerald the Giraffe said from behind him in the third row of seats.

"Oh, I know he will be thrilled to meet you," Turnbull replied.

They continued north and then headed west into what had been the Upper East Side. This formerly wealthy neighborhood had been left out of the secure zone and was now a collection of tenements and charred shells of buildings lit up by squatters.

They passed several pharma vans passing out drugs, and several military trucks with PR soldiers handing out old AKs and a couple mags to anyone who wanted them.

They continued onward, slowing to let the occasional rickshaw go by or zombie stagger out of their path. A van that appeared to be from the Upper East Side Workers' Party pulled onto the road and was slowly proceeding ahead of them as they prepared to turn west at East 79th Street. It was also flying the blue truce banner. After a few moments, it came to a sudden stop and Karla slammed on her brakes – though at their speed there was no danger of a rear-ender.

Turnbull pulled up his rifle, lifting the muzzle out the open window beside him.

Gunshots in the distance. Lots of gunshots.

The Upper East Side Workers' Party's van door swung open and the passengers began to spill out with their rifles, not in a threatening manner but in a cautious one.

"Out!" Turnbull ordered and he pushed his door open. Gibson leapt out into the road and Turnbull stepped through, recce rifle ready. The others followed, though Gerald was having trouble moving quickly in his fur suit.

"What's going on?" Turnbull yelled to the UESWP militia ahead.

One of them, with a pentagram hanging around his neck over his plate carrier, turned. There was a rumble from up ahead. Turnbull could not see much past the van between the darkness of dusk and the smoke of cooking fires and a million bongs hanging in the air.

"People are coming. Running!" the guy with the pentagram shouted.

The first runner came out of the dankness and past the van, not slowing, followed by more and more of them. Most were armed, and all were wearing the blue armbands. They ignored the idling vehicles and streamed past in small groups. There was more shooting from up ahead.

"What is this?" Comrade Chico asked Turnbull. Turnbull decided to find out.

A young man in what looked like a modified school girl uniform was sprinting by close to the SUV. Turnbull threw out his leg and the runner tripped and sprawled. His skirt bunched up and Turnbull involuntarily grimaced at the sight. None of the others stopped to help the fallen schoolgirl/boy up. Turnbull walked over as the man got onto all fours. Gibson circled him warily.

The young man had no weapon, and he was clearly shaken. Turnbull bent down and lifted him to his feet. The man's eyes were red and glassy – he smelled like a Jamaican toboggan team's locker room after they celebrated coming in twelfth.

"Sorry about that," Turnbull said. "An accident. You okay?"

"I think so. I fell."

"Yeah, you fell. So, why are you running?"

"It went to shit, man."

Comrade Chico was now by Turnbull's side, his own AK-47 ready.

"What went to shit?" Turnbull asked.

"We were waiting to go to our meeting in the park, getting high, grooving on the unity. I was digging it, and then someone started shooting and it went to shit."

"Happens a lot," Turnbull said. "Who did the shooting?"

"Crazies maybe. Racists. Who knows? But there's no truce anymore. Everyone's trying to get home. I mean, screw that noise. Get home and get ready to fight the reds, right?"

"Yeah, I can dig that," Turnbull replied. The man stared into his eyes.

"Who are you?"

"The POUM," Comrade Chico said proudly.

"The Poo?"

"The POUM!" Comrade Chico insisted loudly.

"I don't know them," the stoned scholar said. Turnbull pushed him off and he stumbled away to the east.

"If the truce is really off, we have got a problem," Turnbull told Comrade Chico. "We're a long way from home and I don't know how much longer these blue armbands are going to protect us. We need to get inside the secure zone tonight because this out here could turn into a real nightmare."

"The north wall runs along East 72nd," Comrade Chico said. "It cuts across Central Park. Our friends have access underground into the part of the park inside the Zone. We just gotta get to them."

"Where are they?" asked Turnbull.

"The former steakhouse on Lexington and 74th. It was the old Museum of Meat Murder, but now they use it for themselves. Some people call them smugglers."

"Let's go," said Turnbull, motioning for Gibson to hop back inside the SUV. The dog did. Gerald, who had not managed to make it out, settled back in his seat with his head on.

As Turnbull went to get back inside, there was a burst of fire up ahead, this one close. Two wild-eyed men in ragged clothes, both wearing truce armbands, were running past the UESWP van and they simply opened fire on the occupants. The pentagram guy who had answered Turnbull's query was hit and thrown against the side of his vehicle into the pattern of his own blood-splatter.

Homie is going to have some explaining to St. Peter to do about his pentagram fashion accessory, thought Turnbull as he brought up his tricked-out M4.

The crazies kept running past even as the surviving UESWP folks scrambled for cover. They got two steps before they saw Turnbull had a bead on the first shooter.

Turnbull fired twice and the man went down. His running buddy pivoted to bring his AK to bear but Turnbull's red dot was on his chest first. Turnbull fired twice, quickly, and the man staggered two more steps before dropping to the street dead.

Turnbull slid back into the SUV, but kept the muzzle out the window.

"Move!" he ordered.

The others settled in and pulled their doors shut and Karla pulled around the UESWP van and the dead man beside it.

"What will we do about our equipment!" Comrade Chico said, morose. "How will we get our share of the equipment now?"

"Trust me, I'll take care of the POUM," Turnbull lied.

14.

Karla drove slowly and carefully though the mass of humanity clogging the streets. No one shot at them, but they got some hard looks. Turnbull also noted several towed Type 90 Chinese dual 35mm anti-aircraft cannons in a parking lot. Some militia members were taking charge of them. The PR was upping the game beyond just passing out rusty AK-47s.

In normal times, the groups could have walked to their objective faster than the time it took for the SUV to drive to what had once been the home of the BLT Prime Steakhouse at Lexington and 74th. The buildings on that block were low, three to six stories, and there were no lights in any of the windows breaking the gathering gloom. Except for a steel door, the old restaurant itself was fully bricked up in front, a new addition to the façade constructed with the materials obviously scavenged from the decaying hulks of buildings in the area. The brick wall was designed for security – the frontage was clearly several bricks thick and it covered up the former windows.

Out on the sidewalk in front of the former restaurant, a half-dozen unusually well-dressed toughs with rifles walked the block. They were not packing old AKs either – there were some M16s, some M4s and at least one FAL. The guards were clearly effective. There were no passersby. Unlike most of the city outside the secure zones, there was obviously someone in charge here, and the locals knew it and stayed away. Turnbull doubted that anyone messing with them got away in one piece.

The zombies and hobos were completely absent.

Karla parked off the block at the intersection with 74th, and Comrade Chico turned back to Turnbull.

"I should go up and talk to them. They can be hostile, and I think they are capitalists, but we have a good relationship. At least until the revolution is complete and we can eliminate all of the social parasites like them."

"Social parasites are the worst," concurred Turnbull.

"Let me come," Paloma said. "I can use their cis against them."

"I'll come too," Turnbull said.

"I don't know if that is a good idea."

"I'll roll the dice," Turnbull said. He opened the door and ended the debate.

Turnbull, Comrade Chico, and Paloma walked slowly down Lexington, Gibson at Turnbull's heel, earning the full attention of all six of the toughs. There was movement high and Turnbull noted a couple more gun thugs up on the roofs silhouetted against the smoky night sky and the nearly full moon.

Tight security. He made no sudden moves.

An AH-6 helicopter flew past above them toward the secure zone to the southwest. The toughs paid it no mind – they were clearly used to fly-bys. There were gunshots in the distance from all directions. The war of all against all in Manhattan was underway and probably would not let up until it became a war of all against the American invaders, whenever the red invasion force finally showed up.

All three had their weapons slung and walked slowly with their hands out in the open. A pair of toughs approached. The bigger one, with a broken nose and a saint's medal around his neck, spoke first.

"Youse guys clear out," he ordered, but added "Nice doggie."

"We're here to see Lou," Comrade Chico said.

"Does Lou know youse coming?"

"He'll know the POUM."

"The poo?"

The POUM," snapped Comrade Chico. "The Party of the Urban Marginalized. I mean the United Marginalized."

"Sounds like a bunch of assholes. Clear out or we'll clear ya out."

Comrade Chico seethed.

"Are you sure?" Paloma said, batting her eyes.

The tough paused, as if he wasn't sure, but then thought the better of it.

"Move on or we'll move ya."

"Hold on," Turnbull said. "This is a business proposition. We need to talk to Lou."

"He don't wanna talk to you. Though he does like doggies. What kind is that?"

"Belgian Malinois," Turnbull said. Comrade Chico seemed annoyed.

"I had a Beagle named Rags," the tough said. "Back before the Split, before people started eating dogs."

"Worst case, Lou talks to us and he gets to pet the dog," Turnbull said. "How many dogs you see around here anymore?"

Paloma did her fluttering eye thing as well.

The tough looked at his running buddy and nodded. The running buddy trotted off to the old steakhouse and was let in the steel front door. In the meantime, Gibson submitted himself to being petted by the tough and listening to his baby talk.

"Good doggie," the man said, rubbing the animal's ears.

It took about two minutes for the runner to return.

"Lou says bring them in. Especially the dog."

The pair of toughs escorted them to the front door. It was painted black. The dog lover gestured for them to enter after it creaked open. There was a large interior space with an exposed ceiling that had been the dining room at one time. There was a loud rumbling too – generators churning somewhere in the back.

Several more toughs stood about around with their higher-grade weapons, wary. They eyed Turnbull's recce rifle and one literally licked his thick lips.

"You want to hold onto my piece?" Turnbull asked.

"Not necessary," answered a wide, sturdy gentleman who the toughs cleared a path for. He had to be the legendary Lou. He was clearly well-fed – all the toughs were, but Lou was positively thick. He had swagger, and wore a blazer and slacks.

"I figure you can count guns," Lou told Turnbull, ignoring Comrade Chico. Turnbull had counted the guns, and calculated his odds. He figured he might get one or two besides Lou before they shot him to bits.

"That is a nice gun, though," Lou observed.

"We appreciate you seeing us," Turnbull replied.

"Lou, you remember me? I am Comrade Chico, he/him, of the POUM," the militia leader announced. Lou turned and looked at him quizzically.

"Settle down," he directed, then looked at Gibson. "Now that's a good dog. You was right, Mikey."

Mikey, the dog-loving tough with the broken nose, beamed.

"May I?" Lou asked.

"His name is Gibson," Turnbull said as the *padrone* bent down to pet the animal's head. Gibson sat perfectly still.

"Anti-racism dog, huh?" Lou said, reading Gibson's harness. He looked at Turnbull skeptically. "And you?"

"Comrade Eddie is the People's Republic liaison to the POUM!" Comrade Chico declared.

Lou stayed polite, but he was also clear.

"Mikey, take Comrade Chico and this young lady back to show them the old displays from when this was the Museum of Meat Murder. I think they'll like that."

"Okay, boss," Mikey said. Another gentleman gently helped Comrade Chico away. Mikey led Paloma off, and not toward the exhibits.

When Comrade Chico and Paloma were out of earshot, and their conversation was covered by the roar of the generators, Lou spoke to Turnbull once again.

"Okay, who the hell are you? Because just looking at you and your gear and that weapon and the fact you aren't telling me about what freaking gender you are and who youse like to bang tells me that you are not whoever Comrade Circus Clown thinks you are."

"I was under the impression you and my friend had a close relationship," Turnbull replied.

"We probably smuggled someone or something in or out for him and his crew once or twice. I see a lot of these kind of guys these days, punks with some guys and a big head, and I'm not friends with any of them. Now, what do you want?"

"I need to get inside the Secure Zone. Then I need out again."

"Use your fake ID. I know you got one. My dad taught me how to sniff out an undercover long before everything went to hell. That dumbass and that tramp you're with might not see it, but I do, plain as day. You're a red, buddy. And that is a dangerous thing to be around here."

"I could get in alone with my ID, but I need these guys – there's two more back in the car, including one who thinks he's a giraffe – to hook me up inside there and provide some bodies in support to do what I need to do."

"And what's that?"

"Bring someone out. Someone the blues have."

"Rescue mission, huh?"

"Something like that."

"Now you want my help getting through the wall and inside Midtown?" Lou said. "I know it's not going with the flow around here anymore, but I'm a capitalist. I think your pal thought I'd do it out of the goodness of my heart, but my heart is all out of goodness these days. What do I get for helping out?"

Turnbull had considered this. He paused for a moment before he responded.

"You get gratitude."

"Gratitude?" scoffed Lou. "What do I need your gratitude for, Cap'n America? How many broads or bottles or whatever can gratitude buy me?"

"You know what's coming, don't you?"

Lou's jolliness visually diminished. Clearly Lou had some idea of what was going to happen. Turnbull continued.

"At some point, really, soon, the entire red US Army is hitting this island. It's going to be a freaking mess."

"You think I can't get off the island?" Lou asked.

"I'm sure you can. But do you want to? I mean, the Americans are going to wipe out everyone who opposes them and then occupy Manhattan. That's going to happen."

"It'll be a bloodbath. The blues gave every psycho with a trigger finger their very own AK. And that wrecked that part of my business."

"The reds will eventually win, and if it's harder they'll be meaner when it's over. But Manhattan is a big island and they will need friends. That's where the gratitude comes in. Imagine in the aftermath, during the occupation, you having the new bosses owe you one."

Lou considered the proposal. Turnbull went on.

"Think of the opportunity. You lay low during the fight, then come out of it with a monopoly on what's left because the new management will be more than happy to work with anyone who has shown they will work with it."

"You got that kind of heat to make that kind of deal?"

"No," Turnbull conceded. "But the guy I'm grabbing does."

Lou began to imagine the possibilities of operating under a friendly red regime. Under the blues, the lack of order kept the government largely off his back, but he had to expend extraordinary resources on security against the various factions and militias, as well as other criminal groups. The American occupation would eliminate that cost. And the rebuilding funds, because Americans always poured money into any place they conquered, would provide limitless opportunities for graft.

"What do you need from me?" Lou asked.

"Can you get us into the Secure Zone unseen?"

"Of course. We go in and out all the time. That's what we do."

"Do that for me. Maybe give me some intel. And keep the guy in the giraffe suit on ice here. He's a liability."

"A guy in a giraffe suit?"

"Yeah."

"Are there like two of them in the suit, a front guy and a back guy?"

"No, just one, it's a two-legged giraffe."

"So, it's not a realistic giraffe?"

"No."

Lou shook his head.

"Some of us are good family guys. It's been hard since the Split. All the weirdos and perverts are running rampant. Used to be if you diddled kids they found pieces of you in five different vacant lots. Now, if you're a minor attracted person you're some kind of freakin' hero."

"I'm nostalgic for the good old days too," Turnbull assured him.

"The Americans are going to put an end to all this weirdness, right?"

"Oh yeah," Turnbull assured him. "We do not play that. We tried tolerance and they tried to molest our kids. Furries, race hustlers, angry fatties, especially pedos – there's none of that in the red."

"Good. I hate that weird stuff. Okay, I'll get your crew inside. The dog too. Now tell me, where is this guy you're looking for?"

"The old Mandarin Oriental, I think."

"No shit," Lou laughed. He was clearly amused.

"What's so funny," Turnbull asked.

"The Mandarin – I don't know what they call it now, some commie nonsense name – well, the chef there buys my meat."

"Your meat?"

"Yeah, my meat. Meat is a big part of my business model. You hear that?" Lou paused, opening his arms wide. The sound of the generators hummed in the background. He went on.

"Those generators power the old restaurant fridges. I store meat in there that I bring over from the mainland. Beef, chicken, pork. Good stuff. They buy it from me in the zone because the PR can't get it to them and the bigwig guests they have don't want to hear any excuses about why they can't have a medium-rare filet mignon."

"So, you're not just an economic criminal but a climate criminal? And a furryist."

"Damn straight, Eddie, if that is your real name."

"It's not," Turnbull said.

"Yeah, well when the Museum of Meat Murder kind of stopped being a thing, we moved in, fixed the reefers left over from when it was a steakhouse, put in generators, and *voila* – worked perfectly for my business. I get stuff inside and out of the Midtown Secure Zone, anything, including people – that's no doubt how I met your dumbass pal over there looking at the old Museum exhibits. Guns too. And normal porn. But meat is my biggest product. It's a great play – people are sick of eating bugs."

"Bugs?"

"Where do you think the protein comes from in that community gruel crap they truck in to feed to the schmoes? Ground up beetle, cockroach, grasshopper, whatever. Bugs."

Turnbull's stomach churned.

Evidently Paloma was still busy when Comrade Chico came back alone with his escort, beaming.

"They showed me the exhibits from the Museum of Meat Murder. There's so much history here," he said. "You know, this is where the World Economic Forum helped pioneer the work on adding arthropod protein to the community gruel?"

Turnbull ignored his question.

"Lou is sending us over tonight."

"I'll probably need you to carry over some pork chops or something when you cross," Lou noted.

"That's fair," Turnbull agreed.

"Pork chops?" asked Comrade Chico, blinking.

"It's for the struggle," Turnbull assured him. "Now, get the rest of them in here. We need to move. And tell Gerald the Giraffe he needs to stay here to watch the Chevy."

Turnbull stripped the blue truce cloth off his arm.

"Won't be needing that."

The entrance to the tunnels was located back in the kitchen. The hole in the floor was wide enough for two at a time, though there was only one steel ladder bolted to the wall heading downward. The generators that ran the refrigerators and freezers also powered a string of incandescent lights that ran downward into the tunnel.

"Where did you get all these bulbs?" Paloma wondered aloud. Her hair was tousled. Lou and the others ignored her as they stood in a group around the entrance.

"The tunnel drops into the sewer lines, but don't worry." Lou explained to Turnbull. "They are big and dry. The ones we use are cut off from the main tunnels. We blocked them off years ago, and as you can imagine there's not a lot of maintenance down there. Mikey will lead you. The entrance you come out of is in some woods in Central Park on the other side of the wall. It's dark. I don't expect a lot of people to be there, except maybe some people having normal sex. They can get arrested for that, so they do it out in the dark."

"Like cis sex?" Karla said, theym face scrunching up in disgust. They looked at Paloma, who ignored they.

"What else?" Turnbull asked the mobster.

"You deliver the meat in those packs to the Mandarin. The chef is named Tom Lopez. Tom Lopez, got it? Pink hair, tatt on his forehead. A freak, but okay. He's not expecting another shipment quite so soon but he won't turn it away. Tell him you're new and that my boys will be around to collect for it later. Anyway, that will get you close to the Mandarin. Just don't drag him into your shit because he's a good customer."

"Understood," Turnbull said. "What about security?"

"Tighter around the Mandarin lately. We noticed that. Low-key, though. And weird foreigners. Russians maybe."

"Ukrainians?"

"What's the difference? All the vodka jockeys all look the same. Now, a lot of people are taking off and clearing out of the zone ahead of the invasion. You think your guy will still be there?"

"I think they will keep him there until the last minute." Turnbull did not add that he suspected that it was because Scott was hoping that he would appear.

Lou handed him a cell phone, a basic PR model. Turnbull flipped it open. There was a signal.

"You call Tom Lopez on that and arrange the pick-up. The number is loaded. They're listening, so tell him you have the stuff but don't mention meat."

"Got it."

"You better get going," Lou said. "Dawn is coming. And if you get caught, you best forget about our tunnel." He gave Gibson one last pat.

Turnbull hooked Gibson's harness to his gear and carried the dog as he descended the 30-foot ladder to the tunnel itself, unhooking the animal at the bottom. Gibson sniffed around, taking it in doggie stride. The others came down after him while Turnbull waited with Mikey, their guide. Up at the top, Gerald, his giraffe head off, looked down sadly at his departing comrades.

The sewers were, in some ways, less appalling than the streets above. They were relatively dry and well-lit, and high enough that none of them needed to stoop. The tunnel smelled musty, but that beat the alternative. Clearly, Lou's smugglers had put some work into them over the years.

Comrade Chico, Paloma, and Karla each carried a pack filled with meat and ice. Turnbull carried his own ruck.

Mikey took the lead, and Turnbull went second, his recce rifle out and its white light activated. He doubted there would be a problem, but took no chances. The others followed, making too much noise, and occasionally talking. Turnbull briefly reconsidered whether he actually needed them, but decided he would wait and see. Three extra pairs of hands might come in handy. But three extra mouths that rarely shut up might also get him killed. He deferred any terminal decisions for the moment.

After a long walk, past a number of branches and some doors, they came to a dead end. Another ladder rose up into the dark – the string of lights cut off a few dozen feet behind them so there would be no white light escaping the hatch. Mikey pointed upward and Turnbull told them to wait.

He climbed up into the dark and found the hatch. He listened for a few moments and, satisfied, carefully pushed it open. It was of heavy steel, and attached to the hatch's top there was a piece of plywood with sticks and leaves apparently glued to it. It was still dark, and very quiet. Turnbull listened again. There were some noises in the distance, including gunfire far away, but nothing close. After five minutes, he gently let it close and came back down the ladder.

There was no way he was going to let the POUM people secure the top side – he could think of a dozen ways they would screw it up. He had them wait and re-attached the dog to his rig, then began the long, slow climb back up.

It was miserable and difficult, though Gibson cooperated by not squirming. It took Turnbull several minutes to get to the top and, once there, he again pushed open the hatch. Nothing. He waited two minutes, his arms and legs burning with Gibson's dead weight, before pushing it open more and climbing out onto the surface. Once on the bed of leaves surrounding the hole, he freed the dog, who gingerly and carefully sniffed around and then took a leak. Turnbull pivoted back to the hole.

"Come up," he whispered down into the dark.

"What?" someone shouted from down below, probably Comrade Chico.

"Shut up!" Turnbull hissed. "Climb!"

They came up and as they came out Turnbull set them out to provide security for around the hole – Comrade Chico at twelve to four o'clock, Paloma at four to eight o'clock, and the last one, Karla, took theym position guarding eight to midnight. The team waited for twenty minutes as Turnbull listened and they acclimated to the noise of the early morning. From where they were, they could see a portion of the wall cutting through Central Park to their north. Beyond it there was increasing gunfire. Manhattan was going off and the real war was not even upon it yet.

Turnbull wondered when the war would come here to Manhattan. He looked into the sky and saw something small fly across the face of the full moon.

A drone.

It would happen soon.

"We need to go," Major Vasilev told General Scott. "Remaining here is madness."

Behind Scott, through the window, one could see where the lights of the secure zone cut off in a line across the island. Beyond the wall it was darkness, except for some fires. There was occasional flashing off in New Jersey – the US forces were on the way.

But where was Kelly Turnbull? The general could not abide that the American who humiliated him was still breathing.

"Give them some time," Scott said. "Turnbull and his pal will come for their friend."

Clay Deeds sat on a couch, his eye swollen and his hands cuffed with a white zip tie.

"You should hope not," he said.

"Still feisty," Scott observed. "I like that. Regardless, I need to be here. A leader is at the front of the fight, and within twenty-four hours, Manhattan will be the front."

"You're leading the fight now?" Harrington said, the line of mockery just beneath the surface in his manner of letting the recipient imagine that the politician *might* be mocking him, but not quite making it clear enough to invite a reaction. "I thought the plan was that no one led the fight."

Scott stiffened in his seat and pushed the plate holding a half-eaten ribeye away. Video monitors and computers flashed around him. The soldiers operating them hunched down and tried to be invisible. They did not want to be in the midst of this. When Godzilla and King Kong fought, it was the little guys in Tokyo who inevitably got smushed.

"This is not a traditional battle, Harrington," he said. "But it is my plan and I want to see it through."

Vasilev snorted and turned toward his client.

"The American Pathfinder forces will be on the island within hours. You can see yourself, they are massing in New Jersey. If we stay here, we risk being cut off.

"Well, *I* am certainly leaving once we finish here tonight," Harrington said. "Of course, I am not a professional military man. And I have no personal interests at play, like killing your Kelly Turnbull."

"Lucky for you," Deeds observed.

"Mr. Deeds, you are becoming tiresome," Harrington said. "I would have had your fingernails out and you begging for death already if not for General Scott, so you should consider being more polite to him. And to me."

"Kiss my ass," Deeds said genially.

"Do not give me any ideas. You might not like how they play out."

"Stop it, you two," Scott interjected. "Harrington, your mercenaries have choppers on the roof and they can get me out in plenty of time. But I need to see the battle. It is a general thing. You would not understand."

Harrington sighed. Clearly, Scott wanted to watch his handiwork unfold. He supposed that he could say the word and have Major Vasilev and his Ukrainian thugs drag the flag officer to a waiting helicopter for evacuation, but there were a dozen ways that could go wrong and leave him without the key to his whole plan. Plus, there was the necessity of maintaining the farce that he and the general were equal partners.

"I would not presume to tell you where you should be in a battle, general," Harrington said. He turned to Vasilev.

"The general stays here until he decides it is time to go. And you will stay with him."

Vasilev scowled.

"I need to go check my men," the mercenary leader said. "And to make sure the helicopters on the roof are ready for when this turns to shit."

The Ukrainian turned and left the room. Scott gazed at the monitors. The American forces on the maps were all over Northern New Jersey and creeping toward the city.

"They will not stop," Scott said. "They will keep coming right over the water. The boats are with the forward support elements. The idea is that they cross the Hudson by bridge, tunnel, and watercraft without pausing for long on the Jersey side. Speed. Momentum. But the Pathfinders will come first in their own helicopters, but maybe airborne. That means by parachute."

"Which we are prepared for."

"They are not expecting us to be covering the landing zones, nor our anti-aircraft guns and missiles, or the Kurylenko choppers for that matter. We'll defeat them in the sky and the American main assault force will land blind. Blind and vulnerable."

"I daresay your idea about arming the crazies is delightful."

"They will expect a cakewalk and reap the whirlwind."

“They will step off their landing craft into a quagmire,” said Harrington with considerable pleasure.

“Exactly,” the general replied. “I expect to see the Pathfinder forces land in Manhattan within hours thinking they will disrupt any organized defense.”

“But there is no organized defense,” Deeds interjected.

Scott chuckled.

“No, Mr. Deeds, there is only chaos. Chaos that I foresaw, and that, because America betrayed me, I will now allow it to walk into. I want to assure you, though, that I will have mixed feelings watching my own army wrecked as it tries to secure this island.”

“You’ll feel bad, I’m sure,” Deeds said. “Unless Kelly Turnbull blows your brains out first.”

15.

They kept to the edge of the trees, moving slowly as the sun came up in the east. Ahead, the high-rises surrounding the park were mostly dark even inside the zone, but some of their windows betrayed that the electricity was still on in the zone.

The portion of Central Park within the Midtown Secure Zone was not the home to the unhomed, as the park was outside the walls. Shanties were not tolerated here in the zone, and the housedism that was forbidden when exercised outside the zone was tolerated inside.

But the park was not totally empty. Gibson stopped and alerted and growled, and a frightened and deeply embarrassed adult male/female couple emerged from the brush.

"It's not what you think," said the one who had clearly been assigned male at birth, raising his hands. "I thought she was genderqueer! I'm not a pervert!"

"I thought *you* were genderqueer!" the one apparently assigned female at birth insisted, refusing to take the fall. "And a minor!"

Paloma evaluated the male-assigned one and her face betrayed a hint of approval.

"Perverts," Karla hissed. She started raising theym weapon but Turnbull interceded.

"Put your pants on and get out of here," he told Romeo. The man obeyed and quickly left with the one who had been assigned female at birth.

"No shame at their cisnormativity," sighed Comrade Chico as the band continued on. "The People's Republic is far too tolerant of deviations."

"And so is the POUM!" Karla snapped.

"Be quiet!" Comrade Chico said.

"Unfortunately, we have a mission and no time to deal with these social parasites," Turnbull said. "I say that as a person of genderbenthood, so this is traumatic to me."

"That cisnormative paradigm is exactly what the red will impose on us if it wins," Comrade Chico said as they began moving. "I hear they persecute anything else, even MAPs."

"Yeah," Turnbull said. "The red paradigm is that if you are a minor attracted person in red America, they shoot you."

"Savages."

"Yeah, it's a real tragedy," Turnbull said. He paused, then pointed past the trees. "Is that the old Mandarin?"

The hotel formerly known as the Mandarin occupied floors 35 through 54 of the former Deutsche Bank Center at what had once been One Columbus Circle until mentioning the explorer's name became a felony. It was now officially called Megan Rapinoe Circle – though the former soccer player herself had, like so many others, vanished sometime post-Split with no official explanation. There were rumors that her incessant whining and complaining had become so irritating even to the Marxist powers that be that she was disappeared into the gulags. Still, the giant sculpture of her at the circle remained. Turnbull could just see the purple top of the colossus's head from where he now stood.

"Yes, that's the People's Asian American and Native Hawaiian/Pacific Islander Hotel New York," Comrade Chico replied – he knew the place from the old days. After his disappointed parents cut him off, he supplemented his income from the coffee house as an Uber driver during the years immediately after the Split but before private cars were largely banned.

"It was a temple to capitalist greed. Now we have turned it into a worker's retreat," he continued wistfully. "All this progress is at risk because of the racist greed of the red wreckers."

"My feet hurt," complained Paloma. She was staggering along under the weight of her meat-filled pack, hardly demonstrating the warrior pride of her alleged people.

"I am so proud of your strength," Comrade Chico told her. "You are showing the great power of womyn and indigenous folkx!"

Turnbull thought he heard Karla whisper something like "whore" under theym breath, but not loud enough for anyone else to hear the illegal anti-sex worker/slut shaming slur.

Turnbull considered whether he still needed his three companions and briefly evaluated the pluses and minuses of shooting them here in the park, but he thought better of it. Who knew how this would play out? And besides, someone had to carry the pork. That would get them in the door.

They moved along carefully. It was just after dawn, so they did not expect many people, but there still seemed to be fewer people on the streets than would have been expected. No doubt the evacuations were well underway – in fact, the bulk of those who would be going were probably gone. The remaining entitled inside here could still get a pass off the doomed island, while all the schlubs outside the walls got was a rifle and some bullets and a one-way ticket to meet their maker. Equity, not equality, or something.

They kept moving until they hit the edge of the park near the old Trump International Hotel & Tower New York at 1 Central Park West – the street had not been renamed, at least not yet. Of course, the building was not the Trump International anymore. It was not even a cautionary memorial. The name "Trump" had not just been wiped from every building but was barred from the history books, with all books by or referring to him stripped from libraries and publicly burned. Book banning was called "literary hygiene" and was eagerly approved of within the

People's Republic as part of its commitment to democracy and free thought. They took the "T---- Cleansing" campaign seriously. In fact, children had been urged to report whether their parents had retained copies of the unspeakable one's forbidden tomes in their own personal libraries, though that became unnecessary when the personal library licensing laws came into effect and blue government inspectors could see for themselves that the libraries did not contain illegal materials before granting the approval to privately possess books.

The Trump International was now simply an empty shell, with every window on every one of the 44 floors broken out by a mob unleashed on the building during one of the official "Campaigns of People's Outrage" orchestrated in the mid-2020s to divert attention from the nation's myriad real problems. Rolls of concertina wire surrounded the front, and several People's Security Force thugs with AKs stood watch to prevent anyone from putting flowers on the wire, as used to happen before the 24/7 guard posting.

Behind it, the old Mandarin and current People's Asian American and Native Hawaiian/Pacific Islander Hotel New York rose into the sky. He did not risk approaching closer than he was. There was a cordon on the streets around the building, and Turnbull made several plainclothes Slavic-looking guys lurking around outside the perimeter. He could also see across the street to a building with several occupied windows overlooking the front of the hotel. Snipers.

The trap was set. They would ID him at the cordon, then probably ambush him in the lobby with the cordon turning inward to form a perimeter he could not escape from. The hotel itself was 35 floors up; if the bad guys got their way, he would never get there. Turnbull needed a different plan than going in the front door.

He headed the little group away from the buildings. The guards paid scant attention as Turnbull, Gibson, and the three others walked south toward the looming statue of Megan

Rapinoe at the former Columbus Circle. The PSF officers simply assumed the group was supposed to be there; it was inconceivable that a bunch of people with guns and a working animal companion would be walking about nonchalantly if they were not authorized to.

The Rapinoe statue featured her with a soccer ball in one hand and a book in another – the book's title was "Womynx History" and the legend on the base identified them as "Greatest Person of Fútbol Ever (They/Them)," since "soccer" was a term of colonialist appropriation.

The top of the statue's head was bright purple.

"They inspire me every day," Paloma said as the group passed by, bowing her head to the scowling figure on the concrete plinth.

The team headed across the empty traffic circle to 8th Avenue and continued south. The Secure Zone was waking up listlessly as the sun rose higher. The literally blue-collar workers, in their blue shirts and cheap blue jeans, were still being admitted into the Secure Zone at the gates despite the oncoming war, and some were already at work on the many menial tasks that allowed the zone to function. They knew what was coming, but they dared not risk their precious jobs with the invaluable access to the Zone that their employment gave them by staying home and hunkering down.

"Where are we going?" Comrade Chico asked Turnbull as they walked. The workers studiously ignored them, the occasional guards – so far – ignored them, and the few actual inhabitants who passed by never saw them through the tinted windows of their black cars.

"Gotta find a place to lay up, figure out a plan," Turnbull said. "You said you have contacts in there?"

"Sure, there's a worker from our area who has a Zone pass and works maintenance at the People's Asian American and Native Hawaiian/Pacific Islander Hotel New York. He will help us."

Turnbull grunted, wondering why the anarchist said the full name of the hotel. Not doing so was probably illegal somehow. And Turnbull expected that the worker would help, or else.

They continued on, and the Zone came somewhat more alive around them as the sun rose still higher. It was smoky and hazy even in here, but at least the power was on. The workers still ignored them – in fact, they averted their eyes. And, so far, so did the PSF officers they occasionally passed.

Their luck did not hold.

There were three of them, PSF officers with AKs slung, standing at the corner of 8th and West 51st Street, near the former Gershwin Theater. The venue was now the Forum of People's Justice and used for public trials of racists, imperialists, and pronoun criminals. The PSF officers were hassling a pair of workers, who were trying to satisfy the goons with their ID cards as Turnbull approached. The victims turned over some of their money and the PSF officers let them go, laughing. Now the government thugs were looking around for fresh marks. Apparently the coming invasion was not enough to disrupt their business model.

The team was mid-block when they noticed the PSF men – assuming they identified that way – up ahead. Turnbull would have to have the team do a 180 or cross the street to avoid the three stooges. Those were obvious evasive moves and would draw attention. So was unslinging his rifle. Once again, he decided, he would bluff his way through.

One of the PSF sized them up as they approached down 8th, paying particular attention to Gibson and to Turnbull's weapon. Most of the PSF who had seen Turnbull thought better of it; the big, armed man with the dog was clearly trouble. But this PSF guy – with eyes so wide apart that his mom had probably downed a fifth every night of her pregnancy – did not give much thought to that, or to anything much at all.

"What's this shit?" he asked his buddies as Turnbull closed the distance. Now all three dull faces were looking at him.

Turnbull assessed two of them as probably native PRers. The third looked like one of the foreign immigrants they were letting into the Force – aliens actually got priority in hiring. The guy had his boots on the wrong feet, and the laces flopped onto the filthy sidewalk. None of them were STRAC, but this one looked like he fell into his uniform.

Turnbull did not avert his eyes and kept walking. As he did, he ran through his plan. It was a pretty good plan, considering the time and logistical limitations, and if it worked it would eliminate the immediate threat. The second order threat, not so much.

"Comrade Eddie," Comrade Chico began in a whisper.

"Stop talking," Turnbull hissed.

At ten feet, Wide Eyes made his choice.

"Hold up," he directed. "Who the hell are you?"

"Who the hell are *you*?" Turnbull retorted. "Because I'm People's Bureau of Investigation, and I don't have time for this."

Another decision point. The smart play for the PSF guy would be to wave them past. But Wide Eyes was on a losing streak.

"You got ID?" he demanded.

"Yeah," Turnbull said. He reached his left hand into his pocket and pulled out the fake credential, holding the ID card with his picture out for the thugs to squint at.

Wide Eyes's mouth moved slightly as he squinted to read "Edward Peyronie."

Another decision point, and another bad decision.

"Let me see it," Wide Eyes said, reaching out a paw. His companions were getting uncomfortable. After all, this guy would not be strolling through the secure zone carefree with that dog and that gun and those papers if he was not for real. But Wide Eyes was walking a crappy beat jamming up janitors for a few bills for a living and this guy, well, this guy thought he was better than them. Him and his dog and gun and PBI job.

Turnbull cocked his head a bit, as if he was considering whether Wide Eyes was insane.

"Hey, let them go," the other native PSF man said nervously.

"Shut up," said Wide Eyes, never breaking his eye-lock with Turnbull. "I told you to hand it over, and theirs, too. We're calling it in. See if you're for real."

"You sure?" Turnbull said, offering Wide Eyes one last off-ramp.

"Right now," Wide Eyes growled.

"Hey man," the nervous one said to his companion, catching and correcting himself. "I mean 'person.'"

"Now!" Wide Eyes shouted, eyes locked on his prey.

Turnbull sighed, and tossed the card into Wide Eye's face.

Turnbull's right hand dropped down to the handle of the Centurion Beretta at his waist. Wide Eyes was blinking and blocking the ID card coming at him when Turnbull pulled up the Wilson-modified M9 and pivoted the barrel to his front, firing two shots into Wide Eyes's chest.

The wounded PSF man staggered back as Turnbull brought his left hand to the grip and canted right. The nervous one was center mass behind the red front sight. Turnbull fired twice into his chest then brought it up and put one in the face of the falling thug. Then he turned on the foreign PSF thug, who was trying, and failing, to bring his AK-47 to bear. Turnbull shot him once in each lung then through the forehead.

"Holy shit!" Paloma said. The other three were frozen. Gibson sat and scratched his ear as Turnbull walked up to where the groaning Wide Eyes lay on his back. There were lots of faces turned his way up and down the street, mostly workers. They would not volunteer any information, but if pressed – and the PSF would press – they would sing like canaries.

Turnbull picked up his ID card with his left hand then brought the M9 to bear and shot Wide Eyes right between them. It was an easy shot.

Turnbull was reloading a fresh mag as he addressed his team.

"Now we really need to find a place to lay up," he said. "Let's go."

Gibson started wagging his tail, but the three POUM fighters just stared at him for a moment before following him down the street.

Deeds sat uncomfortably on the couch, his hands a bit swollen from the zip-ties his Ukrainian merc minder had wrapped around his wrists.

"Dimitri, why don't you loosen these," Deeds asked.

"Shut up," Dimitri said, looking up from his phone. His brand-new 5.56mm AK-19 Kalashnikov Assault Rifle was leaning against the chair. There was a .45 Heckler & Koch USP pistol in his holster. Vasilev had used some of the substantial payments Harrington made for the delivery of General Scott and Clay Deeds to upgrade his crew's weapons, and both guns were brand new.

Deeds shut his eyes. He was trying, and failing, to sleep when, sometime around ten in the morning, one of the colonels in the People's Republic Anti-Colonial Military Land Forces (he/him) working in the command suite came in and interrupted General Scott's breakfast of bacon and eggs to hand him a paper.

Scott put down his fork and scanned the document with great interest, even as the colonel stared at the general's breakfast with barely disguised envy. This was a pretty luxe meal even inside the Midtown Secure Zone.

"And they have not caught the perpetrators?"

"Not yet, sir. It's unclear how many there were. Some of the witness statements do not make sense. There were two, there were a half-dozen, they were walking dogs. You know how stupid workers are."

Scott grunted and kept reading.

"Three dead, two shots in the chest and one in the head on each of them and none even got off a shot," the general summarized.

"That's what the report says," replied the major, not sure if that was the answer his commander was seeking.

From his couch, Deeds began to laugh. He knew what Scott was thinking, so it gave away nothing. Scott looked over, grim.

"Kelly's here," Deeds said.

"Maybe," Scott said. "But I'm glad. He's coming for you."

"No, he's come for *you*, general. I am a fringe benefit."

"He will never get in here. He will come and we will take him, and then you stop being useful, which is bad news for you."

"I'd double my guard, if I were you," Deeds said. "And even then, I don't think it will be enough."

"So, he's James Bond times Rambo times Dirty Harry?" sniffed the general. The People's Republic Anti-Colonial Military Land Forces colonel knit his brow. The last two were alien to him, but he knew James Bond. She was a differently-abled trans-lesbian who had been assigned male at birth and fought red colonialist racists in the movies.

"No, he just doesn't care if he lives or dies, and that makes him very scary indeed," Deeds said.

Scott looked him over.

"Dimitri," Scott said.

"Sir," the merc grunted, looking at the general.

"If Mr. Kelly Turnbull or one of his friends should manage to reach our suite, would you kindly take one of your brand new weapons and blow his brains all over this nice white carpet?"

Dimitri turned to Deeds.

"*Tak*," he said, staring dully at his prisoner.

Deeds did not need to speak Ukrainian to know that meant "Yes."

Turnbull had found the perfect hideout for them, a building that was not actually abandoned and still had power, but that was near certain not to have much in the way of foot traffic.

The Joe Biden Memorial Museum and Performance Space was located in the old Ambassador Theater on West 49th Street. The assigned worker, a youngish man who looked fairly healthy, was sweeping the sidewalk out front. He had been most cooperative and allowed the fugitives in, especially after Turnbull told him that if he did not aid them the dog was going to clamp his teeth down on the man's groin.

"Did anyone see us?" Comrade Chico asked as they tried to relax inside. Karla was silent and angry, but it was unclear if that was her usual sullenness or something related to the one-sided shootout and their subsequent rapid escape from the area. Paloma, for her part, was off getting information from the worker. Turnbull figured that would take a while.

"We're probably good in here for a couple hours," he said. "But they will come."

"You killed three People's Security Force officers," Karla said. "They are the vanguard, after the POUM, of the struggle."

"Sacrifices sometimes need to be made," Turnbull replied. "They threatened the mission of freeing Professor Deeds from the revanchist forces holding him. The people appreciate the sacrifice. And we know the POUM will make the hard decisions. That's why the People's Republic intends to award the POUM the island of Manhattan as its exclusive territory."

"What?" Comrade Chico gasped.

"I did not want to tell you before," Turnbull replied seriously. "But you have been on our radar for quite some time."

"I don't know what to say," Comrade Chico sputtered, beaming. Karla, for theym part, seemed less excited and more suspicious.

"POUM!" Turnbull cried.

"Power to the marginalized!" both Comrade Chico and Karla shouted in unison, their fists shooting up.

Tom Lopez, the chef at the hotel, was excited to get the call just after noon. He was not concerned with OPSEC.

"What do you have? I need salmon. You got any salmon?"

"Pork," Turnbull said. "Maybe 50 pounds."

"Well, is it inspected? I mean, it can have worms and your suppliers are not exactly on the grid, though there's not really a grid anymore anyway."

Lopez's freewheeling talk on an open line was disconcerting. Turnbull assessed that he had powerful protectors, or at least thought he did.

"I got what I got from our friend. You want it or not?"

"I want," the chef said. "But you'll never get near here. They tightened security all over the perimeter. Got some bigwigs upstairs, and then there's all this invasion stuff."

"Can you come get it?" Turnbull asked.

"I can send some guys in a truck in a few hours. Where are you?"

"No, our friend said since it's on credit I deal with you. Only you. Face to face. You gotta come."

"I'm a chef, not a teamster. Also, it's a crime to union bust."

"I guess I find another buyer then," Turnbull said. "We done?"

"No, we aren't done. Where the hell are you?"

Turnbull told him. Lopez bitched that he needed to be cooking, not making meat runs. Turnbull was unmoved. After Lopez agreed to come, the call ended.

The team began to get its gear together. Paloma reappeared, bringing the worker around from backstage.

The worker kept smiling at Paloma. She smiled back.

"He did not know anything useful," she said. "He would have told me."

"Is he good? He's not going to make a call once we leave?" Turnbull asked.

Paloma smiled, then lifted her rifle and shot the worker in the chest. Turnbull's hand fell onto the grip of his Wilson Beretta.

The man fell to the floor, gasping. Blood oozed across the front of his blue work shirt. She shot him again in the head and he was still. The ejected shell bounced across the floor, and then it was silent.

"He's good," Paloma said.

"Sacrifices," Comrade Chico said to Turnbull. "I wanted to make sure you knew the POUM was serious."

Turnbull reevaluated his options. He decided to keep them around for now, but it was close.

Paloma began their planning session with a land acknowledgement tracing Manhattan's origins as an island belonging to the Indians. This took about ten minutes. Turnbull again made the conscious decision not to shoot them yet.

"We need Lopez to get us in and up to the 36th floor," Comrade Chico said. "That's where the kitchen is, according to my contact. Then my contact gets us where we need to go."

"Your guy is in the maintenance department?" Turnbull asked.

"Yeah. He fixes things," said Comrade Chico, uncomfortable both that Turnbull had assumed the contact's gender and had done so correctly.

"What's his name?"

"It's probably safer not to say, in case one of us gets captured," Comrade Chico said. The man's goateed face stared at Turnbull's, expectantly.

Was he suspicious?

"Good thinking," Turnbull said. That seemed to satisfy the anarchist leader. But Karla was still scowling.

It was just after 5 p.m. when the white cargo box truck pulled up out front of the Biden Museum. The words "MANDARIN ORIENTAL" showed through the black paint someone had used to blot them out years before; there was no room for the new name so no one had tried to paint that on.

Lopez, true to Lou's description, had bright pink hair and a sunburst tatt on his forehead. His driver wore a blue worker's shirt and stayed in the truck while Lopez got out onto the sidewalk.

Turnbull stuck his head out of the museum's door and scanned the street. No PSF. He gestured at Lopez to come over. The chef sighed and came inside.

"This is a giant pain in the...," he began. He did not get to "ass," much less to sharing his pronouns. Turnbull's Wilson Beretta was in his face.

"You're robbing me when I didn't bring any money?" the chef asked incredulously.

"This is not a robbery. It's a change of plans. You're bringing the pork inside and us too."

Lopez furrowed his brow.

"I don't get it."

"You're getting us through the security cordon to the loading dock. I assume there's an express freight elevator from there up to the 36th floor?"

"The loading dock is in the deliveries garage. You want to walk the pork up to my kitchen?"

Turnbull pressed the barrel into the tatt on his forehead.

"Yeah,"

"Okay, fine," Lopez said. "Whatever."

"We're all riding in back," Turnbull said. "Except for Paloma here. She's riding up front with you in case you get any ideas."

Turnbull handed the woman his Beretta.

"Paloma, what do you do if he does anything stupid?"

She smiled sweetly.

"I shoot him in the kidney."

"So," Turnbull explained. "If you like your sweetbreads intact, you get us in."

"How do I explain her?" demanded Lopez.

"You tell them she's on the menu. And you keep them out of the cargo box by telling them you have dogs back there and you don't want them getting loose. I hear they're a delicacy and your important guests will be mighty pissed if their dinner gets loose."

"That mutt looks a little stringy, but okay. You're still giving me the pork, right?"

"Get in the truck," Turnbull said.

16.

The truck's cargo box had a hardwood floor that was rutted and stained from a couple decades of deliveries. It smelled like an amalgam of foodstuffs, but foodstuffs that had been left out too long. Gibson, however, enjoyed it. He went across the floor sniffing while Turnbull, Comrade Chico, and Karla sat on the floor, backs against the side of the box and weapons on their laps. The trip was bumpy, but only a few minutes long.

The truck slowed to a stop, and the whine of the worn brake pads echoed through the cargo box.

"If that door rolls up, rock 'n' roll," Turnbull said.

"Why are there Ukrainian mercenaries holding Professor Deeds?" asked Karla. She looked as suspicious as usual.

"Because what People's Republic patriot would?" Turnbull answered. She seemed dubious.

The truck idled. Turnbull pressed his head against the side, but could hear nothing. It seemed to be taking a long time. Turnbull instinctively began improvising a new plan in case his current improvised plan went south, as was seeming more likely by the second.

The truck began to move. The anarchists sighed in relief.

"We go up, connect with your guy, find the professor, get him, bring him down and leave the same way we came in," Turnbull said. "Stay together, and don't shoot unless you need to. I'm suppressed, you are not."

He screwed the suppressor on the barrel of his rifle and then took out the FN pistol and screwed its suppressor on, then stuck it through his belt.

Now they were on a slope heading downward. It flattened out again. After a moment, the truck stopped and the engine went off. It was quiet.

"Get ready," Turnbull said.

The door went up and Paloma was standing beside Lopez and the driver facing the three rifles and the teeth of a Belgian Malinois. They lowered their guns.

Turnbull reached out for his pistol and Paloma handed it over reluctantly. Comrade Chico gave her back her AK. Turnbull holstered his piece.

"We're in the loading garage," Lopez said. "You really want to go up to the kitchen?"

"We really do," Turnbull said, jumping down. Gibson followed. The garage was cavernous, with several loading docks. It was dark, lit only by weak lights on the high ceiling. The garage door was closed behind them. There were three or four other vehicles on the floor, which may well have been derelicts considering their shabby condition.

"Why?" Lopez asked.

"I want to see how a kitchen works because I was a big fan of Gordon Ramsay back before the Split," Turnbull said. He did not mention that Ramsay was a fixture in the red and had a very successful Texas mash-up restaurant called "The Gordon Ramsay Signature Whataburger Experience." Turnbull had actually enjoyed his "Shiner-Bathed Fois Gras Double Whataburger," but he refused to admit that to Lorna.

"Then follow me," Lopez said.

They grabbed the pork packs and followed the chef. Lopez led them up the steps onto the loading dock level and to a bank of elevators. They stood in front of the door that had "36 EXPRESS" emblazoned across the doors in fading white paint. Lopez hit the call button.

Inside the elevator, as it began to rise, passing by the ambush on the ground floor, Turnbull relaxed just a bit.

They were in.

"When we are up there in the kitchen," Lopez said, "you need to show me respect. These cooks are savages. You have to be dominant."

"Any of them got guns?" Turnbull asked.

"No," Lopez said.

"Then I'm not worried."

"I mean me," Lopez said. "I have to run this kitchen once you leave."

"Stop talking," Turnbull said.

The elevator slowed and stopped. The doors pulled apart, and revealed a white industrial kitchen with maybe a dozen workers with white hats and white aprons over their blue outside worker uniforms bustling over prep tables, stoves, and sinks.

"Chef on the floor!" shouted Lopez.

"Yes, chef!" they all shouted, not looking up.

Turnbull thought little of it, having been in restaurant kitchens before – hell, he had had gun fights in restaurant kitchens before. But the rest of the POUM crew was stunned into silence as they stepped off.

"Secure the door," Turnbull growled at Karla, but she stood transfixed at the scene, as did Paloma and Comrade Eddie.

It was so many impressions at once that short-circuited their minds. There was the brightness – the power was on – and the cleanliness – it gleamed. But there was also the bounty and variety of food. Chicken, melons, lettuce, cheese, peppers – the three anarchists had not seen anything like it, at least not since the Split. They stood, amazed.

"Go!" Turnbull said, shoving Karla toward the front door of the kitchen ungently. She recovered her senses, dropped her pork pack, and began walking by the boiling pans and heaps of prepped veggies on her way to secure the entrance/exit.

Lopez was already berating his staff for their infractions, ignoring his guests. Turnbull grabbed a step ladder and put it in the elevator doorway so it could not close, trapping the car on the 36th floor. Then he turned and scanned the room, his eyes settling on the walk-in cooler with the thick metallic door.

"This is amazing," Paloma said, her eyes wide at the bounty.

"A triumph of people's economics," Comrade Chico said. "We will all eat like this every day, as soon as we eliminate the wreckers, racists, and looters."

"Yes," Paloma said, taking it all in. "Looters and wreckers."

Lopez came back to Turnbull.

"Okay, you have seen it. Lou can rest easy. Give me the pork and go."

"Get all your people and get in the walk-in," Turnbull said.

"What?" exclaimed the chef.

"You heard me."

"We have a dinner service going on in under an hour!"

"And I have a rifle. Which do you think you should be more concerned about?" Turnbull reached down, picked up Karla's pack, and thrust it into Lopez's arms.

They herded the entire kitchen staff, with the pork packs, inside the walk-in. Turnbull slipped the locking pin into the latch mechanism and turned off the cooling fans. They would not freeze. He also handed them a fire axe and instructed that they could start chopping in two hours if no one let them out earlier. But anyone popping out before then was liable to get popped themselves.

Paloma took a big bite out of a melon slice as they gathered over a prep table to talk. Gibson was busy sniffing around the linoleum.

"Floor 54," Turnbull said. "That's where Lopez says the bigwigs are. And that's where they send a prisoner plate every meal."

"Eighteen floors," Comrade Chico said. "That's a long way."

"We need to go up, find and free Dr. Deeds, then get back here. The express elevator car is trapped here so we can get back down to the ground and drive out in the truck, assuming the alarm does not go off."

"That seems like a lot of assumptions," Karla said grimly. Turnbull turned to Comrade Chico.

"This is where we need your worker to help. We need to know how to get up there. And we need to know what is between us and that floor, and what's on the 54th before we go up there. We need to know where Dr. Deeds is, and especially where the Ukrainian mercs are."

"I saw a phone," Comrade Chico said. "I can call maintenance and have our person sent to us here. I'll tell them a stove is out or something."

"I can do my own reconnaissance," Paloma suggested. "The Ukrainians seem highly cis. I can exploit that."

Karla grunted. Paloma ignored her and continued.

"I will find a phone and call back here with what I find."

Karla scowled but was silent.

"Your dedication is admirable," Comrade Chico said, placing a hand on Paloma's shoulder. She smiled coyly, and took another bite of melon.

Comrade Chico stood guard at the main door to the kitchen, keeping an eye out not just for interlopers but for the maintenance man. Karla stood by, sullen.

"I'm excited for the chance to talk to Dr. Deeds about xis theories," Comrade Chico told Turnbull.

"Oh, xe'll definitely enjoy talking to you," Turnbull assured him.

"I never heard of xim," Karla said firmly.

"It's xe! You've never taken ideology seriously," Comrade Chico snapped. "You have only the barest inkling of Marxist-Leninist-Kendi thought!"

Karla swore and stomped off back to the rear of kitchen.

"They is very immature in theym thinking," Comrade Chico explained about his fellow anarchist. "I see only limited potential for them."

"You, on the other hand, have limitless possibilities," Turnbull assured him. "Assuming we get Dr. Deeds out."

"This is such an honor that the leadership would select the POUM for this mission," Comrade Chico gushed. "And for me to be serving the struggle with an intersectionally marginalized individual like yourself. I only wish Gerald could be here to represent otherkin."

"The struggle is all about sacrifice," Turnbull said.

There was a knock on the kitchen door, and when Comrade Chico answered they found a thin man in a blue worker uniform standing there. Michael Dobbs was in his mid-thirties and holding a toolbox.

Comrade Chico motioned him inside.

"He/him," the maintenance man said.

"I told you I would require a service, Michael," Comrade Chico said after introducing Comrade Eddie.

"What do you want?" Michael asked. He was clearly frightened and wary all at once. Comrade Chico continued.

"You live in the POUM zone and we need you to assist us in a mission of extreme importance."

"I just fix things," the man insisted.

"And you go all through the building to do it," Turnbull said.

The man nodded. He was clearly distressed.

Too bad.

"Fifty-fourth floor," Turnbull said. "What's up there?"

"The Presidential Suite – I mean, it's not called that any more. Like, now it's the 'Rotating Temporary Executive Suite.' But it's been taken over."

"Taken over?"

"Yeah, there's like a headquarters in it. Computers, videos. I had to fix some electrical outlets. Lots of soldiers, too, some speaking Russian."

Turnbull did not correct him. The man continued.

"There's a prisoner, too. In another room. I forget the number, but I know where it is. I had to fix the radiator. He was chained to it."

"You got bolt cutters in that tool box?" Turnbull asked. The man nodded.

"I could cut through. Is that what you need me to do?"

"That's one thing," Turnbull said. "How do you travel through the building?"

"Elevators," Dobbs said. "Sometimes the stairs."

"Is the stairwell locked?"

"I have a key." Dobbs patted his front pocket.

"Guards?"

"Sometimes the Russians use it."

Turnbull considered the options. He checked his watch. 6:32 p.m.

"Put on a waitperson jacket," Turnbull instructed Paloma. "You're going upstairs with dinner. Can you make a sandwich?"

Karla grunted in fury.

"For the struggle, I mean," Turnbull said. "Sometimes we have to conform to gender stereotypes to achieve our objectives."

"I'll make the sacrifice," Paloma said bravely.

"You'll need something concealable," Turnbull said. He held out the compact Glock 30 in .45 and the spare mags. She took them and put them in her pocket.

"Go up, find someone important looking, and get the layout then call us here," Turnbull instructed. "No shooting unless there is no other way. We'll see you up there."

Paloma nodded.

"I'll do what is necessary."

"POUM!" shouted Comrade Chico proudly.

"Power to the marginalized!" Karla, Paloma and Turnbull replied in remarkably tight unison with fists raised.

"You ready?" Turnbull asked.

Paloma nodded just as a series of dull thuds echoed through the building.

Explosions, out there in Manhattan.

The wind whipped through the open door of the UH-60 Blackhawk as it skimmed the deck over northern New Jersey. Junior Ryan's aircraft was flying into battle with a hundred other choppers.

They passed over depots, assembly areas, and artillery firebases each with dozens of 155mm howitzers whose barrels pointed across the river. The roads below the choppers were crowded with US forces – tanks, armored personnel carriers, and trucks. Many of the trucks carried boats. The People's Republic forces between the front line and the shore of the Hudson were now almost non-existent. What had not been pulled out had been smashed by the American iron fist. There was only a short way to go to the river's edge, and this was now less a kinetic battle than a logistical campaign to get the boats in the water for the assault crossing the next morning.

Major Ryan looked to his left and right. Dozens of helicopters fanned out in a line each way, all headed directly at Manhattan, and each with a specific landing zone.

The Pathfinders were coming. Their mission was to set the conditions for the landings. The Army would be crossing at dawn, and the Marines – whose assault ships lay to the east – would join them.

"Dun dun dun dun dun duh," sang a Pathfinder sergeant, clutching his M4. Junior conceded to himself that it would be kind of cool to have speakers blasting some Wagner right about now.

The Valkyries were riding.

The land beneath them vanished, giving way to the dark surface of the river that rippled and swirled in the setting sun. Only a couple minutes left.

Lazy arcs of smoke reached out from behind them and climbed overhead until they descended into the city to their front. Most of Manhattan was dark, but the Midtown and Downtown Secure Zones still had power and therefore lights. Where it was dark, there were flashes where the smoke tracks touched the earth or a building. The drones the US had been flying overhead for a week had identified targets for the Multiple Launch Rocket System's warheads.

PR heavy weapons, arms caches, commo links, command posts – these were the primary gun and missile targets. The problem was that there were not many of such targets to hit. The redlegs were complaining at the division's final coordination briefing that their artillery had little to shoot at. That struck Ryan as disturbing.

It meant the enemy was decentralized. If an enemy is centralized and integrated, you can take out key nodes and resistance collapses. There are no individuals, only units, and units operate as part of a whole. It's like a Jenga tower – you take the right pieces out and the tower collapses. But if the defense is just a bunch of individuals with guns, taking out one piece has no effect on the other pieces.

You have to kill them one by one, person by person.

And Manhattan had a lot of people.

His earphones helped block out the noise of the engines and the rushing air, but the Pathfinder radio net was already active. It was hard to make out who was who.

The city skyline was getting closer as the swarm of OD green helicopters ripped low over the water. Ryan leaned out to look ahead, wind buffeting his face and his ballistic glasses protecting his eyes from the blast. Orange bubbles erupted across the island and even on the sides of some of the skyscrapers as well.

"Sixty seconds until over the deck," the pilot announced.

Now he could see jets above the city skyline, probably doing high-altitude precision guided munitions runs. An orange finger leapt up off the island, shooting skyward. It hit something in the sky above what he calculated to be Hell's Kitchen – there was a bright flash and, a moment later, the American plane was spiraling down in flames.

No parachute.

"Thirty seconds!"

Poking up above the city near the middle of the island was what was the Empire State Building, though the communists called it something else. It was the Empire State on US maps, though, and a key landmark for orienting the attack. There was an orange lick of flame about half-way up on its east face.

He gazed at it for a moment, the cold wind across his cheeks, but then his attention was suddenly drawn to the pencil-thin orange fingers reaching out from the shore near his front, what he knew to be Pier 99. The fire was tracers from some sort of large anti-aircraft weapon. One of the rounds flashed by only a few meters off. Then more passed by, but then one round punched into the cockpit of the helicopter fifty meters off his starboard and the Blackhawk twisted and spun as it fell, disintegrating in black smoke and red flame as it broke apart across the surface of the river.

That was at least a dozen men gone in an instant. A dozen families getting the dreaded visit from a pair of solemn officers making the notification.

Ryan hoped this was worth the price they just paid, and the price to come. Behind him, his fire support officer was desperately calling in coordinates for an arty strike on the AA gun.

"Fifteen seconds!" the pilot shouted over the intercom.

Ryan got ahold of himself and keyed his mic on the Pathfinder Battalion frequency.

"Crimson Tide, this is Crimson-Six, Alabama. I say again. Alabama."

"Alabama" was the code word for breaking ranks and heading toward each chopper's individual objective. Helicopters spun off in each direction, some gaining altitude and others staying low, even as another AA gun on the shore joined the barrage.

"Missile, missile!" shouted the pilot. The chopper banked. Ryan did not see the missile leap off the shore, but he saw it impact into another Blackhawk. The helicopter spun into the water as well.

There were supposed to be search and rescue choppers behind them to grab up shot down Air Force flyers as well as Army aircrews. Ryan hoped there was someone left alive to pluck out of the cold Hudson.

And in an instant they were over land again, the former Henry Hudson Parkway flashing below them as his aircraft headed in toward the former Lincoln Center that lay in the dark just outside the Midtown Secure Zone near the abandoned Fordham University. The PR called all these places something else. The red forces used the pre-Split names on their maps.

The gatling gun beside him erupted as the door gunner hosed down something on the deck. They flew over a block of low buildings and there were people on some of the roofs. From the muzzle flashes, they were shooting into the air with small arms.

The gunner was blazing away at them until Ryan grabbed him and got him to cease fire.

"Don't burn up all your ammo on onesies and twosies," he ordered as loud as he could. The gunner reluctantly nodded.

Other helicopters were landing at various objectives, many of them in the darkness of Central Park outside the Secure Zone wall but some inside the walls in the park. The helicopter reared up over the old Tavern on the Green and came in to land on the Sheep Meadow. Six of the troopers aboard rolled out onto the grass and the helicopter pulled up and away. The men Ryan had just let off immediately began firing at targets all around them. The door gunner saw Ryan's nod and suppressed the enemy with a few blasts from the gatling gun as the chopper rose higher over the park.

Ryan was left with his S3-Air, who coordinated air strikes and his fire support officer, who was in touch with the cannon-cockers back in New Jersey. Both were talking into their own mics on their own freqs, calling in fires in support of the Pathfinders on the ground. He hated that he was not in the dirt with his boys, but he needed to see the big picture and the big picture was only visible from up in the air.

Now, most of the choppers were heading back to New Jersey to pick up the second wave of Pathfinders. A few Blackhawk gunships remained on station for fire support. One of them launched a Hellfire off its rails at something in the dark part of the park. It must have hit its target, since there were secondary explosions.

Down on the ground, there were muzzle flashes and small explosions, likely hand or 40mm launched grenades. The radio net was full of calls giving situation reports or calling for help. A few called for MEDEVAC. To his starboard, bad guys on the roof tops were spraying and praying at the choppers with AKs. Near the edge of the water, by Pier 99, a volley of 155mm shells loaded with DPICM – dual-purpose improved conventional munition – blanketed the anti-aircraft gun positions. There were dozens of explosions as each of the sub-munitions detonated. Those AA guns stopped shooting. But others deeper in the interior opened up.

Ryan's chopper pulled up and to the port side, and it followed the edge of the park uptown.

Operation Overlord had begun.

17.

"Lights out!" Scott shouted across the command post in the former Presidential Suite. Several PR soldiers cut the white lights from the suite's lamps and fixtures, leaving just the glow of monitors and video screens.

"We have to go!" Major Vasilev insisted. There was no fear in his voice, just frustration. The merc's mission was to keep this man alive, and his charge seemed intent on taking unnecessary risks for purely emotional reasons.

"Have your men reported anything around the cordon?" Scott demanded. Behind him, out the windows, the fireballs from missile impact explosions were rising up here and there across the city.

"Your nemesis, this Kelly Turnbull, is not coming. We have to leave!" shouted Vasilev. His aircraft were on the roof, waiting.

"We have time!" Scott countered. But Vasilev knew that there were air and artillery strikes going on. His AH-6s on the rooftop landing pad were sitting ducks – though in Ukrainian, the phrase more aptly translated as "sitting targets."

"Confirmed helicopters approaching over the Hudson!" a People's Republic Anti-Colonial Military Land Forces lieutenant shouted from behind his monitor. Next to him, what appeared to be a female lieutenant looked stricken and howled.

"You deadnamed the river again!" she bellowed. "The Haudenosaunee people call it the Cahohatateaby, and you are literally murdering them!"

"That's not deadnaming!" the apparently male one said before his face was splattered by the brains of the indigenous advocate.

The .45 barrel of Major Vasilev's Heckler & Koch USP emitted a thin swirl of smoke before he returned it to its holster. This was one order from the general – issued via a mere nod – that he was happy to carry out. The remaining dozen People's Republic Anti-Colonial Military Land Forces in the command post looked stricken.

"No more foolishness," General Scott said. The dead LT slumped over then fell onto the white shag carpet, leaving a deep scarlet blemish.

The rest of the soldiers got back to their work, with the river-slandering lieutenant wiping the objector's brain chunks off his mug.

"General, my job is to keep you alive," Vasilev said after gingerly stepping over the dead person and walking over to the general. He nodded at a pair of Kurylenko mercenaries who had watched the events unfold with amusement and they came forward to carry off the corpse.

"And my job is to ensure this operation succeeds," Scott said.

"You are not commanding anything," Vasilev said. "These clowns and psychopaths you have armed down there in the city have no chain of command. You are desperate for revenge, and that will get you killed."

"And that would cut into your bonus."

"Yes," Major Vasilev said, his scar a shadow across his face in the low light. "I care nothing for your quarrels. I do care about both being paid and living to spend it."

"We stay," Scott replied coldly. "Until I determine it is time to go."

"Yes, general," Vasilev hissed. He did an about face and left the room.

"All generals are fools," he muttered to himself in English as he walked past a couple of his men in the hallway. Vasilev was too professional to allow his men to see the full extent of his frustration with the American commander. Vasilev's face was a solid scowl – as usual. His men backed up against the walls to let him pass through. There was a dull thud – something in the distance was exploding. Vasilev ignored it, but he dreaded hearing a detonation from above amongst his helicopters, and that could happen any moment.

Vasilev headed down the hall past the elevator bank toward his room. One of the two men he passed around the corner should have been standing right there instead of twenty meters away. Vasilev paused to reprimand the delinquent when the door opened.

A young woman in waitperson white stepped out carrying a platter with a plate containing a sloppy sandwich and some chips, plus a glass of very dilute iced tea with no ice and no lemon. He had become used to the elaborate dinners provided here, and this looked distinctly downscale. But then, there was a war on.

The woman seemed surprised to see him, and looked him up and down, considering. After a pause, she apparently completed her assessment and batted her eyes at him.

"She/her," she said seductively.

Vasilev appraised her coldly.

"This is for you," she cooed. "Can I take it to your room?"

Vasilev considered the opportunity being presented. Such things were common in poor countries. This woman was obviously impressed with herself, and she was on the high-end of the People's Republic scale. But he was from Ukraine, so he was distinctly unimpressed. In Kyiv, if he considered her at all, it would be after emptying a bottle of Hetman vodka and the clock reading two.

Still, she would kill the time here until the general came to his senses.

Vasilev grunted and Paloma followed him down the hall, tray aloft, as the noise of battle from outside got more intense. She paused to look back at the two giggling Ukrainian guards, who clearly understood their commander's intent *vis a vis* the serving wench. Beyond them was the door to the Presidential Suite. She continued around the corner behind the mercenary major, passing the door to the stairwell. Its sole guard looked bored though he popped to attention when Vasilev appeared.

She made her mental notes and continued on.

Paloma followed the major inside his room carrying the tray, and the door shut behind her. She placed the platter on the black bureau that held the dark video screen.

Vasilev's room was ridiculously luxurious, with various Asian-inspired artifacts and statues on various surfaces throughout. The walls were of dark hardwood, and the doors were all sliding. There was a king bed, unmade. His ruck was on the floor. There were a half-dozen empty vodka mini-bottles on the bureau by the big screen. A sign on the wall by the bed read "THE PEOPLE'S ASIAN AMERICAN AND NATIVE HAWAIIAN/PACIFIC ISLANDER HOTEL NEW YORK APOLOGIZES FOR THE IMPLICATION OF CULTURAL APPROPRIATION AND CISNORMATIVITY."

Paloma read it with a sigh of relief; the quasi-Asian vibe had left her literally shaking. Vasilev looked her over.

"Money or food?" he asked, his accent pronounced.

"Either," she answered. "Both."

The Ukrainian grunted and took the Motorola radio off his pistol belt. Keying it as he walked to the window, he began to speak into it in rapid-fire Ukrainian – he told them he would not be long and to be ready to move in an instant. Paloma stood there, waiting.

Vasilev looked outside his east-facing window, down to the city. The lights were all on in the Midtown Secure Zone, especially the bright lights of Times Square. The lights were also on throughout the sliver of the Downtown Secure Zone he could see at the far end of the island. In between the zones it was dark, except where there was a fire or an explosion.

He released the send button on his Motorola. He could see a few Blackhawk helicopters flying above the city, but below his 54th floor vantage point. He considered his problem – the Kurylenko helicopters on the roof would be irresistible targets for the Americans. It occurred to him that perhaps the best thing to do would be to get them off and into the air. They could lurk in the area awaiting the order to evacuate the remaining Kurylenko men. After all, the choppers were unmarked, so the Americans would almost certainly assume that any blacked out AH-6s were US special ops and not engage.

His plan pleased him, for it combined tactical imagination with duplicity and deception. He keyed the mic again. After he finished barking his instructions to his men and got confirmation of his orders, he put the radio handset down on the table by the window.

Paloma stood by, emotionless, then their eyes met and she smiled. He knew it was a lie – a woman's smile directed at him was always a lie – but he did not particularly care. This was purely business.

"Wait," he said. The mercenary walked past her into the bathroom and slid the door shut behind him.

Paloma stepped over to the phone on the bedside table, where it sat next to a small statue of a samurai, and picked up the receiver. She entered a five digit extension.

"Kitchen," Turnbull answered.

"Two in the hallway with the elevators and the Presidential Suite," she said, forgetting its new name. "One by the stairwell around the corner."

"What are you doing?" demanded Vasilev. She had not heard the door slide open nor seen him step out.

Paloma hung up the phone.

"Calling the kitchen," she said. "To tell them I'll be a few minutes."

The mercenary looked her over hard and without pity. He walked to where she stood by the bedside table. Paloma backed away and he picked up the receiver. His finger found the redial and pushed it. He locked eyes with her as it rang.

"Kitchen."

Vasilev hung up. He had been concerned this was some kind of robbery, though that would have been suicidal. Desperate people do desperate things, though.

But she had not lied. She was just checking in with her boss, who probably took a cut.

"Get undressed," he ordered, and removed his shirt.

"I never wanted to do this," Dobbs complained as they waited in the kitchen. He looked warily at Gibson, who sniffed him and then went to the corner to curl up and rest.

"A lot of persons would be happy for a job in the secure zone," Comrade Chico said, his voice tinged with an edge of offense. "Any job."

"I was assigned it," Dobbs said, more militantly than Turnbull would have expected. "I didn't ask for it."

"You should be grateful you get to serve the revolution!" Karla snapped. "Maybe you should show a little ideological commitment."

"Commitment?" Dobbs said, now fully contemptuous. "I was a Marxist grad student at NYU when the Crisis and the Split happened. I was in the vanguard of the damn revolution!"

"Careful," Comrade Chico said. His grip on his rifle tightened.

"We need him," Turnbull reminded the POUM leader.

"I was going to be a poet in the revolution. Just spend all day drinking wine and screwing my woman – yeah, I'm cis – and writing poems. That was what we all expected from Marxism. And then the PR takes over and they give me a privilege level of one. I step up for my poet job and instead they tell me I'm going to be fixing air conditioners and plastering walls in a hotel for the ruling class."

"I've shot people for less," Comrade Chico said, stone-faced.

"Shoot me then," Dobbs laughed. "I'm going to die anyway of starvation or disease or your damn war!"

Comrade Chico was on his feet, his face a twisted rictus of hate, his gun up. Karla's eyes were bulging. Turnbull leapt to his feet as well.

"We need him," he growled, leaving no doubt.

"He's a traitor!" Karla screeched.

"He's necessary." Turnbull said.

"Yeah, I'm necessary," Dobbs said, grinning with satisfaction. "You and your clown militia, a bunch of morons with guns. You babble about Marxist-Leninist-Kendi thought but you don't know anything about it, like the most important thing – it's all bullshit!"

Turnbull's gut punch made Dobbs gasp and double over. The maintenance man fell to his knees and began retching. He was in no condition to thank Turnbull for saving his life.

"The revanchist traitors holding Dr. Deeds have poisoned his mind," Turnbull announced. Dobbs continued to dry heave on the floor.

"We should make an example of him," Comrade Chico said, apparently forgetting their situation.

"He knows where they have Dr. Deeds," Turnbull said.

The phone on the wall rang. Turnbull and Comrade Chico's eyes locked, and Turnbull grabbed the receiver.

"Kitchen."

He listened for a few moments, then hung up.

"The elevator opens to a hallway and there are two guards. The Presidential Suite is at one end. Around the corner is the stairwell door. There's one guard there." Turnbull kept the fact that Paloma had abruptly hung up to himself.

"So, do we…," began Comrade Chico.

The phone rang again. They exchanged glances. Turnbull reached for the receiver.

"Kitchen."

This time, Turnbull hung up immediately.

"I think someone was checking on Paloma," Turnbull said.

"Indigenous folx cannot lie," Comrade Chico said earnestly. "It is not their way."

"We're up against the most despicable racists imaginable," Turnbull told him gravely. "They deny the integrity of First Peoples."

"They will pay," vowed Comrade Chico.

"I have a plan, but we need to move quickly," Turnbull said.

"The whole north side of the building is the Rotating Temporary Executive Suite," Dobbs said.

"The Presidential Suite?" Turnbull asked.

"Yeah, that's its deadname," Dobbs confirmed soberly. "And their prisoner is kept around the south side in one of the rooms. I have keys to all of the doors."

Turnbull nodded. There was another explosion from somewhere outside. He wished the kitchen had windows so he could see what the hell was going on. He continued issuing his orders.

"I go up in the elevator. The pair in the hallways are mine. Comrade Chico, you go up the stairwell. I'll give you a five minute head start. At exactly 7:05, you come out the door and take out the guard there. You have a watch?"

"Yes," Comrade Chico said. "Though I acknowledge that time pieces attempt to conform us to a western and patriarchal understanding of time."

"Seven-oh-five," Turnbull repeated. He turned to Dobbs.

"Good luck," Dobbs said.

"You come with me," Turnbull replied.

"I'm not a fighter!" Dobbs exclaimed. "I don't want to get any more involved in this."

"I'm not asking you to fight. I'm not asking at all. I need you to find the prisoner and cut him – I mean xir – loose. You do what I want and you're free to go. And free of obligation, right, Comrade Chico?"

"Sure," the militia leader said without emotion.

"He should be shot!" Karla said.

"Stop talking," Turnbull snapped. He turned toward them. The non-binary being was clearly miffed.

Turnbull ignored theym emotional upset.

"You stay here and secure this floor. This is where we rally after we get Deeds."

"*Doctor* Deeds," corrected Comrade Chico.

"Dr. Deeds."

"Who?" said Dobbs, confused. He looked like he was about to speak but Turnbull's death glare silenced him.

Karla saw the exchange, and in theym mind they began thinking about what it meant. Turnbull turned back to the two male-identifying individuals and continued.

"When we all reassemble here, we take the express elevator down to the ground and drive out and away. Apparently World War III is going on out there and hopefully no one will notice one cargo truck departing. Everyone understand the plan?"

Karla grunted. Comrade Chico nodded. Dobbs stared. Gibson scratched his left ear.

Turnbull handed over the FN pistol with the silencer. Comrade Chico took it, and he regarded it in awe.

"Use that, not your AK. Two in the chest, one in the helmet carrier."

Comrade Chico nodded as he slung his rifle.

"Open the stairwell door for him," Turnbull ordered Dobbs. Comrade Chico followed as the maintenance man walked to the stairwell door and opened it.

Comrade Chico stopped at the threshold.

"POUM!" he shouted.

"Power to the marginalized!" Turnbull and Karla responded, raising fists.

Comrade Chico went through and the door latched shut behind him.

"Sir, we have had multiple reports of helicopters on the Mandarin Hotel rooftop LZ," the fire support officer said through the intercom. This was one of several dozen bits of info that MAJ Ryan was trying to process as he oversaw the Pathfinders' fight – really, it was dozens of small fights spread across the island. His big issue at the moment was a Pathfinder platoon that was about to be overrun by a huge swarm of drug-addled sociopaths assaulting the paratroopers' temporary fighting positions in the old Dakota apartment building.

The Dakota was an ornate, German Renaissance revival-style nine-story apartment building built about 150 years before. Critically, the Dakota dominated key ground overlooking two vital crossroads and a gate into the Midtown Secure Zone. That was why the Pathfinders had secured it. And that was why the enemy was determined to take it back.

The Americans called the Dakota "Objective Moptop." John Lennon – generally unpopular in red America for writing the banned song "Imagine" – had died out front on the sidewalk in 1980, shot by a lunatic fan. Now two dozen of Ryan's guys – who knew about the Beatles, if it all, mostly because of their grandparents – were about to buy the farm there, and Ryan's FSO was babbling about choppers on some skyscraper.

Without even having to be told, the Blackhawk pilot was roaring over Central Park toward the big building just outside the Midtown Secure Zone at 72nd Street and Central Park West. As they flew low over the part – drawing small arms fire – Ryan did what every commander was trained to do when presented with an intractable and inconvenient tactical problem.

"Call for fire on the Mandarin!" he ordered, and the FSO began screaming into his mic on the fire support net. Now he could focus on the Dakota battle.

"Crimson-six, this is Bengals-six actual," the platoon leader at the Dakota said. "We're down to our last mags. We are going to be overrun, over."

The lieutenant was not panicking. Instead, he reported the imminent deaths of his entire unit as calmly as he might be ordering a Dos Equis at a bar in the Florida Keys.

"Bengals-six, this is Crimson-one!" Ryan replied. "Wait one, over!"

Ryan pivoted and grabbed the S-3 Air and pulled him close.

"Broken Arrow!" Ryan shouted.

The Three-air stared at his boss for a moment, eyes wide.

"You heard me! Broken Arrow!" Ryan yelled over the sound of the rotors, and the Three-air started nodding and began shouting into the tactical air net.

"Broken Arrow, Broken Arrow! Objective Moptop! Broken Arrow!"

Miles away, the just-established tactical air command post (TACAIR-CP) in Northern New Jersey went dead silent as the provisional Pathfinder Battalion's Three-air began calling "Broken Arrow." The Air Force airmen manning it, assisted by a few sailors and a couple Marines, had just gotten the Air Force essentials of their TACAIR-CP up and running – the air conditioning and the refrigerators for their Cokes. Cool and their thirsts slaked, they were at their stations, and they knew what the call meant. Now, they looked over at the full colonel in charge.

This was a huge decision that moved men and resources across the battlefield. You did not call it lightly. It would change the entire plan. If he got it wrong, it would be his ass. But this is why they paid him the big bucks.

He did not hesitate.

Now it was the USAF's time to shine.

"Okay, we have a Broken Arrow call!" the colonel yelled. "Initiate!"

The CP suddenly went into overdrive with a red flashing light hanging from the tent's roof beam activating and dozens of voices making calls out to aircraft in the skies.

They knew the drill, though it was rare. But when it happened, it was on like Donkey Kong.

An American ground unit in contact was about to be overrun. That could never happen. And every bit of American combat power was going to be focused on stopping it.

The call went out to every United States Air Force, Navy and Marine Corps combat aircraft flying over New York and New Jersey with unexpended ordnance.

Light your afterburners.

Vector in on Objective Moptop.

Now.

On a dozen video monitors, red US aircraft icons suddenly turned around onto a direct course toward Objective Moptop. And they were moving fast.

Scores of F-35s, F-16s, F-18s, F-15s, and several A-10s – leaving aside the B-52s, B-1s and B-21s – all converged on the objective.

Ryan's Blackhawk flew over the firefight. The streets were thick with running and gunning enemies, as well as the bodies of those cut down already. Sadly, his ship had fired off all its Hellfire missiles already. A pair of Blackhawk gunships were hosing down the streets with minigun fire, the orange streaks tearing down and then often ricocheting back up into the sky from the asphalt. But it was nowhere near enough.

Every hopped-up lunatic in New York City was converging on the Dakota. And those men inside were going to die if the game did not change right now.

It changed. Hard.

The rear echelon air controllers at the TACAIR-CP usually got a lot of grief from their Army comrades for their perceived lack of soldierly skills, but not that day. The airmen switched into "Pro" mode on a dime, lining up the incoming aircraft and placing different airframes at different altitudes to await terminal guidance in to dump their ordnance. There were sixty-seven US airplanes in the sky over New York waiting to be called in with more coming.

The People's Republic forces were about to learn what US airpower can do.

On the roof of a nearby high-rise a few blocks up Central Park West, a squad of paratroopers leapt out of a chopper and secured it for a couple of attached Air Force Joint Terminal Attack Controllers (JTAC) to set up and guide in the air strikes. The guys had comms up to the waiting jets within the first minute on the roof. The JTACs decided to start by bringing in a pair of A-10s, callsign Angel.

"This is Sauron-12. Angel flight, you're first at bat, how copy?"

"Roger, Sauron-12. Angel-1 and 2 inbound."

"Plow the streets, out."

The A-10 is a venerable aircraft, an ugly, slow, and squat ground attack jet built around a 30mm GAU-8 Avenger rotary autocannon the size of a Volkswagen beetle. The stubby barrels of the big gun poked out of the front of the ugly hog just under the cockpit. When it fired, the front of the plane was sheathed in smoke.

The A-10s were laden with AGM-65 Maverick missiles and various bombs hanging from hardpoints on their wings. Their twin engines were far back on the fuselage and heavily armored. The pilots flew sitting inside titanium bathtubs to protect them from ground fire. You could shoot down an A-10, but you had to work for it.

In fact, the greatest danger to the Thunderbolt II – lovingly nicknamed the "Warthog" – was the Air Force brass who had spent decades trying to retire the airframe. It was just not cool like an F-35. But the grunts loved it. The plane was designed to sweep through columns of commie tanks in Cold War Europe, opening them up with uranium tipped shells. Now, the jets would sweep through rows of commies here at home. But these commies did not have armor between them and retribution.

These Angels were definitely of the avenging sort.

Most of the beleaguered Screaming Eagles occupying the Dakota were slapping in their last magazines, determined to sell their lives dearly as the wide-eyed fanatics besieging them made their final push. But then the warning came in over the radio net – gun run, A-10s, danger close – and the paratroopers took cover.

Ryan's chopper pulled back out of the Air Force air lanes created by the TACAIR-CP to bring the fighter/bombers in without colliding with Army rotary wing assets. They knew what was coming and wanted to watch.

The A-10s dropped down and flew in from over the Hudson, crossing at the overgrown and abandoned sports fields along the river bank and flying in parallel, one tearing east on West 72nd, the other roaring east on West 73rd. The JTACs took over and brought them in for their final approach. Crossing above Broadway, the pilots lined up their sights and hit the triggers on their sticks.

All the Pathfinders dug-in inside the Dakota heard was a *buuuurrrrrrttttttt*. What they saw was the east-west streets erupt and the mass of sociopathic humanity trying to kill them scythed down and converted to a pinkish goo. Then the next gun run came north-south down Central Park West. More goo.

And then the rest of the planes took their turn, the JTACs vectoring them in with their guns and bombs. It was a slaughter.

Ryan watched it from a distance as the massed enemy was strafed, bombed, and generally blown into its individuals' component parts by air strike after air strike. The Broken Arrow response was quite a sight, so impressive that he did not even notice when the missile strike he had called in on the Mandarin Hotel slammed into the west side of the building and erupted in a pair of orange fireballs.

18.

Comrade Chico had disappeared up the stairwell. Turnbull checked his watch, heedless of how the act of doing so validated the colonialist paradigm.

It was 6:58 p.m. Give him six minutes to get up twenty flights, leaving two minutes wiggle room. Turnbull decided he would grab one of the three main elevators and bring it to the 53rd floor, and hold it there, waiting. Then he would go up and be on 54 at exactly 7:05.

He decided to leave his pack there in the kitchen. Karla could watch it. He did not want to be separated from his stuff, but he was going to need to be unencumbered for this next part. Then he took up his rifle, looking it over and confirming, again, that the suppressor was on the muzzle that pointed down at the linoleum floor.

"Who are you?" Karla hissed from a few meters away.

Turnbull's eyes flicked up and over to them. They had theym AK-47 leveled at him. Dobbs started to walk backwards, wanting no part of whatever this was.

"Don't move," she snapped, but the gun never left Turnbull's gut.

"Is this about having a watch?" Turnbull asked. "Because I reject racist constructions of time."

"It's not just that!" Karla shouted. "It's everything about you. Comrade Chico is blinded by ambition, but I see everything!"

"I'm going to leave," Dobbs said.

"Stay where you are!" Karla shouted, theym eyes flashing. Dobbs stopped, lifted his hands and nodded.

"Put down that rifle," Karla said to Turnbull, adding, "Slowly."

He made no move to comply.

"You're interfering with an important mission, Karla," Turnbull said. "You're interfering with the revolution."

"I'm protecting it from whoever you are! You better put that weapon down."

"I guess I should tell you the truth," Turnbull said. "I'm a red operative here to rescue Clay Deeds, who is not some commie professor. He also has no pronouns. Neither do I. Neither does the dog."

Karla's mouth opened slightly as she processed this information.

"And if that's true, then I fooled your leader. That means the POUM is nothing but a collection of clowns and mutants. Your whole life is a joke, a pointless, ridiculous joke."

"Shut up!" they stammered. "I'll kill you!"

Dobbs stood, eyes wide, listening.

"Yes," Turnbull continued, the intensity in his voice growing. "You will, because you are a revolutionary. You are dedicated to the revolution and you and your cadre would *not* be fooled by some racist, sexist, colonialist intruder. You would have seen it, and you did, meaning I am not some red infiltrator but exactly who I said I was. Because you are the vanguard of the revolution! You are the defender of the gender non-conforming! Of the trans and the quantum-trans and the otherkin and all the rest of the glorious diversity that is the People's Republic. You are the spearpoint of the revolution!"

Karla swallowed, trying to assess what Comrade Eddie was telling her. It made no sense, but in the PR, that meant little.

"And now you have passed the test! You saw through everything! You will be the leader!" Turnbull shouted. "POUM!"

"Power to...," they began, lifting theym hand and theym gun for a moment before they realized that Turnbull's weapon was coming up even faster as he was turning aside out of the track of theym AK's barrel.

Turnbull's 5.56mm round smashed through theym sternum. They heard the whoosh of the suppressed shot and felt the impact, and forgot completely about theym own rifle as they flew backwards and collapsed onto the cold white floor.

It was hard to breathe – they could not catch theym breath, Theym mouth moved even as Turnbull walked over with his rifle. The suppressor on the end of the gun had a black hole, and a whiff of smoke twisting out of it. They tried to speak even as the hole came even with theym face.

Turnbull shot her through the head. Theym leg kicked and went still. Gibson trotted over to give theym body a sniff, then walked away.

"You aren't going to shoot me, are you?" Dobbs whimpered.

"Not if you do what I say. But if you ever point a gun at me, you're done."

"Are you really from the red, or the blue? Who are you?"

"I'm the guy who will shoot you if you don't stop talking."

He hit the elevator call button.

"Where is Doctor Deeds?" Paloma shouted. The small, black Glock 30 was in her hands, aimed at the shirtless chest of the Ukrainian mercenary.

Vasilev chuckled bitterly, as a pistol what not what he had expected her to produce from under her uniform. He theatrically lifted his hands.

"You're with him," he said, as it became clear in his mind.

"What?"

"With Turnbull. He actually got in," Vasilev marveled.

"I don't care about any Turnbull. Where is the professor?"

"Is that what he told you?" laughed Vasilev. "That you were coming to rescue some professor?"

"Professor Deeds is the leading voice of Marxist-Leninist-Kendi thought!"

Now Vasilev was laughing even harder.

"You little whore," he said. "I'll take you to see him. I have him chained to a radiator with my man Dimitri. You can ask him yourself about your Marxist-Leninist-Kendi thought."

"I don't understand," Paloma said, the Glock shaking.

"You're definitely from this ridiculous country," Vasilev explained. "You met a stranger recently, a very tactically savvy one, and he must have convinced you to help him by telling you that you were fighting for the revolution or some nonsense."

"I am fighting for the revolution!" she insisted.

"You are fighting for the reds!" He laughed again and sat on the edge of the bed. "I thought you were a tramp, but I never imagined you were such an idiot."

"Stop slut-shaming me!" cried Paloma.

"Are you going to shoot me?" smiled Vasilev.

She lifted the gun.

"Your one chance, your only chance, is to hand me that pistol. You have no way out. And then my hundred men and I will hunt down and kill your Kelly Turnbull – he is in the building, isn't he?"

"I don't know a Turnbull. But Comrade Eddie is here. He was the liaison from the government. The rest of us are POUM."

"Poo?" he giggled again "You *are* practically feces."

"POUM," she shouted, the gun shaking. "The Party of the United Marginalized!"

Vasilev laughed again.

"Do you think you will survive this? You are now on your own. And I grow impatient. Give me the gun and I let you live. And perhaps even keep you for myself. You are about the best this country has to offer."

"You won't hurt me?"

"Give me the gun. Now."

Paloma calculated her options, then gave the Ukrainian her most seductive smile. His face was stone as he stood up again and extended his hand.

She considered, and then let him take the Glock with his left hand. His right hand smashed into the side of her face and she fell down onto the carpet.

"I reconsidered," he said, pointing the weapon at her face. "You are nowhere near pretty enough."

The gunshot alerted the guard by the door to the stairwell, who faced Vasilev with concern and confusion as the major rushed out of his room, his shirt back on.

"Intruders!" Vasilev shouted. "Stay here at your post!"

The Ukrainian rushed past the sentry, shouting into his Motorola, then turned the corner. One Kurylenko guard was standing watch by the elevator bank and another was by the door to the former Presidential Suite at the far end.

"Intruders!" Vasilev yelled as he ran down the hall. He keyed the mic on his hand radio and began shouting orders to prepare to evacuate the old Mandarin Hotel.

Comrade Chico walked up the cold, dingy stairwell slowly, trying to be quiet. Down below, many floors down, he heard footsteps and undecipherable talking. At the fortieth floor he was tired; at the fiftieth, exhausted. The arthropod-based People's Gruel was not particularly nourishing, and his skinniness did not necessarily translate into aerobic fitness.

Still, he pressed on climbing the endless flights of stairs, inspired by the revolution, of course, but also by his own ambitions. This mission, and the liberation of the esteemed Dr. Deeds from the hands of the revanchist forces, would demonstrate his value. And that value, he was convinced, was greater than his current gig as head of the POUM.

Standing under the orange and blue sign reading "52nd Floor," he checked his watch. It disgusted him to look at the tool of oppression, acknowledging colonialists concepts of time and all, but sacrifices had to be made.

6:59.

He exhaled, rested on the metal handrail for a moment, then began to climb once again.

The main elevator opened on the 36th floor, with Turnbull standing in front of it with his rifle up. It was empty.

"Get in," Turnbull said, pushing Dobbs inside. Gibson followed him in. The doors slid shut, and Turnbull pushed "53."

After a pause, the car engaged, and the elevator began to rise. It was louder than it should have been, with a metallic whine as if no one had bothered greasing the gears.

Dobbs noticed it.

"I don't do the elevators," he said.

Likely, no one had – disciplined maintenance was not exactly in the People's Republic wheelhouse, and what no one owned, no one took care of. The whole country was a living example of the tragedy of the commons.

Turnbull hoped it would not choose now to break completely and send them hurtling several hundred feet down to their doom.

It did not. Instead, it came to an unexpected halt at the 47th floor.

The door opened and four Kurylenko men stood there, AK-19s slung, patiently waiting for their car. Seeing a man with a heavily tricked-out M4 and a leaping Belgian Malinois was not on any of their bingo cards.

Gibson took out the one on the far left, probably the leader since he seemed the oldest and his neck was thickest. The other three went for their guns, but the first two were dead with a burst in their chests before their hands even reached their weapons. The third managed to get the sling off his shoulder before Turnbull put a burst into him.

The leader was screaming something in what was probably Ukrainian as he tried to keep the snapping fangs from his face. His bloody hands were grasping the dog, who did not appreciate it.

"Hit the hold button," Turnbull ordered Dobbs, who complied. It never occurred to either of them that he might not.

Turnbull checked the hallway for additional targets – it was all guest rooms – and, seeing none, walked out of the car into the hallway. He stepped over to the man-dog death match on the floor and pressed the end of the suppressor to the struggling man's forehead.

He fired once and the Ukrainian went limp. Gibson instantly let loose and sat down. Turnbull then put an insurance round into each of the other three foreheads.

Turnbull and Gibson walked back into the elevator. Turnbull dropped the mag from the well and replaced it with a fresh one.

"Guess our secret is out," he said as the doors slid shut.

Gasping for breath, Comrade Chico reached the 54th floor. There was a small window with chicken wire embedded in it in the heavy metal door to the hallway. He crept up and hid beneath the slit, out of sight.

He cradled the suppressed FN 5.7mm pistol in his hand.

Comrade Chico was so amped up on adrenaline that he did not even feel disgusted with himself for looking at his watch.

7:03.

The elevator was strenuously protesting as Turnbull held it open on the 53rd floor, waiting. The other two elevator banks were clearly both working – you could not miss the racket. He heard at least one car pass them heading up.

Not good. That would mean more bad guys.

Oh well, he thought, we're committed now.

At 7:04, he let the door close. The button reading "54" was illuminated.

The elevator began to move.

"We need to go!" Vasilev shouted.

"He's inside?" Scott shouted back, incredulous. Behind him, out the windows, the city was ablaze with tracers, fires, explosions and helicopters. The speakers on the radio frequencies were blaring – some People's Republic forces but most were American freqs. Their Chinese radio equipment was able to identify and lock in on some of the active US nets, even radio networks that were scrambled. A couple of captains in the People's Republic Anti-Colonial Military Land Forces were trying to figure out what "Broken Arrow" meant.

Scott knew, but ignored them. He had more important considerations at the forefront at the moment.

"Have you mobilized your men?" he demanded of the Ukrainian mercenary.

"Of course I have!" Vasilev snapped back, offended. "But that is irrelevant. I've ordered a helicopter to return. We need to take you out of here."

"But Turnbull!"

"You do not need to be here when we kill him!" shouted Vasilev. The dozen PR troops in the room were mortified at his disrespect to the general. One captain, a man with rouge, lipstick and pink fingernails, was actually in tears. But the mercenary did not stop.

"What, do you imagine you will kill him yourself?" Vasilev laughed bitterly.

Scott scowled, but before he could respond, one of the largest men any of them had ever seen entered the room with two other Kurylenko mercenaries.

"Sergeant Drago," Vasilev ordered. "Take the general to the roof. Get him out of here!"

"*Tak cep*," the behemoth bellowed, acknowledging the order. He slung his AK-19 rifle and began walking toward the general.

"Look at that!" one of the majors, who wore a noticeable diaper under his uniform as part of his infantilism lifestyle, was pointing out the window. Far below them, on the West Side near where the Midtown Secure Zone wall left Central Park, a pair of aircraft were doing gun runs along the streets.

And out in the Hudson, there were black shapes.

American ships. Lots of them.

7:04 flipped to 7:05. Comrade Chico was momentarily torn because he understood that a rigid adherence to time schedules was a primary symptom of white supremacy. Was this another test by Comrade Eddie? Was Comrade Eddie trying to flush out hidden racism within him that even the anti-racist animal companion could not detect?

He convinced himself that this was not the case, and that just this once he could do it. After all, these were exceptional circumstances. He reached up with his left hand and took hold of the door. Standing, he moved the handle downward until the lock disengaged and then pushed the door open.

The light from the nearly deserted hallway – he was not used to so much artificial illumination – flooded the stairwell – and then things happened fast. There was a soldier about four meters away with some kind of very fancy AK rifle in his hand, who turned as soon as the door opened and began bringing the weapon to bear.

Comrade Chico had the element of surprise – he had his weapon up first and fired. There was barely a noise – just a *pffft* sound – and almost no recoil at all. He observed no blood spray or splatter from or on his target, and did not see any impact at all. But the man stopped turning and bringing his gun up. He looked surprised, but he was still standing.

Comrade Chico fired again, then again, now concentrating on aiming center mass. The man wobbled but did not fall, yet he was still and his eyes were wide open.

Comrade Chico pushed the door open and stepped out even as he fired two more times. The mercenary took a step back, gasped and fell backwards, but on the carpet he was still moving. There was blood on the mercenary's tunic now.

Comrade Chico kept shooting him – he did not know how many rounds but the magazine seemed bottomless. Finally, he shot the man in the face, and there was a red bubble of blood on the man's forehead. Now he stopped moving.

Comrade Chico caught his breath, and then heard a ruckus around the corner. And gunfire.

The elevator door was not even a quarter open when Turnbull began to pump shots into the Kurylenko man standing in the hallway. The target dropped, the wall behind him painted with abstract red, and Turnbull put the *coup de grace* through his forehead just as the doors locked open.

"Stay!" he shouted to Gibson and Dobbs equally.

"To the right!" Dobbs offered as he cowered in the back corner of the car. His directions to the former Presidential Suite were confirmed by a hail of fire coming down the hall from that direction. It stopped for a moment and Turnbull leaned out – awkwardly, since he was a righty trying to shoot around a right corner – trying to expose as little of his body as he could to the shooter while trying to get a good sight picture through the close quarters optic.

The red dot found a Kurylenko shooter maybe 25 meters up the hall at the corner by some wood double doors. Turnbull fired a burst and the man returned the favor. Chunks of plaster exploded where the 5.56mm rounds – the AK-19 was designed for the export market and shot NATO ammo – hit. One shot dinged the metal doorway of the elevator car, punching a neat hole into it at shoulder level.

Turnbull returned fire with two bursts, and not all the rounds impacted his target. But the background was the doors of the Presidential Suite, and Turnbull did not care about his background. Still, the shooter clearly took a couple hits at least.

Now, from the other end of the hallway, there was more gunfire – distinctly AK-47 fire. Turnbull pivoted to engage, but it was Comrade Chico. Turnbull had him in his sights and considered pulling the trigger, but the voice of Gandalf remarking that even Gollum might have some use yet echoed in his head.

He turned back to the wounded shooter and fired again. The man faceplanted and was still. Comrade Chico still fired again and the rounds went through the door of the former Presidential Suite. There were a number of holes in it already. Bad day for anyone on the other side.

He dropped the mag, abandoning the few rounds left, and snapped in another. Comrade Chico loped up to him, panting.

"You made it," Turnbull said disinterestedly.

Then the building jolted back and forth like some giant had grabbed it and shook it.

A hail of rounds tore through the front door of the suite, hitting one of the Kurylenko men in the back of the head and the diaper major in the groin.

The dead and the howling wounded man did not seize Vasilev's attention. It was the fact that there was no sound of gunfire. Someone was firing suppressed.

Now the guard outside the door – obviously the intruder's target – was firing back with his unsuppressed AK-19. More rounds came through the doors, and if Sergeant Drago had not physically dragged General Scott toward the suite's private staircase leading up to the helicopter pad, it might have ended the red states renegade's career right then.

Vasilev drew his HK USP pistol and took charge even as the general was dragged away. There was more fire, but not AK-19. That was the sound of an AK-47 that he knew by heart. His guards out there were certainly dead.

"Get ready! Weapons on the door!" he shouted. "They're coming!"

Then the entire building lurched.

19.

The two 610mm M57 Army Tactical Missile System (ATACMS) surface-to-surface missiles, each with a 500-pound high-explosive warhead, roared out of the M270 Multiple Launch Rocket System Vehicle belonging to First Platoon, A Company, 2nd Battalion, 80th Field Artillery. The fire control center had been dealing with a problem that was rarely encountered in training – what happens when the target is a skyscraper? But the redlegs – artillerymen – had worked it out, and when the mission came down to suppress a landing zone on the roof of an enemy-occupied building in Manhattan, they came up with a firing solution and fed it to the gunners.

The launcher was parked in the parking lot of what had been the Meadowlands stadium. Soon after the Split, football had been outlawed in favor of mandatory soccer, which itself was later outlawed as "emblematic of the systemic hate crimes against the differently-abled and non-traditionally mobile Otherkin." Militant furries had complained, both in English and in their version of the sounds made by their animal fursonas, that they could not compete while wearing their fursuits. The People's Republic government saw the justice in their pleas, and the answer was to shut down the sport entirely. Thereafter the stadium was occasionally used as a venue for mandatory voluntary rallies against racism and such. Later, it was simply abandoned.

Now the US Army was occupying it as a logistics center and artillery fire base supporting Overlord. The M270 launcher that fired the strike on what had been the Mandarin Oriental was unwittingly parked right above the resting place of the buried body of Jimmy Hoffa.

The missiles, guided by a global positioning system (GPS) navigation system, had a range far beyond the eight-mile distance from the New Jersey launch site. The target was the roof where the Fire Support Officer (FSO) from the Pathfinders had said they had observed enemy helicopters a few minutes before. The gunners had looked at the mission and figured that dropping shells down on the roof was a pretty difficult challenge. In true US Army field artillery branch style, they decided it would be easier to just blow the top dozen floors off the skyscraper.

The twin rockets rose up over the Hudson then dived into Midtown, with one striking the 40th floor and the other the 42nd. The rockets went through the exterior glass windows of the guest rooms they struck and both detonated inside a fraction of a second later at about the center of the structure. Back at the fire control center, the redlegs eagerly waited for the battle damage assessment, for they really had no idea exactly what two ATACMS rockets hitting the high floors of a modern skyscraper would do, but they were very curious to hear.

The dual detonations were so nearly simultaneous that Turnbull did not distinguish them. In fact, he was busy flying off his feet and into the air over the hallway. He slammed back down hard on his face, ears ringing from the roar. It sounded like a 747 crashing into a freight train during a Motörhead concert back when Lemmy was drinking really hard.

The lights flashed off then went on again. Behind him, Gibson barked. Turnbull painfully looked back. The dog was okay. Dobbs was on his face, shaking it off, half in and half out of the open elevator car. Comrade Chico had been running when it went off and he was thrown against a table holding a Chinese vase that had been sitting under an ornate mirror in the hallway.

A curl of scarlet running down his forehead showed where he had hit the vase after being blown off his feet, and the mirror was shattered on the floor, covering him with shards.

The fire alarm went off, a loud, insistent series of head-splitting beeps.

"Was that a bomb?" Comrade Chico asked as he shook off the glass and retrieved his AK-47.

"That or the loudest party ever," Turnbull said, standing up after securing his rifle. Dobbs was getting to his feet as well. There was a rumble and a groan, like steel being bent. Turnbull put his hand against the wall and tried to feel whether the building was tilting. He was not sure.

"Dobbs, check the elevators," he ordered.

Dobbs went back inside the car, which had dropped a full foot. You could see the shaft in the space at the top of the doorway. The doors were not even attempting to close.

"No good," Dobbs said. "The system is offline."

"How are we getting out?" Comrade Chico asked, concerned.

"The same way you came up. The stairs. After we get Deeds."

"Well, where is xe?" Comrade Chico demanded of Dobbs. Dobbs pointed toward the Presidential Suite at the far corner of the hallway.

"Around that corner there."

"Let's go," Turnbull said over the incessant beeping of the fire alarm, leading with his M4. Gibson trotted beside him and so did Dobbs, who had grabbed his tool bag and followed.

"Cover our rear!" Turnbull directed Comrade Chico, who looked back the way he had come. Nothing. He followed.

They moved toward the doors, which had a sign reading "Temporary Rotating Executive Suite" on it. The capital "R" was shattered by a bullet. In fact, there were a dozen holes in the wood. And from the other side, there was noise – voices and an occasional moan. Maybe some of those shots had taken someone down inside.

Good.

They got to the door and Turnbull paused to clear the hallway to the left. Nothing and no one. He took a breath. Now Turnbull's mind went to a meme that Casey Warner had showed him years before during some downtime – he still remembered it even though he only saw it for a split-second before he pushed it away, demanding that his comrade "Get your stupid internet incel crap out of my face."

It was a sweaty cartoon superhero choosing between two red buttons.

Turnbull did not remember what the buttons were labeled in the meme, but he knew his choices here. Behind that door was probably General Karl Martin Scott – and a bunch of armed toadies. He could go through it. The other choice was to go get Clay Deeds.

Red Button One – kill the treasonous son of a bitch. Red Button Two – save his friend.

"Crap," Turnbull said. "Where is Deeds?"

"I think xe's in 54-175 or 54-177."

Of course, that would be at the far end of the hall, past the edge of the suite, Turnbull thought.

"Watch for anyone coming out of that suite," he ordered Comrade Chico without missing a step. Comrade Chico kept turning to ensure no one slipped in behind them.

The lights flashed and the building groaned.

Turnbull kept moving, his weapon up and ready.

The alarm's beeping made it hard for him to be heard, but Vasilev was used to yelling.

"Get up! Get your weapons!" he shouted.

"Is the building going to fall down?" cried one of the People's Republic Anti-Colonial Military Land Forces officers, a young lieutenant – he/him. He had learned in class about how freedom fighters before the Split had once collapsed the World Trade Center, a hated symbol of American imperialism, right here in

New York City. In fact, September 11th, "Deserved Retribution Day," was a school holiday.

Vasilev went to the window, which was cracked but not shattered – all of them were on this floor. Smoke was pouring out of a hole in the side of the skyscraper and curling up past their command post on the 54th floor in thick, black, roiling clouds. Whatever hit the old Mandarin hit several floors down. He had no idea what it was that struck it – a bomb, a shell, a missile – and he did not particularly care.

Vasilev ignored the whimpering LT and surveyed the tableau below through breaks in the smoke. There were orange streaks coming from New Jersey over the water and impacting in the dark of the unsecured areas of Manhattan. Out on the water, there were various shapes briefly illuminated by orange bursts – naval gunfire. One of the ships was much bigger than the others, but from here it simply looked like a giant black sea serpent.

"Redleg-1, this is Pathfinder Gunner, BDA on that Mandarin strike," came a call from the radio squawk box monitoring the American net. Vasilev knew the acronym "BDA" – "battle damage assessment."

"We saw two impacts of your ATACMS, near the top. It's still there, though, how copy?"

"Copy Pathfinder, you want more?"

"Uh, wait one, we got other missions, over," the FSO replied.

A reprieve. He took up his Motorola.

"Drago, the general?"

"I have him, major," replied Drago. The beat of the rotors came over loud in the background.

"Take him to the alternate location. I will meet you there. All other aircraft, be ready to take the rest of the Kurylenko team off the roof when I call!"

"What about us!" whimpered the terrified lieutenant.

"What about you?" sneered the mercenary.

Deeds had been lying on the floor for the last few hours, his hands chained to the radiator under the blinds-drawn window with about two feet of slack. Dimitri had been sitting in an orange chair, tossing dying cigarette butts at him for amusement. He had laid an HK USP .45 in his lap.

"Are you going to let me loose to use the bathroom?" Deeds asked.

Dimitri laughed.

"You can piss yourself, American," he laughed.

"I'll hold it," Deeds replied.

There was a noise in the distance. It might have been a shot, but it was muffled. Dimitri stopped smiling. Deeds watched him. Then there was nothing further, he relaxed again and lit a new Marlboro, the last of his Red American stash.

"Smoking is bad for your health," Deeds observed.

"Shut up," Dimitri said.

"So is screwing with me."

"Shut up!" Dimitri said again, this time more emphatically. He punctuated his comment with a vicious kick to Deeds's leg.

There was a distant burst of automatic fire, then another and another. Dimitri was on his feet now, the pistol in his hand, straining to listen. The gunfire stopped.

He turned and pointed the weapon at Deeds, but paused, considering.

The blast of the two 500-pound warheads several floors below was still enough to lift them both off the floor, though the chain kept Deeds from flying too far. Not so Dimitri – he was lifted a full four feet into the air and he crashed down hard on his back beside Deeds.

The gun bounced out of his hand, but Dimitri did not seem to notice as he got his bearings, shaking his head to clear the fog.

The fire alarm sounded. Beep beep beep – each one louder than the last.

Deeds delivered a vicious kick to the mercenary's face, connecting, then another. Dimitri rolled away, out of range of further blows. Deeds began looking for the gun.

It was there, on the floor, under the orange chair. He pulled his legs over and began maneuvering the weapons with his feet, trying to pull it close, into the range of his bound hands. The lights flashed off then back on.

Dimitri turned onto his belly and pushed himself up. A sticky trail of blood and saliva dripped down from his mouth to the carpeting. There was a groan – not from him, not even human, but the sound of stressed and agonized steel. And the incessant beeping continued.

Deeds caught the butt of the automatic with his heel and pulled it closer, but lost his grip. He tried again, caught it, and pulled it a bit closer again.

Dimitri shook his head again, spraying drops of blood around. He turned his head over at Deeds.

Deeds bent to bring his legs to so they could pull the gun to where his hands were. It was close now. He strained to reach it.

Dimitri rose up to his feet, the blood from his mouth pouring down his shirt. On the floor, his last cigarette was burning the carpet.

Deeds kicked one more time and his fingers touched the butt of the German handgun, but as he sought to close them around it Dimitri was there, ripping it away.

Deeds rolled back, staring his captor in the face, defiant.

Dimitri spit a wad of blood on the carpet.

"I start shooting at your feet and work up," he promised.

There was a noise from behind them at the front of the guest room. Dimitri spun about, bringing the weapon up. Deeds could not see, but even over the endless beeping of fire alarm, he heard two *pffft* sounds.

Dimitri fell backwards, into the orange chair, the pistol falling to the floor. His tunic was already bloody, so it was unclear where he was hit, but he was certainly hit. And probably in the chest. He was gasping for air.

Turnbull came in and swept the room, announcing "Clear" from force of habit.

"I'm very glad to see you, Kelly," Deeds said. Turnbull shook his head "No." Two other men, whom he did not know, one with an AK-47, came in as well. And Gibson trotted over and licked his face.

"Get him loose," Turnbull ordered Dobbs, who approached with his tool kit and began to comply. The other man with the rifle, who looked a bit like Che's dumber little brother, stood at his feet.

"Professor Deeds, it is an honor," Comrade Chico said.

"Okay," Deeds said as Dobbs did his work.

"I am proud to meet the world's foremost authority on Marxist-Leninist-Kendi thought."

Deeds's eyes flicked away to meet Turnbull's; Turnbull's rolled.

"I am Comrade Chico, of the POUM!" he said proudly.

"Of course you are," Deeds said.

"There you go," said Dobbs, snapping the cuffs off. Deeds rubbed his wrists and slowly, carefully stood up.

"Thank you," he said. The beeping was still going on, and the building groaned again.

"I think we got bombed," Turnbull said.

"I assume you have a plan to get us out of here," Deeds said.

"I had one. The elevators are out. Plan B is the stairs. We should go."

"You kill Scott yet?"

"It was that or you. You want me to rethink my choice?" Turnbull sounded like he did.

"Who is Scott?" asked Comrade Chico.

"We're leaving," Turnbull said. He thought about smoking the POUM leader right then, but he could use another gunman.

"Just a moment, I need to do a couple things," Deeds said. He looked around the floor and then bent over to pick up the USP .45.

He leveled it at Dimitri, who was still gasping, but with his eyes open and blinking.

"I warned you that screwing with me was bad for your health," Deeds said pleasantly. Dimitri's eyes bulged as Deeds fired twice into his gut. Deeds waited a moment and the man groaned.

"Look at me," Deeds commanded, and then repeated it louder. "Look at me!"

Dimitri's eyes slowly rose, reluctantly and fearfully, and met his. Deeds shot him right between them. Much of the back of Dimitri's head was now defacing the wallpaper.

"People's justice," Comrade Chico said approvingly.

"Now let's go," Turnbull directed.

"I said *two* things," Deeds replied. "Now, I'm going to use the bathroom."

The four of them went out the door back into the hallway, but continued on the way they had been coming so as not to go back by the Presidential Suite and the potential enemy inside. They made a left. The south hall was empty, and they moved down it fast with weapons up.

The alarms continued and so did the groans of the building. Comrade Chico made no 9/11-related comment – Turnbull probably would have shot him if he had. Instead, Comrade Chico had another question.

"What about Comrade Paloma?"

"She's probably with Karla," Turnbull said, which he felt was probably true in the figurative sense. If they had not seen her running around the floor, she was probably dead.

Dobbs giggled.

"Are you disrespecting her? Unlike you, she's a valuable asset to the revolution!"

"Screw your revolution," Dobbs said.

"See what the lack of ideological discipline has done?" Comrade Chico complained to Deeds as they turned the next corner. The hallway was clear up to the body of the mercenary Comrade Chico had shot multiple times outside the door to the stairwell.

"We must have patience with those whose commitment to the revolution is lacking," Deeds replied smoothly. He had Dimitri's USP in his hand.

"That does not sound like Marxist-Leninist-Kendi thought as I understand it," Comrade Chico said.

"Maybe you just don't understand it," Turnbull said. "Now stop talking."

Comrade Chico fumed, but kept walking, occasionally swinging his weapon to the rear to cover their six.

Turnbull held them up at the sturdy metal stairwell door. He tried to look inside through the glass slit but saw nothing.

"It goes up to the roof, but that door is locked, and of course it goes all the way down to the street," Dobbs said.

"Roof's not going to do us any good," Turnbull said. "Once we're in we need to move fast down the stairs. No lagging, no running your mouths. Just move. Dobbs, you don't have a weapon so stay behind us. Ready?"

Comrade Chico grunted. Deeds nodded.

Turnbull pushed open the door and immediately fired at the half-dozen shapes he saw coming up the stairs. Two Ukrainains caught rounds that splattered the dingy walls behind them with their blood. The survivors struggled to react but the bodies of their buddies fell on them and Turnbull was back through the door and into the hallway before they could hit him with return fire.

The band backed away further down the hallway as AK-19 rounds tore through the door.

Turnbull stood back and emptied his mag through the metal door into the stairwell. If his weapon had not been suppressed, they would probably all be deaf. There were yells and Slavic screams from the other side that they could hear over the beeping of the alarm.

"Can you lock this door?" Turnbull yelled to Dobbs.

"Yeah," he said, scared.

"Then lock it!"

"They'll shoot me!"

"*I'll* shoot you! Lock it."

Dobbs stepped up with his key ring and put one in the slot then turned it. There was a click, and then more bullets punched through. Dobbs jumped back.

Turnbull, back several feet, dropped his empty mag and reloaded.

"Okay, the stairs are out. Any other way off this floor?"

"There's a private access door to the roof in the Presidential Suite," Dobbs said. "I don't know what good that will do."

"Well, it puts some distance between us and these bastards," Turnbull said. "Let's go."

"Sir, we are in the stairwell, taking fire from the 54th floor!"

"Fight through it!" Vasilev shouted into his radio. The building chose that minute to shake and shimmy.

He had two Kurylenko men left in the Presidential Suite command post – he did not count the half-dozen PR soldiers who were in various states of emotional collapse as they pondered the potential for a building collapse. He gestured for his men to come forward to the doors to the hallway.

"The enemy is out there," he whispered to them, aiming his USP.

Perhaps he would finally come face to face with this legendary Kelly Turnbull.

Turnbull sat covering the Suite's doors as Dobbs went back in the elevator car to see if he could get it working. Deeds went with him. Comrade Chico covered back toward the stairwell door where they had come from. There were occasional bursts of fire from that direction.

"No good," Dobbs said, and Turnbull was in the midst of answering when the Presidential Suite door cracked open.

A face appeared.

With a scar.

And a black pistol in his hand.

The man did not fire – the face's eyes bulged.

"You!" Turnbull yelled and he dropped his eye to his recce rifle's optic.

The man's handgun went off, randomly firing as Vasilev pulled back, slammed the door shut, and dropped to the carpet. A swarm of rounds from Turnbull's recce rifle tore through the door where he had been standing a fraction of a second before. The mercenary scuttled out of the path.

He laughed. He found it hilarious.

"So, *you* are the Kelly Turnbull the general kept talking about!" Vasilev yelled. "I am not surprised!"

"That one's the Kurylenko head honcho, Major Vasilev," Deeds whispered from the car. Turnbull was locked onto the doors with his red-dot.

"Scar? Bad attitude? Needs to die?"

"So you've met?" Deeds replied.

"Liberia," Turnbull said. "Did not get along."

"Hello? I know you are out there," Vasilev yelled from behind the door.

"Why don't you send the general out," Turnbull yelled. "I'm old friends with him too."

"I guess your late friend Deeds was right about you. Sorry about what Dimitri did to him. Orders!"

"The best part of Dimitri's head is dripping off a wall. Deeds is with us. How about you send out the general and I let you live?"

"Tempting offer, but the general has flown away."

The building shook and groaned again.

"I think there is a fuse on this discussion, Kelly," Deeds said.

"What is this?" Comrade Chico said.

"Keep watching our back!" snapped Turnbull. Comrade Chico did not respond.

"Why don't you come in and we can chat?" Vasilev yelled. He waited for Turnbull to reply. Then his Motorola cracked.

"Inbound, sixty seconds!" the pilot said in Ukrainian.

Vasilev sighed. The building shook again, settling in a new and unstable posture. He saw one of his shell casings on the floor start rolling toward the windows.

"This is not good," Dobbs shouted as the building shifted.

"When in doubt," Turnbull told Deeds, "go full auto."

He flipped his selector switch and began walking forward, weapon up and on the door.

Vasilev stepped out of the private entrance to the landing pad on the roof and was instantly buffeted by the cold wind. He looked out over the city, immune to the effect of the height. He had started as a soldier fighting Russian invaders as a paratrooper in Ukraine's 25th Airborne Brigade, nicknamed "Sicheslav," with the motto "No One But Us," and he had so many jumps to his credit that he had ceased counting and logging them. The other two Kurylenko men with him were not so jaded – they grew a bit woozy as they paused to survey the chaos below them while their commander shouted into his Motorola.

Smoke was rising from the west side of the building, thick and oily. Beyond it, they could see the firefights clearly in the dark areas outside the Secure Zone walls. But the power was still on inside the Midtown Secure Zone, and as they looked south the lights of the Times Square signs were still flashing.

There were jets above them and helicopters below – mostly Blackhawks. Americans. The men stared even as the major shouted into the Kurylenko radio net.

There was a whoosh of air and a roar of rotors.

A Kurylenko AH-6 flew in through the smoke and landed on the pad.

As Vasilev and his men got aboard, the building shifted again.

It was some small consolation that Turnbull was going to die, even if it was not by his hand.

Turnbull kicked open the door to the Presidential Suite and sprayed two uniformed PR soldiers, one of whom had evidently had surgery to make him look like a badger or some such, before they could bring their Berettas to bear. Gibson slipped in and went straight at the survivors. The wounded one with the bullet through the diaper moaned and the other three surrendered, tossing their weapons away and sobbing.

The dog watched them with bared teeth, The other three members of the crew came inside and Dobbs shut the door behind them.

"Watch the door," Turnbull told Comrade Chico.

"What about them?" the POUM leader asked, nudging his barrel toward the pathetic mass of prisoners.

"Don't waste bullets," Turnbull said. He slung his M4.

"This was the command post," Deeds said. "Scott stage-managed the fight from here."

"The suite covers most of this side of the building. The general's room is that way. There's a private access stair to the rooftop over there," Dobbs added, pointing to a corridor.

The building shuddered. It groaned.

"I think the fuse is burning down," Turnbull observed.

"Crimson-2, this is Crimson-1 actual, over," came a voice over the squawk box.

"Crimson-1, we're getting heavy automatic fire from Central Park, over."

"Roger, call in fire support. Get on the fire support net, out."

Turnbull was baffled. So was Deeds.

"Is that?" asked Deeds. He was smiling.

"Holy crap, it is," Turnbull said. He grabbed a radio handset off a table and made some adjustments to the radio.

"What are you doing?" Comrade Chico asked, baffled. The building shook again. He looked around, scared. So did Dobbs.

"Getting us a ride," Turnbull said. "Crimson-1, this is Turnbull. That you, junior?"

Turnbull had basically set fire to Army radio procedures, but the military had set fire to the building so he felt they were even.

Junior Ryan knew the voice when it came over the ops net. It somehow did not surprise him that Kelly Turnbull would be in the midst of this Manhattan maelstrom. He keyed his mic.

"Last sending station, are you kilo tango?" he said. "Kilo tango was "KT" in the phonetic alphabet.

"Roger that," Kelly Turnbull replied. "I need a lift, over."

"Little busy, over."

"Crimson-1, you bombed our building and now there's no way down. How about a pick-up off the roof lima zulu, over?" Turnbull requested, referring to the rooftop landing zone.

Major Ryan leaned out the open door of his Blackhawk and into the wind over the body of his door gunner. A few minutes before, the poor guy had caught a random round under his chin fired by some strung-out freak with a Kalashnikov blazing away into the sky.

In the distance, there was a lot of smoke and some tongues of flame licking up the side of the old Mandarin Hotel where the ATACMS missiles had punched through.

"Mandarin, over?"

"Roger that."

"I copy, are you up top, over?"

"We will be. When can you execute a pick-up, over?" Turnbull asked.

"Two mikes, see you up top, out." Ryan hit the intercom and told his pilot where to go.

They had two minutes to get up there.

Turnbull put down the handset and, having decided enough was enough, prepared to wheel around and put a bullet in Comrade Chico. But he saw Deeds and Dobbs both looking distressed. He turned, slowly.

Comrade Chico was covering them with his weapon.

"Not again," Turnbull said.

"I want to know what this is!" the POUM leader shouted. The building groaned again. Turnbull weighed his options, and none were good. He put his hands out where the POUM leader could see them. Gibson turned and gave the anarchist a death stare, waiting for the word from Turnbull.

"If that fake anti-racist dog comes at me, he dies!" Comrade Chico told him.

"Are you calling his dog racist?" Dobbs laughed.

"Shut up!" Comrade Chico snapped.

"Word of advice, Chico," Turnbull said. "Do not threaten a man's dog."

"I am in charge!" Comrade Chico declared, though not particularly emphatically.

"This is where you make a decision," Turnbull said. "About living or dying. See, this building is going to come down and us with it unless we get into that US Army Blackhawk that's coming to take us off."

"Who are you?" Comrade Chico demanded. He looked at Deeds. "Aren't you the leading authority on Marxist-Leninist-Kendi thought?"

"Not exactly," Deeds said. He kept his hands away from the USP tucked in his belt.

"You're a red racist transphobe imperialist," Comrade Chico said to Turnbull in a voice entirely free of irony. "You used me."

"Imperialists gonna be imperial," said Turnbull. He did not know what it meant, but it sounded good at the time.

"I thought you were part of the vanguard of Marxist-Leninist-Kendi anarchist thought!" he exclaimed, betraying genuine dismay.

"You understand that Marxist-Leninist-Kendi thought is the precise opposite of anarchist thought, right?" laughed Dobbs. The maintenance man could not help himself. "You utter buffoon."

Comrade Chico pivoted and shot him twice in the chest. The barrel was back on Turnbull before Turnbull could reach his Wilson Beretta.

"Are you going to laugh at me too?" Comrade Chico sneered. The People's Republic prisoners were whimpering. Gibson was eyeing his throat, awaiting the signal to tear it out or die trying.

"I could have killed you a hundred times," Turnbull said, eschewing any sudden moves. "But I didn't. Don't screw up now. We are your ticket off this sinking ship. So think about your next move."

"You're flying me off this roof and flying me back to the POUM," Comrade Chico declared in a monotone. "Or I'll kill you both. And your racist dog."

"You're gonna fly," Turnbull promised. He looked down on the floor at the dead Dobbs, then back to Comrade Chico. "You have my word on that."

Vasilev was monitoring the American ops net from his AH-6. He had already confirmed that Scott was safe on the ground outside the city. He had earned his hefty fee. Now his mission was getting his four helicopters off the island too. They were keeping low, slipping through the concrete canyons of Manhattan, nearing the East River. Luckily, American special ops used the same aircraft, so the American choppers they encountered did not open fire. The quartet of mercenary aircraft were almost out of danger.

Then he heard Turnbull's exchange with Major Ryan.

He considered his options.

"Turn around," he ordered on the Kurylenko radio net. His pilot, veteran of a hundred aerial insertions in the Donbas, pitched left between two skyscrapers and headed back, with the rest of the squadron in tow.

Vasilev smiled at the irony as he realized that for all his frustration with General Scott's single-minded focus, he now shared the renegade's overriding goal.

Kill that son of a whore Kelly Turnbull.

20.

Comrade Chico followed Deeds, Turnbull, and his racist canine nemesis as they made their way up the back staircase that led to the rooftop landing pad's private access door. Both the prisoners kept their hands well clear of their weapons. Comrade Chico was quite agitated, but not so much that he failed to keep his rifle covering his captives.

Turnbull looked for an opportunity to draw or some other way out of this, but he assessed each prospective course of action as too likely to result in a bullet in Gibson or his or Deeds's back – or all three.

The roof was windy, with the cold blowing across the landing pad. There was smoke from the building's gaping wound in its west face. And there was a noticeable lean to the structure now.

On the way out, one of the PR soldiers had asked Turnbull, "What about us?"

He replied, "What about you?"

He was actually wondering, but that was not his problem. However, he did feel good about leaving the cooks with an axe to chop their way out of the walk-in. Without Karla there – well, without Karla there *and* breathing – the worker bees would be able to free themselves and get out.

High over the island, they oriented themselves to the tableau below. Manhattan was a battleground. Angry aircraft dived in and out while helicopters buzzed about in the night sky. A thousand fires burned, and tracers flew up, down, and across all over the dark of the unsecure areas. Improbably, the electricity was still on in the Midtown Secure Zone, and the Times Square lights flashed as they had before, heedless of the war all round them, the only difference being that there was anti-air fire coming from the streets where previous to the Split tourists, grifters, and perverts had cavorted.

After the Split, the tourists were mostly gone.

There was a lot of activity out on the water and along the New Jersey shoreline. The invasion was coming, and the Navy was already there. As Turnbull watched, a huge orange and black sphere erupted around an enormous, dark shape in the midst of the Hudson River. There was no sound because it was so far off, but the flash was intense.

"Never thought I'd see the *USS Iowa* in action," Turnbull said, striking another entry off his bucket list. The battleship had been a floating museum in Long Beach, California, at the time of the Split, but the US took her back to Pascagoula, Mississippi, for refitting before the country broke apart.

The massive dreadnaught was actually at home here – the veteran of World War II and Korea had been launched from the New York Naval Shipyard in 1942. It was bringing only one of its 16-inch guns to bear on a target inside Manhattan, but even one of the nine barrels was devastating. The thunderous boom of the shot hit them seconds later, and off in the northern reaches of Central Park, there was a huge explosion among the trees in the dark – the shell weighed 2,700 pounds.

Turnbull wondered what a full broadside could do.

But the events unfolding below them were lost on their captor. He was concerned with more mundane issues, like not dying when the building collapsed.

"Where is it?" Comrade Chico demanded. "You said it was coming!"

Turnbull pointed. A Blackhawk helicopter was heading in for a landing through the smoke.

"Don't try anything!" Comrade Chico warned, brandishing his rifle.

"I'm good for my word," Turnbull said.

The helicopter set down and the three moved forward. Turnbull recognized Ryan and smiled. Behind the Pathfinder commander were his fire support officer and S-3 Air, both busy on their radios. There was also a body.

Ryan was covering the trio with his own M4. He lowered it and smiled back. Gibson leapt aboard the aircraft uninvited and made his way into the middle of the compartment, where he lay down.

"You brought a dog?" shouted the Pathfinder major.

"Of course," Turnbull said. "And I brought this guy here who's going to shoot us if we don't give him a ride back to his fellow communists."

"I'm an anarchist, a Marxist-Leninist-Kendiist!" Comrade Chico shouted, his weapon not wavering.

"We're going to play it cool," Turnbull told Ryan, who now had his M4 on the POUM leader. "We're getting on and then he's getting off. Nobody's shooting anybody."

"Okay," said Ryan, confused at hearing Turnbull taking a stand against shooting people.

"Me first!" demanded Comrade Chico, sidling up to the aircraft but covering Deeds.

"I've always wanted to load a communist into a helicopter," Turnbull said, gesturing for Comrade Chico to hop in. The POUM leader did, careful to keep his gun on Deeds. He sat on the edge of the aircraft, the gun not moving from its target.

Next, Turnbull helped Deeds aboard and the spy moved back into the interior. Then Turnbull hopped up himself.

"Now we go back to the base!" Comrade Chico ordered.

"I'll drop you off, just like I promised," Turnbull said.

"You better," Comrade Chico said.

"Go," said Ryan into the intercom, and the helicopter lifted off.

Comrade Chico's gun barrel was now pointed directly at Turnbull's liver.

"No tricks," he instructed, as the chopper pulled away from the roof, through the smoke, and flew out over the former Columbus Circle.

"Who is this guy again, Kelly?" Ryan demanded.

"I am the leader of the POUM!" snapped Comrade Chico.

"The poo?" Ryan asked, confused.

"The POUM!" insisted Comrade Chico, breaking his concentration for just enough time to allow Turnbull's left hand to grab and pull the AK's barrel outward while his right cross connected hard with the adherent of Marxist-Leninist-Kendi thought's left cheek. Blood, and a couple teeth, sprayed out into the wind.

Comrade Chico managed to fire a burst at the empty sky, but his grip on the rifle loosened as the reality of his shattered jaw swept over him. Turnbull tore the Kalashnikov from his hands, tossing it out of the chopper into space.

He grabbed the woozy POUM leader by the lapels.

"I told you that you'd fly," Turnbull shouted above the roar of the twin turbines, and threw him out of the Blackhawk. The last Turnbull saw, Comrade Chico was hurtling to the ground back-first, his arms flailing, screaming. He would fall about 1500 feet and accelerate to just about terminal velocity, 121 miles per hour, before landing directly on the top of the Megan Rapinoe statue's purple head and painting it red with his innards.

"Communists and helicopters, they go great together," Turnbull said to Ryan. "At least until the chopper gets to altitude. Then they need to go their separate ways."

"Technically, I think he was an anarchist," Deeds observed.

"Don't care," Turnbull replied, amused by the splatter below.

His amusement lasted for only a second. Then there were sparks and the spray of metal fragments.

"Damn it!" Ryan shouted and the helicopter banked and tore down 8th Avenue. The American pilot, a Chief Warrant Officer 4, had flown missions over Fallujah and Kandahar and did not need orders from some ground-pounder passenger to tell him to get the hell out of there. Four armed AH-6s were in pursuit, and the UH-60 was outgunned.

The Blackhawk had reacted fast to the attack, a spray of 7.62mm rounds from the forward machine guns in Vasilev's lead AH-6 Little Bird. The mercenary had assumed the co-pilot's seat, and while he was not rated on the aircraft he could fly it if need be. But the pilot had extensive experience starting with the war with the Russians and besides, if he wasn't good Vasilev would not have hired him.

"Close in and I'll kill them," Vasilev ordered. He had control of the forward-mounted machine guns.

The Ukrainian pilot accelerated, and the four men hanging off the side with their weapons held on.

"Who the hell are they?" Ryan demanded as Turnbull slipped on the dead gunner's commo helmet. The headphones were integral to it, so Turnbull could now hear the intercom.

"Ukrainian mercenaries," Turnbull said, like that should satisfy the query.

"Why are they trying to kill you?" Ryan yelled. "And now us too?"

"Everyone's always trying to kill me," Turnbull said. More bullets tore by, one in five of them a tracer.

He unslung his rifle from his shoulder and leaned out the open door, then pulled back as another volley of shots tore past.

"There's three or four of them!" Turnbull yelled.

He leaned back out, bringing his recce rifle up and firing two bursts. No effect. He fired again, then pulled back.

The Blackhawk was roaring down 8th Avenue, still in the Midtown Secure Zone so the lights were on. The pilot took them low, maybe thirty feet off the deck and the rotor tips spinning closer than Turnbull liked to the high-rises lining the street.

Down below, people were running to and fro – and some were firing upwards at the helicopters.

Vasilev was in the lead helicopter, Kurylenko-1, and it followed the Blackhawk down into the concrete canyon. The challenge was that 8th Avenue was nowhere near wide enough to fly two aircraft abreast, meaning only his AH-6 could bring its front-mounted machine guns to bear. The American pilot was good, really good. If Kurylenko had been a fan of American movies, he might have thought the warrant officer was using the Force, but he was no fan of American cinema, or anything else American.

"I have you now!" Vasilev yelled. As co-pilot he was operating the mounted machine guns. He fired, and the tracers launched from the aircraft's sides, joined by bursts from the riflemen plinking as best they could while leaning out of the aircraft.

No apparent effect, but the same was true of the American leaning out the side of the Blackhawk to shoot back at him with a rifle.

Turnbull fired again at the lead pursuer, the brass spilling out of his weapon's breech and falling to the ground.

"Take the gun!" Ryan yelled into the intercom.

"The gun?"

"The minigun!"

Turnbull noted the unmanned mounted multi-barrel electric cannon.

"Yeah, makes sense," he conceded, slinging his recce rifle and flipping on the weapon system. Ryan pulled something around his gut – a safety strap.

"I'm not having you fly out," he said into the intercom.

"I'm no commie," Turnbull said. He saw he could not bring the weapon to bear on the aircraft directly behind them. He could only fire to the starboard side.

"We need to change the dynamic," Turnbull said to Ryan over the intercom. "Can he take a left?"

"Close in!" Vasilev ordered his pilot. "We have to get closer!"

The pilot obliged, gunning the engine. The little aircraft began to make up ground. Below them, the Secure Zone wall cut in and began running north-south down the middle of 8th Avenue.

Then the Blackhawk swung left heading east above West 50th Street, a much narrower road. Vasilev's chopper was going too fast and could not make the turn, but the remaining aircraft in line did.

The Blackhawk pulled up and then to the right once it was down West 50th, clearing the lower buildings on the south side – the north side was dominated by a skyscraper.

The American aircraft turned hard, with Deeds grabbing onto the dog so that the puppy did not slide out. Turnbull was at the minigun, which he could now target against one of the enemy helicopters.

"All yours!" the pilot said over the intercom.

The target was Kurylenko-2, a pursuing AH-6 Little Bird with Ukrainians sitting in the doorways on both sides. Its pilot was heading east down West 50th below them, having not seen the Blackhawk's maneuver. The gunners in the right-side door did though, and they were firing on full auto at the hovering American aircraft above them and to the right.

Turnbull ignored the *ping* of an AK round puncturing the sheet metal and brought the minigun to bear.

"Adios," he said.

The minigun fired about 3,000 rounds a minute, raining the empty shells on the buildings below. Turnbull only had it going for about two seconds, enough for a hundred rounds to stitch across the left side of the enemy aircraft. The bullets shredded the two Ukrainian pilots and actually tore up all four of the mercenary shooters sitting in the doors – the two facing out the other way never knew what hit them.

The Ukrainian aircraft kept flying unguided and veered right, smashing into the side of the Brill Building at Broadway and West 49th. The Brill Building was the one-time hub of early Sixties popular music and was currently the home of the People's Republic's "Popular Music Review and Licensing Board" that approved or disapproved all musical recordings and performances. In fact, the Little Bird crashed into the floor housing the "Anti-Cultural Appropriation Protection Division" which, among other things, enforced the PR's bans on white rappers, Asian classical musicians, and black barbershop quartets.

The third and fourth AH-6 made the turn east onto West 50th Street just in time to see the ship in front of them riddled with minigun rounds.

The lead chopper, Kurylenko-3, pivoted and launched a missile from its side rail, a Hellfire that was not designed as an air-to-air weapon but that still got the Blackhawk's attention. The American pilot pulled right hard back over the street, with the rocket shooting past them closer than Turnbull would have liked. The missile launch spoiled his aim and now the two aircraft were behind him and he was unable to bring the minigun to bear.

The Blackhawk picked up speed as the two choppers chasing it sought to bring their front-mounted machine guns to bear. High-rises flashed by on both sides. Passing over 6th Street, Turnbull could see the deep hole where the Fox building had once stood. After the Split, PR tore it down and sought to replace it with "Anti-Disinformation Park," but never got around to building it.

The American helicopter picked up speed, with the former 30 Rock – the enormous Rockefeller Center – passing on its right. It housed NBC before the Split, and it now held the fully nationalized and licensed NBC, which endlessly spouted leftist propaganda and anti-American hatred. In other words, there had been no significant changes at the network since the country fell apart.

"You still got rounds?" the pilot yelled over the intercom.

"Yeah," Turnbull yelled back. "Just get me a shot."

"Hold on!"

At 5th Avenue, the Blackhawk banked left hard, with everyone but Turnbull grabbing onto something to keep from spilling out onto the street below. Turnbull kept hold of the minigun's grips, waiting for the pursuing AH-6s to come into his sights.

They passed in front of the former St. Patrick's Cathedral, which had been deconsecrated after the Roman Catholic Church had lost its religious organization license for good, with the final straw being its refusal to consecrate abortion until the "eleventh trimester," or two years old. The PR then confiscated all church property, giving much of it to the government-approved People's Catholic Church but, in the case of St. Patrick's, turning it over to a consortium of druids, satanists, and Methodists.

The soaring twin spires were still standing upright even if their religious iconography had been stripped off. The Blackhawk banked again, this time to the right, making a hard turn around them and using them for cover. The two pursuing Little Birds flew left at 5th too, and found their target gone for a split second before it reappeared above them from behind the towering spires.

Turnbull opened up with the minigun, the fingers of fire leaping from the rotating gun barrels and the *whirrrrrr* of the engine spinning it filling the chopper. The lead helicopter, Kurylenko-3, caught the full brunt of the fusillade, with Turnbull keeping the spray directed at the pilot's cockpit. The helicopter burst into flames and plowed straight into the glass and steel high-rise next door to the ex-church. A fireball erupted out of the side of the building where the helicopter had gone in.

The other chopper wisely kept going, heading uptown on 5th Avenue. Turnbull sprayed a burst after it, but then the gun stopped shooting.

Dry.

"Crap," said Turnbull.

"Let's get out of here!" Ryan ordered the pilot. Then the sound of metal hitting metal filled the compartment, along with smoke and spraying oil.

Vasilev depressed the trigger and the guns erupted. The AH-6 kicked as it flew up 5th Avenue on a straight line course for the Blackhawk hovering over what looked like a giant gothic church. Having missed the turn down West 50th, he directed his pilot to go down another block and shadow the chase. He had heard what happened to Kurylenko-2 on the radio and he had witnessed the destruction of Kurylenko-3 as he came up 5th Avenue from the south. But that sacrifice had allowed him to get into position to unload on Kelly Turnbull's helicopter.

And it was clear that the rounds hit home. The Americans' cockpit was shattered and there was smoke trailing from the body of the Blackhawk, but the chopper still tore away and flashed past him, heading southwest.

"Kurylenko-4," Vasilev called on the radio. "Come back and follow me. He's wounded and we will finish him!"

The rounds from Vasilev's chopper had not just ripped up the Blackhawk. The fire support officer had caught a couple in his lower chest. He was turning pale.

"My co-pilot's dead," said the pilot over the intercom. "And I'm hit too. Both engines are hit. We're losing power. We're going down."

Turnbull leaned out the door. The bright lights of Times Square were ahead. It did not strike him as odd that the power had not yet been cut in the secure zone, because nothing struck him as odd in the People's Republic anymore. He looked back and saw two dots in the distance.

Vasilev was still coming.

There were billboards and signs with flashing lights ahead in the distance. The damaged Blackhawk was going toward them. Then the aircraft dropped behind some of the high-rise buildings and disappeared from view.

Vasilev urged his pilot on. He turned to the right and looked out his cockpit. Kurylenko-4 was now back with him, its shooters hanging off the side waiting for the chance to engage the American chopper.

Two on one.

Vasilev liked his odds.

The two General Electric T700-GE-701 turboshaft engines sputtered and kicked. Turnbull could feel the helicopter becoming unstable and they crossed over several high-rises and began dropping into the concrete canyon that was West 46th Street.

"I can't...," the pilot began, but he did not finish. The gears ground and strained, and the engines went silent. The ship's four-bladed rotors slowed appreciably, running out their inertia. There was smoke, a lot of it.

They were coming in for what looked like a reasonably soft landing and then, at perhaps 15 feet above the deck, the Blackhawk lurched forward and downward.

"Brace for impact!" the pilot shouted.

The wounded helicopter smashed cockpit-first into a building's front overhang, then dropped about ten feet to the sidewalk. The jolt was tremendous – the wounded fire supporter groaned. Deeds had a hold of Gibson, or perhaps it was the other way around. They seemed okay when Turnbull looked them over. Ryan was good too.

He undid his restraining strap and stepped out onto the sidewalk. The helicopter was smoking from its engines, but not yet burning. That might happen anytime.

"Get them out," he told Ryan and unlimbered his rifle. There were people in the streets, and they stared, not quite processing how a helicopter had just dropped down on their street from the sky. None of them seemed armed, and none of them seemed to be hostile, just curious. That would not stay true forever, but it looked to Turnbull like they had at least a little time before trouble started and the bad guys showed up.

He went around to the front of the chopper, toggling his selector switch from "AUTO" to "SEMI." Ammo was now officially a precious commodity.

The UH-60 had smashed into the overhang, taking much of the structure with it down to the ground. It was clear that the pilot and co-pilot were toast.

He walked back to where the rest of the survivors were getting out of the aircraft. The fire support officer was standing with his arm around the Three-air, but he looked bad.

Movement ahead.

Two men, carrying Kalashnikovs and wearing People's Security Force uniforms.

"Hey!" shouted the lead one.

Turnbull's suppressed M4 was up and the red dot alighted on the target's chest. He squeezed twice and shifted his aim even before the first target staggered. The dot found the other PSF officer and Turnbull shot him twice too.

Ryan was up with his weapon, assessing.

"We need to recover my guys," he told Turnbull.

"I know we leave no man behind, but your FSO dies if we don't get him MEDEVAC'd. We're not doing Mogadishu Two because it sure as hell is not having a happier ending here and now," Turnbull said. "We'll recover them later. Right now, I got a mission to complete."

Ryan did not like it, but he knew Turnbull was right. There were no extra forces – or helicopters – to launch an unplanned search and rescue mission for one little crew of one little Blackhawk. Command was about making hard choices, and leaving three bodies behind – the pilots and his door gunner – was one of the hardest.

"Which way?"

"West," Turnbull said. "The Secure Zone wall runs down 8th Avenue below West 52nd Street. Then it's not too far to the Hudson where the Army and Marine Corps are going to be landing at dawn. We stabilize your guy, see if we can get a MEDEVAC chopper in, and hunker down until the cavalry comes."

Ryan nodded. They started moving, with Gibson trotting along beside Turnbull.

"What the hell are those lights?" Ryan asked, looking west.

"I forgot that you're too young to have been here before the Split," Turnbull said. "That's Times Square."

21.

The pair of Kurylenko choppers flew over the streets, looking for their wounded prey. They had lost sight of the Blackhawk as it dropped between the tall buildings, but Vasilev knew it was not going far, not shot up the way it had been.

Kurylenko-4 found it first and called him over. The Ukrainian Little Bird was hovering over the wreck of a UH-60 on West 46th street. It looked like it smashed into the front of a building. There were people in and on the wreckage. He toyed with the idea of using one of his Hellfire missiles to annihilate the hulk, but then he would not be sure he had killed Turnbull.

"Take us down," he ordered the pilot in gruff Ukrainian.

The two aircraft had each dropped their four shooters, and Vasilev, then took an overwatch position hovering above. Vasilev had his AK-19 but wore no helmet. The bright light from Times Square was such that none of the others dropped their night vision devices down. Vasilev did not have to tell them to spread out and secure the perimeter around the derelict aircraft.

They could now see it was local people crawling on the wreckage – simply because they were in the Secure Zone did not mean they were not inclined to loot whatever they could take if given the chance.

"Go on, get away!" yelled one of the mercenary sergeants at a pair of looters trying to make off with some treasures from the passenger compartment. They moved too slow, so the Ukrainian shot them. That convinced the others to run.

Vasilev came forward for a closer look. He noted blood on the sidewalk, blood that could not have come from the newly-dead looters. He peered inside the compartment. Besides the wasted looters, there was a dead American soldier. He walked to the cockpit, and noted a couple more bodies.

None were Turnbull.

"Sir," one of his men called over the Motorola. "Two dead cops." The Ukrainian word was the same as the word in English.

"Two rounds each in the chest, tight groups," the mercenary continued.

Kelly Turnbull is alive, he told himself.

"Aircraft, scout ahead. We follow them on foot."

Times Square was named after the *New York Times* in 1904 and was still named after it. Following the Split, the People's Republic embarked on its campaign of endless renaming of things in order to eliminate any vestige of support or affirmation of the United States of America. Considering the political inclinations of the *Times*, there was never any consideration at all of renaming it or the Midtown attraction that bore its name.

In a land of the bland and the dull, Times Square was meant to be the showplace for the blue, the demonstration of progressive potential and a promise of the prosperity and innovation that would inevitably follow from the revolution. So, it was a festival of lights, signs, and massive video monitors – all manufactured in China and maintained by Chinese technicians. The techs had fled when it became clear that Manhattan would be the target of an American invasion, but the power was still on and without the Chinese techs there were no blue Americans who knew how to turn the gaudy displays off even if the PR had been inclined to do so.

The occasional American jet passed over them, and there was an occasional burst of anti-aircraft gunfire reaching up into the sky, but otherwise, life seemed to be going on as usual – or as usual as it could be in Times Square terms. The hordes of tourists had long been gone, a combination of poverty, ennui, and tight carbon travel credits that kept most blue Americans tethered to their homes. Most of the businesses had reverted – by official policy – to what they were in the Eighties before the fascist Guliani regime swept them out – bars, pot dispensaries, and sex worker enterprises. Most of the pornography offered was approved and licensed, appealing to the furthest acronyms and symbols of the LGBTQA2S*@€∞÷7, etcetera, spectrum. However, the discerning pervert could still find illegal cis porn – naughty cheerleader and sorority girl–themed material smuggled in from the red was very popular among the true degenerates.

There was no PSF presence. Having law enforcement present in Times Square, even of the marginal type the People's Security Force provided, "was traumatizing to sex workers, otherkin, pharma-pioneers, gender minorities, and the unhomehaving." For their part, the PSF officers were perfectly happy to avoid the place.

The myriad signs flashed and changed, often advertising luxury goods and travel no actual blue American could ever buy or experience. There were silent music videos too, usually androgenous band members lip-synching their latest approved tunes. One exception was a wizened Jon Bon Jovi, who danced awkwardly to his new hit, "I Don't Need a Penis to Love You."

And there were the messages, like the warning to "TURN IN FAMILY MEMBERS WHO HARBOR CLIMATE DENIAL AND TRANSPHOBIA."

Another advised passersby to "EAT YUMMY BUGS."

A large screen featured a dozen very thin people, and a hugely obese one, and the words "EXPERTS SAY THAT EXTENDED FASTS ARE THE KEY TO HEALTH AND DEFEATING ENVIROMENTAL RACISM."

Turnbull stared as the main video billboard informed the masses that:

FAITH
FAMILY
FREEDOM
IS
FASCISM

The inhabitants were out that night despite the coming invasion, hundreds of them lurking and loitering across the Square, but keeping back from Turnbull and Gibson. The big man with the big gun and the big dog looked like nothing but trouble. The other Americans followed them, with the fire support officer being helped. Turnbull had them spread out, so that they did not stand out, which was validated when an AH-6 flew over the square but did not seem to pick them out of the crowd.

No shooters hanging out of the sides, Turnbull noted.

"They're on the ground!" Turnbull told Ryan. "Take your guys and Deeds and keep heading west until you hit the Secure Zone wall at 8th Avenue. Look for a gate or some way to get over. Head north until you find one. I'll follow."

"You're going to delay them alone?" said Ryan.

"No, I got my dog and my rifle," Turnbull said, before heading back east across the square.

The Ukrainians were having no nonsense as they entered Times Square from the east. A bum made the mistake of speaking to one of the sergeants and got his nose broken with the butt of an AK-19 for his trouble.

Vasilev used hand signals to have his men spread out. They did not have to be told the plan – the first one to see one of the renegades would engage him and seek to pin the fugitives down. The rest of the group would head toward the gunfire – none of them were using their suppressors – and flank the targets. Then it was simply a matter of rolling the surviving Americans up and killing them all.

Gibson lay down beside Turnbull as he took up a position outside a low-rent theater catering to the lowest of the degenerates that promised "HOT GIRL AND GUY ACTION," using a cement flower box that was full of trash to steady his rifle. The locals watched, somewhat amused, as if it was a movie and as if no random round might ruin their day. Perhaps they just did not care.

Turnbull saw his quarry. Two of them, coming west fast. One hundred fifty meters away.

Turnbull sighted through the distance optic, placing the crosshairs on the one walking behind his buddy. He fired, then fired again. The Ukrainian staggered and fell on his face; his buddy stopped and looked back, thinking his comrade had tripped. The mercenary noticed the blood seeping out from underneath when Turnbull put two more into him. He dropped too.

The flower box exploded with shattered concrete and kicked-up dirt and trash as two of them to the left fired a couple of bursts his way. They were running toward him, and their fire was poorly aimed, designed to suppress him. From the right, two more were coming, flanking him. They were more deliberate and therefore more dangerous.

He flipped his selector switch to "AUTO" and unloaded most of his mag at the two on the right. They both stopped being deliberate, one because he dropped to the filthy pavement to avoid the bullets and the other because a lucky 5.56mm round punctured his throat and blew out his spinal column.

Vasilev heard the shooting to his south, and waved the men with him in the direction of the guns.

The guys on the left were still firing and charging. Turnbull put a burst in their direction with no effect and went dry. He hit the mag release and was sliding in a replacement freshie even before the empty stopped clattering on the ground, then took down the guy on the right who had stood back up.

Then he realized that Gibson was gone.

Another burst came in-bound and Turnbull dived. Chips of broken cement settled over him, and in the background a hobo screamed as one of the off-target AK-19 rounds pulverized his femur.

Turnbull rose up and saw that two of them were still coming, now within fifty meters. Even praying and spraying, one of them was bound to blot his ledger.

He put a burst into the one on the left. The guy's head let out a puff of red as he dropped, but this was his comrade's chance for vengeance. The man stopped and aimed through his optic.

Turnbull was pivoting with his rifle but he was not going to make it.

Gibson leapt at the mercenary from the man's side, the Belgian Malinois's mouth open like a bear trap. It sprang shut on the Ukrainian's face. The mercenary forgot all about shooting Turnbull; he forgot all about his gun too, dropping his AK-19 and using both hands to try to get the canine attached to his face detached.

They fell to the pavement together, the guy screaming something in Ukrainian that did not need translation. It was pretty obvious that he wanted Gibson to stop using his noggin as a chew toy, and it was equally obvious that Gibson had zero intention of complying. Turnbull sprinted over and yelled for Gibson to come. It took two yells – Gibson was enjoying himself, but the moment the dog was clear, Turnbull put a burst into the mercenary and the Ukrainian stopped moving.

Vasilev's Motorola pinged as he passed two of his dead men. He ignored it, but it pinged again. The shooting ahead had died out, but he could not see either his surviving men or Turnbull.

He grabbed the radio.

"Major Vasilev," the voice said. It was Harrington.

"I am busy," the mercenary shouted, though he knew Harrington would not be on the line personally if it was not serious.

"Vasilev! I need you! Get out of New York now!"

"Turnbull!" was all that Vasilev could utter.

"I don't care! Get out now and return to me immediately! Or say good-bye to your money and your life if Turnbull doesn't kill you first!"

Vasilev shook with rage. He keyed the Motorola again.

From the number of surviving Little Birds, Turnbull knew there could not be many more Ukrainians, but he still stayed ready. Then the Motorola on the body of the dead Ukrainian sounded. He heard the entire exchange with Harrington. The next burst was in Ukrainian, and a few moments later one of the AH-6s came in to land at the other end of Times Square.

Turnbull snatched the Motorola and started heading west with Gibson.

The helicopter was only on the ground for a moment. It took off and began heading east fast with the other Kurylenko bird right behind.

Turnbull could not resist. He keyed the mic.

"Hey Vasilev," he said. "You forgot a half dozen of your men."

"Turnbull!"

"Yep," Turnbull replied.

"Now I understand why General Scott wants you to die so much!"

"Well, give him my regards, and tell him that he and I have unfinished business," Turnbull said. "And so do you and I."

Turnbull did not find his people where West 46th ran into the Midtown Secure Zone wall running down the middle of 8th Avenue. He turned north and caught up with them at the abandoned gate at West 50th Street.

"What happened?" Ryan asked. His Three-air was giving the wounded fire support officer some water while Deeds was keeping watch with his purloined USP.

"Shot some guys," Turnbull said.

"So, the usual?" said Ryan.

"Yeah, the usual. How's it look out there?" Turnbull asked, looking through the gate.

"It's dark, no street lights. It's three or four long blocks to the water's edge. The Marines land in this sector at dawn."

"Any luck on a MEDEVAC?"

Ryan shook his head.

"They can't spare one. The best we can do is go out there, find some cellar somewhere and wait out the invasion. The jarheads will have medics with them, or Navy corpsmen, as the case may be."

Turnbull nodded. He did not point out that "corpsmen" – "core-men" – was officially pronounced "corpse-beings" in the People's Republic Anti-Colonial Military Naval Land Forces, their version of the Marines, because Barack Obama had pronounced it "corpse-men" pre-Split and the PR government did not want to concede that the ex-president and writer of erotic autobiographies was an idiot.

Turnbull did a quick ammo check. Just three 5.56mm mags and whatever was in his M4 now. He counted three 9mm mags plus the one in his Wilson Beretta. That was not so good – he wished he still had his pack. Then he mentally counted up the other guys' ammo. The FSO and S-3 Air had their SIG 9mm pistols. Deeds had his .45 USP with three mags liberated from Dimitri. Ryan had an M4 and four mags or so. That was not so good either.

"Okay," Turnbull said. "Let's move out."

They pushed open the gate and crossed the road into the dark.

The formerly gentrified Hell's Kitchen was hellish once again. Its buildings were dark and foreboding, with lots of broken windows and boarded-up lower levels. There was a high-rise at 8th and 50th that used to be the Longacre Apartments. It looked deserted, though many of the boards on the ground floor had been torn off. There was a subway station on the ground floor on 50th, a yawning hole leading downward.

No thanks, thought Turnbull.

They moved forward, slowly and quietly. But he felt the hair on the back of his neck standing at attention.

So did Ryan.

"You feel like we're being watched too?" he asked.

"Yep," Turnbull said.

They continued down the block, the uncanny quiet broken only by the occasional explosion or sound of gunfire from the battle primarily going on to their north. But that was just for the present – tomorrow, a few blocks to their west, the Marines were going to Iwo Jima the hell out of Hell's Kitchen.

They kept close to the buildings lining the street, hopefully protected from attack on that side, but Turnbull could hear noises from inside the structures – scratching, breathing, bumps, whatever. No one came outside though. Maybe it was civilians trying to shelter in place until the nightmare was over. Turnbull did not want to find out.

They reached some trees among the buildings, dead ones. No one maintained them since the Split, though someone was certainly assigned to and getting rations for doing so. This place looked more like a graveyard than a city.

Gibson alerted first, and Turnbull instantly raised his weapon. There was an animal howl, a scream that should not have been human but was. For a moment, the group froze there on the sidewalk, and then there were a dozen howls.

Shapes were coming down the road from the west, some firing rifles, others just carrying them. They ran and yelled like madmen, and they probably were. Certainly they had taken the drugs the PR had distributed – maybe angel dust? Who knew? And who cared? They were coming to kill Turnbull and his men.

Maybe these are the crazies I keep hearing about, Turnbull thought to himself as he brought up his rifle.

He fired, dropping the first one, then he moved to the second and shot him too. Ryan was firing, bursts, and Turnbull gave in to the inevitable and began firing bursts as well. Next to him, Deeds took careful aim with the .45 pistol and shot one dead who got within 20 feet of them.

In a matter of seconds, the attackers were all down. A few were twitching and moaning, some both, but Turnbull did not finish them off. He was too busy listening to the much louder gunbattle up the street and around the next corner.

"I think this way is probably no good," Turnbull said, dropping his empty magazine and inserting a new one. Two left.

"Sounds like an infantry platoon," Ryan said as the battle raged out of sight. There was some machine gunfire – at least a couple M240Bs. "Can't be us. We don't have anyone here!"

"Start heading back," Turnbull directed Deeds and the Three-air with his wounded buddy. "We will backtrack and go around."

The trio moved out, going back the way they came. Ryan stood by him with Gibson, who was hyper alert, watching.

Up ahead, about a dozen figures turned the corner and began moving their way. It was hard to see them – they were wearing pattern-disruptive camo. And they were not a howling cluster of crazies. They were a squad, moving as a unit.

"Sling it," Turnbull said to Ryan. "Sling that weapon now!"

Ryan did not need to be told. He slung his M4 and put his hands out like Turnbull did.

Half the troops passed them without engaging, going down a few meters and taking up defensive positions. Turnbull noted the floppy boonie hats in place of helmets.

The other half of the squad covered them with M4 rifles.

The leader, a tough looking guy who was clearly a noncommissioned officer, stepped forward.

"Who the hell are you?" he demanded. He had his rifle leveled at Turnbull and Ryan.

This might be one of those times his official rank came in handy, Turnbull thought.

"I'm Lieutenant Colonel Turnbull, and this is Major Ryan, US Army," he answered. "Who the hell are you?"

"We're the US Marine Corps, sir!" he said, uttering the word "sir" in that special way an angry sergeant could such that it sounded like he was telling you that your mom worked the bus station restroom for quarters.

More Marines were coming their way, though the fire was still continuing around the corner. They were doing a retrograde in good order, and you could safely bet that whoever was pushing them back was paying for every inch in blood.

A thin but tall Marine with noticeable bearing ran to them, his radio man struggling to keep up with a ruck full of commo as well as his basic kit and ammo. Nearby, a couple other Marines with radios took a knee and provided security with their rifles.

"Sir," the sergeant reported. "These two say they're an Army colonel and a major."

"Our helicopter went down," Ryan interjected. "We have a wounded officer back that way and a high-value civilian we just rescued. You got corpsmen?"

The officer looked them over. Ryan was in his uniform and Turnbull wasn't, but to his Eagle, Globe and Anchor mind, Army operators tended to be undisciplined cowboys anyway, so that did not raise any red flags for him. The dog was a bit odd, though.

"I'm Captain Smith," the jarhead said, then he turned to the NCO. "Sergeant Betley, police up their wounded and their civilian. We need to keep moving until we can find a good defensive position."

Betley nodded and moved out smartly.

"I thought the Corps landed at dawn," Turnbull said.

"We're Marine Raiders doing a recon before the landing."

"Looks like it's not a covert recon," Turnbull observed. To their front, the rest of the platoon was coming around the corner, continuing the fighting retreat. "Who's chasing you?"

"Same freaks it looked like you just wasted," Smith said. "These buildings, they're packed with them. All of them. Thousands. The civilians are gone. Anyone you see here is trying to kill you. If we had not come ashore to recon the area, they would have sprung a trap on our guys and who knows how many that would have gotten killed."

"That's not good," Turnbull said.

"No, it kind of sucks. They seem to be keeping most of the fighters inside and undercover, but if they open these buildings up and let them all out, we're screwed. And because the buildings are already occupied, there's no place for us to dig in."

The last of the Raiders came around the corner. Another squad had set up about fifty meters down the road and the last guys in contact ran past them, and then past their captain and Turnbull. Now the new line of defense opened fire on the bad guys coming around the corner.

"There's a subway station back a block or two," Turnbull said. "Your boys can clear it and we can defend the mouth – if they don't fling open the doors and let all these bastards out," Turnbull said.

"Let's go!" the platoon commander shouted to his men. "Move out!"

Turnbull and Ryan trotted along with the Marine command section, with Turnbull occasionally turning to watch the Marines wasting a seemingly never-ending supply of drugged up crazies. The M240B machine guns were getting a workout. Turnbull wondered how much ammo they had left.

The lead Marines swept up Deeds, the Three-Air and the wounded officer, and a Navy corpsman immediately set to work on him. The squad occupied the sidewalk and street in front of the 50th Street subway station, forming a fan with their backs to the former Longacre Apartments high-rise.

The rear squad was bounding back down the road – one would set up, then the other would fall back and set up behind it and so on, so that there was always a line of Marines in contact and firing on the attackers. The bad guys were doing their best, firing wildly, and occasionally a Raider would catch a round. If they could, the Marines would fight on. If not, their buddies would carry them back, dead or alive.

Won't be needing this, Turnbull told himself as he unscrewed the suppressor from the business end of his rifle.

They were moving faster now, trotting down the road. The pressure was increasing, but Turnbull was concerned with an attack into their flank from the buildings lining the street beside them.

He had reason to be.

The board that covered the missing door of what appeared to be an abandoned Italian restaurant began to shake from kicks from inside, and then it broke open and wild-eyed men with AK-47s began to pour out, screeching and gibbering. On the other side of the street, the same thing happened, only from a former Duane Reade store.

Turnbull engaged immediately, firing a burst into the first two who stepped out of the former spaghetti joint. They were blown off their feet, but there were more behind them firing. Their bullets went everywhere, including at times, into the back of other blue fighters who had the misfortune of standing in front of the over-enthusiastic shooters.

Ryan joined in, blasting away with controlled bursts. Smith smoked a couple with his weapon, and his radiomen were fighting too.

"Keep moving!" the platoon commander shouted, before taking aim and dropping another blue.

Turnbull punched out his empty mag and inserted a new one. One left. Then he shot dead one guy who had hit a Marine in the thigh. Gibson was at his side, looking for the chance to join in the fight.

The Marine platoon was building up its forces in front of the subway station entrance, but the bad guys were coming in increasing numbers. They could not shoot well, but they could shoot a lot. One shot Ryan in the calf.

"Damn it!" he yelled as he fell to the pavement. He emptied his weapon at an oncoming trio of fighters, and immediately reloaded and engaged again. Turnbull bent down and swooped him up with his left arm, firing his recce rifle in bursts with his right hand. It was sub-optimal, but he caught one of the blues in the pancreas and he fell screaming.

"How bad?" Turnbull asked.

"Muscle, not bone," Ryan said through a grimace as he searched for targets.

Turnbull reached the entrance perimeter and let Ryan down. His uniform trousers were soaked with blood below the right knee.

Smith was organizing the defense.

"Gunnery Sergeant Betley!" he shouted. The NCO appeared.

"Sir?"

"Take a squad, go down those stairs and kill everyone you see," he ordered. Betley knew the civilians were gone, and understood the order.

"First Squad, on me!" he yelled, and led them down the long steps of the long-dead escalator into the dark of the subway station.

The perimeter of Marines was fully engaged as bad guys approached from every direction. Turnbull continued to fire, but switched to semi-auto as he inserted his last magazine.

The enemy was increasing in number, and in volume of fire.

A Marine came running out of the station, breathless from the climb.

"Sir, Sergeant Betley says it's all clear!"

"Get the dead and wounded down there," the platoon commander shouted. His men got to it, but Ryan waved off evacuation.

Turnbull shot another couple fighters, but it made no difference. More replaced them and he killed them too. The enemy's combat power was growing every minute and the Marines's combat power was shrinking every time a 7.62x39mm round connected.

Turnbull surveyed the battlefield. There was a dark swarm in the distance coming toward them. It looked like they had released the Kraken.

"Damn," Smith said as he reloaded. He might go down, but he and his jarheads were taking a bunch of these bastards with them.

"We can't hold the entrance," Turnbull said. "There's just too many of them."

"Then we'll die on heaps of brass," Smith said, aiming and firing. The second squad was now pulling back into the station and down the steps.

Turnbull thought through the situation. There was only one option he could think of.

Not a great option, but it was an option.

He fired off the rest of the rounds in his rifle, shooting until it locked back empty. He killed a couple more, but it made no difference to the big picture.

They were all going to die.

"Captain Smith," Turnbull said. "You got an ANGLICO team?"

"Yes, sir, those two guys with radios," Smith said. Seeing they were being discussed, the pair moved forward.

"Okay, Captain Smith, I'm assuming command."

"What?"

"I'm the senior officer present and I am assuming command. Everything that happens from here on in is on me, do you understand? It's all on me."

Smith didn't understand – he thought he was being relieved.

"No, Captain, you've done great. If you live, you should get a medal. But I'm taking command because of what I'm going to do now."

"What are you doing, Kelly?" asked Ryan, attempting to stand up.

"ANGLICOs, come here!" Turnbull ordered. The two liaison Marines from the Air Naval Gunfire Liaison Company (ANGLICO) got close to the weird, unshaven colonel in the civilian clothes, half because he ordered them to and half out of curiosity.

These were the guys who orchestrated the naval gunfire from the Navy ships cruising off Marine Corps battlefields.

"No time to call in a Broken Arrow," Turnbull said. "I need a fire mission,"

"We can do that sir!" said the lead ANGLICO, taking his mic in hand.

Turnbull looked him in the eye.

"I want a nine-gun broadside from the *USS Iowa*, and I want it right now. Here's the tricky part. I want it on my position."

"Are you nuts?" Smith asked.

"Yes, he is," Ryan said. "I can testify to that."

"Sir, they won't fire that mission," said the lead ANGLICO.

"Do it," Turnbull said. The ANGLICO shrugged and got on the radio while his buddy figured out the target grid coordinates. As in, the grid coordinates they were standing on.

"This is Lancelot-7, calling Thor-7, priority special fire mission, over," he said.

This is Thor-7, go," called the *Iowa's* fire control center.

Turnbull pivoted away from the ANGLICOs who were trying to explain to the *Iowa's* gunners that the grid coordinates they were at were also the grid coordinates that they wanted nine 2,700-pound shells to drop around.

"Pull your men back down underground into the station, Capt. Smith," Turnbull ordered.

"I can't – someone's got to hold the entrance until the fire mission," the platoon commander said.

"Yeah, and that's going to be me," Turnbull said as one of the remaining machine gunners fired off a long burst then shouted that he was out of ammo belts. "Commander's prerogative. I leave last."

"I'll stay too," Ryan said, unsteadily on his feet.

"No," Turnbull said. "You go with them. Protect Deeds and take care of my doggie."

"Kelly...," Ryan began.

"My call, my job to see it through," Turnbull said. "If it goes south, you talk to Lorna for me. You'll know what to say better than me."

"Sir," the ANGLICO said handing the mic to Turnbull. "They want to talk to you."

In the fire control center of the *USS Iowa*, the fire control officer, Lieutenant Commander (LCDR) Steinman, waited.

"Thor-7, this is the commander on scene. We are about to be overrun. Fire the mission as called, over."

"Identify yourself, over," said LCDR Steinman.

"Lieutenant Colonel Kelly Turnbull, US Army," Turnbull said. "I am in command. I am calling for the strike on my position. I say again, I understand that I am calling this strike on my position. This is my responsibility. Fire the mission now, over!" he said.

The fire control officer pursed his lips.

"Get me the captain!" he shouted.

Turnbull handed the mic back to the ANGLICO. The Marines began pulling their last squad back into the subway station. The blue fighters were inching closer, using cover more than the dead ones had. It was a twisted form of natural selection, where the really crazy crazies died first. But they were still coming, inexorably, though when one would try to fire he usually got shot. But then two more would pop up to replace him.

This is like Hercules fighting the hydra, except instead of two new heads whenever he cuts one off, it's two new assholes, thought Turnbull.

The last of the squad disappeared down into the depths of the subway station. They helped the wounded Ryan, who took hold of Gibson's harness.

The dog would not move.

"Go on, Gibson," Turnbull said. "Good dog."

Gibson looked at him and Turnbull was sure he was sad. He let Ryan take him down the frozen escalator.

On the *Iowa's* bridge, Captain (CAPT) Sauer knocked his Annapolis ring on the metal arm of his captain's chair as he waited for the fire control officer to get back to him with answers to his questions. It occurred to him that his ring knocking habit was a little too on the nose.

"Captain, I have your info," LCDR Steinman said through the speaker mounted on the wall. "The ANGLICO team is attached to a Marine Raider platoon. That means there are twenty, thirty Marines at that grid."

"And the commanding officer stated that he knows the strike is on his own position?"

"Yes, sir, he said *specifically* that he is calling for the strike on his own position." The fire control officer did not need to mention that every word in the fire control center was being recorded so when the inevitable investigation happened, no one would be able to say that this Kelly Turnbull guy did not know what he was asking.

"And the target area?"

"Assessed as green, free fire," Steinman replied. Before the battle, drones had observed the evacuation of civilians and the fires maps declared the entire area open to any kind of bombs, rockets, or naval gunfire that the invasion force chose to call down.

"Do you have a firing solution?" CPT Sauer asked.

The fire control officer did not need to be prompted to do his job.

"Roger, the firing solution is in the computer and ready if you give the order."

Sauer considered the situation. Earlier in his career, before Annapolis, he had been an enlisted Marine himself, and later he had spent time operating with ground pounders and knew their culture better than most surface warfare officers. He understood the gravity of the situation that had forced this Colonel Turnbull to make the request. And its urgency.

It was one hell of a decision, but he did not get command of a battleship by avoiding making them.

"We have a commander in the field in *extremis* calling in a fire mission," CPT Sauer said into his mic. "Fire it."

"Sir," the ANGLICO said, his eyes bulging, looking up at Turnbull. "They're firing the mission."

Turnbull turned to Smith.

"Get going."

Smith saluted and took his radio man and ANGLICOs down into the subway station with him.

Turnbull drew his Beretta and shot a fighter across the street who made the fatal error of lifting his head over a stoop.

But up the street dozens, maybe hundreds, were coming.

All nine guns slewed to starboard to aim at Manhattan. In the innards of the ship, and in all three of its massive turrets, each of which held three independently targeted 16-inch cannons, the crews ran through their thoroughly trained and rehearsed firing procedures. The shells were loaded into the breeches and the bags of propellant – not many were needed at this distance – were pushed inside behind it and the breeches shut.

Each of the nine guns had its own targeting coordinates. The mechanical computer used prior to the last decommissioning had been replaced with a computerized one. Each gun now adjusted to exactly the position that needed to be in to drop its shell right where it was wanted. In this case, nine shells would fall in three rows of three, with the center shell right on the old Longacre Apartments building that housed the entrance to the 50th Street subway station.

On the fire control officer's computer screen, the readiness status of each gun tube was tracked separately. The nine started red, but one by one they flipped to green. Then all nine read green. LCDR Steinman licked his lips nervously. The cramped room in the bowels of the battleship was dead silent - every sailor in the fire control center knew exactly what kind of request the battleship was fulfilling.

The fire control officer exhaled.

"Fire!"

Turnbull engaged the enemy even as rounds blew chunks off the walls around him. Three of the fighters sensed that Turnbull was alone and sprinted at him, their weapons blazing. Turnbull dropped each, though the third one took two rounds to stop.

Now, the slide on the Wilson Beretta locked back empty. He hit the magazine release and the empty dropped to the sidewalk.

He was pulling out his last loaded mag when the horizon down the street toward the Hudson River silently illuminated like a bright orange dawn.

The sun was not coming up for several hours.

Turnbull spun and ran down the frozen escalator staircase.

He got about halfway down it before the entire world became nothing but noise and darkness.

22.

Turnbull kicked the industrial metal chair across Deeds's bland office. It hit the wall and bounced off. He had been back in Dallas for three days, most of that time spent in debriefs, and now this.

"They're playing footsie with this bastard!" he yelled. Deeds's face was still not completely healed, and still showed the marks where the late Dimitri pummeled him. He stood beside his desk and allowed his operative to vent. Whether he felt the same was something his face did not reveal. But his mouth did.

"I'm as mad as you are, Kelly," he said. "And I have made my views known at the highest levels."

"They didn't listen, did they?"

"No, not this time. And I expect they will have cause to regret it."

"Scott's plan worked," Turnbull said. "It *worked*! Our Army is drowning in quicksand and now he's pretending to throw us a life line."

The news from the front was not good. Sure, the American forces would win the battle for Manhattan, eventually, but they would win ugly. There were a whole lot of red casualties, and the international media was focusing on the blue "civilian" ones. But those *faux* civilians had to be shot down one by one. The problem with doped up sociopaths was that they did not know when they were defeated.

Worse, sometimes they would get lucky wildly spraying their AKs and punch a red trooper's ticket. Sure, the ratio was 20:1, but it was those ones that mattered to the people in the red, and they were adding up. America was getting sick of burying blood citizens.

Overlord's operational success would ensure strategic defeat.

"Wait, Kelly," said Casey Warner, up and out of his hospital bed and back at work again on light duty. "I think we're burying the lede here. You called in a broadside from the *USS Iowa* down on your own position and lived?"

He had, barely. The subway station did not collapse in on them though several blocks around the station entrance were flattened, along with the fighters waiting inside to ambush the Marines landing at dawn. Turnbull and the Marines had moved out north through the C Line tunnel and eventually linked up with the invasion force at the station near the former Columbus Circle. Not long after, he, Deeds and Gibson were evacuated to the US Air Force forward airfield at the former Newark International Airport for transport back to Texas. As the Army Blackhawk flew them over the Hudson River to catch their flight, Turnbull saw that the engineers were already working to remove the facial hair, Adam's apple, and crotch bulge that the People's Republic had added to the Statue of Liberty.

"Focus, gentlemen," Deeds demanded. "The facts are the facts whether we like them or not."

"And facts don't care about your feelings," Casey added. This was the motto on the coat of arms of Ben Shapiro University in Nashville, formerly known as Vanderbilt.

"The peace conference starts in 24 hours," Deeds continued. "The truce is going into effect in twelve hours all along every front. No bang-bang while the bigwigs jaw-jaw."

"London," Turnbull said bitterly. "I hate London." Getting nicked in the butt by a sniper with an Armalite hiding out in a wrecked double-decker bus near Piccadilly Circus would sour anyone on the British capital. But his British special ops pal

Kirby's laughter at his situation had been even more annoying than the minor wound. The Second British Civil War was miserable.

"The conference is being held in the Tower of London, to be exact," said Deeds.

"I know it," Turnbull said. It was where his team had dropped off Queen Meghan to be held for trial. The last thing he heard from her as he walked away after turning her over to the guards was her demand for organic vegan meals. He remembered how peaceful and happy her husband looked, all alone in his cell.

Turnbull continued.

"The Tower is good as far as security for the conference. It's got double castle walls and it's solid. You can secure it easily," he said. Then he frowned. "You know, they ought to go with history and cut Scott's head off. Or, even better, draw and quarter him. The Brits used to know how to deal with traitors. We should learn from them."

Faux Queen Meghan had not been beheaded, though several judges voted for that. Instead, she was exiled to Napoleon's old haunt of St. Helena. She asked if there was "a vibrant and diverse arts community" on the island. When her husband was sentenced to be exiled along with her, he looked like he would have preferred the headsman's axe.

"London is a drag," Casey said. He was sitting on Deeds's couch, his Walther automatic in a hip holster, still moving a bit slowly as he recovered. "London is damp, English food's bad, and the chicks just aren't hot. But maybe I can catch 'Hang In There, Baby.' It's my favorite Joy Division cover band."

Turnbull ignored him.

"Clay, this guy is suckering the politicians in. He's playing us."

"I know, Kelly, but you need to understand the power of telling other people what they want to hear. He claims he can make a peace and both sides gave him 72 hours in London to get a deal between our president and their, well, whatever they call their president these days – rotating chief executive or something."

"That Richard Harrington lowlife. I'd like to cap his ass, too."

"Kelly, is there anyone you don't want to kill?" asked Casey.

"At the moment, no."

"Focus, gentlemen," Deeds said.

Turnbull grunted.

"We're kind of screwed, Clay," Casey said. "Karl Martin Scott is playing mediator between the red and the blue and half our population thinks it is the greatest news since Taylor Swift joined OnlyFans."

"They don't know who Karl Martin Scott really is," Turnbull said.

"They don't know that he's conspiring with the blues," Deeds said. "They do know there's an election coming, and they are afraid of Ric Grenell or some other candidate winning off dissatisfaction with the war."

"So you're saying politicians are selfish and dumb," Turnbull said.

"And predictable," Deeds continued. "Obviously, the talks will go to the wire and then, at the last minute, he will put himself forward as the one compromise candidate both sides can embrace. Us, because most people here do not know what a traitor he is, and the blues because they will be told to do it."

"Maybe he'll come out as gendertwerked to get the blue masses actively liking him," observed Casey.

"Gendertweaked," Turnbull said absently. "I don't think there is such a thing as 'gendertwerked.' Might be wrong, though."

"Maybe we frame him somehow," Casey suggested. "Didn't he shoot some pedos in California when he was a general? That will crush him with the blues."

"They'll just announce pedos are racists and that will excuse him," Turnbull said. "No, the solution is obvious."

"What is so obvious?" Deeds asked. "Wait, let me guess."

"I go to London and shoot him in his smug face," suggested Turnbull.

"That's your answer to everything," said Casey.

"No, just to a lot of things," Turnbull replied. "If I had shot Scott after he grabbed the nuke this never would have happened. But I had to trust the system. Like an idiot."

"Yeah, that was pretty dumb of you," Casey observed. "You need to be more black-pilled like me. @FullMetalGalt's catch-hashtag is #TrustNo1."

"Stop talking," Turnbull snapped. He turned back to Deeds. "Send me to London. Let me end this."

Deeds walked back behind his utilitarian desk and sat down.

"Well, *I* am going to London," he announced. "The powers-that-be think they might need my advice, though if they listened to me this farcical peace conference would not be happening."

"I'm coming with you," Turnbull stated.

"Me too," Casey added. "We can be part of your close security team."

"As my security?" scoffed Deeds. "Gentlemen, we are not going to turn a peace conference into a blood bath."

"I just want Scott," Turnbull said.

"It'll be more like a blood sink," suggested Casey. "Not a blood bathtub."

"You know you need us there. Just in case," Turnbull argued.

Deeds considered the situation.

"Kelly, you do provide me a certain level of flexibility in case I need a drastic option."

"Yeah, I'll give you options."

"And are you recovered enough to go?" Deeds asked Casey. Casey nodded.

"I can shoot and I can tweet."

"I get a five-man security team inside the Tower complex. You two can come if you give me your word you are not going on a killing spree."

"You mean an unprovoked one?" asked Turnbull.

"I'm serious, Kelly. This is a delicate, diplomatic mission, and while we want to stop Scott, we cannot do it by starting World War III."

"I'll be chill," promised Casey.

"Yeah, that," Turnbull said. "Me too."

"Fine," Deeds said reluctantly. "But no gunplay."

"I'll try," Turnbull promised. He did not bother crossing his fingers.

"Yippee, London," Casey said. "You bringing the dog again, Kelly?"

"No, Gibson's staying home this time."

"Get packed," Deeds told them. "We leave in three hours. Kelly, I assume you'll stop off and see Lorna. Tell her I'm sorry for taking you away just a few days after you got back."

"If I mention your name to her, Clay, she'll probably shoot me and make this all moot. If I go missing, that's why. Also, I need to make another couple stops before we go."

"Where?" Deeds asked.

"If I'm going to England, I want one of those fancy Chef Ramsay Whataburgers first," Turnbull admitted.

"Oh, those do kick ass," Casey said, licking his lips.

"And," Turnbull said, "I need to stop by Ernie Smith and pick up my .45."

The People's Air Airbus 320 lifted off from the former Hartford-Bradley International Airport in Connecticut, which had initially been renamed post-Split for Democrat Senator Richard Blumenthal. He had been greatly pleased, especially by the statue of him in a loincloth raising aloft a torch that the PR government installed out front. But it did not last. The Womyns Cadre for Decolonialization raised a tremendous stink about his vaunted military career, labeling him a "running dog lackey of the imperialist warmongers who waged war on the Asian-identifying folx of Vietnam."

No matter how much he tried to explain that he had actually never been anywhere near Vietnam, he was disbelieved because of his pre-Split admissions of wartime heroism.

They then renamed the airport for Rosie O'Donnell because of her "cis/anti-fatist abuse by the racist whose name cannot be spoken" and "service to humynkind as a being of heft and gender nonconformity."

The jet was cleared on a direct flight plan to London that would take it far to the north over Greenland. When it crossed into Greenland's airspace, the red American controllers on the USA's newest possession allowed the PR flight to pass without being intercepted.

General Karl Martin Scott sat in his luxury seat, sipping sub-par champagne delivered by a silent, nonbinary flight attendant. This was one of the jets reserved for the *nomenklatura* of the People's Republic, with every seat what used to be called a "first class seat." Now, in a classless society, the upper class simply called these seats "seats," and the regular subjects either did not know that such seats existed or knew enough not to talk about them.

The plane was crowded with diplomats and staff and several security men who were obviously from Kurylenko. The general now had his own coterie of attendants. He was, after all, the man of the hour. He was the man – the only man – who could bring peace to the sundered United States. The minions around him on the plane all treated him accordingly, solicitously briefing him, praising him, and offering him a rather staggering set of erotic options.

But there was no time for that. He was deep in thought about how he would pull off his coup. And about the steps that would follow.

A woman sat down next to him. She was wearing a cream-colored suit, exquisitely tailored, and she displayed no apparent piercings, tatts, or blemishes. She could almost fit in back in Dallas.

Her face was icy and serious, her bearing imperious. The minions were clearly terrified of this formidable woman-identifying woman.

Scott knew who she was.

"Secretary of State and Decolonialization Camile Cochran," he said. "I guess I am supposed to ask your pronouns."

"She/her," Cochran said.

Interesting, thought Scott. From intel reports he saw before the current unpleasantness, she – now it was she – used to be "zhe/zir" for many years.

"I am glad we have a chance to talk," she continued, her eyes piercing through him. "It seems Temporary Rotating Executive Harrington has been keeping you all to himself."

Scott assessed this not as flirtation but frustration, not sexual but political. He was good at identifying factional rifts inside organizations, and he fancied himself adept at exploiting them. Scott was a general, and there was no greater pit of striving vipers than the Old and the New Pentagons where he had flourished.

Scott further assessed Cochran as eager to rotate into the executive role, and not necessarily temporarily. This could be useful down the road.

"I am at the service of the entire People's Republic leadership," Scott said. "And the United States. I am a neutral, after all, simply working for peace."

"Working for peace," she said, as if trying the words on to see if they fit.

Scott wondered if she knew about the plan. She definitely suspected something.

"I just find the idea of initiating a conference like the London talks without involving the Secretary of State to be...."

Secretary Cochran paused.

"Unusual," she finally said.

"You are involved now, fully part of the process, and that's proper," Scott said. He noted that she had not used her full title.

"It probably would have been best if the entire Supreme Political Bureau had had the opportunity to meet with you before embarking on these talks, and not simply the Temporary Rotating Executive," she said.

"I'm sure if we come to a fair and mutually-beneficial agreement in the Tower, the Bureau will approve it. You are a part of it and will certainly be able to win support for whatever solution we negotiate."

Secretary Cochran smiled cryptically .

"I hope we can talk more in London," she said, standing. Scott smiled.

"We will."

She smiled coldly in return and vanished into the rear of the aircraft.

Scott returned to his thoughts, now with more to think about. The pieces were coming together in his mind.

Harrington sat down daintily in the empty seat across from him not so quickly after Cochran departed that he looked desperate, but soon enough that it was clear his visit from the back of the plane was connected to her visit. He wore a tailored Savile Row suit with bone buttons and held his own glass of champagne.

"How is our mediator doing?" Harrington asked, facing the general but not bothering to keep his voice down.

"Excellent. And our future vice-president?"

Harrington smiled coldly. Scott noted that he did not bring up Cochran.

"Your Overlord operation has had the desired effect," the Temporary Rotating Executive said placidly. "The Americans are stunned by the casualties, and the fact that the fight is not over already. The reds were mentally unprepared for the welcome you arranged for their troops."

"Arming mindless thugs and lunatics and passing out intoxicants is a classic military strategy," the general said. "And, as a fringe benefit, every one of these creatures that the red forces kill is one less useless eater."

Harrington smiled.

"I have always respected your utter ruthlessness," he assured his co-conspirator. "Even when it was directed at my country."

"I am merely an unjustly persecuted patriot seeking to end a terrible war and undo the tragic Split that the politicians engineered," Scott said. He finished his champagne with a long sip even though it tasted like bubbly turpentine.

"It will be good to reunite the country," Harrington said, "Perhaps we can once again have adequate wine instead of this Massachusetts swill." He placed the nearly-full glass on his tray and the non-binary flight attendant swooped in and took it away.

"How do you anticipate the negotiations will go?" Harrington asked. "Since you are the allegedly neutral intermediary."

"I anticipate acrimony on the first day," Scott said. "The second day, concern that the conference may fail, and by the third day, desperation for a solution. That's when I will cease being the mediator and selflessly put myself forward as the solution to the impasse we have engineered."

"We will leverage their enthusiasm for peace to attain reunification," Harrington said. "And make you our new president – I suppose we have to call you 'president' and me 'vice-president.' Your red citizens will insist on the traditional titles, regardless of their legacy of cis-imperialism and so-forth. My people, however, will do as they are told."

"Are you sure?"

"Among those on the Supreme Political Bureau, there are some who might oppose this – call them 'traitors,' because I will," Harrington said. "My allies will eliminate them when the time comes. And do you anticipate problems among the reds? After all, you tried to kill hundreds of thousands of people in a coup."

Scott smiled.

"My supposed crimes are all state secrets. For the chance at peace, the US leadership will put aside my attempt to seize power after destroying Dallas. All will be forgotten and forgiven."

He smiled.

"But I will not forget or forgive," he said coldly. "Once in office, I will naturally have to impose certain controls to protect the newly reunified country from the threat of disinformation and dissent," Scott said. "Reasonable limits on speech and the press. And, eventually, the confiscation of weapons."

"Red fanatics outraged by those common sense policies helped cause the Split in the first place," observed Harrington.

"Yes, but back then a Split was just talk, a fringe hypothetical. Now they must face the reality of the war and economic ruin the Split brought," the general said. "Now they actually have to pay a price for their so-called rights, so let's see how much they are willing to pay when they can give them up and get peace and safety in return."

"You obviously know your own people," Harrington said, smiling his enigmatic little smile. "And I know mine. We will make a fine partnership."

"I would propose a toast," Scott said. "But my glass is empty and yours is gone. I do have one concern."

"Yes?"

"Security at the conference. There are factions within the red that might wish to stop us."

"Deeds and Turnbull?" Harrington's question held the hint of an accusation.

"And others," Scott said defensively.

"Our friends from the Kurylenko Group are already in London. They will oversee our security."

"You don't trust your own people, Mr. Vice-President?" Scott said smugly.

Harrington smiled and got up. The Temporary Rotating Executive of the People's Republic felt no need to tell General

Scott that he did not trust anyone. Not Secretary of State and Decolonialization Cochran, and certainly not him.

"I guess this is the life we've chosen," Lorna said.

"I think it chose us," Turnbull replied. He pet Gibson, who sat between them. His Wilson Combat CQB .45, cleaned and primed by Ernie Smith, was back on his hip.

"I am not asking where you are going, but I do watch Fox. Enjoy the fog and the terrible food."

"I'll be back in a few days," Turnbull said. "Then we can get back to wedding planning."

"*If* you get back."

"I always come back."

"Yeah, but usually shot, beat-up, or diseased."

"At least I won't vapor-lock in an easy chair watching a Dallas game."

"That actually sounds like a pretty good way to go," Lorna observed.

"I don't think there is a good way to go."

"You're the expert on getting people gone," Lorna said. She bent over to a brown paper shopping bag on the floor and pulled a pink, gift-wrapped box out of it. Turnbull looked at it, then looked at her.

"A wedding present. It's early, but I thought I should give it to you now." She handed it over, and he accepted it carefully.

"It's not a bomb," she said as Turnbull examined it. "If you were Deeds, maybe."

It was heavy. Turnbull tore off the pink wrapping. The box said "WILSON."

"I think I'm going to like this," he said, opening it up.

"That's a Wilson SIG WCP365X," Lorna said. "It was going to be your wedding gun."

"How did you know this is what I wanted?"

"I checked your browser history. It's all guns and ammo. Thankfully."

"Sweet," Turnbull said, carefully examining the compact automatic. It was about six inches long and just under five inches high, black-bodied with a gray slide. The slide was cut with X-Tac pattern cocking serrations all around for ease of racking.

"It has spring mods, a Grayguns trigger, and it's action-tuned. Twelve round capacity, plus one in the pipe. I didn't get you an optic because I know you're picky."

Turnbull racked the pistol; it was crisp and tight, and the beveling gave him a firm grip on the slide.

"I love it," he said.

"I figured you could take it as your back-up gun. It's nine-mil, though, and I only have one SIG mag at the moment."

"I'm only carrying .45 right now," Turnbull said.

"You can have some of my 9mm." She took one of the spare mags for the Smith & Wesson Military & Police 2.0 she was carrying from her purse. Turnbull started emptying it with his thumb, silently counting out thirteen hollow point bullets into a golden pile on his lap.

"Just one thing," she said. "Try not to die, okay."

"How am I going to die when I'm carrying this?" Turnbull asked, smiling.

"You'll definitely die carrying something," she said.

"This is a great wedding gun," Turnbull said, loading the mag. "And it will go with my suit, right?"

"I'm not having your gun clash with your suit," Lorna said. "We're not barbarians."

Turnbull inserted the loaded mag, racked one into the chamber, dropped the mag again, topped it off with the thirteenth shell, and slid the magazine back in to the well.

"I'll see you soon," he said, standing up and stuffing his new automatic into his belt at the small of his back.

Lorna looked up at him.

"Just make sure you see them coming at you first."

The Tower of London sat on the north bank of the Thames, with the iconic White Tower rising out of the green inner courtyard. The White Tower once contained, among other things, the British crown jewels. They disappeared during the Second British Civil War and had still not been recovered. But the famous ravens still dwelled there. Legend said if the ravens ever left the Tower, Britain would fall. So the birds got taken good care of, even during the height of the recent war.

It was the perfect location for the conference, a spectacular backdrop within an at least nominally neutral country. But it was also a readily defensible venue. After all, William the Conqueror had built the White Tower in 1078 as a fortress.

The double walls of the Tower complex themselves stood tall behind several cordons of security, and the Tower Bridge to the southeast was closed and guarded. Brit cops, who now carried guns, were manning the outer perimeter. The inner perimeter, which was still outside the walls, was guarded by Royal Commandos. Inside, the Americans – both red and blue – took the lead on the security.

Turnbull and Casey left Deeds at his hotel room at the Ritz, where the US president had a suite. The blues, who moved more slowly in arranging logistics, were consigned to the Rosewood.

Their driver met them at the entrance to the Ritz, where the staff icily ignored them. The lobby was full of buffed New Secret Service agents with dark glasses and earpieces. Like the Old FBI, the Old Secret Service was totally disbanded in the red after the Split as irredeemably corrupt. Media star and pizza magnate Dan Bongino had returned to the agency as Director of the United States New Secret Service in order to rebuild it. Among other things, now all agents had to bench a minimum of 300 pounds.

For their part, Kelly and Casey wore sport jackets and button-down shirts over slacks, without hiding the bulges at their hips, and looked exactly like what they were. So did their driver.

"Hello, Kelly!" Derek Kirby said from what Turnbull's mind involuntarily assessed as the wrong side of the black car. It was some sort of late-model Jaguar sedan.

"I knew you'd be in on this," Turnbull said as he slid into the passenger seat, moving the black Heckler & Koch MP7A1 submachine gun poking out from under the sport coat Kirby had lying between the front seats out of his way.

"I'm now a glorified chauffeur for a couple of yanks," Kirby complained. "Beats my last job, though. Close protection for Sir Morrissey against militant anti-vegans."

"Cool," said Casey.

"Who's your mate?" the Brit asked.

"This charming man is Casey," Turnbull said while his partner got into the back.

"I'm impressed," Casey said.

Kirby lurched away and into traffic. Turnbull could not look forward – the wrong-way driving made him edgy.

"So, you Americans are going to kiss and make up, huh? Well, we've been trying to do that here – not with the bloody Scots though. They can have their moors and sheep and communism."

"Yeah, I'm pretty excited about it," Turnbull said, though he clearly wasn't. He wiggled a bit, as the new WCP365 was digging into his back.

"Well, your hosts, us, are giving your people the royal treatment."

"You mean you're talking smack about our president in the newspapers?" asked Casey.

"I mean we got enough security on the ground to stop Armageddon. I assume you two have a dedicated protectee, or are you floaters?"

"We got a guy," Turnbull replied. In the backseat, Casey was taking in the sights. He would probably tweet about them later.

"Can you tell me who?"

"No, but it's not the president."

"I'm here with some of my boys, you know, just in case all hell breaks loose and you yanks can't handle things."

"So you're going to rescue us?" Turnbull said. "Like you did in World War II?"

"Hey, who saved your arse when you got shot in the arse?"

"You got shot in the ass?" inquired a suddenly interested and delighted Casey.

"He sure did. Sniper. Blew a big chunk out of his left bum cheek!"

"Hey, stop talking about my ass!" demanded Turnbull.

It took a while for the security men to get through security. They had to obtain their credentials, and then have them checked what seemed to be every ten minutes. Turnbull noticed that Kirby's identified him as "Noel C. Gallagher." But Turnbull had no grounds to complain, since his identified him as "Paul T. Westerberg." Casey was happy to be "Marky V. Ramone."

The trio walked the grounds of the complex, their conference ID credentials hanging around their necks. The actual conference would be held in the White Tower in the center of the complex, but there were dozens of smaller towers, buildings, and other structures along the walls. On the south wall was the Traitor's Gate, in the St. Thomas Tower that faced the river. Kirby pointed out another tower with a flat top surrounded by battlements.

"That's Wakefield Tower," he said. "One of four alternate helicopter landing zones and the only one on top of a structure. The main landing zone is right out front of the White Tower and the participants who fly in – pretty much the presidents and our prime minister – will use that. MEDEVACs will use it if something happens. The other three alternate LZs are around the courtyard. I'll show you them all. If one takes fire, you can call in a chopper for your boy at another one. Just remember, if the shit hits the fan, the gates shut tight. No one in, no one out, except by air."

They continued through, examining the sight lines and looking for egress routes. There were fewer bodies than he would like on the ground inside, but when the conference started tomorrow, all the security would be in place. He observed a team of explosive ordnance demolition techs and some bomb dogs pass by.

"Snipers?" Turnbull asked as they walked by the Chapel Royal of St. Peter ad Vincula on the northwest side.

"No real good sight lines from outside," Kirby said. "We closed the bridge and have guys on the towers, so that's a no-go for shooters."

"Inside here?"

"The snipers on the outside wall point out. None of ours are authorized to engage inside. Both your guys and the blues insisted."

Turnbull understood. Can't have foreigners with high-powered rifles overlooking your protectees.

He stopped, his hand falling instinctively to his Wilson .45. Kirby and Casey halted too, their eyes following Turnbull's to his target.

About ten meters away was a cluster of six men, clearly out of place in ill-fitting civilian jackets and slacks. One was a literal giant. There was an HK USP in each of their holsters and blue security credentials hanging around their thick necks. All were stocky, all close shaven. One, clearly the leader, had a scar along his cheek.

"It's them," Casey said. "The bastards from Flesh."

His hand was on his Walther.

"Did I miss something," Kirby asked as his eyes flitted from the Americans to the Ukrainians and back.

"Just a firefight in New York City," Turnbull said.

"And one in Dallas where these jerks capped me," Casey said.

Major Vasilev was smirking.

"Kelly Turnbull, back again," he called. "We have a saying in Ukraine about a problem that continues to follow you."

"Shove your saying," Turnbull said, "right up whatever the Ukrainian word for 'your ass' is."

Vasilev did not find this amusing. His hand made a fist and it shook.

"Mad, Ivan?" Turnbull enquired. He smiled. "Then draw."

Vasilev spit out a string of words that did not need translated, though one did seem to be English.

"Cowboy."

"Ye-ha," Turnbull said.

Vasilev nodded and the Kurylenko crew moved on. The major looked back over his shoulder.

"I will see you," he called out. "And then we finish this."

"Cannot wait," Turnbull called after him.

"Looks like we were about to go high noon here in the Tower," Kirby said.

"Could have taken them," Casey said.

"Soon enough," Turnbull said.

23.

The morning of the third day of the London Peace Conference, Turnbull and Casey knocked on the door of Deeds's room at the Ritz. There were several New Secret Service agents on the floor, each with a gizmoed-up M4, keeping guard.

Deeds answered, in a suit, unsmiling. He had a locking briefcase. Turnbull noted it and said nothing right then. Casey, like Turnbull dressed in slacks and a blazer with no tie, went ahead to the elevators and hit the buttons. Turnbull had his Wilson in a discreet belt holster, and the four extra mags divided between the front pockets of his sport coat. His WCP365 was nestled in a holster in the small of his back.

Turnbull silently walked Deeds along the hallway. They got into an elevator car after Casey cleared it and together went down to the lobby.

Turnbull was the first out. The lobby was sealed off from regular civilians, but it was packed with both New Secret Service and reporters – red, blue, and international. Out front, the rest of the close protection team had Deeds's two black Chevy Suburbans idling in front of the door. One of the guards was out on the walkway with his M4. The security team numbered seven, but only five could enter the Tower complex. The other two would spend the day watching the SUVs in the parking area outside the walls near Tower Hill, where the Brits did most of their head-chopping back in the good old days.

Turnbull pivoted back to face Casey, who was holding Deeds in the open elevator car, and nodded. All clear. Casey brought their high value target out and joined up with Turnbull in a beeline through the front doors to the waiting SUVs. The reporters saw the crew passing, but had no idea who Deeds was, and went back to whatever they were doing. At the Suburban, Turnbull opened the back door for Deeds to get in and then Turnbull and Casey followed.

Deeds sat in his seat, thinking about the smug look Scott had greeted him with when he saw Deeds was part of the American delegation. The mediator was secure in the knowledge that Deeds was under strict orders to remain silent about everything Scott had done, including launching the Overlord debacle that was still killing American troops. Everyone else, starting with the President, was focused at (purported) peace at any price. Only Deeds, the keeper of Red America's secrets, managed to curb his enthusiasm.

"So, how are the peace talks coming?" Turnbull asked as the little convoy maneuvered through London's streets. He had asked the same question of Deeds during the drive back to the Ritz the previous evening, but he understood that much of the actual work happened at night far from the conference table in the White Tower. Everything could have changed overnight, and judging by Deeds's grim demeanor, it had.

"It went well," Deeds said. "Too well, in fact. There was some movement overnight."

"Good movement or bad movement?" Casey asked.

"Bad, from our perspective," Deeds said. "Scott proposed that the parties expand the scope of the talks from ending the war to reunification."

"That's what you said yesterday afternoon," Turnbull observed.

"Well, last night both sides agreed to talk about it," Deeds said. "The conference ends tonight. That means there will be tremendous pressure to come to some ill-thought-out understanding in order to leave London with something concrete."

"How the hell can our government want to reunify with these blue lunatics?" Casey sputtered.

"Because they don't know them like we do," Turnbull said. "They still imagine that these are just fellow Americans with a quirky pronoun fixation."

"Obviously, there's no time at this conference to work out the details of reunification," Deeds said. "So what they are going to try to do is agree on the big issues. Will we reunify? What kind of government? And who is in charge?"

"I'm guessing who will put himself out there," Turnbull said. "A man of the red, loved by millions, but persecuted and given shelter by the blue."

"I expect that will be the proposal our neutral mediator will be making this morning," Deeds said. "And our leaders know what he tried to do, how he tried to nuke them and take power, and they are willing to look past that for what they hope is peace."

Turnbull snorted at that notion.

"Let me guess, he's the president nominally representing the red, and that Harrington bastard is the veep repping the blue," said Turnbull. "Harrington gets himself and the People's Republic out of the Chinese sphere of influence and puts himself in line for the big prize.

"Is Scott that dumb?" asked Casey.

"Scott's an ass, but he's not dumb," Turnbull said, shifting himself in his seat to get comfortable in his stifling sport coat.

"I do not know if I can stop Scott – everything he did is Top Secret, and without some revelation that would change red minds that's beyond us, he's a shoe-in. But Vice-President Harrington can't happen," Deeds said. He cradled the briefcase. "I need to let our leadership truly understand who Temporary Rotating Executive Harrington really is – the man behind much of the death and chaos that has happened since the Split."

"There's another option," Turnbull said. "A terminal one."

"Even if I was inclined to allow it, and I admit I'm torn, you would never survive even if you got past that phalanx of Ukrainian gun thugs," Deeds said.

"It's worth it," Turnbull said firmly.

Turnbull waited with Casey in the Americans' preparation room, along with the other dignitaries' security – as a relatively minor participant, Deeds was allowed two men within the White Tower – while Deeds was inside the conference room itself during the sessions. There was no security inside the main conference room by common agreement.

"I gotta take a leak," Turnbull said, putting down his Styrofoam coffee cup.

Casey grunted. He was annoyed and bored because everyone except the bigwigs had to check their cellphones at the entrance of the Tower complex and he was unable to tweet or do anything else Gen Z people typically did to pass the time.

Turnbull walked out into the hall, where there were several blue and red guards at the door to the conference room.

Major Vasilev was escorting a statuesque woman down the hall and into the conference room. When she slipped inside, he spotted Turnbull and approached.

Turnbull stretched out the fingers of his gun hand. He hated having the sport coat on – it felt constricting and that's the last thing he needed in a gunfight.

"You, again," Vasilev said, stopping in Turnbull's path.

"If it isn't my favorite Slavic military rent-boy," Turnbull said. "Say, I've got a twenty. Can I buy you for a couple minutes? I'm going to the loo and I need something wiped."

The mercenary gritted his teeth, trembling with anger. His hand hovered over his Heckler & Koch USP.

"Are we going to do this here?" asked Turnbull innocently. "Because I'm good with that."

"Not here, not now, but soon," Vasilev promised, nodding.

Turnbull smiled.
"I cannot wait."

The sessions broke for the parties to confer, with the Americans retiring to their preparation room, the blues to their own, and the mediator to his room where he could be alone during the fifteen-minute break. Scott walked out of the White Tower conference room stone-faced and with all the bearing he could muster. It would be beneath him to pretend that the great honor being bestowed upon him was anything but an Atlas-like burden that he would reluctantly – for the people of red and blue America together – accept and bear.

But he had gotten exactly what he wanted for himself, what he had planned and worked for, and it was so easy. The American president had even been the one to suggest it, offering to sacrifice his own position for the good of his country.

"General Scott, I have an idea. What if *you* would accept the presidency of the reunited United States? You are trusted by red and blue, you are a proven leader, and frankly, there is no way the blue might accept me or anyone else from the USA that I can think of. Would you consider it? For your country?" the president had asked, his mind mulling over how history books henceforth would portray him as the greatest statesman of the era for sacrificing his own position and ambition to bring America together once more. Of course, there was that whole unpleasantness with Scott, but the H-bomb and the coup were in the past – and that secret was safely buried. Water under the bridge. Time to move on.

Scott had taken a moment, his face registering his shock at the mere idea of this outside-the-envelope compromise – a look he had practiced intensively in anticipation of just this moment.

"If that is what the people of the United States and the People's Republic ask me to do in order to reunite our great nation, then I will do my duty," Karl Martin Scott replied solemnly. "Of course, that means my vice-president must be from the blue."

Now, as Scott walked out of the conference room toward his private preparation room, Harrington was behind him and coming fast, his face a rictus of rage.

Scott walked into his room and turned to greet the wide-eyed Temporary Rotating Executive.

"You bastard," Harrington spat.

"I raised your name," Scott said. "And the Americans rejected you. You saw it. They will simply not accept you as vice-president."

"Then you should have *made* them accept it!" Harrington said, not quite shouting but not quite not.

"I am a mediator," Scott said. "My job is to find solutions to disputes, and I did."

"You suggested that bitch Cochran!" Harrington hissed. "And I know you planned it. How long have you been working together?"

"We have been working together to serve the People's Republic," Secretary of State and Decolonialization Cochran said as she strode into the room. Her normally icy visage betrayed the hint of a smile.

"I can put you in a grave with the snap of my fingers," Harrington said to her coldly.

"I doubt that," Cochran replied. "I have my instructions from the surviving members of the Supreme Political Bureau."

"Surviving?" Harrington said, confounded.

"Yes, the traitors on the Bureau who you were counting on to assist you have been tried, found guilty, and executed, all in the last thirty minutes," she said pleasantly. "The Temporary Rotating Executive role has been rotated to me – temporarily – until I assume the vice-presidency of the reunited United States."

Harrington's eyes were wide and his mouth twisted. It amused Scott to see him like that. The debt Harrington had incurred his petty slights and passive microaggressions were coming due and would be repaid in full.

"Do you imagine I have not prepared for this, you ridiculous fools?" Harrington said.

Neither Scott nor Cochran reacted. Major Vasilev entered the room with Sergeant Drago, the giant.

"As I said, I will put you in a grave." He looked at the Ukrainian, who seemed bemused.

"I regret to inform you, Mr. Temporary Rotating Executive," the mercenary said, "that I have a new employer.

"He is no longer the Temporary Rotating Executive," corrected Cochran. "I am."

"And I am his new employer," Scott announced.

Vasilev shrugged disinterestedly. Harrington looked stricken.

"You're dismissed," Scott said. "With no leadership role, you have no seat at the table. I would suggest that you try to stay in London for a while, though I expect your expense account is closed, and wait to come home until the amnesty that will no doubt accompany the reunification takes effect."

"You are luckier than your allies on the Bureau. Consider that mercy as recognition of your service to the People's Republic," Cochran added. "Now get out before we change our minds."

Harrington looked back at Vasilev, who nodded toward the door.

"You will regret this," Harrington said walking out. "Mark that."

Scott and Cochran returned to the conference room. Before the dust-up with Harrington, he had floated the Secretary of State's name – leaving out the "and Decolonialization" portion of her full title in a sop to the Americans. During the break, the US delegation considered her normal appearance and her current pronouns and determined that they were unlikely to do any better. She was the best of a bad, blue lot.

The American president was giddy, feeling his place in history secured. The primary American dissenter was the mysterious man referred to only as "Mr. Deeds." In the poll in the preparation room, he was a "No."

But Deeds was out-voted.

It would be President Scott and Vice-President Cochran presiding over a newly reunited United States of America. There were a few more general points to agree on, like the truce and the basic timeline for reunification, as well as the procedures for making the tens of thousands of decisions involved in merging two very different countries.

There was the question of the unified government. To the delight of the red American delegation, Scott and Cochran both argued that the US Constitution and its Bill of Rights should provide the general framework for the new unity government. But both of them knew that the devil was in the details, and they had a legion of those to unleash.

If he could not have victory, Harrington told himself as he walked alone across the courtyard in front of the White Tower, he could have vengeance.

He had prepared his insurance from the get-go, assembling a doomsday device to be used as a threat to compel compliance. The problem was that Scott had acted *before* Harrington could use it to deter the apocalypse. Their deal was done and being executed before Harrington could even issue his threat.

Mutually assured destruction only worked when the other side knew it was mutual before pushing the button.

Otherwise, it was just destruction.

Scott had already pushed the button. Now Harrington would too.

He smiled cruelly at the thought.

"So be it," he said, drawing his private cell phone from his pocket.

Inside the conference room, Deeds felt like the guy who stopped off at a Christmas party on the way home from putting his golden retriever puppy to sleep. For the last half-hour since reconvening, the other negotiators had been excitedly yammering about how the reunification would work, throwing out ideas and suggestions – most of them terrible – about how to manage the process. Others were helping draft the joint statement to the world announcing the success of the peace conference.

"Clay," said the president, taking him aside. "I know you have qualms."

"A multitude of them, sir," Deeds replied.

"This is a chance to bring the country together, to drive out Chinese influence, to become what we were again."

"Sir, you know what Scott did, what he *is*."

"And it's vital that only we know," the president said. "You do not make peace with friends. You make it with enemies."

"But you don't make enemies your president," Deeds said. The President did not reply. He just looked at Deeds, and Deeds knew that look. He was going to be retired – honored, praised, even rewarded – but retired and excluded from any power or influence in the new government. That was the price of dissent, and he accepted it.

"What the hell?" said the Secretary of Defense. He was looking at his iPad 23. A moment later, a green-haired nonbinary People's Republic delegate's phone beeped with a message – xe had failed to silence xis ringer. Its owner looked at the screen, xis eyes went wide, and xe began tapping links.

More people looked at their phones, first mostly the reds but then the blues too.

At the middle of the table, President-To-Be Scott surveyed the growing chaos.

"Everyone, we need to focus on the process...," Scott declared, but no one paid him any heed. That offended him. These politicians needed some iron discipline, and he resolved to deliver it soon enough.

Then the sound went on from someone's phone.

It was Harrington's voice asking and Scott's answering.

"And the reds? What do you expect from them?"

"I know the outlines of what you were really imprisoned for, and it was not overzealously prosecuting the war on the People's Republic."

"And what do you think that was?"

"I think that you were plotting a coup. And I think you expected to kill many thousands of your own countrymen to do it. I am not sure of the details, but that is what my information tells me. Now you tell me, since we must be transparent – is it true?"

"It is. I sought to overthrow the feckless American government, and I intended to sacrifice tens of thousands of innocent Americans to do it. Is that what you wanted to hear? Is that enough to convince you that I am willing to do the same thing on a larger scale with a reunited United States?"

Scott's mouth dropped open after the first few words. The room fell silent. Deeds looked over on the SecDef's iPad screen. Apparently there was video too, taken in what Deeds recognized as Scott's suite in the former Mandarin Oriental Hotel. The video seemed to come from a camera worn by Harrington – the former Temporary Rotating Executive was off-screen, and Scott was facing the hidden lens.

Harrington had taped their conversations. That was his insurance.

"And a second clip provided to Fox," the anchor said, "shows General Karl Martin Scott apparently on a blue aircraft while flying to the peace conference."

"My supposed crimes are all state secrets. For the chance at peace, the US leader will put aside my attempt to seize power after destroying Dallas. All will be

forgotten and forgiven. But I will not forget or forgive. Once in office, I will naturally have to impose certain controls to protect the newly reunified country from the threat of disinformation and dissent. Reasonable limits on speech and the press. And, eventually, the confiscation of weapons."

"Fox News has come into possession of several more shocking clips, all from the same reliable source," the anchor said breathlessly. "Including one clip in which General Karl Martin Scott and People's Republic Temporary Rotating Executive Richard Harrington plan to draw the United States into undertaking Operation Overlord, which had already cost thousands of American casualties, in order to create the conditions for him to be named president of a reunified United States at the peace conference currently underway in London."

Deeds turned away from the screen – the room was dead quiet except for the video clips that entranced the delegates – and he looked up to the center of the negotiating table.

Scott was gone.

When Scott ran to him in the hallway, pale and enraged, Major Vasilev had been in the process of watching the bombshell video clips on KyivNews.com. He took a moment to assess his options.

He made his decision. Desperate men paid better than anyone else. And Scott was the most desperate man he had ever seen.

"Come on," Vasilev said, grabbing the general's arm and calling to his men in Ukrainian. They broke out their AK-19 rifles and followed him out the exit past several puzzled red and blue security guards.

Vasilev put his cell to his ear after hitting a favorited number.

Ahead was the Traitor's Gate and Wakefield Tower.

"Kelly!" Deeds shouted as he burst into the red preparation room. Turnbull looked up from the screen of a phone that one of the president's guards had snuck in.

Turnbull was grinning ear-to-ear.

"He's running, Kelly!"

"Green light?" asked Turnbull.

"Take him!" ordered Deeds.

That was all Turnbull needed to hear.

He tore out of the room, with Casey following for about five steps before it was clear that his healing gunshot wound was not going to allow him to follow.

"You see a bunch of thick-necked assholes?" Turnbull shouted to several red security men loitering in the hallway, none with a phone and therefore completely ignorant of the earth-shattering developments underway beneath their noses. "Which way did they go?"

The baffled men pointed to the west exit and Turnbull sprinted to and through the door and out into the courtyard and the sunlight.

No London fog today.

There were figures down by the Wakefield Tower door – and gunshots. The figures went inside and one body in red lay on the ground. Turnbull started sprinting, and tossed off his hated sport coat as he did.

He drew his .45 as he ran.

The courtyard was nearly empty as they sprinted south across the grass. The Ukrainians reached the foot of the Wakefield Tower with their man in tow. A British Yeoman Warder sergeant, in his dress red tunic and towering beefeater hat, was at the open door with an SA-80 rifle and stared at them.

"What's all this then?" he demanded. Vasilev shot him three times in the chest with his pistol. The sergeant crumpled.

Vasilev pushed the general inside and the rest of his men went through the door behind him. The ground floor was evidently some kind of museum. Suits of armor stood on pedestals around the circular walls, and various swords, maces and lances were displayed about the room. Several glass cases showed off other ancient weapons. A spiral staircase headed upwards at the opposite wall.

"Captain," Vasilev said to one of his men. "To the roof. You two, security in the upper hall." The three took off – they had scouted the Wakefield Tower prior to the conference and understood where their commander wanted them.

Vasilev looked out the open door back toward the White Tower. There was a man running from there toward them, and he was tearing off his sport coat.

Turnbull.

It was a pity he could not do the job himself, but he had priorities.

"Drago," he said to the giant Ukrainian merc. "Kill him. But make it painful."

Drago smiled and tossed his leader his AK-19 rifle. Vasilev almost pitied his opponent not having the mercy of a bullet.

Almost.

The merc major pushed Scott ahead, ignoring the general's objections to the rough handling. Beggars could not be choosers. The pair disappeared up the stone stairs.

Drago's eyes settled on a fine two-handed sword hanging on a display rack and he snapped the thin metal wires holding it on as he pulled it off. Next to it was a mace, a wooden handle with an iron cylinder on the end used to pummel enemies into puddles of goo. He took that too.

Then his eyes settled on a suit of plate armor standing in the corner, and Drago began to laugh.

Turnbull saw the dead Beefeater sprawled on the ground outside the door to the bottom floor of the Wakefield Tower. It was a crappy way for an experienced old soldier to go – you had to serve at least 22 years to get one of the coveted Yeoman Warder gigs.

More reason to cap that Slavic schmuck and his minions too. Of course, it was one against five, and one of the five was a literal ogre.

Turnbull did not slow down, but he dropped the safety on his locked and cocked Wilson .45.

Then he realized his extra mags were in the blazer he had discarded on the way.

"Guess you go to war with the Army you have," he muttered.

Turnbull crossed the threshold and the mace slammed into his gut, but not hard enough to kill him. That would be too easy.

The blow knocked the wind out of him, and more important, it knocked the Wilson .45 out of his hands. The pistol skidded across the floor as Turnbull went down on his knees on the stone floor.

He recovered quickly and turned. There was a giant standing there with a mace. Moreover, he was wearing a steel helmet and a metal breastplate clearly liberated from one of the displays.

And the troll was laughing.

"Are you kidding me?" Turnbull said, looking around.

"I will break you," the mountain bellowed.

Goliath lumbered forward with the mace.

Turnbull scrambled backward. He glimpsed his .45 and made for it, even as the monster saw the gun too and accelerated.

Turnbull, though wanting to toss his cookies from the blow, jinked behind one of the glass displays featuring a selection of ancient daggers even as Sergeant Drago brought the mace down on the case with both hands, not holding back. The glass shattered and sprayed them both, and the wooden case collapsed in a V-shape. Drago, his vision restricted by his helmet, looked around for his quarry for a moment before picking up the pursuit again.

But Turnbull had his Wilson and he swung around firing two shots at a giant who was moving very fast. The rounds punched into a suit of armor standing on the far wall.

Drago was gone. The bastard was quick when he wanted to be.

There was a flash of movement and Turnbull fired again, the hollow point blasting the glass of another display case.

Then the flying mace hit the slide of the gun and tore it from Turnbull's hand.

Drago, his face hidden by the steel mask, laughed heartily. He rose up, looming.

Now he had a broadsword.

A two-handed broadsword that was as tall as Turnbull, and Turnbull was tall.

"You have not begun to hurt!" it bellowed.

Oh, I've got a good head start on that, Turnbull thought to himself as he moved toward the wall. His gut ached, but if the mace had connected higher right now he would be dealing with splintered ribs.

Where the hell was his .45?

Wait, he thought. He reached to the small of his back.

But Sergeant Drago was on him, swinging the giant blade. The sword arced through the air and came down. It was dull from the centuries since someone last sharpened it, but the tip was pointy and the blade was heavy enough to slash through Turnbull's left forearm when he raised it in his defense.

Blood spurted out and across his chest.

Turnbull fell back, but the monster advanced. The challenge for the ogre was the weight of the huge sword. It was so big and unwieldly that it took a long moment to prepare the next swing.

Turnbull pivoted and grabbed a round shield from another suit of armor with his bloody left limb. The next blow came in and, if it had caught him dead-on, likely would have split the shield in two along with his arm. Even the glancing impact was still enough to send a shockwave of pain up to his shoulder.

Turnbull staggered and fell in the glass beneath the destroyed dagger case – and saw a sweet little six-inch number which he grabbed.

Drago stepped out in front of him, holding the enormous blade with two hands behind him and hefting it up and over with the clear intent of, if not removing a limb, of cleaving him in two.

Turnbull gathered all his remaining strength and pushed up and forward, leading with the shield. It impacted with Drago's own gut just as the sword came over his head and knocked the ogre off-balance. This spoiled the sword swing and Drago staggered backwards under Turnbull's weight, colliding with a suit of captured French armor that fell over in a loud avalanche of metal and fabric.

Turnbull took the opportunity to drive the dagger into the side of Drago's left thigh until the crossguard was flush and a geyser of hot blood spurted out.

Turnbull jumped back as the monster howled, and kept backing up to gain distance.

Drago ripped the metal helmet from his head, snarling.

"No more games! I kill you now!"

"Yeah," Turnbull said. "No more games."

He drew the WCP365 from the small of his back with his right hand and put six shots into the steel chest plate. The holes in the metal showed a remarkably tight shot grouping under the circumstances.

Drago staggered and fell to his knees. But then he began to stand. Did he have a Kevlar vest under that plate, or was he just that enormous?

Turnbull fired two more times center mass, followed by two in the face.

Sergeant Drago stopped and swayed, and then fell forward on his chest, but then he flipped over to his back. His eyes were shut – there were holes in his cheek and forehead. He was still. Turnbull looked over the man-mountain's body for a moment, from a few feet away.

"Nah, I saw *Game of Thrones*," he said and put the last three rounds into Drago's brain.

Blood was pouring from the gash on his left forearm. There was a little desk area where an attendant usually sat when the tourists came through. Turnbull staggered over and opened the drawers one after another. There was a silver roll of industrial duct tape in the third one. It would have to do.

He used his pocket knife to cut off his shirt sleeves and then stuffed the fabric into the slice on his forearm. He did not see bone, luckily. He then wrapped the field expedient bandage with the duct tape over and over again, tightly to compress it and stop the bleeding – or at least slow it down.

That took about a minute, but he had time. Turnbull doubted the bastards upstairs would be going anywhere until their ride arrived. The roof of Wakefield Tower was one of the designated helicopter landing zones. No doubt Vasilev was calling for help.

His WCP365 was empty and the slide was open. He shoved it in his pants pocket with the pocketknife. No way he was going home without his wedding gift.

Of course, he thought, some would argue there was no way he was going home, period.

He looked around the room and saw his Wilson .45's butt poking out from under a pair of steel greaves knocked over in the fight.

Turnbull picked up the handgun and headed toward the spiral staircase.

24.

Turnbull charged up the Wakefield Tower's stone stairwell, his weapon up and pointed ahead, looking to acquire targets. There was noise emanating from the stairway somewhere up above and ahead, footsteps, but no one to shoot.

Not yet.

There would be soon enough. Vasilev and Scott had a head start, but eventually they would run out of floors. And then Turnbull would blow both their brains out.

That thought energized him. But his sliced and diced left forearm was now radiating a dull throb all the way up to his shoulder. He glanced down at his field expedient bandage. Red was oozing between the duct tape that pressed down on the cloth, but the bandage would hold for a few minutes.

Enough time to finish this job or bleed out trying.

Turnbull paused on a landing under a sign telling him not to smoke. Except it smelled like someone had been smoking – evil Balkan tobacco. The mercs were here too. He shook off a wave of lightheadedness and stood, his back against the cold granite wall. Through a window, he could see Tower Bridge in the distance. The London bridge was not falling down. At least something was not going all to hell.

He took a moment to check his mag, sliding it out of his Wilson CQB and counting the golden shell cases through the holes bored in the eight-round Wilson custom magazine.

Five shots plus the one in the pipe.

That was not great.

He slapped the mag back into the well.

Shouts above – definitely Scott, and the general was definitely mad about something.

Oh, he was going to learn about mad.

Turnbull launched forward and upward, moving fast, going around the twisting staircase that corkscrewed up to the roof of the Tower. He made a tentative plan – kill everyone he met – but he had still not figured out exactly how to make that happen, not with just six slugs.

One-point-two bullets per schmuck.

Screw it. Scott was not slithering out of payback again. Not this time.

Turnbull came to another landing with a hall going left, and there were more noises. Footsteps and yelling.

Turnbull spun around the corner, his weapon finding its target, a Kurylenko merc with an AK-19 barreling down the hall toward him, maybe twenty feet away. Turnbull acquired a center mass sight picture and fired – the first shot tore straight into the Kevlar plate on the Ukrainian's chest, the second shot into his face.

The mercenary went down and his AK-19 scattered on the stone. Turnbull leapt toward the freshly ownerless gun and he got three steps before the dead man's comrade down the hall brought up his own assault rifle.

Not good.

Turnbull retreated back to the next flight of stairs and rushed onto it while a flurry of rounds impacted where he had been standing just a moment before.

A rifle with a full mag would have been pretty sweet right now, Turnbull reflected as he paused inside the stairway. There was a heavy oak door at the foot of the stairs, and, with some effort, he pulled it shut behind him. With more effort, he slid the ancient iron bolt into the slot and tested the hold. That door was not opening for anyone. Probably.

At least the Kurylenko shooter could not follow behind him. He had enough to contend with to his front.

Turnbull pivoted and continued upwards, slowly now, his Wilson leading in his two increasingly bloody hands. There was another window up ahead, again looking out over London toward the bridge. He glanced out, then away, then back again at something that caught his eye.

A black speck.

Coming fast.

A helicopter, an AH-6, the Kurylenko Group's favorite. The general was going to get away again unless Turnbull caught up with him first. And he intended to.

Turnbull moved upward, careful. There was some sort of room up ahead at the top of the spiral staircase.

And there was noise coming from that unseen room. An argument, a pretty intense one. Scott's voice and then Vasilev's too, both shouting.

Trouble in paradise.

It was hard to hear them clearly, but one thing was clear. Vasilev was renegotiating.

Turnbull paused and considered his options. He could charge up with his four rounds. But he would almost certainly get smoked.

He had an idea. It was a bad one. Turnbull pulled his knife and the empty Wilson SIG WCP365 from his pocket.

It was a really stupid idea.

He went with it anyway.

"Vasilev!" Turnbull yelled up the stairwell to the top floor landing to the hidden merc. "I want to come up and talk."

"Kill him!" Scott demanded from somewhere in the room.

"Be silent," Major Vasilev snapped at the general. Then the mercenary shouted down the stairway.

"Turnbull? Is that you? I have a rifle. You have no chance."

"I have a deal."

"You promised me...," Scott began.

"Shut up!" Vasilev bellowed. "You're worth the same with a bullet in your leg as without!"

"I'm coming up," Turnbull said. There was pounding on the oak door down at the bottom of the stairs behind him. It had held for centuries – hopefully it would hold for a few more minutes.

Vasilev was lurking around the top of the stairwell, but was wisely keeping back and out of sight.

"Throw up your pistol," the major yelled down the steps.

Turnbull tossed up his empty Wilson SIG WCP365. The pistol clattered on the stone floor above.

Vasilev looked the weapon over. The SIG's slide was locked open, and was blood on it.

"That pistol is my wedding gift," Turnbull said.

"Congratulations," Vasilev shouted back. "Does your bride know that she will be a widow if your deal is unsatisfactory?"

Turnbull ignored the jab.

"By the way, major, I shut the door at the foot of the stairway, so your boys are stuck on that last landing. There are fewer of them than before."

"Come up, Turnbull – slowly!"

"Kill him!" demanded the general, still from somewhere further back in the dark.

"Say another word and I'll kneecap you!" hissed the mercenary.

"Yeah, general, shut your pie hole!" Turnbull shouted. The flag officer had to be hating being told to zip it by a couple of field grades.

"Slowly!" the Ukrainian yelled. His accent was more pronounced under stress. "Hands behind your head!"

Turnbull licked his lips and walked carefully up the stairs, hands in the air, fingers intertwined on the back of his head. Blood was flowing fast down his left arm as the improvised bandage fluttered loosely.

Turnbull's eyes broke the plane of the top of the stairway, and he could start to see inside the room at the top of the steps. It was a large, dark space with a stone floor and a single, open oak door across on the opposite wall that obviously led up and outside to the roof.

Scott was near the opposite doorway, furious that he was forced to stand there with his hands behind his head like some common prisoner. Turnbull continued upward, a step at a time. Vasilev stepped into view – his AK-19 leveled at Turnbull's face. He was smiling. Improbably, the scar on his cheek seemed to make his grin even wider.

"If you even twitch...," Vasilev hissed.

"I'm too tired to twitch," Turnbull replied. His blood had now run down his arm to his shoulder.

"Stop there," the major commanded. He looked Turnbull over, then his eyes settled on Turnbull's left arm.

"I see Sergeant Drago cut you nicely."

"You should see Drago about now. He's not looking too good. Lead poisoning. He was too dumb to know he was dead until I emptied my mag into his skull."

Vasilev's smile vanished.

"Watch your mouth, American."

"You should hear me out," Turnbull said. "Because I'm your best chance of walking away both alive and rich and not hunted by guys like me for the rest of your life."

"I'm listening," Vasilev said.

"You damn mercenaries, you have no honor!" Scott shouted.

"Stop talking," Turnbull shouted at the general as he walked slowly up the last few stone steps and emerged fully onto the landing. He kept his hands folded behind his head as the mercenary kept the jet black AK-19 aimed directly center mass. A green designator dot danced across Turnbull's chest.

"It seems that I am in an enviable position," Vasilev said. "I have two competitors vying for my services."

"We can rewrite our arrangement," Scott said. Was that an edge of fear in his voice? "I can give you whatever you want. Anything. You know there are still many rich and powerful men who support me."

Outside, the sound of the approaching Kurylenko chopper was getting louder.

Vasilev considered this for a moment.

"That sounds like a fine offer, general, yet perhaps Mr. Kelly Turnbull can offer me something more. As a businessman, I have an obligation to maximize my profit."

"I can," Turnbull said.

"But I am also a soldier," Vasilev continued. "Mr. Kelly Turnbull has killed many of my comrades and I, lamentably, take such things personally."

"You should still hear my offer." Turnbull said. "But first, are you a fan of American movies?"

"What?"

"Cinema. Films. Hollywood. I mean old Hollywood, not the new woke one. In particular, actions films of the late Eighties?"

"Your American culture is primitive and poisonous," Major Vasilev scoffed. "It was even before the Split."

"For the most part, you got me there," Turnbull conceded. "Anyway, I was just curious."

"Your offer, Mr. Kelly Turnbull?" Vasilev demanded impatiently.

"Oh, that," Turnbull said, the blood from his forearm wound now running down his shirt below his intertwined fingers. "Here it is."

He paused.

Vasilev nodded.

"One," said Turnbull.

"One what? One million dollars?"

"You sure about not knowing American movies?" Turnbull quelled the urge to put his little finger to his mouth.

"One *billion* dollars?" the Ukrainian laughed.

"No. One."

Vasilev squinted and his smile faded.

"One what?"

"One hollow point," Turnbull said, ripping the duct tape holding his Wilson CQB off his upper back as he dodged left and brought around his black pistol.

Vasilev fired first, the 5.56mm round digging a furrow through his moving target's right side. But now Turnbull's Wilson pistol was up and the forward sight danced on the mercenary's forehead.

Turnbull fired.

The .45 caliber Speer GDHP 200 grain hollow point round hit dead center between Vasilev's eyes, flattening on the Ukrainian's skull and pushing through the mushy pink brain matter until it hit the wall of bone in the back. The bullet still had enough energy to punch through and take a good part of the contents of his head and splatter them on the stone wall to his rear.

Vasilev dropped, his weapon falling away even as the noise of the descending chopper filled the room.

Turnbull reoriented to cap Scott then and there, but the general leapt through the doorway and sprinted up the stairs to the roof. Turnbull had no shot.

The noise from the helicopter was frightfully loud now. On the floor, Vasilev's body twitched and kicked. Turnbull resisted the urge to blow the smoke from his barrel. His side hurt where the Ukrainian's bullet grazed him.

"Bruce didn't get shot when he did it," Turnbull complained to the dead mercenary.

Taking a deep breath, Turnbull followed the general up and out to the White Tower's wide roof. The helicopter's rotor wash was beginning to blow up a fierce dust storm. Through the chaos, Turnbull's eyes went to another target, the Kurylenko captain who had been waving in the chopper. The merc was bringing up his rifle.

Turnbull shot him through the neck as Scott dodged behind a stone chimney. The dead man sprawled.

Turnbull's eyes went up to the helicopter – one shooter was on the side, feet hanging out. There was motion on the roof and Turnbull's eyes darted back – Scott was grabbing the dead captain's A-19 and pulling back behind the chimney.

The AH-6 was nearly overhead now, the rotor wash kicking up even more dust and debris into a thick, grey, gritty vortex. The shooter on the side of the chopper was taking aim. Turnbull put a round into him and pivoted back to Scott.

He had no shot at the general. Scott was behind the chimney, with the rifle barrel peeking around the corner in order to take Turnbull out.

"There's no happy ending to this movie for you, Turnbull!" Scott yelled, bringing the gun to bear.

Turnbull raised his pistol high, and Scott paused in confusion. Then he realized Turnbull's plan.

Turnbull took aim at the face of the Ukrainian pilot and squeezed the trigger. The round punched through the canopy and through the man's helmet visor but did not come out the other side. Instead, it bounced around inside his skull. The helicopter jerked up, then down, as Scott looked upward in terror.

Turnbull dived back down the stairs into the room as the chopper crashed down on the rooftop, the whirling rotors disintegrating in a millisecond one after the other on impact with the stone of the roof, but not before they annihilated the four star meat sack in their path. The left part of General Karl Martin Scott's head would later be found a quarter mile away having smashed through the front window of a local pasty shop. Most of the rest of him was never found, at least not in any recognizable form.

Turnbull was face down on the stone floor of the room as the Little Bird tore itself and the general to pieces. When the noise stopped, there was even more smoke and dust, but Turnbull still had his task. He took Vasilev's rifle and went back out onto the roof, avoiding the piles of fiery debris, to make certain that it was over.

The chunky red smear by the remnants of the chimney demonstrated that it was. The cleanup crew would spend hours hosing the goo that once was a decorated officer off of the roof and battlements. It would flow down the gutters, and into London's sewers.

Turnbull's forearm was now a clump of blood-soaked red cloth, and he tried to use the remnants of the duct tape he had used to hide the pistol behind his back to hold the bandage tight once again. Then he remembered he had been shot in the right flank too. That gouge across his side started to hurt and the blood from it was flowing under his belt and down his leg.

"Look at yourself, Kelly. You're a mess," he said aloud, swaying. "But not as big a mess as these assholes."

Things got blurry and he steadied himself on the battlements, looking down over the wall at the grass where a dozen Brits with rifles were running at full speed. Was that Kirby leading the charge?

Turnbull fell back onto his fourth point of contact and, before he passed out, wondered if they would be able to figure out how to open that thick oak door. He hoped that Kirby would not snag his wedding SIG because Lorna would kill him.

When Kirby and his squaddies burst out on to the roof, Turnbull was dancing on the edge of unconsciousness, but he was laughing. Satisfied the rooftop was clear of threats, Kirby negotiated past the wreckage and the red smear to his giggling friend's side.

"I bet this mess is your gen-gen," he said, kneeling. Turnbull was still chuckling even as his eyes were going glassy. "What's so bloody funny?"

Turnbull coughed and chuckled again, putting his hand on Kirby's rig and pulling him close.

"Guess now we know why they call them 'choppers.'" He began giggling again and then passed out.

"Can you pop this open?" Turnbull asked Lorna, handing her a cold brown bottle of Shiner Bock. "Everything hurts."

She took it, pried off the cap and handed it back. Turnbull carefully sat down in his chair. His arm and his side were bandaged, professionally this time. Gibson sat next to him on the porch, sniffing the BBQ smell in the air and ensuring the other dogs understood that the place of honor next to their master was his alone.

"You supposed to be drinking that with all the drugs they have you on, Kelly?" asked Junior. He was back in Texas on rehab leave too.

"Just antibiotics. I don't like painkillers. They make me dull, and stop up the works worse than MREs," Turnbull said.

"You're still not supposed to drink with antibiotics," Junior replied.

"Arrest me," Turnbull said and took a swig.

"Kelly does not play by anyone's arbitrary rules," Clay Deeds said. Off a discreet distance away was his new, dozen-member security detail. Deeds was not going missing again if the powers that be had anything to say about it. He knew too much.

"Just one," Lorna said to her fiancé. "One beer."

"We aren't even married yet," Turnbull complained, taking another sip.

"I am asserting preemptive nagging rights. After all this, you're not going to die on me from a drug reaction."

Turnbull sipped again. He was carrying the Wilson SIG WCP365 today. Kirby had found it on the floor of the Wakefield Tower's top room and returned it to its rightful owner.

"When do you go back?" Deeds asked Junior.

"Couple weeks. I have to rebuild the battalion. The war's not near over."

"No," Clay said. "We're still split in two, with the US in big trouble. Not like the PR, but it's dire. And the Chi Coms and the Russians and every other bad actor on planet Earth is maneuvering to take advantage of our misfortune."

"How did it come to this?" Lorna asked, taking a sip of her own Shiner.

"Stupidity," Deeds said. "A failure to learn from history. Greed. Too much prosperity. Social media."

"Hey," Casey Warner said, offended. His next project was a @FullMetalGalt podcast where his voice would be electronically disguised.

"Regardless, guys like my troops end up paying the price," Junior said bitterly.

"Yeah," Casey said. "I did a long @FullMetalGalt thread on Twitter about it. I mean 'X.' Elon Musk changed it back to X from Twitter again last week."

"Remember how people used to be sick of endless wars, Clay?" Turnbull asked. "Well, I gotta say I'm getting a little sick of this one."

"The whole country is. The whole world is." Deeds said. "Everyone, except for the people in charge."

"Oldest story in the world," Turnbull said. "I remember, back when I was little, when we weren't fighting anyone."

"I'm a lot older than you," Deeds said. "And I can barely remember that anymore."

"I don't remember a time when we weren't fighting someone somewhere," Junior said. "Not ever. My whole generation never knew, I guess, peace."

"Normality," Lorna said. "I don't think anything has been normal in America, in the whole world, since 9/11. And I am too young to remember that."

"Turnbull likes them young," Casey said.

Turnbull glared.

"Not like People's Republic young," Casey backpedaled. "Oh, forget it."

Turnbull took a final swig to finish his Shiner Bock, then told Casey, "Just stop talking."

AUTHOR'S NOTE

I've said it before and I'll say it again... Let's try really hard to make sure this book's predictions don't come true. The other seven are already too damn close to reality.

KAS, October 2023

Kelly Turnbull will return

in a new adventure in

2024

Also, look for a brand new series of conservative action novels in

2024

ABOUT THE AUTHOR

Kurt Schlichter is a senior columnist for *Townhall*. He is also a Los Angeles trial lawyer admitted in California, Texas, and Washington, DC, and a retired Army Infantry colonel.

A Twitter activist (@KurtSchlichter) with over 480,000 followers, Kurt was personally recruited by his friend Andrew Breitbart to write for his Breitbart sites. His writings on political and cultural issues have also been published in *The Federalist*, the *New York Post*, the *Washington Examiner*, the *Los Angeles Times*, the *Boston Globe*, the *Washington Times*, *Army Times*, the *San Francisco Examiner*, and elsewhere.

Kurt serves as a news source, an on-screen commentator, and a guest host on TV and on nationally syndicated radio programs regarding political, military, and legal issues, at outlets including Fox News, Fox Business News, CNN, NewsMax, One America Network, and on shows hosted by Hugh Hewitt, Larry O'Connor, Cam Edwards, Chris Stigall, Seb Gorka, Dennis Prager, Tony Katz, Dana Loesch, Dan Bongino, and Derek Hunter, among others.

Kurt was a stand-up comic for several years, which led him to write three e-books that each reached number one on the Amazon Kindle "Political Humor" bestsellers list: *I Am a Conservative: Uncensored, Undiluted, and Absolutely Un-PC*, *I Am a Liberal: A Conservative's Guide to Dealing with Nature's Most Irritating Mistake*, and *Fetch My Latte: Sharing Feelings with Stupid People*.

In 2014, his book *Conservative Insurgency: The Struggle to Take America Back 2013-2041* was published by Post Hill Press.

His 2016 novel *People's Republic* and its 2017 prequel *Indian Country* reached No. 1 and No. 2 on the Amazon Kindle "Political Thriller" bestsellers list. *Wildfire*, the third book in the series, hit No. 1 on the Amazon "Thrillers – Espionage" bestsellers list and No. 122 in all Amazon Kindle books. *Collapse*, the fourth book, hit 121, while *Crisis* hit 29. His previous novel, *The Split*, hit at least 43. *Inferno* hit 59 overall and No. 1 on "Political Thrillers."

His non-fiction book *Militant Normals: How Regular Americans Are Rebelling Against the Elite to Reclaim Our Democracy* was published by Center Street Books in October 2018. It made the USA Today Bestsellers List.

His Regnery book *The 21 Biggest Lies About Donald Trump (and You)* was released in 2020 and hit Number 1 on an Amazon list.

His Regnery book *We'll Be Back: The Fall and Rise of America* was released in July 2022 and hit Number 1 on an Amazon list.

Kurt is a successful trial lawyer and name partner in a Los Angeles law firm representing Fortune 500 companies and individuals in matters ranging from routine business cases to confidential Hollywood disputes and political controversies. A member of the Million Dollar Advocates Forum, which recognizes attorneys who have won trial verdicts in excess of $1 million, his litigation strategy and legal analysis articles have been published in legal publications such as the *Los Angeles Daily Journal* and *California Lawyer*.

He is frequently engaged by noted conservatives in need of legal representation, and he was counsel for political commentator and author Ben Shapiro in the widely publicized "Clock Boy" defamation lawsuit, which resulted in the case being dismissed and the victory being upheld on appeal.

Kurt is a 1994 graduate of Loyola Law School, where he was a law review editor. He majored in communications and political science as an undergraduate at the University of California, San

Diego, co-editing the conservative student paper *California Review* while also writing a regular column in the student humor paper *The Koala*.

Kurt served as a US Army infantry officer on active duty and in the California Army National Guard, retiring at the rank of full colonel. He wears the silver "jump wings" of a paratrooper and commanded the 1st Squadron, 18th Cavalry Regiment (Reconnaissance-Surveillance-Target Acquisition). A veteran of both the Persian Gulf War and Operation Enduring Freedom (Kosovo), he is a graduate of the Army's Combined Arms and Services Staff School, the Command and General Staff College, and the United States Army War College, where he received a master's degree in strategic studies.

He lives with his wife Irina and their monstrous dogs Bitey and Barkey in the Los Angeles area, and he enjoys sarcasm and red meat.

His favorite caliber is .45.

The Kelly Turnbull Novels

People's Republic (2016)

Indian Country (2017)

Wildfire (2018)

Collapse (2019)

Crisis (2020)

The Split (2021)

Inferno (2022)

Overlord (2023)

Also By Kurt Schlichter

Conservative Insurgency: The Struggle to Take America Back 2013-2041 (Post Hill Press, 2014)

Militant Normals: How Regular Americans Are Rebelling Against the Elite to Reclaim Our Democracy (Center Street Books, 2018)

The 21 Biggest Lies About Donald Trump (and You) (Regnery, 2020)

We'll Be Back: The Fall and Rise of America (Regnery, 2022)

Made in the USA
Monee, IL
09 February 2024

53147745R00213